W9-CAH-975

THE LONG SILENCE

A Selection of Recent Titles by Gerard O'Donovan

The Tom Collins Series

THE LONG SILENCE *

Mike Mulcahy and Siobhan Fallon Mysteries

THE PRIEST
DUBLIN DEAD

* available from Severn House

THE LONG SILENCE

Gerard O'Donovan

severn
House

This first world edition published 2018
in Great Britain and the USA by
SEVERN HOUSE PUBLISHERS LTD of
Eardley House, 4 Uxbridge Street, London W8 7SY
Trade paperback edition first published
in Great Britain and the USA 2018 by
SEVERN HOUSE PUBLISHERS LTD

British Library Cataloguing in Publication Data
A CIP catalogue record for this title is available from the British Library.

ISBN-13: 978-0-7278-8774-0 (cased)
ISBN-13: 978-1-84751-889-7 (trade paper)
ISBN-13: 978-1-78010-951-0 (e-book)

All Severn House titles are printed on acid-free paper.

Severn House Publishers support the Forest Stewardship Council™ [FSC™],
the leading international forest certification organisation.
All our titles that are printed on FSC certified paper carry the FSC logo.

Typeset by Palimpsest Book Production Ltd.,
Falkirk, Stirlingshire, Scotland.
Printed and bound in Great Britain by
TJ International, Padstow, Cornwall.

For my mother, Jo, who taught me to read and gave me the world

'Do you remember the Taylor case?' he asked Maigret abruptly. 'You probably don't read American papers. Well, Taylor, one of the best known movie directors, was murdered in 1922. At least a dozen people's names were mentioned in connection with the case – stars, beautiful women and so on. But no arrest was ever made.'

A Man's Head, Georges Simenon

Extract from a deposition discovered at the home of the deceased:

A guy once told me secrets are the best insurance on earth. I thought then he meant moneywise. Like when you know something a body doesn't want anyone else to know, you can always lever some dough out of them when times are tough. That was the game this guy was in, and I helped put him away for it. But that is blackmail, and there is a difference. I was a kid back then, a big Mick rookie in a baggy blue uniform, barely off the boat. But the idea stuck.

Folk always wanted to whisper in my ear. Maybe because compared with some of the other apes on the job I was the quiet one. At the end of a day dragging in deadbeats, when we'd drop into Dooley's or some other Irish joint, it was always my ear got bent by the mournful drunks at the bar. Maybe I was the only one who'd listen to them. But, like I say, the idea stuck. A few years later, after I left all that behind and switched coastlines and cities, a uniform for a suit, and found good times in a place where looks are everything and lies are the order of every day that dawns, that's when I really got to know the secrets business is a good business to be in.

Back in the time I'm thinking of, I hitched my wagon to the fortunes of a man called Zukor. He took a real shine to me for a while. That was 1917, just a couple of months after Wilson joined the war in Europe and Congress passed the Draft. Good men were hard to come by. Said he'd pay me five times what I made as a cop and make sure I wasn't called up. I didn't need to think about it.

Southern California was pretty as a postcard back then. Never saw blue like it, first time I took the tram out to the shore. But as God himself found, soon as you start putting people in paradise, things begin to sour. Sure, the rot set in long before we got there – Los Angeles was already a hard little city with plenty of hard city problems – but we were the ones helped it take hold. All the money and dreams and high living. There were benefits to be had sticking on the edges of it.

All that's gone now. And they're all dead. Most of them forgotten, though they were known across the world once. Even Zukor is gone. Saw it in the paper last week. No man has a right to 103 years on this earth, even if he did invent half the dreams of the twentieth century. Must have begun to think he was immortal after all. And I'm not so far behind I can let this lie any longer. I've kept my long silence long enough.

Thomas J. Collins, June 16, 1976

ONE

As soon as he wrestled Swann's lifeless form into the roadster, he clambered in behind the wheel, reaching across and holding a hand out to the girl.

'Tom Collins,' he said. 'Get in.' It was the only invitation he was going to give her.

She stared at it a moment before grabbing on and pulling herself in. 'Colleen . . . Colleen Gale,' she said, not quite meeting his gaze.

'That your real name?' He raised an eyebrow. He'd been in the business long enough.

'Since I came out West. I'm used to it now.'

'It's not so bad. Has a nice Irish ring to it. It'll look good up on a marquee someday.'

Her eyes followed his thumb and forefinger as they traced out the oblong against the city lights below. She was nineteen, maybe, straw-blonde hair bobbed and curled at the bangs, eyelids smeared with kohl, lips rouged and raw-looking.

'My mom and pop are Irish – came over in the nineties. You too, I guess?'

'A little later than that,' he laughed, wondering how old she thought he was. But she wasn't short of smarts, clocking the accent like that. 'You got the right idea, anyhow. Irish is a good thing to be in this town, so long as you don't overplay it.' He flicked the ignition and the motor coughed into life, lamps illuminating the dirt wall of the passing place he was parked in, midway up the hill.

'He's Hank Swann, ain't he?' Her tone was more matter-of-fact than curious about the short, plump, extravagantly mustachioed man propped between them, his face alabaster, eyes like blown bulbs seeing nothing, belly like a circus sea lion swelling out from under his shirt. 'I seen him in those Keystone comedies. You in the business, too?'

None of that needed answering. Instead, he asked if she would grab a hold of Swann while he steered the auto back on the road. Once they got going, the wind through the open cab bit down on them like fangs.

'Where you from, Coleen Gale?'

'Grinnell, Iowa.'

'Iowa, she says!' That cracked him up. 'Well, I don't reckon we'll be getting you back to Iowa tonight. Don't you have anywhere closer?'

She shook her head, embarrassed, as if she didn't know.

'Look, I gotta stop off at a pal's place first – make sure knuckle-head here's safe away. After that I'll drop you where you want, OK?'

She nodded and sat chewing her bottom lip, drawing the lapels of the jacket close beneath her neck, arms across her chest, shivering.

'Maybe we can do something about that, too. Meantime, take this.' He fished behind the seat, pulled out his beaver car coat. A remnant of better times.

Once she got that on, the girl did a better job keeping Swann from sliding as they twisted down the steep incline, yellow head-lamps carving a route through the dark. The cold air was working into Swann, and though his head still rolled like a skiff in a squall, his legs at least were planted on the floor. The first drops of rain fell as they eased out on to Franklin, and came down steady the rest of the way.

By the time they parked out front of Sennett's apartment building, they were wet through and bone cold. There had been blizzards in the mountains for days, newspapers packed with stories of rescue parties in the high passes and marooned autoists. But here on the coast, not a snowflake. Only rain. Swann was semi-conscious now. Hauling him out of the roadster was easier than getting him in, but he hadn't mastered staying upright, let alone walking. Nobody this side of heaven would guess he was clown enough to pull in $1,500 a week capering in front of movie cameras. Carrying him was the only option.

Sennett's was one of the newest buildings on the Boulevard, towering several floors above its low-slung neighbors, the facade looming white out of the dark a block or so east of Gower. Seemed like every time Tom passed that way, something newer, taller, fancier had shot up. Ten years earlier, you couldn't have slingshot the distance between the houses, and the hotel up the street was a sleepy old health resort nestled amid orange groves and pepper fields. So they said. Nothing left of it to see. Every last foot of streetfront snatched for some upstart enterprise to soak the movie-making hordes: ration houses, milk bars, clothiers and drug stores – even the banks looked half built, flung up in the rush for easy money.

'Your pal must have quite a place,' the girl said, wide-eyed.

Inside the heavy teak doors, the lobby was even more imposing: polished marble, fancy French mirrors, a chandelier burning electric light despite the hour. Most important, there was an elevator. Sennett occupied the penthouse, though it wasn't his real home. That was a white-pillar palace over in West Adams, with enough land to stable horses and keep a few head of cattle – which his mother, so he claimed, liked to raise. That was its downside: his mother. So he had this place, too. As if he didn't have a whole studio to get away from her in Edendale.

Soon as he knocked, the door opened and Sennett filled the frame, six foot one with a broad barrel chest that seemed to cleave the air in front of him. His eyes were wide and steely, the sense of metal heightened by a shock of prematurely gray hair. The wide farm-boy face might have been handsome but for a fleshy upper lip that looked permanently wet. Standing there, in a blue plaid bathrobe that barely covered his union suit, feet bare and a five-cent cigar between his teeth, movieland's king of comedy could easily have passed for a spud-sucker straight off the boat.

'Where the hell you been, Tom? I was beginning to . . .' Sennett's booming basso trailed off, not so much for having Swann's ass shoved in his face on the way through to the parlor as the half-naked girl in the corridor behind. He swung the door shut, loped over to where Tom was unloading Swann on to an overstuffed davenport. What the hell's going on, Tom? Who's the, uh . . .' He stopped again, noticing the pallor of Swann's face and the low moans he was emitting. 'Jeez, what the hell's wrong with him? Will he be OK like that?'

Where other men took calm stock of a situation, Sennett fussed like an old maid. It never failed to get Tom mad. But he wasn't going to make matters worse by snapping back at him. 'He'll be fine, Mack – in time.'

'What's the damn fool been drinking?'

'It's not booze. He's graduated to more exotic pleasures. I found him in a fun palace up by Franklin. The old Bernheimer place, remember?'

Didn't so much find him as snuck in and dragged him out before the peddlers who laid out the dope could stop him. A risky business, especially when the girl insisted on getting out too.

Sennett shrugged, no interest in the whys and wherefores. Swann groaned as Tom unbuttoned his vest and rearranged his limbs in more natural order.

'Well, someone with a sense of humor must've bought the old place,' Tom said. 'Cos they've turned it into a Chinese-theme party house: liquor, girls, gambling and – guess what?

'Hop?' Sennett's grimace had less to do with Swann's delinquency than the threat exposure would have on the studio's bottom line.

'Stupid clown's smoked enough opium to floor a mule.'

'Anybody see him at it?'

'Whoever peddled him the stuff, I guess. Nobody much saw me get him out, except for the girl. She was working there.'

'Working?' Sennett's complexion, already blotched by the news that one of his best clowns was a dope fiend, went a vein-riddled purple. 'And you brought her here? Have you taken leave of your senses? With Hank like this? What if she goes to the papers?'

The newspapers were Sennett's latest obsession, and with good reason. For six months the trial in San Francisco of comedy star Roscoe 'Fatty' Arbuckle, over the death of Virginia Rappe had been exercising the imagination of every screaming headline writer in America. Holding Hollywood up for a beating by every God-bothering preacher and mothers' union in the country. There wasn't a producer in the business who wasn't running scared of what a scandal might do to their prospects. And while Tom had reasons of his own to regret that turn of events, there was no denying it was also the one thing that had kept him in work for the last few months. He looked around. There was no sign of the girl, but Sennett was staring at the back of the door as though he could see right through it and wasn't liking what he saw.

'For Christ's sake, Mack, you could've asked her in. It's freezing out there. She won't say anything. I wouldn't have got Hank out without her.' He strode over and yanked the door open. She was standing there, shivering, eyes down, seemingly unconcerned. 'Colleen, this is Mack. Mack, Colleen.'

She came in, clutching the car coat tight around her waist, eyes wide now, never once taking them off Sennett.

'I just told Mack here you were a big help to me and the least he could do is let you borrow some clothes.' He turned to Sennett, enjoying his discomfort. 'You must have some clothes lying around? Costumes? Something one of your girls left behind?'

Sennett nearly choked on that one. 'Not funny, Tom.' He scowled and flicked his eyes towards the girl again, gave her a gnarled approximation of a smile. 'Would you excuse us a moment, my dear,' he said to her and draped an arm around Tom's shoulder, steering him to the far side of the room. 'I don't know what the hell you think you're playing at, Tom,' he whispered, angry. 'But I want you to stop it, right now. Don't you forget who pays who in this arrangement.'

'Look, it's been a long day, OK? I'm done in.' With Sennett, the problem with overstepping the mark was never knowing where the mark was.

'Yeah, well, get rid of the girl. We need to talk.'

'Are you kidding me? Can't it wait till morning? Hank won't come to before then and my bed is crying out for me.'

'I'm not kidding. And I'm not asking either,' Sennett growled. 'You're going nowhere. Not yet. Didn't you see the papers?'

'I've been out chasing down that damn fool all day,' Tom said, nodding towards Swann. He was running out of patience. Much as he needed the work, the whole point of his 'arrangement' with Sennett was that it was freelance. That way, Sennett, notorious penny-pincher that he was, didn't have to bear the cost of Tom's idler moments. And Tom didn't have to take any of his claptrap.

'Goddamn!' Sennett's face was turning a deeper shade of plum, on the verge of popping a whole new batch of blood vessels. It had to be something bad to get him so worked up.

'Look, I said I didn't see any papers today.' Tom's tone was more conciliatory now. 'If you're so desperate to talk, I'll stay. But I promised the girl I'd take her home. I won't go back on that. Why don't you go dig out some clothes for her? We can talk private as you like while she's dressing.'

TWO

'You pay if she steals anything,' Sennett muttered as he emerged from the bedroom, a thumb jerk indicating Tom should follow him into the kitchen. Copper pots, cast-iron pans and fish kettles, every imaginable culinary vessel hung from racks and sat on shelves, unused, probably shipped in wholesale from one of his sets.

He shot a glance back through the doorway before turning to Tom with the same anxious expression as before.

'Bill Taylor's been killed.' His voice cracked in trying to say it low. So low Tom couldn't be sure he was hearing right.

'Who's been . . . What?'

'Taylor. Bill Taylor for Chrissakes,' Sennett hissed. So close now Tom felt spittle spray hot on his ear. 'He's been murdered. Shot dead in his own parlor.'

Even spelled out, it took a moment to comprehend. Bill Taylor – or William Desmond Taylor as he was known to the world – was one of the top directors in town, and among the most respected. A tall, handsome guy with a commanding presence, he'd been president of the Motion Picture Directors Association and was under contract to the studio Tom had come out to Hollywood to work security for, Famous Players-Lasky. He had run across him plenty, inevitably, and always found him a bit remote, a bit cool. Tom the muscle, Taylor very much the artist. They didn't exactly run with the same crowd. Apart from being Irish, they had nothing in common. And even that Taylor preferred to play down, preferring to put himself across as some kind of English gent about town. Still, you could be whoever you wanted to be in the colony. That was the deal. And if Taylor's reputation was to be believed, you couldn't meet a nicer, more refined guy. Or imagine anyone wanting to hurt him.

With one glaring exception: Mack Sennett.

Something in Tom's expression must have betrayed the thought because Sennett took a step back, wiped a look that bordered on satisfaction off his face, and grabbed a copy of the *Los Angeles Evening Herald* from the table.

'See for yourself.' Sennett thrust the paper at him, front page first. 'Found dead in his place over on South Alvarado this morning, shot in the back. Whole place's in a flap about it.'

An oversize headline blared from beneath the *Herald*'s spread-eagle masthead: *Mystery Gunman Kills Film Director Taylor.*

Tom stared at the first two words, their significance wrestling all other thoughts out of the way. 'They don't know who did it?'

'Not a clue,' Sennett said emphatically. His countenance was changing now, as if telling Tom was a relief somehow. 'Maybe it was the butler,' he said, snickering and jabbing a finger at the bottom of the page. 'The ex-butler, I mean – this guy Sands. But nobody believes that.'

Tom's swimming vision followed the fingertip to a report claiming that a valet the director sacked six months before had been named as a possible suspect. It was too much to take in.

'They're getting nasty about it, Tom, trying to draw innocent people into the net.'

The note of self-pity in Sennett's voice rang like an alarm bell, and Tom's brain shifted into gear and caught up with the reality of the situation.

'What're you talking about, Mack? Who's getting nasty?'

'The papers, the stupid papers. They're jumping all over it. The evening editions were bad enough, but God knows what they'll print tomorrow morning. I ain't kidding. It's like Arbuckle all over again. Their blood is up. I had J.A. over in Mabel's place all day fighting off calls. All the news boys want is to dig up dirt.'

J.A. Waldron was Sennett's studio manager, Mabel Normand his top star – the biggest box-office comedienne in the movies and worth millions. As the pieces fell into place, Tom cursed himself for being so slow. For the past six months, all the gossip columns and movie magazines had been clamoring to get Normand to announce her engagement to Taylor, the two had been seen going about together so much. At the same time whispering about whether her employer, and former fiancé, Mr Mack Sennett, would give the match his blessing.

'You're not telling me Miss Normand had something to do with this?'

'Of course not,' Sennett snapped. Catching the skeptical look in Tom's eye, he shook his head emphatically. 'She didn't, I tell you. But she did have the misfortune to be the last person to see him alive. Now they're all jumping on her like she's the killer.'

'That's one heck of a misfortune, Mack. Did she have the misfortune to be alone in the room with him when he was shot, as well, maybe?'

'Goddamn it, how can you even ask that?' Sennett shot him a look sharp enough to stick in his neck. 'She was miles away, in her own bed, when it happened. You know as well as I do, Mabel wouldn't hurt a fly.'

Tom knew no such thing. He never had much to do with Mabel Normand either personally or professionally, but he had ears to hear rumors the same as anyone else. And he heard plenty about her being one very troubled lady. But for all that, he had to think she made an unlikely murder suspect. Not that it would make a difference to the press boys. All they lived for was to build folk up in order to tear them down again twice as hard.

'What do the cops say?'

'They went round and questioned her earlier,' Sennett sighed. 'One advantage of being a major star. They come to you. Can't drag you away in chains on a suspicion.'

'They go heavy on her?'

'Naw, I got that attorney Zweiss to sit in with her. They had to be nice.'

'What about you? They call you, too?'

'Me? No, why would they?'

There was nothing to do but laugh in Sennett's face. 'Oh come on, Mack, get real. It's not like every gossip on the West Coast hasn't been trading on your feelings about her and Taylor.'

And they had, even if a good eighty percent of the stories had been planted by Sennett's own publicity department.

'You know there's nothing between me and Mabel anymore.'

'Yeah, sure. Apart from that great big hole in your heart you're so fond of telling us about.'

'That's just baloney for the fans, and you know it.'

Tom did a double take on that one and was totally unprepared for the big man's response.

Sennett bared his teeth, snarled like a dog and poked him in the chest. 'Now, you listen, Tom. You just shut up about that. That's between me and Mabel, nobody else. And that's how it's going to stay. OK?'

There was much to dispute in that assertion. But with the agitated state Sennett was in, Tom could see now was not the time to argue. He took another tack. 'You'll still have to deal with the papers. Has anybody been in touch? Anyone connect your name to it yet?'

Sennett glared at him again, as though he was going to contest that too, but then seemed to change his mind. He heaved a laugh out of his big barrel chest. 'Oh, you know. Some guy from the *Times* called me at the studio but all he wanted was a quote. I gave him the usual spiel, about what a great artist and a fine fellow my good friend Mr William Desmond Taylor was, what a tragedy for the movie world that a director of his celestial caliber should be taken from us so untimely and all. Seemed happy with that. Didn't ask for more.'

A small miracle, but Tom knew it was only a matter of time before they would return, probably to fling those fine words back in Sennett's face. The tiredness of the long day began to swamp him and, despite the tension, his concentration began to drift. Sennett wasn't helping, yammering on now like a clockwork toy let loose.

'Half a million bucks I put into *Mollie O,*' Sennett was saying. 'I can't take a wallop like that, Tom. If they withdraw it from the theaters, I'm finished. The banks are tightening up. Even looking at the fifty grand I've already laid out on filming *Suzanna*, we're in trouble – that's sure to be held up by weeks now. We got to have something to throw back at them when they come at us.'

'What are you proposing?' It was a question he instantly regretted.

'Ain't it obvious?' Sennett said, exasperated. 'You've got to get out there and find something to prove Mabel had nothing to do with it.'

'Me?' Tom laughed. 'You're better off putting some lawyers on it, and fast. What do you think I could do?'

'More than any chickenshit lawyer, that's for sure,' Sennett insisted. 'I don't see any other way. If the papers come down hard, Mabel's name will be box-office poison. We'll all be going down the chute if that happens. It's no good saying she didn't do it; we gotta show she absolutely couldn't have done it. Beyond doubt.'

Tom knew very well how dangerous it was to go sniffing at holes the cops already had their noses in. 'That's crazy, Mack. You said yourself this thing could be dynamite. You're better off sitting back, waiting to see what happens. If she's innocent, she's innocent. No argument. But if anyone spots me out there asking questions, the finger will point straight back at you. And you know you don't want that.'

Sennett put his hands up. 'I got nothing to hide. Anyhow, there'll be so many cops and hacks out there rooting around, no one's going to notice you. If they do, you got friends in City Hall, no? And I'm paying you, ain't I? You know I'll make it worth your while. I'm telling you, Tom, you're the man for the job.' He said it sweet, but with a layer of vinegar on top. 'And if you can't see your way to helping me, I might be obliged to call in the note on that rent you owe me. I got to have some way to recoup my losses. Every drop in the ocean and all that.'

Tom gave him a long stare. It was all he had. 'That's low, Mack.'

'That's life, Tommy boy.'

A shuffle from the doorway made them turn sharply. It was the girl, looking more womanly now in a green cotton dress and a silk tailor-waist jacket that might have been made for her. Taller, too, in heels, and she'd found the means to make up her face. There was a strained silence as the two men tried to figure how much she might have overheard – until Sennett stepped in to fill it.

'Ah, there you are. And very lovely you look, too, my dear. Better than Tom's old beaver, no?'

She smiled, embarrassed. 'Thanks. I will get them back to you.'

'Oh, don't worry about that, just, you know, uh . . .' Sennett trailed off, not interested enough to say any more.

It was as good an opportunity as any to get gone. Tom led her back under the light in the parlor. 'I said he'd fit you out. And how. Let's get you home now.'

Sennett followed them out from the kitchen. The matter was obviously settled in his mind, all his attention switched back to the davenport as if he had forgotten Swann was even there.

'You be sure to put a blanket over him.' Tom said. 'You wouldn't want him catching his death. Not tonight.'

THREE

The street outside was quiet as a Sunday stockyard and the rain had eased to a soft drizzle. When they reached the Dodge, he felt a tug on his elbow.

'You'll be wanting this.' She offered up his car coat.

He shook his head but took it anyway, held it open for her to put on. 'You have it. I'm already wet as I'm going to get. You got those nice fresh clothes on. Leastways, I hope they're fresh.'

She smiled weakly and slipped her arms in the sleeves without protest. As she bent her gaze to do up the buttons, he let his eyes roam her face, the curve of her cheekbones high and childish, and wondered how long that smooth complexion would survive Hollywood.

'So, where we going?'

If she gave an answer, the motor's roar drowned it out as he stepped on the starter. He waited for it to settle to an idling clatter and asked again. But it wasn't the subject foremost in her mind.

'I can't believe I just met Mack Sennett and I didn't ask him for a tryout. I didn't even tell him how much I love his movies.' She barely got the sentence out for the sob she was trying to suppress.

He had seen people react strangely to Sennett before. The man was as coarse as a ranch hand yet had the power to make millionaires of wage clerks and shop girls. That colored everybody's view of him. But it was after one in the morning now, and Tom was running short on sympathy.

'Don't worry about that,' he said. 'I'm not sure he'd have been receptive tonight, anyway. He's got a lot on his mind. You're better off saving it for next time.'

'Next time?' She gazed up at him. Much the same look she gave him when she begged him for help at the fun palace. What could it hurt to give her a crumb of hope?

'Sure, why not? He knows who you are now. You can lay on the charm when you take this stuff back to him.'

He plucked at the collar of the borrowed blouse and her face lit up like a child's. 'I hadn't thought of that,' she said, and bounced right up in the seat, touching his arm momentarily.

He slipped the machine into gear. 'Right. So where to, kid?'

'Can't I come with you?'

His foot slid off the clutch and the machine jerked forward, crunching to a stop. He slapped the steering wheel hard in frustration. 'Taking you home means what it says. Your home, not mine.'

'I'm sorry, I really am. I don't mean to cause you any more trouble, but at my rooming house they lock the door at ten every evening. Landlady says no decent girl stays out later than that.'

'Don't you have a pal – somebody who'll let you in? That's how folk usually manage it.'

'Sure, but it's a small place. Just me and one other girl, and she's away working just now. I didn't think it would matter when I went to that place . . .' Her face clouded over at the memory, but she quickly collected her thoughts. 'Please, I'll sleep in a chair, on the floor, any–anywhere you like.'

Her meaning was painfully clear, but instead of being angry, he found himself praying he would never be so hard up for a place to lay his head.

'If I had any sense, I'd dump you here in the street right now.'

'But you're too nice for that.' Smiling now that she saw his resolve crumbling.

'How do you know I don't have a wife waiting at home?'

'It wasn't the first thing you said when I asked.' She said it low, beneath her breath. 'And you don't have the look of it.'

He cocked an eyebrow at her, amused. Too fatigued to argue further. Who would it hurt? It was his place. He could do as he liked. And Fay was out of town, so no need for awkward explanations. Why shouldn't the kid have the parlor couch for a night? Who would know?

'Just one night.'

'Sure,' she laughed, her relief conspicuous. 'Why would I stay any longer?'

FOUR

Had the sun not roused him, he might have slept another two, three hours. He was so attuned to it still. After days of cloud and rain, the immaculate blue sky and strong clear light would have movie studios across Los Angeles twitching, coughing, convulsing into life. Even as he rubbed his eyes, canvas was being stripped from cameras and scenery, backlots and glass-roofed stages were blooming with activity, ready to be transmuted into entertainment for millions by the alchemy of sunlight, glass and celluloid.

Already, crews would be on the road, caravans of trucks piled high with props and players, setting out for Griffith Park, the canyons and arroyos surrounding Hollywood, the beaches of Malibu and Santa Monica. Or simply setting out to see what opportunities the streets and suburbs of the city might provide. Directors barking, cameramen cranking, carpenters sawing and hammering. Scene-painters transforming flats, screens and scaffolds into sleek Manhattan apartments or the catacombs of ancient Rome. In long runs of studio bungalows and scattered offices, roofs would be steaming in the heat, artists would be sketching set-ups, writers scribbling scenes, producers wheeling, dealing, lying through their teeth on telephones. And ruling them all, the money men supplicating the great lord Mammon to grant the eternal cycle of outgoings and incomings, receipts and expenditure, prosperity and continuance.

Christ, how he missed being at the heart of it. For five years, this had been the life blood that ran through Tom Collins's veins. And every morning for the six months since he was sacked, he woke and stuffed his face deeper in the pillow, allowing himself a drift of fantasy that he might reawake and have his old job at Lasky's back, and for things to be exactly as they were before. But that could never be. So instead he reconciled himself to the likelihood that what lay ahead might be another unsatisfying day. But as good a day as he could make it.

He shook his head, shuffled on a robe and went out to the kitchen.

The place was a mess. Eating out was wearing a hole in his pocket. Evidence of his unskilled efforts to feed himself lay in a trail from stove to sink. He drew off a glass of water, and thought again about what he needed to do. Not that he had much choice. He clicked the wall phone's cradle arm twice, and over the crackle and hiss of an open line got the operator to repeat the number he wanted and put him through.

The voice that answered was unmistakable, its soft Munster lilt and high pitch as familiar as a brother's.

'Hello, yes?'

'Thad, how're you doing? It's me.'

A pause, followed by a gasp of surprise. 'Jesus, Tom. Are you all right, lad? I didn't recognize you there for a minute.'

'I'm OK. A catch in my throat, I guess. Hour of the morning.'

'Or the late hour last night, knowing you,' Thad Sullivan chuckled. Then, as if remembering himself, lapsed into chiding seriousness. 'Eleanor and me were beginning to think you'd been run out of town, you know. Especially when we didn't hear from you over the holidays. Where've you been all this time?'

Tom felt a stab of guilt, apologized and said he'd been busy getting the new business up and running. That wasn't the whole of it, but now was not the time for explanations. A late night and a bottle of whiskey would take care of that.

'Listen, Thad, are you downtown today? Can we meet?'

'Sure, if you want. I'm on from ten today. If it's urgent, I—'

'Before you go in would be good. Are you working the Taylor murder by any chance?'

Sullivan's intake of breath echoed down the line. 'Sure I am. The whole detective squad's been called in on it. All hands to the pump. Woolwine is going crazy. Why? Do you have something for us?' His half-suspicious, half-hopeful tone was pure cop.

'No,' Tom laughed, embarrassed now. 'It's kinda the opposite.'

That arranged, Tom cooked up a pot of coffee on the stove and headed back, cup in hand. In the parlor, the girl was fast asleep, barely visible on the couch, a few wisps of tawny hair and the rhythmic shush of her breathing the only evidence of a body beneath the bunched-up blankets. Closing his bedroom door, he sat and took a long draught of the reviving brew. In the wardrobe mirror he caught sight of himself, hunched on the edge of the bed, arms a jumble of angles and bones, hair a sleep-mussed mess of black curls, lips pale against the shadow of another day's beard. He rubbed his eyes again with the heels of his hands, before dragging a large leather suitcase out from beneath the bed, just as he did every morning, his gaze catching inevitably on the big yellow transit label on the lid, his name stencilled on it, care of Famous Players-Lasky on Vine Street – another painful echo.

Snapping the case open, he pulled out a loose-leaf notebook and scribbled an account of his movements the day before: names, places, times, expenses. Other crumbs too about Swann and the girl, the faces he'd seen gambling and whoring at the fun palace the night before. He replaced the notebook, shut the case, checked his wristwatch. Time to wash, shave and dig out some decent duds. Bathroom-bound, he stopped at the parlor door and took another look. She was asleep still but had turned over, her shoulders bare, much of the blanket bunched on the floor. He stepped in, draped it over her again as she murmured dreamily into the upholstery.

FIVE

South Alvarado shimmered, indifferent. Up and down the steep-sloped street, stucco storefronts and white-painted homes gleamed as if laundered overnight. Sitting on a low wall midway up the hill, Tom looked up as a bright-yellow trolley car approached, rumbling and squealing, clanging a warning as it braked on the incline, packed to standing with shoppers and office workers heading downtown. He turned back to his *Los Angeles Times* and the latest news on the Taylor murder. Compared with the bold headlines and shrieking speculation of the previous evening's *Herald*, it was a model of reserve.

The story took up but half the front page, allowing for the possibility that some readers might be more interested in the failing arms talks between China and Japan, the conclave of cardinals electing a new Pope in Rome, or the latest news on Arbuckle's retrial in San Francisco – the jury deadlocked, again. Even so, the main picture was of Mabel Normand, looking rapt and alluring in a studio publicity shot, swathed in off-the-shoulder furs and an enormous velvet hat, her glamour undercut by the melodramatic headline *Linked in Sinister Drama of Mystery* and a caption suggesting she had been questioned in connection with the murder.

Tom drank in the detail. Beside the picture of Normand was one of Taylor, a quarter the size, and a graphic photo-diagram reconstructing the murder: a crude sketch of the gunman and his flailing victim superimposed on a crisply focused photograph of Taylor's front room. The gist was how *Times* investigators had dug up four witnesses who saw a stranger behaving suspiciously near Taylor's home the evening of the murder – one even provided a detailed description of the man's clothing. All very convincing, but nobody could doubt that what most readers would remember was the photo of Miss Normand.

He looked across the street at the fashionable residential block opposite. Alvarado Court. It was a five-minute stroll from the modest frame house he rented, but it could have been a million miles away. Eight elegant duplexes grouped around a pretty courtyard garden open to the street. Wrought-iron balconies added a slash of Spanish zest to the white walls and green tile roofs. A central flower bed eased the eye towards a vine-clad sun pavilion. Stillness enveloped everything. The place was built to exude peace, solidity and discreet wealth. It did the job well: not a sign remained of the outcry raised twenty-four hours before when Taylor's murdered body was found by his manservant arriving for work.

A honk from a dusty black Ford pulling in across the street. Tom smiled as Thad Sullivan began to dismount awkwardly from under the tattered canopy, rear first, the machine groaning and listing on its springs, the footplate creaking under his weight. He walked over, hand outstretched in greeting, delighted to see his old partner again. It really had been too long.

'Fine morning, Detective Sullivan,' he said in his best brogue.

'Ah, shur 'tis,' was the even broader reply. It never failed to amaze Tom how decades in New York and four more years in Los Angeles had so little impact on Sullivan's broad Kerry accent, even when he wasn't kidding around.

Sullivan slammed the car door and crammed a hat over his graying hair. He cut an impressive figure. It wasn't so much his height as the fact that he looked to be equally wide as well, and at the shoulders rather than round the belly. The huge frame was topped by a head so rock-like it could have been hewn from a cliff face. Back in the old days in New York, when they worked the Eighteenth together as patrolmen, he had seen men mistake Sullivan's bulk and shambling manner for slowness or stupidity. It was an assumption they invariably came to regret.

'Looking stylish as ever, I see.'

'You always could spot a man of refinement,' Sullivan laughed. His wife, Eleanor, never let him out of the house unless he was as spick and span as any man on a detective's salary could be. 'How's it going, anyhow?'

'OK, I guess. Business is a bit slow.'

'Can't be bad if you're on to this already,' Sullivan said. 'What's your line on it? Are you Lasky's promise of unlimited resources?'

He pointed at the *Times*. Tom had read the front-page vow from Jesse Lasky, co-founder with Zukor of the studio, to subsidize the police investigation to 'any extent that might hasten the capture of the assassin'. He had guessed that would not go down well with Los Angeles' finest, implying that they weren't up to the job. Still, the question took him by surprise. How could Sullivan think he was working for Lasky's again?

'C'mon, Thad. You know that's never going to happen.'

'So who're you working for?' Sullivan demanded. 'Or am I not supposed to ask, now you're a private inquiries man?'

'You can ask,' Tom laughed. 'But you might be left hanging for an answer.' It was awkward, and if Sullivan had pushed, Tom probably would have told him straight out about Sennett. But as it was, the detective gave him a crooked sort of glance and muttered something about knowing your pals. Tom didn't catch it all, but saw a chance to change the subject.

'The press boys got a run on you with these witnesses, didn't they?' he said, pointing to the *Times* again.

'Get away, would'ya,' Sullivan growled, taking the bait. 'It was we gave 'em all that. "Investigators for the *Times*", my arse. We took the statements from Mrs MacLean and her maid within hours of Taylor's body being found. And the service station guy and the streetcar conductor came forward to us, not the blasted *Times*.'

It was always thus. Everyone stole the credit when the cops did well, and screamed blue murder when they didn't. Tom followed

Sullivan through the pretty courtyard garden until he stopped outside
the last house in the corner on the left.

'This is Taylor's place,' Sullivan said, searching his pockets for
the key. Between this duplex and the one cater-cornered to it was
a passage running out to some garages and the adjoining street. He
followed Tom's gaze down along it. 'Reckon that's where our killer
waited his chance to get in – we found a mess of smoke butts under
the jacaranda out back. Everything points to him leaving that way,
too.'

'Makes sense,' Tom said, twisting round to look at the windows
and balconies overlooking the gardens all the way round the courtyard. 'Anyone out of place would've been spotted down here. It's
like a fishbowl.'

'You said it,' Sullivan agreed. 'It's mostly movies living here,
and you know how picky they can be.' It was one of Sullivan's
favorite gripes – the snootiness of movie folk. 'Fancy people, right
enough. Main witness is married to that actor fella, Douglas
MacLean – you know him? And that other one – Edna Purviance
– she lives next door along.'

'Seriously? Purviance was here?' That was a surprise. She was
one of Charlie Chaplin's leading ladies. Made a big splash just the
year before in *The Kid*, his biggest hit to date. A name for reporters
to get excited about.

'I didn't see that anywhere.'

'One of the first on the scene,' Sullivan confirmed. 'But she kept
her name out of it. Must have a good publicity man. Not that she
saw anything. It was the MacLean woman got the goods on the killer.
Lives right there.'

Sullivan pointed at the house on the adjacent corner, its entrance
no more than fifteen feet from where they were standing. 'She got
a grandstand view as our man came out the door, right here, and
walked round into the alley. Looked her straight in the eye, cool as
you like.'

'Guy must've had balls of brass,' Tom said. 'Why didn't she call
the cops? Surely she must've heard the shot?'

Sullivan shook his head. 'You know how it is in a place like this.
They don't expect bad things to happen. The MacLeans' maid said
she heard a shot but Mrs Mac overruled her. Decided it was an auto
backfiring and refused to hear any more of it – not even when this

tough walked past a few minutes later. Wasn't until Taylor's man Peavey arrived in the morning she realized she'd been a helluva lot too polite.'

He grunted and unlocked the door. 'Come on in, and mind where you walk.'

SIX

T he curtains were shut to keep out prying eyes, but the sun forced its way in, illuminating the interior with a spectral light. They stood taking in the dead man's parlor. The only indication that anything amiss had occurred was an upturned chair beside the antique writing desk, and a small dense stain on the carpet in front of it.

'So, mister private inquiries man,' Sullivan said. 'What do you make of this?'

Tom ignored the jibe, determined to play along, certain Sullivan would already have forgotten the diagram on the front of the *Times*.

'Well, in the absence of a body, you've got the advantage over me, Thad. But at a guess, that stain on the carpet is where Taylor leaked his life away when he was shot. And unless you and your boys have been messier than usual, he was sitting in that chair when the bullet hit him, or he knocked it over as he fell to the floor.'

'A regular little Pinkerton, aren't you?' Sullivan scoffed. He strode over to the window and pulled one of the curtains back, flooding the room with a disconcerting air of normality.

'That's where he was lying, all right. Laid out like the mortician had already been in. Suit coat buttoned up, arms by his sides, legs together. The cops on the call didn't even figure he'd been shot until the morgue van arrived to take away the body. Some fool decided early on this was natural causes, and because the body was so neat and tidy, everyone believed it. They only spotted the bloodstain and the hole in his back when the coroner's man arrived and lifted him. Add to that, there was a two-carat diamond ring on his finger, a platinum watch in his vest, a silver cigarette case and a wallet with seventy-eight dollars in his pocket. More cash and a checkbook in the bureau, and a pile of gold jewelry in a drawer upstairs. So robbery wasn't the motive, and it's not like the killer was disturbed and had to make a quick getaway. Any ideas?' Sullivan stared at him, an eyebrow cocked quizzically.

Tom shook his head. 'Ne'er a one. What do you reckon yourself?'

'To be honest, I've no clue either. For the shooter to walk out in front of a witness like that – I never heard the like. Unless he was an out-of-towner brought in for the job and didn't fear being recognized. But even so.'

'What about this Sands guy – the one the papers are talking about?'

'DA would love us to think it was him,' Sullivan said. 'That would make it nice and easy. Sands was Taylor's valet until August last, when he took off for no obvious reason with his master's auto, clothes, cash, and went on the lam – forged checks, the lot. Heavy damage to Taylor's bank account. One curious detail was Taylor took four months to swear out a complaint. Why wait so long? We'll have to review that too now, I guess. But sure, Sands is nice for this, except for one big problem.'

'The witness?'

'You got it. Sands worked here every day for a year. Got real cozy with Mrs MacLean next door. She says categorically it wasn't him.'

'She's not covering?'

'For murder? Why would she? Anyhow, the service station guy knew Sands, too. He agrees it wasn't him. And it figures: why would Sands ask directions to a house he worked in for a year?'

Tom thought about it. He knew the guys at the gas station. It was where he always filled up his Dodge. Real friendly every time, and they always called him by name. Those guys made a big point of knowing their customers.

'What's the DA say to that?'

Sullivan's smile was skeptical. 'Woolwine? Not a lot. All he wants is to give something to the papers and get them off his back. Look, I've got to check the stove in the kitchen, so you have your look around. And in case you've forgotten, that means look only – don't disturb anything while you're about it.'

Tom curled his lip at Sullivan's back, then poked his head into the neat little dining room next door. Nothing much to note, except along one wall a line of framed photographs of movie stars: Mary Pickford, Constance Talmadge, Betty Compson. There were men there, too – among them Wally Reid and Jack Pickford. All the pictures were inscribed. The one nearest the door was from a pretty, virginal blonde: *For William Desmond Taylor, Artist, Gentleman, Man! Sincere good wishes, Mary Miles Minter.* Lasky's biggest up-and-comer, they said. The next Mary Pickford, they said. Except they'd been saying it a couple of years now and she showed no sign yet of knocking the queen of Hollywood off her throne.

Back into the parlor, more photographs. In pride of place on the bureau, one of Taylor posing beside a fine McFarlan auto, big as a charabanc, a liveried chauffeur behind the wheel – the defining symbol of movieland success. Beside it was a smaller portrait in a delicate silver frame. This was of Mabel Normand. There was another of her on the bookshelves by the wall, and a third, largest of all, mounted in a polished walnut frame on top of the piano. Tom examined it. She was an odd-looking creature, with those huge, half-hooded eyes. Beautiful, no doubt about it, with that little-girl ringlety innocence so favored by the movie-going public. Once, at a party, he saw her light up a room with her laughter. A comical kind of beauty, he supposed.

In the kitchen, he found Sullivan bent over the potbelly stove, poking around in the ash. Time to broach the crucial question.

'You see all the photographs of Mabel Normand out there? Not exactly the face of a killer, you think?'

'Can't be ruled out.' Sullivan rolled a shoulder stiffly as he straightened up and replaced the lid on the stove. 'Even if she didn't do it by her own hand, the killer most likely slipped in when Taylor walked Normand out to her car. Her driver was waiting where I parked just now. Question is: what was she doing paying Taylor a visit anyway?'

'Didn't he invite her over?'

'Only she knows that. Says she phoned him from her bank downtown and came over to pick up some book he'd bought for her. But Taylor's driver says he was sent over to her place with a book earlier. Why didn't he take both at the same time?'

'Maybe Taylor sent the wrong book?'

'Yeah, maybe. It was Ziegler and Wallace interviewed Normand last night. Said they didn't get much of a sense of her. She was so darned upset. But I say guilt never stopped anyone sobbing. And she is an actress.'

'Which, as you're always telling me, is as far from real life as anyone can get,' Tom insisted. 'Besides, I can't see why she'd do it. I mean, everybody says she was practically engaged to Taylor.'

'Everybody but her, you mean. You saw what she said in the *Times*: "Just good pals." But, you know what? He had a photo of her in a locket in his breast pocket. I wouldn't mind having a good pal like that.'

Sullivan harrumphed and made an obscene gesture. 'Something funny was going on. Why else would she deny it?'

'They're all running scared since Arbuckle, I know that,' Tom said. He also knew he wouldn't get as good a chance again to find out whether Sennett's name was in the frame.

'Do you think she's maybe protecting somebody? Yesterday's *Herald* said the squad was following up a jealous ex-lover angle.'

'The *Herald*, is it?' Sullivan gave him a withering look. 'Well, there's a steaming pile of gospel truth in that rag every evening, isn't there? But you know these guys. You can be sure he had more than one iron in the fire. And him old enough to be—' Sullivan stopped himself, gave a loud tut and another disbelieving shake of the head before continuing. 'Look, if Normand claims she wasn't engaged to Taylor, what's to be jealous about? It doesn't add up. Especially when no one even noticed he'd been shot. It's like they were all so busy trying to clean the place out, Taylor was the last thing on their minds.'

'Cleaning it out? How?'

The big man threw his hands in the air, exasperated. 'Look, you know it was this Peavey, Taylor's negro man, who found the body when he arrived for work at seven thirty, right?'

'Yeah, so?'

'Well, this Peavey calls himself a valet.' Sullivan raised his eyebrows meaningfully. 'But from what I've seen he's more the chambermaid type. He woke half the neighborhood with his shrieking when he found Taylor. That's when Purviance and the MacLeans got involved. Came over to see what was the matter, saw the body and – good citizens of movieland that they are – got on the telephone immediately to report it to . . . guess who, Tom?'

Sullivan's sarcasm was enough to give him an idea of what was coming next, but he shook his head just the same and invited Sullivan to enlighten him.

'It wasn't us – that's for sure. No, they called their pals over on Vine.' There was bitterness to Sullivan's tone now, as if he'd never cease to be astonished by the depths to which movie folk would sink. 'I mean, who calls the police any more just because they've got a corpse on their hands?'

'You mean the guys from Lasky's got here before the cops?' Tom said, not a little impressed. 'They must've moved pretty damn fast.'

'All I know is your old boss, Charles Eyton, was standing in the doorway like he owned the place when I arrived.'

'I read something about Charlie putting in an appearance, but not like that.'

'Damn right. Directing operations like it was one of his bloody productions. You'd think he was the Chief of Police himself. There were more of his fellas here than ours. Swarming all over the place, they were.'

For the first time in months, Tom was relieved he no longer worked for Lasky. He could only imagine how many cops' toes Eyton had stepped on, and just the thought of it made him uncomfortable.

'They were probably looking for love letters or something compromising like that, Thad. Stuff that could embarrass the studio.'

'Or the evidence, as some of us still call it,' Sullivan said. 'We found almost no personal correspondence belonging to Taylor, and that sure as hell can't be right. For one thing, Miss Normand told Ziegler and Wallace last night that Taylor had a whole stack of letters from her wrapped in ribbon. There was nothing burned. I just checked the stove and it's clean. But some smart boy was spotted running off with Taylor's stash of liquor, so Christ knows what else was in the crate. You wouldn't know anything about that, would you?'

The hair prickled on the back of Tom's neck. 'Me? Why would I know anything about it?'

'I'm just surprised. You tell me you don't know any of this already, and then you come up with that stuff about the letters.'

'It was an educated guess, Thad. I know how these people think, remember? They would remove his booze and anything else that could reflect badly on him or the studio. You said yourself, even the cops on call didn't know Taylor was shot until the coroner arrived. How would the studio benefit from trying to cover up a murder?'

'I have no idea,' Sullivan admitted. But it wasn't enough for him. 'Sure as hell, something's not right here. I asked you earlier if you were working for Lasky's and you sidestepped it, so I took that to be a yes. Because we're old pals, Tom, I thought I wouldn't push it. But I didn't think I'd have to stand here and listen to you talk bull to me into the bargain. That's not on. We go too far back for that.'

Tom felt the color rising in his cheeks, and tried to keep his voice level. 'Hey, old pal, I told you on the phone, I'm just making a few inquiries on behalf of a client.'

'Yeah? Well, maybe you'd better go back to this *client* of yours and tell him your cop friend doesn't appreciate being treated like an eejit. Do you hear me?'

How could he not? The man was bellowing like an ox. But Tom didn't get a chance to argue it. Sullivan put a hand on his shoulder, turned him like a top and pushed him towards the door. He was outside in the sunlight again before he knew it, Sullivan on his heels, pulling the door shut behind him with a thud.

'I'm sorry you think that's as far as you and me go, Tom. I really am.'

He turned to see Sullivan ham-fistedly struggling to turn the key in the lock, and couldn't help but laugh – as much from shock as anything else. 'You gotta be kidding me, Thad. Come on, seriously? This is me you're talking to.'

'I'm glad you find it funny,' Sullivan growled, turning the key at last. 'Because I sure as hell don't. Look, I know you're hard up, and I don't blame you for wanting to make a quick buck while you can. But I can't help being sore at you using me to help out those rotten pups at Lasky. They've done so much damage already, interfering with the proper course of this investigation. It's not right.'

'You think I'd try and dupe you for a few lousy dollars? How can you even think that?' Tom glanced away a moment, as much to keep his anger in check as to decide how much more he could afford to reveal. 'Look, Thad, you know damn well I would never stiff a pal. Not you, and not the guy who's asked me to look into this for him, either. But especially not you, for Chrissakes. How far back do we go? If you *must* know, the reason I never said I was working for Lasky's is because I'm damn well not. And if I was, I would've been straight with you and told you so.'

Sullivan flushed to the edge of his hairline and put his huge hands up. 'Quit your hollering, will you? You're not supposed to be here, so calm yourself down.' He ran a quick eye around the courtyard to check for twitching curtains and saw none. 'Look, maybe I shouldn't have gone jumping to conclusions like that. But what can I say? You're not confiding in me, are you?'

'I can't yet,' Tom said, as they began walking back towards the street. 'But it won't affect your case, I promise you. OK?

'All right, whatever,' Sullivan muttered, embarrassed now. They reached the sidewalk and he put a hand on Tom's shoulder. Easy this time, a confidential look in his eye. 'Look, I'm sorry. I was out of line. But there's a load of shite going on with this investigation that I don't understand. All sorts of muck coming down from the top, and I don't like the smell of it. It makes me jumpy.'

'Coming down? From where? From the Chief?'

Sullivan shook his head non-committally.

'From the DA?'

Again, Sullivan said nothing, a confirmation in itself. District Attorney Thomas Woolwine's links to the movie industry were, some said, entirely responsible for his rapid climb to the top branches of Los Angeles' law enforcement tree.

'Well, Taylor was a big cheese, wasn't he?' Tom offered. 'Those guys are sure to feel the heat with so many headlines in it. It'll settle down in a day or two.'

'Maybe. But if you ask me, the whole affair stinks. Whoever your pal is, take my advice, Tom, get shot of this right now. Don't get dragged in.'

'Ah now, Thad.' He tapped Sullivan's shoulder and smiled broadly. 'You know if you say that to me, I won't be able to keep my nose out.'

'I'm serious, Tom. It isn't worth it.' Sullivan nodded towards his machine. 'I got to get going. Look, we should organize that evening out. Maybe do the fights one Friday. I've haven't been out in Venice since that last time with you. Stonefist Miller, d'you remember? What a smacker!'

A smacker it certainly was. The knockout punch set Tom's ears ringing ten rows back. He laughed and watched as Sullivan bent and cranked the ancient Ford. Engine spluttering to life, he removed his hat and clambered in, accompanied by a squeal of protesting springs.

'Let me know if you hear anything,' Sullivan shouted over the clatter, then eased away from the curb, turning in a wide arc and chugging down the hill.

Tom watched him go, and breathed free for the first time in an hour.

SEVEN

D own the hill at the intersection with Sixth, across from West Lake Park, people thronged between the stores, going about their business and daily chores. He pushed through the door of the Lago cafeteria and tapped a nickel on the gleaming zinc countertop. A small dark man, thin and bald, with ears hairy as cactus stalks, appeared from nowhere. He rubbed his hands on a crisp white apron and beamed at Tom.

'*Ciao, Tomas, come stai?*'

'Hey, Luca. Do me a coffee and a glass of water, would you? And while you're at it, can I use your telephone?'

'Sure, Tom, in back, same as always.' The Italian jutted his chin towards the swing door behind the counter and stepped aside.

Tom spun the coin, listened to its whirr and the slap of Luca's hand as he walked through. Beyond the door was a small storeroom packed with coffee drums and dry goods, and a narrow unlit passageway that doubled as a basic kitchen. On the dividing wall was the telephone.

'Wilshire one-zero-eight-nine,' he asked, and had to repeat it. The exchange must have been trying out the deaf that morning. He wrapped a finger idly round the brown cloth cord as he waited for the connection to click through, winding and unwinding it twice before someone picked up. Sounded like a big negro woman.

'Miss Normand ain't receiving calls today,' she said sternly. 'Not on the telephone and not in person.'

She didn't offer to take a message and broke the connection before Tom had time to ask any more. He cursed at the earpiece, clicked the cradle and repeated the process again. This time he didn't give the woman a chance to get in first. 'Look, I'm calling on behalf of Mr Sennett. Is Mr Waldron there?'

A pause at the other end of the line. Then: 'No, he ain't. Not since last night.'

Again he cursed, but knew he had to be quick. 'Thank you, ma'am. But look here, Mr Sennett wants me to meet with Miss Normand. Can you tell her that, for me? My name is—'

'I don't care what you name is, or for who you calling. Like I say, Miss Normand ain't seeing nobody today. Not you, not Mr Sennett, not nobody.' And that was her last word, followed by the clunk of disconnection.

'Here you go.' Luca slid the coffee across the counter and a tall glass of water. 'You wan' anything to give it kick?' He waved a hand vaguely under the counter.

Tom looked at his wristwatch. 'Plenty of kick in it for me already, this time of day. But I'll buy you one.'

'No, *grazie*, I got work to do,' Luca said, and disappeared through the swing door without another word.

'Like I don't,' Tom muttered, and caught a broad smile from Luca's wife who was wiping down the far end of the empty counter.

He gave her back his best, knocked back the brew and walked out the door with a wave of his hat. Ambling down into the shallow bowl of Westlake Park, he appreciated the soft touch of dirt beneath his shoe leather as he made his way through the gardens towards the Wilshire Boulevard exit on the far side. Young mothers and nursemaids thronged the walkways, airing infants in perambulators, pulling knock-kneed tots by the hand. The fountain hissed a tall feather of mist across the boat lake, its plume brushed out by the morning breeze. On he walked, out again into the brisk city streets until, rounding the corner of Vermont, he stopped, balking at a huddle of men up ahead outside the canopied entrance to Miss Normand's apartment building. He had expected a couple of newsmen to be hanging around, but nothing like this. At least thirty reporters were standing on the sidewalk, laughing and smoking, chattering among themselves.

It was all they could do. At the top of the steps, two burly patrolmen stood, arms folded in silent defiance, blocking access to the building. Tom approached to see who he knew among the hacks and find out what was going on. But when he reached them, he didn't recognize a face. All out-of-towners to judge by the accents, shipped in to grand-stand on the fall of another star. He walked on, following the building round the next intersection until he came to a gap in the street front shielded by a high wooden gate. He crossed, selected a lamppost to lean against, unfolded his newspaper and settled down to wait.

It couldn't have been more than fifteen minutes before his luck came in. The gate swung open, pushed out by an elegant chauffeur in smart blue livery and cap who straightaway disappeared again. Seconds later came the subdued roar of a motor and a long, silver-gray limousine with an open cab and closed tonneau behind rolled out on to the street. It wasn't Mabel Normand's; he knew that for sure. The machine stopped, reversed a few feet and, instead of jumping down, the driver reached out, gave the gate a heave and drove off before it was fully home. Tom ran over, inserted a brown brogue just in time and squeezed inside.

A glint of chromium beyond assured him he was on the right track. The passage opened out into a wide enclosed courtyard where a row of snazzy automobiles were parked – a Bugatti, a Mercer, an enormous Pierce Arrow. Beside a gleaming lavender sedan, a man in knee-boots and britches, stripped to the waist, was bent over a bucket of foaming water, wringing out a cloth. Garish even by movie colony standards, the sedan was one of the best known in town: the Rolls Royce that studio boss Sam Goldwyn had gifted Mabel Normand when, a couple of years before, she signed up with him following a row with Sennett. The deal with Goldwyn didn't last but, as everybody knew, she sure as hell kept the automobile.

'Hey, you, driver? What's your name?'

The startled chauffeur jumped up, holding the wet cloth to his belly. 'How'd you get in here?'

'How do you think?' Tom cocked his head towards the gate. It didn't take much figuring. 'Now answer the question, and be quick about it.'

'You a cop?'

'What does it look like?'

That was usually enough for most folk, and so it proved for this one.

'Davis,' the driver said grudgingly. Mid-height, early thirties, he was wiry rather than skinny, a thin face and an upturned nose giving him an odd boyish look. Stripped of his shirt, the most noticeable thing about him was a livid purple scar snaking all across his stomach, like he'd had his gut ripped or been bitten by a shark.

'What've you got for me, Davis?'

''Bout what?'

Tom moved closer, chest out, stared him down. 'What do you think? Two nights ago. The dead guy. Miss Normand?'

'Hey, lay off,' Davis protested, but half-heartedly. He took a step back and found he had nowhere to move, glanced behind, saw nothing but gleaming lavender and glass. 'I already told your bull pals everything. Why would I have anything more to say?'

'Maybe I got a better price for you.' Tom pulled out a roll of bills, peeled off a couple and dangled them under Davis's nose.

'You ain't no cop.'

'Does it matter?'

Not if the look in Davis's eyes was anything to judge by. The driver glanced over his shoulder again, this time towards the windows overlooking the yard. 'Look, pal, it's not like I don't want the dough, but you ain't gonna get value for money. You could just as easy read the morning papers.'

'I already read them. Tell me something different.'

'Like what?' Davis tried to make a laugh, but all that emerged was an anxious rattle in his throat.

'Like what really happened over at Taylor's place.'

The man looked oddly relieved, and Tom noticed the hint of a smirk form on his lips. He reached out for the bills but they eluded his grasp.

'Not so fast. What you got?'

'Like I told the cops, I waited in the street while Miss Normand went in.'

'You were in the car all the time?'

'Sure. I mean, I got down to brush out some peanut shells she shucked on the carpet on the way over. That black boy of Taylor's came out; we traded some words. A couple minutes later, Taylor walks her out, and off we drive. Didn't hear nothin', didn't see nothin'. Except her blowin' kisses at him out the back window.'

'You came straight back here?'

'Where else?'

'And she wasn't acting strange.'

'Nope, not a bit.'

'So, when did you hear Taylor was dead?'

Davis swallowed, glancing at the bills again, checked they were still there. 'Not till yesterday morning. I heard a racket comin' from the apartment and ran in. Saw Miss Normand shrieking and weeping and all, Bessie trying to calm her.'

'What time was that?'

''Bout eight thirty. I waited inside until the doctor come. Bessie told me Mr Taylor'd been found dead in his front parlor. Didn't hear till later he was shot. None of us did.'

Looking at the man's face, Tom could accept he was telling the truth. It sounded about right.

'So where's she now?'

'Somebody came and picked her up earlier . . . Don't ask me who, cos I didn't see. Last time I saw her was last night. Up at the Cocoanut Grove—'

'She was at a nightclub last night?' Tom asked, unable to conceal his astonishment. 'That's a strange way of grieving.'

Davis didn't like that. 'What the hell would you know about it? People have different ways. Miss Normand, too. So she went out and tried to drown her sorrows.'

Quick as it had risen, the anger died in his eyes and for a moment he seemed lost, his face a blank. Then he began again with a vague shrug of the shoulders. 'Like I say, she must've been having a high ol' time because it was past midnight when she came out and told me I could go.'

'You left her there?'

'Why not? It's not like it's a million miles away.'

He wasn't kidding. The supper club at the ritzy new Ambassador Hotel was only a couple of blocks up on Wilshire. Even so, no way would Mabel Normand, international movie star, walk to or from anywhere.

Davis caught the skeptical look on Tom's face.

'Look, it happens all the time. She wants to go on somewhere with a bunch of pals – what's the point of me trailing after her? I gotta sleep too, you know. She was with Harry Williams, Lew Cody and that gang. They're a wild crowd, like to party big time. She's always going off with them one place or another.'

'And sending you home?'

'Sure. Unless she wants to take them some place. Then I drive. She's the boss.'

'So what time did she get in?'

'No idea. Only, Bessie said she went out again this morning. Picked up, like I say.'

Tom looked at his wristwatch. This was going nowhere.

'OK, Davis,' He handed him the ten bucks. 'I guess you weren't holding out on me after all. Do you have any ideas yourself about Taylor? Ever see anything going on when he was with Miss Normand?'

'Hey, I look like a detective now? For all I know, it could've been you shot him.' Again the smirk broke out on Davis's face and his hand went to his waistband where he'd tucked the ten-spot. 'Look, I'm not risking my job to get one over on you, pal. 'Course, if you wanna guarantee that—'

Tom shot a hand out and grabbed a thick clump of Davis's oiled black hair, the grunt of shock turning to a yelp of pain when he whipped the driver's head around and smacked it against the hood of the car. With his free hand, he grabbed Davis's arm and jerked it up in a lock behind his back. Out the side of his eye, he noticed a peppering of tiny scars on the underside of the forearm.

Bending over him, Tom breathed heat into his ear. 'You dumb ass. Don't try to get smart with me. You got your money, now spill all you got or you'll find your job's the least you lose. Understand?'

Davis was still bucking like a jackrabbit when, all of a sudden, he stiffened like a spring and let out a low, unearthly wail. Unsettled, Tom loosened his grip enough to let the man turn his head. His face had turned a sickly shade of gray.

'OK, OK,' he whined, his voice thin and wracked with pain. 'Go easy, will you? I can't take this. You saw my belly; if it splits again, that's it, I'm dead.'

It hit Tom then: the marks on his arm, the rip in his belly. The stories he had heard about war veterans; the rumors about Mabel

Normand. And what it was connected them. He released Davis and stood back, putting a hand under his elbow now, helping him turn.

'Can you stand?' Tom asked.

Davis shook his head. Bent double, he crooked his right arm around his stomach, his face creased with pain. Tom leaned into him, taking his weight, easing him down on to the limousine's running board, waiting as the pain subsided slowly and some dabs of color returned to Davis's cheeks.

'You get that in Europe? In the trenches?'

'Argonne Forest,' Davis gasped, trying to control his breathing, hands on his belly clenching and unclenching. 'Shell took my whole unit out. Half my guts with it.'

Tom tried not to picture it. Too much pity in that. He pointed at the needle marks on Davis's arms. 'That the reason you use dope?'

Again a nod of confirmation.

'And why Miss Normand chooses you to drive her around? You keep the stuff coming in nice and regular, so she never has to get her hands dirty? I'll bet you know every dope dive in town, don't you?'

Davis cast his eyes down to the rough concrete of the yard, as if he knew they would betray him. 'Look, I don't know anything about that, all right? What she does in her own time ain't none of my affair. I just ferry her about.'

'No. I don't think so. I'd bet the bank on you knowing every move she makes, inside that apartment and out. Just like every driver and maid between 'em knows all there is to know about the boss.'

Davis breathed a long, resigned sigh. 'So maybe I used to get her a bit of stuff sometimes. But not now, OK?'

'You saying she's not hooked on it?'

Tom had never seen any sign of it himself, and it sure wasn't something you could talk to Sennett about. But he'd heard plenty of stories, and every gossip column in the country had traded on rumors of Mabel Normand's ill-defined 'illness' for a couple of years now.

'Jesus, guy, what'ya want me to say? That she's got a yen for it? Well, yeah, like that's not exactly news, is it? There ain't hardly anybody in the business doesn't know that. Just don't drag me in. I got enough problems.'

Davis had recovered enough to start feeling sorry for himself again. Tom said nothing, just stared at him knowing the rest would come soon enough. And it did.

'Look, so I used to get her some powder. So what? It wasn't a regular thing. You're wrong about her. She likes to go get it for herself. Likes that kinda thing, you know. Gets off on the seamy side of it. But that ain't always advisable in her line. So she used to be at the studio or out on a shoot and ask me to run and get a few bindles for her, and maybe some for me, too. You think I was gonna say no to that?'

Davis lapsed into silence, his eyes blank, snagged on some memory.

'Don't go all misty-eyed on me,' Tom said. 'Sounds like a pretty nice set-up, for you. So why no more? What happened to stop it?'

'What'ya think? She's trying to quit, of course. Lady's trying to kick it.' Davis went to raise his hands in a show of mock innocence, but winced and thought better of it. 'Like I say, none of mine. I ain't getting in the way of that.'

'Come on. You expect me to believe you'd say goodbye to a meal ticket that easy. Like you don't know full well that if she does get free of it, you're the last person she's going to want working for her. I don't think so.'

'Aw, what's the goddamn use?' Davis dropped his shoulders with a heavy sigh. 'Look, you want it so much. Here it is, straight down the line: it was Mr Taylor – yeah, him – he paid me not to get her more.'

'Taylor?' Tom's jaw gawped. 'What the hell did Taylor know about it?'

'A lot more than you, pal. You think you wouldn't know if your woman was sousing herself with powder? Gimme a break.'

'So what're you saying? Taylor was giving her the stuff himself?'

'No. Why would he? Man was trying to get her to kick it. He was crazy for her. Said he'd give me a bill every week – a fifty for Chrissakes – pay for mine if I left her alone. Gave me a big speech – some garbage about friends not feeding off of each other. Sure, and look where it got him.'

'So did you? Leave her alone, I mean?

'What do you think? Like some rich fool wants to pay my way, and I'm gonna say no? Sure, I played along, I had nothin' to lose. Didn't make any difference, though. She can't stay off it for long. I mean, she tries and all, but it's hard, you know. You can't imagine. Don't know what the hell I'm going to do now.'

'Save the sob story, brother. Tell me more about the dope. Where was she getting it if not from you or him?'

Davis shook his head again, past caring now. 'Shorty Madden, I guess. That's who she usually went to.'

Tom recognized the name, but as a bootlegger, a small-time liquor merchant to the stars. It was news to him that Madden dealt dope as well, but since Prohibition pretty much everything came in the same way. Booze, cocaine – it was all one.

'You reckon maybe Taylor tried to buy him off, too?' Tom asked.

'More than reckon,' Davis nodded. 'I know it. But Madden, he didn't like Taylor interfering with business. I mean, he *really* didn't like it. Told Taylor go to hell and keep his sermons to himself.'

'They had words?'

'Words?' Davis got the beginnings of a guffaw out, then stopped, holding his belly again, eyes tight with pain. He gulped hard, easing his breath back. 'Not just words. Those two had a good ol' rumble right here in this yard. Miss Normand near had a fit trying to drag 'em apart. Seems she made some arrangement with Madden to bring the dope to the gate, there, when Taylor turns up unannounced. I only caught the tail end cos I was inside having my supper, but with all the hollering I came out and found them trying to kick seven kinds'a hell out of each other.'

'Was he hurt?'

'Taylor? Nah, he was a big guy, you know, compared to Shorty. Good shape, too, for an old guy. Looked to me like he was makin' the running. 'Course, he was fortunate Madden didn't out with a blade and do him on the spot. Heart mustn't have been in it that night. Soon as we got 'em apart, they flung a few more cusses at each other, then Madden turned on his heel and stomped on out of here.'

'And that was it?'

'Far as I know. Mr Taylor came back in, dusted himself down and had a sup of brandy while Bessie mended his jacket. Face like thunder on him. We heard him and Miss Normand arguing in the parlor. Soon as Bessie finished stitching, he stormed out.'

'When was this?

'Right before New Year, I guess – yeah, must've been cos I remember Miss Normand thanking the good Lord most of the neighbors were away for the holidays.'

'Cops know anything about this?'

Davis gave him the skeptical look again. 'Not from me.'

'Do you think Normand might've told them?'

'No way. She'd have to be—'

'Crazy. Yeah, she would, wouldn't she?' Tom couldn't see Mabel Normand wanting to tell the cops about any of her dirty habits. If the press got hold of it, she'd be finished, instantly. He gave Davis a long look and asked the obvious question.

'You reckon Madden's good for Taylor?'

'How would I know?' Davis scowled. 'Thoughts like that, y'know, it don't pay to have 'em.'

'So, where can I find this Shorty Madden?'

Davis looked like he was about to swallow his tongue. 'You don't want to go after Shorty. Anyhow, if he had anything to do with it, he'll be long gone.'

'Let me be the judge of that. Where's he operate from?' Tom stuck his hand in his pocket again, skimmed another couple of sawbucks from his roll and held them up, rubbing them slowly between finger and thumb. 'I'll leave your name out of it.'

Davis's gaze went no further than the money. He rubbed his belly where the scar met his waistband and crumbled. 'He usually works out of that Irish place on Virgil, over on East Sunset. Hannigan's. You know it? Used to be a saloon. Still is if you knock right. Won't find him there yet, though – it's nights mostly in his line . . .'

Davis's voice trailed off and he was gasping again, staring into somewhere Tom was glad he didn't have to follow. He stood up, patted the driver on the shoulder and threw the bills in his lap.

'You've been real helpful, soldier.'

EIGHT

As he turned the key in the latch, Tom was still trying to settle on what to do next. In the ten minutes it took to walk back from Normand's, all he thought of was calling Sullivan and telling him what Davis had said about Taylor's clash with this bootlegger, Madden. It was a hot tip, and he owed it to Sullivan to pass it on. But with only Davis's word to go on, something held him back. Handing on this nugget untested might do more harm than good. Not least for Miss Normand. If her connection with Madden got out to the press – and it would for sure once the detective squad got hold of it – that would be the end for her. Just like Arbuckle. Only worse, because she was a woman. Forget evidence. Forget the law. The way things were, every hack and reformist zealot in the country would be baying for her dope-tainted blood on every front page from Portland to New York and all points in between. And Sennett's long association with Normand might well be enough to drag him down with her. Everyone in the business knew how parlous studio finances could be, and Sennett's more than most. No way was Tom going to have that on his conscience. Not without hearing the whole story.

He pushed the door open and stopped. The girl was not there, but her presence was everywhere. Gone was the bundle of blankets on the couch. Gone, too, the scattering of papers, ties, books, cups, odd socks, ashtrays and other garbage that normally littered the floor. The meager stock of crockery on the dresser had been rearranged to look almost homely. The sound of a chair-leg scraping drew him in as far as the kitchen door. It was the same in there. The griddle was missing its crust of grounds, grease and egg spatter. A stack of cups and plates gleamed on the drainer. Colleen was sitting at the little bench table, jacket all buttoned up, absorbed in scribbling on a piece of paper. So pale, a few flecks of pink on her cheeks and eyes red-rimmed. Almost innocent in the daylight.

'You do all this?' he said, tapping on the doorframe.

She whirled around and stood too quickly, kicking the chair back with a clatter. He raised a hand to calm her, saw her hurriedly fold the paper she'd been writing on and stuff it in her jacket pocket.

'That for me?'

Her cheeks fizzed red. 'I wanted to say thanks for taking care of me last night and, well, you know, say goodbye and all. I didn't think you'd want me here when you got back, so, uh . . . I mean, really, thank you.'

He held a hand out, thumb rubbing across his fingertips. 'Aren't you going to give it to me now you've written it?'

She fished the paper out of her pocket and handed it over. 'I didn't think you'd be back, so maybe I said too—' She broke off.

'If you want, I can read it later, the way it was intended.'

She nodded and looked relieved, so he folded the note and put it on the table.

'I better be getting out of your hair,' she said.

He stood aside to let her into the parlor, wondering why she was in such a rush. 'You never did get round to telling me how it was you got to be in that place. How'd you get in a bind like that?'

She glanced around the room, looking for something to fix her eye on and spotted a small, framed picture on the wall. The only thing hanging there, it was a faded photograph of a stern, sharp-featured woman of advanced years, a high lace collar tickling her chin.

'Is that your mother?' she asked.

'You think she looks like me?' The idea made him laugh.

'Maybe.' She shrugged. 'Looks kinda tough for an old lady.'

'Sure does. I wouldn't mind having some of that steel in my jaw. But she's no relation of mine. Maybe Mr Sennett's – he rents me this place. She was up there when I got here and I just let her be.'

'And that one? She one of his girls?' There was a defensive note of sarcasm in Colleen's voice now. She was pointing at the studio shot of Fay on the dresser, inscribed to Tom and signed with all her love. Fay had laughed when she gave it to him, hiding her embarrassment, claiming the way her career was headed there might not be a next one to give him. But he had it framed and kept it propped there on the dresser all the same, where he could glance at it of an evening while she was away.

'She's a friend,' he said, as non-committal as he could. No point telling her the whole of his business.

'Millions'd believe you.' She turned away. Her tone implied she wasn't one of them.

'You didn't answer my question, *Colleen*.'

He drew her name out, not just to make it sound like a secret, but also because it fell oddly from his lips – not *a* girl, not *any* girl, as his mind translated it to and from the old tongue. But this girl, here, in front of him, now. 'What were you doing in that place? And what's your real name, now we're getting so personal?'

'Mae,' she said, flat, as if it meant nothing to her. She dropped her gaze and tucked a lock of yellow hair behind her ear, fingertips brushing back across her cheek again. 'I'm not proud of what I did,

you know,' she blurted. 'I tried my best to get movie work, true as
God I did. Tried four months solid but there are so many pretty
girls in this town, and every one of them looking for the same.'

He knew the truth of that and told her so. No one could walk in
or out of a movie studio without noticing the long lines of deluded
hopefuls outside the gates every morning, hoping for a bit part, the
chance to be discovered. So many, there wasn't work for a fraction
of them, and more crowding in behind every week. The lucky ones
recognized straight off the crazy odds against success, when they
still had the money to get on the train back to Grinnell or Hickville
or wherever they came from, nursing their bruised dignity and shattered illusions. It was the ones who stayed got hurt, who believed
the pap in the fan magazines about never letting anything stand in
the way of their dreams, clinging to the hope of a miracle occurring
just around the next corner.

'Only had sixty-five bucks to start with,' she said. 'Most of that
went first month, before I found a good-price rooming house. Didn't
take long for the rest to dribble away. Then a girl I met at a casting
said she knew a guy who'd pay us to go to parties. Five bucks a
time, and we could eat and drink all we wanted. Sounded too good
to be true.'

It was, of course. He made a pot of coffee, sat her down again
and let her tell her story. How she met a guy called Joe at this party,
who was real nice and picked her out special with another girl to
go upstairs to a room where these swells were drinking and smoking,
and she would get an extra five bucks just to dance. And that was
all she had to do, first few times. But soon Joe wanted more for the
money. She was too embarrassed to go into detail, and he didn't
really want to hear it: how she had been exploited and abused,
coerced and threatened. Didn't tell her either that he heard it all
before, seen what desperation, disappointment, hunger does to
people, too many times. Sometimes it's no solace knowing your
troubles are not unique.

'I'm real sorry,' she snuffled. 'It's not your problem. But you
asked and it's been so awful these past days. I was sure I'd die if
I didn't get away from that place and, all of a sudden, there you
were, like you'd been sent to me, and I . . .' She buried her face in
her hands, the only thing other than pride between him and her
tears.

'It's all right,' he said, uncomfortable now, his mind on more practical matters, like how he might help her without getting taken for a ride himself. 'How bad are you stuck on that stuff?'

From what she told him, this Joe had been dosing her on heroin, building up her need, then demanding money when she sickened for more. Tom knew about that poison. Cocaine and morphine were more common around the studios, but it took people the same way. Got its hooks in, fought like fury to never let go.

'They got you using a needle yet?'

She shook her head. 'Joe tried to make me couple of nights back. Said it was cheaper than a capsule. He used it on a girl who came by in real bad shape. Tried to make me use it after, but I saw her blood in the syringe and screamed. Nothing would've got me to then, so he stopped. Guess he thought he'd have plenty opportunity to try again.'

Tom rubbed his eyes. What the hell was happening to this city? The most beautiful place you could ever want to be – warm sun, gentle sea, fertile land, a cast-iron land of plenty. And so many bent on dredging the depths instead.

'You think you can shake it?'

'I don't know,' she said. 'I'm sick in my stomach now for the want of it. But I guess I don't give in and see what happens.'

'Good, that's the attitude.' He doubted it would be so easy, but he would not discourage her. 'Now, look, you've got to be honest with me. Have you got a place to stay for real, or were you putting me on last night?'

She looked genuinely surprised he could ask it. 'Sure I do. Out in Hollenbeck. It's a good place, like I said.'

'This Joe guy know you live there? You know you'll never get free of that poison long as he's around. You realize that, right?'

'Sure, but what can I do? Move? I got no money to go anywhere else. I already owe three weeks.'

'What about if I find you somewhere to stay?'

She stared at him, her lips parted, unsure of what he was suggesting.

'Not here,' he said, strangling that possibility. 'I have friends who could maybe help. Until you're back on your feet again, I mean. But you'd have to stay away from Joe, and from that stuff. You'd have to make me that promise.'

He wasn't sure why he was saying any of this. He might not even be able to produce the little he was offering. But he wanted to help.

'I can ask around about some work for you, too, if you do OK,' he added. 'Might not be acting, but it'd get you started. Would you quit it for that?'

Her eyes lit up and she threw her arms around his neck. 'Oh Lord, I knew you were—' The rest was lost in his coat. He pushed her off, embarrassed.

'Hang on. All I said is I'll try. Let's wait and see how it goes, yeah?' He raised her chin with his balled fist, fixed his eyes on hers. 'It might take a day or two to organize. And you have to do it proper. No second chances. Meantime, you can stay here. Anybody asks, say you're my niece, visiting.'

She flashed an uncertain smile at him. 'Actually, you know. Somebody did ask. Earlier.'

He stared at her, puzzled. 'Someone called?'

'On the telephone.' She grabbed the note on the table, unfolded it, held it out to him. 'I wrote it down here and forgot to say. Mr Sennett called, wants you to go see him at the studio.'

'Did he remember you from last night?'

Her bottom lip trembled as she tried to force a smile. 'Sure he did. Said something mean about having a feeling I'd be here. Said I could hand in his clothes any time at the studio front office. Just as soon as I got them laundered.'

NINE

Tom gunned the roadster over the crest of the hill and took in the movie-making sprawl spread across the vale beyond. Seen from the high ground to the south-west, Mack Sennett's studio in Edendale looked as ramshackle and chaotic as any of his pie-throwing Keystone Kops two-reelers. But as so often with Sennett, reality was the opposite of how it seemed. Over ten years the studio had grown steadily from two acres to well over twenty and now it was a dense warren of offices, workshops, open sets and canvas-covered stages, packed on to three blocks either side of Glendale Boulevard. On one flank, a collection of sagging timber shacks, storehouses and barns, torn-down scenery flats propped against every surface. On the other side, a scattering of concrete buildings had sprung up, testament to the fact that Sennett aimed not so much for permanence as permanent expansion. Yet it all ran as efficiently as a well-maintained machine.

Finding a space amid the ranks of autos parked nose-in along the street, Tom jumped down and walked back to the main gate. A dust-smothered truck drew up out front and discharged a gang of chattering actors and actresses back from a shoot. Within a minute they'd disappeared noisily beneath the mission-style arch that spanned the entrance, pausing only to collect a pass from the hands of a man in a tweed suit standing in a sentry box, a cast-off prop from some long-forgotten actioner. By the time Tom reached the gate, the man was sitting back inside. All that could be seen was a pair of gnarled hands poking out, clutching the sports pages of the *Herald*.

'Hey, Al,' Tom said, rapping hard on the side of the box.

A small, grizzled head in a brown derby turtle-necked out above the newspaper, the deep-lined face bearing a smile of recognition.

'Evening, Mr Collins,' the gateman replied. 'You see Young Brown give that Coffey guy a pummeling at the Stadium last night?' He pointed towards Fane Norton's *Fighting Words* column in the paper. 'Sounds like a real doozie.'

'I'm too busy for any kind a pleasure these days, Al.'

The gateman liked that. He smiled wider and tipped his forehead with a finger. 'Sure, sure, know what you mean,' he said. 'You in to see the old man?'

'For my sins.'

'Proceed, sir.' The gateman swept a hand out and down, a mocking courtly gesture. Tom smiled, took the pass and made his way along the lot's main strip towards the four-floor tower from which Sennett controlled his empire.

Despite the failing daylight, all around the air still rang with hoots of mirth, shrieks of surprise and occasional bursts of rollicking mood music. Clutches of actors and actresses loitered in costume, gossiping and smoking: a buccaneer swapping gags with a turbaned potentate, a mustachioed villain in top hat and tails sweet-talking a

princess in high-piled wig and billowing gown. As he passed the
commissary, a waft of warm and aromatic stew caressed Tom's
nostrils. Thick, meaty goulash bubbled like a mirage in his mind.
Studio commissaries invariably reflected the people who used them.
Lasky's had pretentions to refinement, Metro's to austerity. Sennett's
excelled in hearty, belly-filling fare. Tom peered in at the crowds
of crewmen and players waiting in line to be served, or seated at
bench tables chowing down on bowlfuls of steaming stew, and
became aware of the chill air of the dying day and a yawning cavern
in his stomach. He checked his watch, licked his lips and succumbed.

TEN

The elevator bell clanged and the doors opened directly into
the top-floor office. Straight ahead, a wall of glass flared
with the gaudy drama of sunset. In the center of the room,
Sennett was perched on the edge of a long table listening, if it could
be called that, to a clamoring band of gagmen, directors and players.
Bug-eyes, buck teeth, bugle beaks, every one had a face born for
comedy. And all shouting across each other. Sennett alone looked
up and registered Tom's arrival. He glanced at the gold pocket watch
he held open in his hand, and back at Tom again.

'Good, you're here. About time, too,' he shouted, and waved him
in. The racket subsided and all eyes turned towards Tom, though
with one or two the optics were so skewed it was difficult to tell.

'Gentlemen, take a lesson from Mr Collins here,' Sennett drawled.
'Punctuality will always buy you a seat at my table. Now get your
sad asses out of here and wrap things up for today. Anyone still
desperate to see me, make it tub-side, in forty minutes.'

The clamor broke out again as Sennett rose and began herding
them towards the elevator. Tom crossed the plush red carpet to the
wall of window and stared out at the studio below. The pulse of
activity along its arteries was slowing now as evening triumphed
and production was at as much of a standstill as it ever reached. A
faint rhythm of hammering and sawing drifted up as sets were struck
and preparations made for the next day's early start. Electric lamps

flickered on here and there, glowing beneath the long lengths of muslin stretched across the tops of open stages. It was all so peaceful he hardly noticed Sennett come stand beside him.

'Beautiful, isn't it? And people wonder at me because I gaze down on it from my tower. Don't you think they would, too, if they had a tenth of it?'

'I guess so.' Tom knew for certain he would. 'But maybe it's not the gazing that they wonder at, Mack. Maybe it's that you do it while you're scrubbing your back.'

Tom nodded back towards the doorway in the wall beside the elevator. Beyond was another room, identical to this but for a fold-back roof, containing the huge tin bath in which Sennett spent a substantial part of every day and from which he conducted much of his business.

Sennett boomed out a short deep laugh. 'Well, maybe so, maybe so. But I always said the tub's where I do my best thinking. And if that's what it takes to keep this show on the road, then let 'em wonder all they damn well like. Hell, half of 'em wouldn't do any wonderin' at all if we didn't stick it up on a screen for them.'

Sennett put a hand on Tom's shoulder and gave it an unusually amiable squeeze. 'Come, sit down and have a drink. What've you got for me? Is Mabel in the clear yet?'

The telephone rang and Sennett snatched up the instrument, turning his back on Tom. He listened a moment, barked orders into the mouthpiece, then hung up and slammed it back down on the abused leather surface of the desk.

'Hank goddamn Swann again. Heaven send me patience. Like he didn't cause enough trouble last night. They just found him curled up round a bottle of laudanum over by the cyclorama. Out for the count.'

'Sounds to me like the man could do with some time off.'

'What, and give him the chance to kill himself properly? It would save me the trouble of sacking him, I suppose.' Sennett pondered the consequences of that, then headed straight for the drinks cabinet, rattling the cover as he unlocked it. 'What'll it be? Whiskey? Bourbon?'

'Irish, if you've got it.'

Sennett plucked two bottles from the many. He poured and pushed a glass across the desk, waiting for Tom to sit before he eased himself into his broad leather desk chair, a balloon of French brandy in his hand. Whereupon he fixed Tom with a sharp stare.

'Speaking of Hank, what the heck was the matter with you last night? I didn't think you were fool enough to have a soft spot for whores.'

The hair prickled on the back of Tom's neck. 'She's not a whore.'

'That's why she was running around Hollywood after midnight wearing nothing but a car coat, right?'

'Look, she's a good kid, just lost her way a bit. Could do with some help. I was going to ask if you could maybe fix her up with something?'

'Oh, Tommy boy, what she do? Ride your brains out? You know the rules.'

'I thought you might push something her way.'

'Nothing I don't want getting the pox, I won't.'

Tom breathed deep, knowing Sennett was deliberately riling him. 'There's no need for that, Mack. I'm telling you, she's not a whore.'

'Well, if she's not, she must be a damn good actress then.' Sennett boomed a salty blast of laughter at him. 'Maybe I should take her on after all.'

'Maybe you should. All I'm asking is you give her a chance. After she's cleaned up. As a favor to me. But what do I get in return? Cheap goddamn shots.'

'Hey, calm down there, Tom. I was only having a joke. It's what we do around here, in case you didn't notice.' Sennett patted the desktop hard with the palm of his hand, the frown slowly loosening on his brow. 'If the little floozie means so much to you, give Waldron a call and tell him I said try her out somewhere. But if she so much as—'

'She won't.'

'Any bills from the pox doc go straight to you,' Sennett muttered. 'Now, for heaven's sake, let's get on with what matters. How's Mabel doing?'

Tom took a breath. 'I have no idea. I tried her at the apartment a couple of times but she wasn't home and her maid wasn't helping any. Said she was out and wasn't expected back. Guess you can't blame her with all those newspaper hounds sniffing about.'

'You mean you don't know where she is?'

Tom shook his head. 'Haven't a clue. From what you said last night, I took it you wanted me to concentrate on looking into what happened to Taylor. On that, I've come up with some interesting stuff. I spoke to that chauffeur of hers – Davis – and he said—'

Sennett broke in. 'Forget that streak of misery. I only pay his wage because Mabel feels sorry for him and wouldn't let me hire her a proper driver. I want you to get out there and find her, for Chrissakes.'

'That's not what you said last night, Mack. And, anyway, what does it matter where she is? You don't think she's run off, do you?'

'Why would she?' Sennett shook his head. 'She's got nothing to hide. Anyway, you don't know her like I do. That wouldn't be Mabel's style.'

'So what's the problem? She'll be fine. She's probably holed up somewhere with some pals, keeping away from all the fuss.'

Sennett wagged a finger across the desk at him. 'No. It's getting serious for her now, Tom.'

'But it's no different from yesterday, Mack.' He tried to mask the irritation in his voice. 'I spoke to my guy in the detective squad and it's all looking peachy for her. He was confident she wouldn't be in the frame.'

Sennett was not impressed. 'So, if the cops don't think she's involved, why in hell won't they say that? Why's all this muck still being raked over the front pages?'

'You know the cops won't do that, Mack. They're not ruling anything, or anyone, out at this stage. No way is Miss Normand in the clear yet. I'm just telling you what my guy reckons.'

'Did you see what they're saying in the *Herald*?'

Sennett pulled a copy from his desk drawer and showed Tom the headline: *Beauty Hired Slayer in Murder.*

'I've already read it, Mack. It's garbage, right? You know they make it up.'

Sennett didn't want to hear. ''Course they don't come right out and accuse Mabel by name. Cowardly bastards. But that's not all. Look, look . . .'

Sennett wrenched the newspaper open and pored over an inside page. 'Here it is. Just listen to this: "Jealousy is believed by police to have been the motive for the slaying." And it goes on: "Taylor may have been shot by the discarded suitor of a woman friend." That's me they're talking about. You know it. They want to have it both ways. They're accusing me now, too!'

'Oh, come on, Mack. Get a grip. We said last night this was bound to happen. And I don't see your actual name anywhere in there.'

'More's the pity,' Sennett snorted. 'Or it'd be my lawyers I'd have up here now, not you.'

Distracted by some activity on the ground, Sennett's expression changed to intense concentration as he strode over to the glass wall, opened a section and bellowed a string of imprecations at some underling below. He was still tutting when he returned his glare to Tom.

'Did your cop pal say anything about me?'

'Nope, and I wasn't encouraging him to think that way.'

Sennett sat down again and had another nip at the brandy. 'Look, Tom, let's be honest here. It's not entirely like I said last night. It's not only money that I'm concerned about. Word is coming in that theaters are starting to pull *Molly O* already. Which is bad enough. But it's the effect on Mabel, too. I'm not sure she can take it. If she's gone off somewhere to drown her sorrows over Taylor, she could do herself real harm. I know I pretend not to notice, but she's been fragile of late, not her old self at all. Everyone says so. And that bunch of derelicts she's been hanging around with – Lew Cody and his gang – they don't give a goddamn about her. They just see her as a ticket to another night's partying. I'm telling you, you have to go out there and find her for me.'

This time Tom didn't bother covering his exasperation. 'Look, Mack, before I came out here, I telephoned everyone I know – everyone *we* know – and nobody's seen her. She could be anywhere.'

'Don't argue with me on this, Tom.' Sennett put his big paddle hands up to his face and rubbed his eyes. 'Think on what you said to me just now about favors. You're going to have to do the rounds of all the joints tonight. She's bound to be out there in one of them. Try the Cocoanut Grove, Joey's, the Turnpike . . .'

He rattled off the names of more clubs, dance joints and fashionable eating places. Tom knew them all, and more. He could check them out, but he knew she wouldn't be in any of them, not if she was blasted off her noodle on dope. She was too well known. Far more likely she would be lying low somewhere quiet, away from gossiping acquaintances, away from prying cameras and, most of all, away from her intolerably easy life. Finding her would make no difference at all.

'OK, Mack, if that's what you want. I'll do what I can.'

'Good.' Sennett drained his glass. Then he was up on his feet again, pulling the bulbous bottle from the cabinet. 'I should've married her ten years ago when I had the chance, Tom. That way, at least I'd know why she was causing me all this misery.' Sennett gave a hearty laugh but Tom saw his anxiety, heard the brandy bottle rattle on the rim of the glass as he poured. 'You'll have another whiskey?'

Tom held his glass out. 'You always did have the best bar in town.'

Sennett smiled as he freshened Tom's drink. 'Well, this rum-runner of mine is the bee's knees. He can get me pretty much anything I want – at a price, of course. Case of Haig last week, the only one on the Pacific coast, so he said.'

'His name's not Shorty Madden, by any chance?'

'No.' Sennett shook his head. 'Why?'

'Oh, you know, this Madden guy – his name came up.'

'In connection with Mabel?'

'Yeah.'

Sennett frowned again and made his way back behind the desk. 'Never heard of him. He a bootlegger?'

'Among other things.'

Midway through lowering himself into his chair, Sennett gripped the armrests hard. 'What do you mean, "other things"?'

'You know, dope. Hop, powder, those sorts of other things.'

'What the hell are you trying to say?'

'Nothing. You're the one asked me. I'm saying this guy sells dope as well as booze.'

'And to my Mabel, in particular – is that it?'

'Well, that's what I was trying to tell you earlier. I spoke to her driver this morning. He said there was trouble a few weeks back over this Madden guy delivering dope to her.'

Sennett was on his feet again, his face flushing from pink to plum, his voice leaping up an octave or two. 'Don't be ridiculous. How in hell would he know anything about it, eh?'

'Well, for starters he's an A-class dope fiend himself.' An image of Davis lying, guts out, screaming, in a foxhole in France, flashed through Tom's mind, followed by a pinprick of guilt.

'Don't be crazy. Mabel'd never employ anyone like that. Even if he is, it's obvious he's lying. Trying to take advantage of the situation. Type like that'll do anything for money. I'll soon put a stop to that.'

Sennett went to grab the telephone, but Tom put a hand out, held the earpiece down in its cradle.

'Don't waste your time, Mack. That's not what this is about. Davis wasn't after anything. He was trying to protect her.' He hesitated over what he said next, but knew he had to say it. 'The problem is with her.'

Sennett loomed over the desk, shoulders forward, arms rigid, the knuckles of his clenched fists pressing into the tooled leather. 'Shut your mouth!'

'Come on, Mack. You know everybody in the business has some story or other about her taking—'

'Shut up, I tell you.'

'For God's sake, if you can't face the truth, how the hell do you expect—'

'Shut your mouth, I said,' Sennett bellowed. 'Before I goddamn shut it for you. I will not have you repeating those slurs to me here in my own office, in my own studio. She told me herself she doesn't take that stuff. She promised me she wouldn't. That's good enough for me. She promised . . .'

With that, Sennett seemed to run into a wall, or out of steam at least. His body sagged, his head dropped. Tom watched as he closed his eyes, rocked his bull's neck slowly left and right, and exhaled a massive rush of air. He stayed completely still for ten, maybe fifteen seconds, then, tensing his arms again against the desk, lifted his big head and breathed in slowly, pumping strength back into his straightening spine, his tightening shoulders, his taut, hardening features. A thin smile formed on his lips before he opened his eyes. Tom felt something like hatred coiled in them.

'Right, enough of this codswallop. I don't want you bringing it up again. Now get the hell out of here, Tom, and don't come back until you've found her.'

ELEVEN

I n any other circumstance he would have laughed out loud when the slot in the wood door snapped back and the pair of goggling eyes appeared glancing left, then right, before settling on him suspiciously. It only lacked an intertitle and harmonium accompaniment to be a close-up from one of Sennett's screen capers.

'What'ya want?'

Muffled by the door, the voice flopped weakly into the deserted street. Tom was standing outside a low-slung dilapidated block of shut-up stores a couple of doors down from the corner of Virgil and De Longpre out on the frayed edge of East Hollywood. He could see lights from the traffic on Sunset in the distance, but here all was dark, still and silent. The rain was back, drifting in thin sheets along the street. He had rattled the chains on the door of the boarded-up saloon, its windows like so many others whitewashed out, though not enough to obscure the ghost of a name on the glass: Hannigan's. Then he spotted the hatch cut in the next door along, and knocked.

'Come on, open up.' Tom shuffled his feet and rubbed his hands impatiently. 'I'm getting wet out here.'

Somewhere near here, a year or so before, he sat with a thousand other happy revellers, picnicking on a sunny hillside, watching and cheering as Babylon was brought to its knees when the vast sets for David Wark Griffith's *Intolerance*, which had stood moldering on the Fine Arts studio backlot for years, were finally torn down – the wrecker's ball smashing the high wooden towers and vast plaster citadels like the wrath of some scornful god. Perplexed as to why Mabel Normand would come all the way out to this bleak industrial sector to do her drinking and doping, the memory of that day brought an explanation. A block or two further east was the old Triangle studio that Sennett had once re-leased to satisfy Normand's yearning for a studio of her own. No more than two minutes' drive away, perfect for a break in shooting. Short of being on the lot, Hannigan's couldn't have been more convenient.

'Who d'hella you?'

Tom tutted loudly and fished in his trouser pocket, pulling out a couple of crumpled bills. He smoothed them and held them up towards the dim light. 'I'm the man with the money.'

There was a grunt and the slot slammed shut. A couple of locks snapped back, what sounded like a chair being dragged aside, and the door swung open. The man was older than expected, thin and stooped. Gray hair ebbed lank down the back of his skull over a greasy shirt collar and a moth-eaten gabardine vest. Tom put a foot in the door, handed over the money. The old guy seemed happy enough, opened wider. The dim light inside revealed nothing more than a three-legged stool and a long hallway with a steel door at the far end. The street door slammed shut behind him.

'Got any heat on ya? Leave it here; pick it up on the way out.'

Tom shook his head. 'Not tonight.'

'Your funeral,' the old guy croaked, and shrugged like he could care less.

'Shorty Madden in the house?' Tom asked.

The old man looked him up and down before replying.

'See for ya'self. In the back bar, down there.' He jerked his thumb over his shoulder towards the other door, as if there was a choice.

His knock brought immediate results: a brute in a too-short suit and a too-small derby opened the door and grunted at him to come through. He saw plenty not to like as he stepped inside. A thick fog of tobacco smoke penetrated only by a handful of flickering wall lamps kept the long, narrow room in a seemingly permanent state of gloom. It looked like the old saloon had been hurriedly chopped in two, and this side got the raw end of the deal. Along the length of one wall ran an ornately carved bar counter. Behind, the mirrored shelves were tarnished and empty but for dust and a stack of glasses one end. The few drinkers sat at widely spaced tables, identities blurred by the murk but emanating an air of hard men: ex-cons, soon-to-be cons or just plain treacherous types. One table was occupied by a handful of poker players, the noise in the room made up for the most part by their low murmur of calling and bidding, the chink of coins tossed into a pot. The only other sound, emerging indistinguishably from the lightless depths, was a rasping booze-sodden snore.

One man stood leaning against the counter, away from the rest. Like the others, he'd turned and looked as Tom entered, but unlike them his curiosity hadn't been satisfied and he continued to stare.

Tom met his gaze and walked over. He was short – five three, five four, at most – mid-thirties or thereabouts, of medium build, though maybe thinner under the double-breasted suit. His pale, lean face and corn-color side-cropped hair had the look of a man alert and ready, someone who'd learned life the hard way on the streets.

'You Madden?' There was something familiar about him, a sense, a memory of someone loitering in a corner of the Lasky lot.

'Maybe. Who're you?' He looked Tom up and down, assessing the nature of his need, the depth of his pockets.

'Collins. Got your name from someone said you might be able to help me find a friend of mine.'

Madden's face flooded with skepticism. 'I look like a missing persons bureau to you?'

Tom stuck an elbow on the bar and glanced round the room. 'Looks like a few of these guys might be on your books, all right.'

Madden liked that. His shoulders rose, fell and rocked in a laugh that never made it to his eyes. 'A wise guy, huh? So, who's this Joe you're looking for?'

Tom put his other elbow on the bar and hunched over, speaking confidentially. 'It's a Joe-ess, actually. Movie lady. A class act. Twenty-four-carat star, in fact. And she's got this habit, I'm told, of coming over and doing business with you.'

Madden stiffened but kept his mouth shut.

'Her driver gave me your name,' Tom went on. 'Says he's a good customer of yours, too.'

'If he's her driver, how come *he* don't know where she is?'

'I guess she gave him the slip.'

'Well, I don't know what you expect me to do about it.'

'I thought you maybe helped her find some peace and quiet, or maybe you got called in to help the party along, if she's with pals.'

'Don't mean nothing to me. You better go find yourself someone else to help you. A novelty store maybe.' Madden turned away and raised his empty shot glass to the barkeep.

'Let me get that,' Tom said, motioning that he'd have one too.

'Your money.'

The tender took a glass from the shelf, blew some dust out, filled it and Madden's from a wide-necked jar containing clear grain alcohol. Tom took a slug and winced as the back of his throat ignited. 'Jesus, they don't make it like that where I come from.'

'Extra strong for us tough boys,' Madden smirked. 'Can't you handle it?'

'I've had rougher.'

'You sure about that?'

Tom ignored him. 'Look, are you certain this lady doesn't ring any bells?'

'None of the right ones,' Madden said gruffly. He looked Tom up and down again. 'You don't dress like a cop.'

'That's because I'm private.'

'Well, it don't make any difference. Means nothing to me. None of my business.'

A hoot went up as someone won a big hand at the card table behind. Tom kept his eyes on Madden. He was getting bored with the cat-and-mouse act. 'This driver was pretty sure you're the man who'd know.'

'Well, you go back and tell him to watch what he's insisting. Could get a fella into trouble.'

'I know what you mean. We had a long talk. He gave me a hot tip about your dealings with another friend of the lady in question. A recently deceased friend.'

Madden jerked back as though he'd been struck. 'You wanna watch your mouth, mister,' he growled, teeth clenched.

Tom didn't budge. Out the side of his eye, Tom saw the barkeep's hand sneak under the counter, ready for trouble. On his back, he felt a roomful of expectant stares.

'Like I said, I'm no cop. All I'm looking for is some help here. You scratch my back, and I'll—'

'Yeah, I'll scratch it all right, all the way into a box.'

'I don't think so.' Tom stared hard at him. If he'd been going to do anything, he would have started before. Already the room's attention was drifting away. 'Strikes me you're smart enough to want to stay out of the spotlight just now.'

Madden turned away again and leaned into the bar. He sniffed, pinching his thin nose. A vaguely defensive note entered his voice. 'You got the wrong idea. I didn't go anywhere near the guy,' he said, pushing his empty glass out in front of him.

The barkeep filled it silently. Tom declined with a hand flat across his glass. As Madden went to drink, he noticed for the first time the scuffed wear on his shirt cuffs. He checked out the man's collar and the jacket. Same thing there. For a dope peddler to the stars, maybe Madden wasn't doing so good.

'So, like I said, I don't care about that,' Tom said. 'I'm only trying to find the lady. If you can help me, there's money in it for you. My client has plenty. Enough for you to disappear for a while, if you want. Wait for the storm to blow out.'

Madden put his head in his hands and stared at the cracks in the wooden counter, thinking hard. He was feeling the heat all right. 'How much?' He asked it firmly, like a man who's made up his mind.

'A hundred bucks.'

'Make it two, I'll make some inquiries.'

'That's kind of expensive – for inquiries.'

'Yeah, well, take it or leave it. Mexico can be pricey this time of year. For two fifty I can maybe take you to her myself. Maybe. You got wheels?'

'Sure I do, but I don't carry that kind of money on me.'

Madden scowled. 'Money up front or no deal.'

'OK, but we have to go get it.'

'No, *you* do.' Madden shook his head. 'I gotta make a call first anyhow. You go get the moolah; I'll see you out front in, what – say, a half-hour?'

It was going a little too easy now, and Tom couldn't help wondering if Madden was taking him for a ride. But he couldn't risk being wrong on that. He'd just have to play the hand and see how it came out.

'Two fifty, half an hour, outside.'

'Y'want the lady, that's the deal.' Madden spat on the floor for emphasis. 'And remember, I see the dough before we go anywhere.'

TWELVE

It was teeming down outside, pattering a racket on the Dodge's canopy. Sitting in the open cab, staring back at Hannigan's, Tom was thinking too hard to care about the rain squalling in on him. He didn't have two hundred and fifty bucks, and wouldn't give it to Madden if he had. As soon as he clapped eyes on him, he knew he wasn't right for Taylor: too short, too young, wrong build for the description given by the witnesses. Nor did he appear to smoke. After speaking with him, he was convinced. Sure, he was good at the tough-guy act, but Tom had met a few killers in his time and he wouldn't have ranked this yellow-head street rat in their number. Not for a thought-out job anyway. If Madden was in the dope business – and there was no reason to doubt it – it had to be storefront, selling goods on for someone bigger, taking a cut. That way, it even made sense he was anxious to get out of town. If the cops were sniffing around and he really had been dumb enough to trade punches with Taylor, it couldn't stay a secret for much longer. He would know in his bones that a small fish like him would fry up nicely if the DA needed someone quick in the pan.

One other thing seemed certain: Madden would not take him to Miss Normand. Not knowingly, anyhow. Either he was awaiting Tom's return with the intention of getting him somewhere quiet to rob him at gunpoint, or it was a ruse to get rid of him and he planned to hightail it out of Hannigan's just as soon as Tom was gone. That had to be the more likely, because he would have insisted on going with him to get the money otherwise, to be sure he didn't bring any cops back. If Madden really did know where Normand was holed up, he would have cottoned on, too, that he could squeeze a lot more than two hundred and fifty bucks out of her to stay quiet about it if she really didn't want to be found. One way or another, Tom was expecting to see Madden walk out that door any second. And he was ready to follow him, on four wheels or on foot.

But Madden didn't emerge. After twenty minutes or so, Tom was starting to think he might need to reassess his plan when he saw a pair of yellow headlamps cleaving up the dark street towards him. He slid low on the bench seat, watching as a dark, fully enclosed Packard tourer pulled up across from the speak. It didn't so much park as sit there, lights doused, engine running, steam rising from the hood as it idled in the rain. Another minute passed, slow as a dirge. Then a wedge of light angled out across the sidewalk as Hannigan's door opened and Madden – he was wearing a hat, but it was him for sure – emerged into the street. Buttoning his jacket against the rain, Madden pulled his brim down and ran across to the waiting tourer. One foot on the running board, he leaned in to speak to someone in the back through an open window. Tom strained to hear but was too far away, the hiss of the rain and rumble of the engine baffling the voices.

He had to know what they were saying. Sliding across the seat, he eased the door open and dropped on to the sidewalk. Crab-like, he scuttled along in the shadow of the auto in front of his, and the next, until he ran out of autos and slipped into the deep recessed porch of Bergmann's shoe store, keeping the Packard in sight through the curving plate glass of the display windows. By now he could hear Madden's voice raised in argument, and saw him begin to walk away, gesticulating angrily and cursing. The only other word Tom thought he caught was – could it be? – 'Taylor'.

What happened next was so fast he only recalled it later in magnesium-bright fragments: Madden striding back across the street, the Packard's headlamps flaring, the auto pulling away, the sheen of a long-barrel revolver nosing out the open window. Stepping out from the porch, for Tom, was an act of pure instinct. As was his shout of warning. But the yell only confused Madden, who swung round, panicked eyes fixing on Tom emerging from the shadows, and only then looking back over his shoulder, too late, catching nothing but muzzle flash.

The first round thumped into Madden's back by his left shoulder blade, sending him into a spin that halted abruptly when a second blew a dark gout of blood from his chest and he catapulted back as though his feet had been sliced from under him. The third slug smacked into his skull as he fell, the back of his head evaporating in a spray of red rain as his body attempted one last mid-air convulsion.

Tom dived as the Packard came level, loosing off at him now. He did his best to become one with the sidewalk as a couple of shots hit the storefront behind, and the plate glass shattered and fell, crashing to the paving in shimmering cascades all around. Above the crystal din, he strained to distinguish the Packard's engine. If it stopped, he'd have to get up and run for cover elsewhere. But the roaring motor passed on, a squeal of tires on the wet street signaling a corner turned. He stayed down. Stayed down until all he heard was the rain again, a hissing on the street broken only by his own heartbeat and the pop and crash of falling glass.

Only then did he drag himself up from the ground, standing as best he could and using the hood of the nearest automobile for support. He patted himself down, examining his limbs and torso for injury or rupture, shaking glass and rain from his coat. He was unscathed but for a graze on his left wrist where he'd hit the sidewalk awkwardly and a bloody scratch on his right knee, the worst of which was a four-inch rip to a good pair of suit pants.

He was OK. He didn't need to look to tell the same could not be said for Madden. But look he did, unable to keep his eyes from the rain-spattered heap lying sprawled in an expanding stain of blood, his narrow frame contorted beyond nature and any possibility of life. As Tom stumbled over to the body, he became aware of other presences on the street now, peering down from unlit windows, out from cautiously opening doors. A burble of shocked and excited voices leaked from the light-filled doorway of Hannigan's, the raw, stupefied 'Jesus Cwyst, Jesus Cwyst' of the ancient doorman joining the muttering figures spilling into the street, circling the dead body at a distance.

Still shaking as if the ground was moving under him, Tom looked up and around and shouted as best he could.

'For pity's sake, stop gawking and somebody call the cops.'

THIRTEEN

Whether anyone actually called the cops or they were out patrolling the area, Tom never heard. All he knew was as soon as the two officers came pounding up the street, boots splashing, slickers swishing and handguns at the ready, most of the onlookers evaporated like wraiths, melting into side streets and doorways and the dark folds of the night. The handful of the grimly curious who remained were loudly and pointlessly instructed to keep back as the patrolmen took a look at what they'd got: one dead body spread-eagled in the street, and a tall guy sitting, head in hands, on the running board of a Dodge in the rain.

A pointed finger and a hurried conference followed. The younger of the two officers was dispatched to find a Gamewell box to call for assistance and a meat wagon from the morgue. The other stood well back and kept his weapon trained on the only obvious suspect present. Tom looked over, held his hands up to shoulder height and broke the silence. 'It's OK, I'm not armed. All I did was try and help the guy.'

The officer stepped up on the sidewalk and under a storefront canopy and signaled Tom to approach him. 'OK, sir. Why don't you come on over here, and keep those hands of yours where I can see 'em.'

Tom did as he was bid, slowly, and allowed the cop to pat him for a weapon.

'Mind if I get my smokes out?'

He pulled the pack from his pocket, lit up and took a good look at the officer: a jaw grim with years on the job, eyes and hands still and steady. He was no more than a couple of years older than Tom, who guessed that beneath the rain slicker he'd probably have three stripes on his left cuff, one for each five years of service.

'You ready to tell me what happened here?' the cop asked. That the 'sir' had been dropped was not a good sign. The cop had been doing a character evaluation, too.

'Yeah, yeah, I think so,' Tom stuttered, his brain still fogged by the shock. All he'd done since the shooting happened was spool it back over and again in his mind like some endless looped projection reel. But how much it was wise to say to the cop was a different matter. He didn't feel sharp enough to think through the implications. Keep it to the minimum for now, he reckoned, would probably be for the best.

'I'm listening.' Already the note of skepticism in the cop's voice.

'The shooter was in a Packard tourer,' Tom said. 'Big one, fully enclosed. Dark color – green maybe. I didn't see the plate. I only noticed it because it was idling there, for five minutes, lights off, like they were waiting for someone to come out of that place.'

Tom indicated the doorway of Hannigan's, certain that the cop would know exactly what trade went on inside, and that he probably supplemented his pay by ignoring it. But that wasn't what he fixed on.

'They?' The cop was evidently surprised by his candor. 'You mean you saw who shot him?'

Tom shook his head. 'Too dark, but the shooter was in the back of the Packard; somebody had to be up front driving.'

'Go on.'

'This guy' – Tom indicated the lifeless pile in the street – 'came out, had a talk with the guy in the auto. Like I say, I didn't see who, but pretty soon they began squawking at each other, and when this one started walking away, the guy inside the Packard started shooting. Took a pop at me too – when I ran out.'

Even that was more than he wanted to say. But the old ways of the cop in him, the need to do things right and by the book, were kicking in automatically, insisting he couldn't risk being caught in a lie. The guys in Hannigan's, if any were left in the joint, would be happy to squeal that they'd seen Tom talking to Madden a quarter-hour before he was killed – if only to draw the heat away from themselves.

'And what was it you were doing out here?' The cop's eyes narrowed. 'In the dark and rain.'

'Waiting for him.'

The cop's reaction was much as he expected – eyes widening, the peak of his cap dipping as his eyebrows rose to meet it. 'You . . . you were waiting for this man?'

'That's right, I had some business I wanted to do with him. He never made it, as you can see.' Tom breathed out heavily as he said it, knowing this was not a good way to go.

'You knew the victim?'

'No, not exactly, but—'

'You know his name?'

'Sure. Madden – nickname Shorty. I don't—'

The cop drew a sharp breath, and looked back at the corpse as if understanding something for the first time. 'And I guess you're familiar with the kind of business Mr Madden conducted, seeing you were planning on doing some with him?'

'You know him, then?'

'Oh, yeah,' the cop smiled. 'I know Madden. Him and his rotten "business" interests are well known to all us cops round here. But I don't recognize you, mister.'

Mister. And a growl in his voice. That was it, then. This square-jawed protector of the people was going to use all his years of experience to jump to the wrong conclusions.

'Look, officer, you're getting the wrong idea here. I've got nothing to do with this, other than I witnessed it.'

The cop smiled a hard smile and nodded at him knowingly.

'I'm just working a job,' Tom continued. 'My business with Madden was legit. I wanted to get some information from him. Now, I'm happy to help you out but—'

He might as well have said he was an assassin. It couldn't have gone down any worse. 'Private, are you? Well, that's just dandy. You'll be able to help us out plenty, won't you? But let's save it for the station, yeah. You'll be coming with us soon as the wagon arrives to clear up this mess.'

The cop refused to say any more to him, putting a hand up every time Tom opened his mouth. When the junior patrolman returned, he was instructed to stay with Tom while the senior went and spoke to the remaining onlookers. Tom's spirits plunged when he saw the cop hammer on the door of Hannigan's and drag the old doorman out. It wasn't looking good. The younger officer – a rookie, twenty at most – seemed mesmerized by the sight of the bloodied corpse lying in the road, so much so that at one point he slipped off his slicker and muttered something about covering it. Tom put a hand up to stop him.

'I wouldn't do that, son. He's past caring anyway.'

The young cop turned on him, a rush of anger reddening his farm-boy cheeks. 'You'd know, would you? Done this kinda thing before, mister?'

Tom stared back at him, unmoved, remembering the first murder victim he'd seen, throat cut to the gizzard in the stinking privy of a Battery brothel years before. Rage had been his first response, too, and he didn't imagine that fellow lived any more worthwhile a life than Madden.

'Look, I used to be a cop myself,' he said firmly. 'You'll only have to take it off again. The coroner's men will want pictures.'

The kid made no answer to that, but made no move to go in the street either. They waited there in stone-hard silence for the time it took the backup men to arrive in a rackety old Dodge half-tonner. The eight cops hanging from it spilled into the street before the vehicle came to a halt. Given a bunch of old-style coats and felt helmets, Sennett could have signed them for Keystone on the spot. The coroner's wagon pulled up a couple of minutes later and a pair of newsmen swept in behind them, tipped off no doubt, cameras at the ready. More and more, the coroners relied on press men to record murder scenes, not always having the photographic equipment themselves, especially for night work. Once they were done, the wagon driver and bearers peeled Madden's sodden remains from the roadway on to a stretcher and covered him with a rubber sheet. From the dull-eyed, matter-of-fact look on their faces, Tom guessed they must have seen worse in their time, maybe in the trenches in France. It was the kind of work given to veterans, men inured to horror.

Once they finished, Tom approached the officer who had taken charge, a short, thin martinet, cap brim low to shield his eyes even at this hour of night.

'Officer, I was wondering if I might leave now, go back to my place and dry out, come into you again in an hour or so to make a statement. I'm kind of all done in. Collins is my name. I'm an ex-cop myself – New York. You can rely on me to show up.'

The cop looked Tom up and down. A nervous tic of the lips or a barely suppressed amusement set the corners of his mouth twitching. 'Thank you, Mr Collins, but as you're the only real, uh, witness to this incident, it's out of the question for you to go anywhere except straight to the station with me. I guess you can appreciate the necessity all the more, given your experience on the job. You can dry out there.'

The words were polite enough, but there was an air of chill insistence to them, making it clear no further argument would be brooked. Tom nodded grudgingly. He wouldn't have played it any different in this guy's position. Still, he didn't like the idea of being dragged in at night by a bunch of beat cops eager to make an impression. Or a reputation. He knew how the later the hour, the more dangerous a station house could be. Boots and billyclubs had a way of finding employment in the hours of darkness. But he forced himself to resign to it as any resistance on his part would only make matters worse. As the cops bundled him into the back of the old police wagon, it occurred to him that at least this was a cut-and-dried murder. The case would have to be handed over to Central and the detective squad more or less immediately – and him with it. That had to be about the best chance he stood of getting home before morning.

FOURTEEN

With its tile-and-beam overhang roof, fancy mock turrets and mission-style bell tower, Los Angeles Police Station No. 6 on North Cahuenga was, even by night, a striking if inelegant building. Shared half and half with the Fire Department, it had an air of brick-built solidity and radiated the kind of strength and municipal authority the good citizens of Hollywood respected, and the not-so-good knew to be wary of. During his time at Famous Players-Lasky, Tom had devoted many an hour to ensuring the studio's precious cargo of talent never got anywhere near its stout wooden doors, or those of any other calaboose in the area. But on those occasions when one of his people did fall foul of the law, a mention of the Lasky studio name, and a hint at its munificent line in gratitude, was usually enough to ensure a quick exit, miscreant movie asset in tow.

This time, he was certain his experience would be different. He wasn't so much escorted as frog-marched into the vestibule with its vaulted ceiling, drab cream walls and high wood-panel booking desk. The place was damnably busy, the room crammed with the usual Friday-night troublemakers and dregs, drunks caterwauling and crooning, waiting to be processed. Tom's guardians swept him straight to the front of the line where the booking sergeant – an older, commanding gray-haired man of fifty or so – stood impossibly tall on the platform behind the plinth.

'In for questioning, Sarge. Murder.'

'Oh yes, we've been expecting you.' The sergeant stepped back to study Tom with a detached professional curiosity before asking, 'Name?'

'I'm a witness,' Tom said, shrugging off the hand one patrolman still clenched around his elbow. 'I'm here voluntarily. I haven't been arrested.'

The sergeant looked up from the ledger in front of him and put his pen down, staring critically at the patrolman. 'Is this man under arrest, Cornell?'

'Not yet, Sarge.'

'OK,' he said, turning to Tom again. 'That's noted, but unless you want to disappear in this station, with no one knowing who you are or how long you have been here – and I would strongly advise against that – you better give me your details.'

Tom gave the man his name and address and at the same time took a closer look at him, recognizing something in the face, in the German accent that should have been a cue, but he couldn't place it.

The sergeant had been having similar thoughts, but with more success.

'Collins?' he said, scrutinizing Tom again, looking satisfied with himself. 'Yeah, I know you. You're with one of the studios, no?'

'Lasky,' Tom nodded. It couldn't hurt if they believed he still worked there.

'Sure, I remember now. I worked traffic before I got the desk last year. You used come in to spring movie types. Another time, too – couple years back – I saw you over in Hollenbeck, some St Patrick's do – you were with that Sullivan guy from detectives, no? You Irish sure stick together.'

'Sullivan and me do, yeah,' Tom agreed, liking the way this was going. 'Used to work a beat together in New York, back when I was in uniform.'

If the sergeant put any value on that, he chose not to show it. 'Sure, I never forget a face. But another guy comes in from Lasky's now, no? Luther or something?'

'Roy Luther,' Tom agreed. 'He's a good man.'

However he said it, the sergeant's eyes narrowed. 'Too good? He get your job?'

'Something like that,' Tom agreed. There didn't seem any point saying more, knowing if his flush wasn't busted already, it was about to be.

'So you're working where now?'

'Nowhere. For myself, I mean. Private.'

The sergeant raised a skeptical eyebrow. 'Private, as in gumshoe?' The sergeant shook his gray head and turned away, muttering something about 'old pals', but Tom didn't catch it.

And that was the end of the conviviality. Formalities complete, the patrolmen took him by the elbow again, pushing him through a set of heavy double doors and down a steep wood stairway towards the back of the building. They were on home ground now, and a cockiness was beginning to show through. Halfway along a dim-lit corridor, they stopped and flung open a door, shoving him into a small room empty but for a table, two chairs and a bare electric light hanging from the ceiling. One of them barked at him to sit, and they left him there, the key grinding in the door as they locked it.

He wasn't so troubled by the lock as the chill atmosphere. Walls bearing the barely literate scrawls of men who had spent fretful hours incarcerated, waiting, staring up at the tiny window set high against the ceiling like a mouth gasping for air. Caution kept him on his feet, pacing the raw concrete floor, frustration bringing greater awareness, excoriating himself for not having torn through the dull veil of compliance that had settled on him since the shooting, blunting his edge. He should never have admitted to knowing Madden, given himself up to them like that. He'd been dumb, his brain all fuzzed up as if he had a concussion. Must have banged his head when he hit the sidewalk. He ran his fingers over the back of his skull, but there was nothing to confirm it.

Resuming his pacing, he began retracing the evening again, minute by minute, event by event, ensuring he had his story straight and undeviating in his own mind. Then he began whittling away at it, calculating what he could and couldn't afford to say, feeling stronger, more in control, formulating a plan at last. Still the time dragged, and after an hour he succumbed to the temptation to sit, whereupon the boredom of confinement began to gnaw away at him anew. He was studying his wristwatch, a silver Waltham, trying to remember the name of the soldier he bought it from – a pitiful, whistle-breathed young veteran come West in the hope California's remedial air would restore his gas-ravaged lungs – when he heard a coarse shout and a heavy tread coming along the corridor outside.

Something about it caused the hair to fizz up on his neck, a pin-sharp spike of memory he didn't want to acknowledge, convinced it was the product of an over-anxious imagination. But as soon as the door swung open, and he heard the voice again, unmuffled, he realized with a fresh jolt of shock that his worst fears were about to be made flesh. And flesh was the only word to describe it, as into the room lurched the corpulent form of Sergeant Aloysius

Devlin – a sight that, had Tom not been sitting down already, might have floored him with astonishment.

If there was one man Tom had optimistically counted upon never meeting on the West Coast, it was Devlin – the rottenest apple he had ever encountered, and that from quite a barrelful. His presence in the room simply didn't make sense. Last time he had seen Devlin was six years before, two thousand miles away in New York, when Devlin had sworn with unshakeable conviction that he would tear Tom limb from limb if ever he clapped eyes on him again. And with good reason, as Devlin had only minutes before been shackled and indicted on major corruption charges based largely on evidence gathered by Tom. That Devlin not only escaped prosecution subsequently but was reinstated in his job in the New York police department was down to an unrivalled network of corrupt connections. And the certainty that he would try to exact vengeance was one of the primary reasons Tom had eagerly accepted Adolph Zukor's offer of a job riding shotgun for a movie studio out in peaceful, remote California. Knowing he wouldn't have to spend the rest of his days looking over his shoulder for Big Al Devlin only made Tom's journey West all the sweeter.

How in hell's name the man came to be standing in front of him now in the basement of Hollywood Station and apparently in a position of authority, was beyond Tom's powers of reasoning.

'As I live and breathe, it really is you,' Devlin said, licking his lips in anticipation. The rest of his face was a globular mass of dewlaps and jowls quivering above the strained confinement of his high-collared uniform.

With a snort, Devlin dismissed the patrolman waiting outside before shutting the door behind him and leaning back against it. For a moment he stood there, breathing deep, as though he could hardly believe his luck, pale-lashed blue eyes glinting out from behind drooping flesh-folds. Then, without warning, he crossed the floor at a rate miraculous for a man of his girth. Tom leapt up, too late. A brain-rattling haymaker caught him full on the jaw as he was rising, every pound of the sergeant's bulk pumped into it. It was like being struck by a side of ham tossed from a railcar. Pain exploded behind Tom's eyes as he was thrown back, wind knocked from his lungs, his skull colliding with the wall behind. He staggered, fell to his knees, struggling for breath and vision, crooking an arm up to fend off a following blow – that didn't come.

'I heard upstairs they had a Collins in on suspicion.' Devlin's voice was high and breathy as he stood over him, his accent a mix of all that grated in his native Boston mingled with decades lived in the Bowery. 'I swear, boy, my heart soared.' He turned and glanced around the room, then lowered his voice anyway and whispered malignantly, 'I heard you were here in Los Angeles and I've been looking out for you since I arrived, praying you'd stray my way. But this – you and me alone down here – it's a bloody dream come true.'

How could it be happening? How was it even possible? Tom squeezed his eyes shut and forced himself to get a grip, to fight through the pain and daze, to concentrate, to comprehend. Devlin was in uniform, so he was there in some official capacity. Which made one realization stand out more than any other: if Devlin held any sway in this building, his life wasn't simply at risk. It was as good as over. If Tom didn't do something, and the sooner the better, he would never make it out of the station alive.

'What happened, Devlin?' He spat a gob of bloodied mucus on the floor, just inches from the man's high-polished boots, struggling to get his breath back. 'Not enough extortion and racketeering in New York? Have to keep your hand in while you're on vacation?'

Devlin wheezed out a laugh like a punctured accordion. As he bent to his level, Tom felt acres of flesh wash about above his head.

'Vacation, is it? Are ye blind as well as dumb?'

Next thing, the sergeant's hand was around Tom's throat, tugging the chin up, forcing his eyes open to take in the yards of blue serge over his belly, the brass badge bearing the legend *Los Angeles Police* on it.

'You think they keep this size in stock, boy? I'm here for good.'

This time, Tom saw the punch coming but couldn't avoid the pile driver that slammed into his belly. Through the rush of blind pain and dumb panic at his sudden inability to draw breath, he was aware of Devlin's thumb on his throat, pressing hard as a piston, the stench exuding from the sergeant's skin at the same time as noxious as smelling salts.

'Remember I said I'd kill you, Collins? Well, I've had plenty of time to think about how. And you can be sure it won't be easy on you.'

As Devlin tightened his grip, through the cloud of choking need and confusion, the only choice left to Tom was between surrendering to strangulation or putting all he had into one last effort to escape from the suffocating bulk. Attack was his only hope. Flattening his hands on the floor beneath him, Tom marshaled every ounce of strength he possessed in his legs and thrust upwards from the knees, pistoning into the soft mass of the sergeant's belly with his shoulder.

Devlin let out a wheeze and staggered back, cursing, leaving enough room for Tom to scramble upright, stumbling sideways, catching only a glance of the heavy blow Devlin aimed at his back. This time, his legs held, but there was nowhere for them to go. Already Devlin had retreated beyond Tom's reach, planted himself solid, back to the cell door, drawing a long black nightstick from his belt.

'Don't push your luck, Collins,' he snarled. 'Or you'll suffer the worse for it.' Stick in hand, he pointed at the chair. 'I said it wouldn't be quick, and it won't be. So you sit down now and ready yourself. And tell me what I want to hear or you'll live just long enough to regret it. Understand?'

Tom understood all right and told Devlin what he could do with his threats. It was a weak resistance, but it felt better than obeying.

'You make me weep,' Devlin said, laughing enough to make his stomach roll. 'You just don't get it, do you?' Stepping forward, slapping the heavy wooden nightstick loud against the palm of his hand. 'There's only one way you get out of this room, Collins, and that's in a box. How long it takes is all we have to decide.'

Devlin took another step forward, raising the stick above his head now, a snarl of pleasure building in his throat. But before he could deliver the blow, a commotion erupted in the corridor, followed by a furious banging on the door and a clamor of arguing, affronted voices congregating outside. Even as Devlin turned and cursed, a Titanic blow from without ripped the lock from the frame and sent the door crashing inwards. Thad Sullivan's granite-gray head followed, angrily scanning the room, behind him the desk sergeant from upstairs and several other flustered faces. What followed, Tom could never have described in detail, short of Devlin and the desk sergeant bellowing at each other like a pair of bull moose, and Sullivan pushing past to drag him by the arm into the corridor, propel him towards the stairs and roar at him to run.

FIFTEEN

Bent at the waist, supporting himself on the rear fender of Sullivan's jalopy, Tom emptied a quart bottle of water over his head, shook it off and prayed the jag of pain lodged behind his eyes would be cast away with it. No such luck. Up front, Sullivan set the springs squealing like a cat orchestra as he hauled himself in behind the wheel. In the chromed radiator grill of a Mercer parked behind, Tom tried to assess how his face had weathered Devlin's ministrations, but there was too much dirt and too little light for a good reflection. The street lamps didn't stay on much past ten, and the luminous hands on his watch were giving off a V of almost two in the morning. Running his fingers over his face, he found a small cut above his right eye and decided the damage couldn't be as bad as it felt.

'Come on, you're as ugly as you ever were,' Sullivan hissed down at him. 'Let's get going before they figure out what's happened.'

He climbed into the cab and slipped the empty water bottle under the seat, his ribs aching as Sullivan maneuvered the machine out into the empty street, turning back towards East Hollywood and downtown. Tom tugged a handkerchief from his pocket, spat on it and pressed it to the ragged wound on the back of his head. It hurt like hell.

'So, are you going to tell me what all that was about back there?'

Tom looked at him askance, wondering if he'd heard right. 'I was assuming you'd tell me. I mean, Devlin . . . in Hollywood for Christ's sake? In uniform? How in hell did that come about?'

'Bet you never thought you'd owe your neck to a Kraut.' Sullivan hawked a gob of phlegm up from his throat and spat into the street. 'All I know is I got a call from Kohl, that desk sergeant, saying you'd been pulled in for questioning, and to come over quick if I thought your hide worth saving.'

'And what about Devlin?'

'That's just it. Kohl didn't mention Devlin. When I got there, he starts jawing on about how some guy was gunned down on Virgil and you were in the frame for it. He wanted to hand it over to the squad right away. Then he drops in, casual as all hell, how "dat fat schmuck Devlin"' – Sullivan caught Kohl's lugubrious German accent to a tee – 'insisted on having a go at you first. I nearly had a stroke when I heard that. I didn't stop to think. I belted in there and grabbed you. Just in time, too, by the look of you.'

Sullivan slowed as they approached an empty intersection, nothing but darkness bearing down from all directions. 'I tell you, this kind of thing's not good for the heart, lad. I need a drink – a proper one, and safe. The Hib's somewhere near here, isn't it?'

Tom told him to take the next right. He knew at least three other speakeasies that were closer, but he also knew that by 'safe' Sullivan meant somewhere you could get proper bonded liquor rather than the pestilential rotgut sold in most joints around. And where the sight of a leading member of the Los Angeles detective squad downing shots of the devil's own brew wouldn't ruffle any feathers. The Hib fitted the bill. He sat back and imagined the booze in his belly, its flare in his brain, and relief rushed from his lungs.

As the stores, homes, trees and telegraph poles of Hollywood Boulevard receded into the distance, Sullivan began quizzing Tom about the shooting, but the only thing Tom had any interest or concern for was Devlin. And why the hell Sullivan wasn't fixating on that, too.

'Aren't you avoiding the obvious here?' he said, at last. 'Where in hell did Devlin come from? I mean, of all the bad pennies to turn up, Thad. You know every cop in Los Angeles. How the hell could you not know he was here?'

Sullivan stared fixedly ahead, his posture stiff and uncomfortable. 'Well, y'know, maybe I did hear something to that effect, all right, now you remind me.'

'You what?' That was not the response Tom was expecting.

'I did hear of him being out here, yeah.' Sullivan shifted in his seat, never taking his eyes off the darkness ahead, affecting a show of concentration.

'And you didn't think to tell me? Have you lost your mind, man?'

Again, Sullivan was silent, only the mechanical clatter of the engine filling the night air. Then, in a rush: 'You got to understand I didn't want to worry you, Tom. All that stuff with him was so long ago, so far back in New York. I thought maybe, you know, maybe . . . maybe he'd got so much bad going on he'd forgotten it. What can I say? I didn't want to stir up all that blood and dirt again, you know? And it's not as if you were likely to run into him.'

'Not likely to run into him?' he gasped at last. 'Are you stone crazy? You knew that fat fucker threatened to rip my head clean off my shoulders if ever he laid eyes on me again. Do you think that just fades away? For Chrissakes, Hollywood is where I do my business. How could you think I wouldn't run into him here? The miracle would be if I didn't.'

'But that's what I'm trying to tell you.' Sullivan was reaching towards him, hand outstretched, conciliatory. 'He's not in Hollywood. Even Kohl didn't know what he was doing up here tonight. Devlin's stationed down in San Pedro, with the port police.'

'San P? He's stationed there? But his uniform was—'

'They use the same one. But it's a separate division and chief. In theory, they're a law unto themselves. Just how he likes it.'

The niceties of police politics were hardly what Tom was focused on and he said so in no uncertain terms, barking at Sullivan now to tell him what he knew.

'Look, you're upset, Tom. You're not thinking straight. All this happened four or five months ago, not long after they let you go from Lasky's. I didn't want to add to your troubles by telling you about it, did I? Sure, I intended saying something once you got settled again but, come on, man, I've hardly seen you since. And, anyway, how often do you get down to San Pedro, huh?'

Tom had to concede that he rarely if ever set foot in the port area, twenty-five miles or so south of downtown. But that was no comfort. All he saw was the big picture.

'He's been out here four or five months?'

'Which proves my point exactly,' Sullivan said, grasping at the straw. 'Look, I'll be straight with you. I got as big a shock as you did when I saw in the *Gazette* that he'd been brought in as deputy chief down at the harbor.' He lowered his voice, adding in boosterish tones, '"Straight from New York, bringing a new level of professionalism to policing in Los Angeles' booming world class port."' He followed up with a derisive growl. 'Jesus, I thought, they're in for the shock of their lives, that lot. I mean I was appalled, for sure, but more for the guys down in the harbor than for you, Tom. That's the honest truth of it. Apart from the inevitable rumors that the dirty sleeveen's been taking a slice off everything that moves through the port since he got his fat ass through the door, I'd almost forgot he was there. Like I say, I guess I never had a good enough reason to break the bad news to you. It's not like we've been seeing a lot of each other, is it? C'mon, man, what more can I say?'

Tom had no answer for that. Sullivan was not the kind to spend time fretting over Devlin. And no matter how upset he was about it, there was no escaping that Tom had to some extent brought it on himself by not keeping in touch with Sullivan, the man he called his best friend in the world, and who'd just proved it more than adequately.

They rode on in silence towards downtown, taking a left on to Third before turning eventually into a shadow-swathed side street and coming to a halt outside a commercial block, the glass in the store fronts black and lightless, apart from one flickering electric bulb illuminating a sign with a gilded harp beside a green door. The Hibernian Grill.

Sullivan cut the motor and sat back in his seat, still gripping the steering wheel. 'Look, I'm sorry I didn't tell you. I should've, OK? That can't have been easy for you tonight. But I got you out of it, didn't I? That's what matters.'

'For now,' Tom said sullenly, unable to think any further into so bleak a future.

Sullivan grinned and tousled the top of his head like he was a six-year-old. 'C'mon now, let's get that drink into you. You'll feel the better for it. I know *I* will.'

SIXTEEN

The Hibernian looked abandoned from outside, but pushing in the door, they encountered an unlikely sentry in a yellow check suit and green homburg, sitting in a cane chair that looked like it was being slowly absorbed into his capacious rear end. He uttered a grunt of either recognition or threat; it was hard to tell which. Sullivan didn't even break stride, flipped the guy a dollar and marched straight on into a cavernous dining hall lit by three low-hanging chandeliers that didn't do much to dispel the gloom. But a homely aroma of roast meat and vegetables permeated the air like a warm embrace, and beneath it a malty, peat-laden undernote of hard liquor. The customers sitting among the rows of linen-laid dining tables were mostly off-duty patrolmen in belts and blues, and a scattering of others in shirtsleeves and loosened ties. Coppers to a man. Only a burst of shrill laughter from a closed booth at the far end of the room gave any indication of a female presence other than that of a black-aproned waitress sashaying towards them, the sway of her hips generating enough heat to fog up the room.

'Boys, what can I get you?'

Sullivan threw his hat on a booth table and slid in behind it. 'A couple'a Irish,' he said, barely looking at her.

'I can see that.' She gave Tom a flash of big, snaggletoothed grin.

'In cups, with coffee, if you would,' Sullivan added. 'And some chops if you have 'em? You hungry, Tom?'

The waitress tutted and said there was only beef stew this time of morning. Tom hadn't eaten since his trip out to Sennett's studio and, despite the pain in his head, just the thought of hot food made him ravenous. 'Yeah, I'll have some of that.'

'You look like you been in the wars, honey,' the waitress said to him, a trace of disapproval in her voice.

'I better go tidy up, then, I guess.' He winked at her. 'If you'll excuse me.'

As he loped off to the men's room, he glanced back and saw Sullivan chatting animatedly with her now, laughing at something, as if he knew her but hadn't wanted to admit it in front of Tom. By the time he'd washed his face and got back, there was no sign of either of them at the table, but two steaming coffee cups sat alongside a half-pint of amber liquid. Picking up the bottle, he examined the gold-backed red diamond label: John Power & Son, Dublin Whiskey. He twisted the cap off. It was the real thing. Best he'd sniffed in a while. One look around the room answered the half-formed question in his mind. So many in here, the place was probably run by cops. And if they couldn't get hold of some proper Irish liquor, no one could.

'Had to use the telephone,' Sullivan said, sliding heavily back into the booth. He looked flushed, his shirt collar in slight disarray.

Tom raised an eyebrow, thinking of the waitress and his old pal's ability to stray, but before he could say anything the big man raised his cup and offered a toast. '*Sláinte mhaith!*'

Tom responded in kind and gulped down half his cup, the layered heat of coffee and whiskey searing his throat, slipping like liquid peace into his belly. For the first time in hours, the fog in his head began to clear and the pain drifted off to a faraway place.

'Thanks for coming to get me,' Tom said. 'I mean it.'

Sullivan shrugged, muttered something about Kohl again and topped up the cups with two more slugs of whiskey. 'It's not like I don't owe you,' he said. 'I'd never be able to give Eleanor and the boys the life they have here if it hadn't been for you convincing us to come out. Eleanor knows it, too. I think she'd lay down her life for you herself.' Sullivan leaned forward and laid one of his massive paws on Tom's forearm. 'She wanted you to know how sorry we were that we couldn't help more over the past months. But you . . . you didn't seem reachable.' Sullivan looked up. 'You never did tell us why you had that bust-up at Lasky's. You were so well in there – Charlie Eyton's golden boy and all that.'

'Get off me, would you!' Tom shook off Sullivan's hand. 'Eyton's golden boy is one thing I never was, and well you know it. He was never more than a boss to me – and he proved it good and proper when it came to all that shit over Arbuckle.'

Sullivan looked surprised. 'Arbuckle? What'd he got to do with it? You told me it had to do with that skirt you were involved with? What was her name?'

'Fay. And she sure as heck is no bit of skirt.'

'Still with you, then, is she?' Sullivan eyes were already glinting with whiskey-fueled good humor. 'Jesus, the woman must be a glutton for punishment.'

'Still with me and still with Lasky, even if I am not.' He said it with only a hint of bitterness. 'That was the deal and I got the better part of it, as far as I'm concerned.'

'If that's how you want it,' Sullivan grunted. 'I just don't get what Arbuckle has to do with anything. You weren't even there, were you?'

Whether it was the drink, or maybe he was just sore and dog-tired, but another surge of emotion was building in him, and he was determined not to be pulled under by it. All the doubts, fear and hurt of the last six months, his dismissal from Lasky's, Sennett's financial hold over him, the everyday struggle just to make a crust, the awful aching doubt that had eaten away at his soul these past months, convincing him that even here, on the threshold of paradise, nothing in life would go right for him. And now Devlin to top it all off. He wasn't sure how much more badness he could take.

'Look, Thad, I've got too much racing through my mind right now to want to go dragging all that up again.' What he wanted was to push it away, let the drink ease him. 'Let's save it for another time. Soon, I promise, we'll have a proper catch-up.'

'Ah, go on with you,' Sullivan said, grabbing the bottle and pouring. 'That call I made there was to Central, to tell them I have you with me. It's as well I did. Devlin's already been on to them, kicking up a shit storm. You know there's no way I'll be a part of the investigation with you involved; it wouldn't be right. But I spoke to Gab Ramirez who's on duty tonight, and he reckons it'll fall to him. He's a good man. I explained why you're with me. He's OK with that, for now. But he wants to talk to you tomorrow. It'll look a lot better for both of us if you go down to Central and see him without me, and make your statement voluntarily.'

Tom caught his drift and nodded. 'Sure, I will. I'll even call ahead, make certain of when he's on duty.'

Just then the food arrived – great steaming bowlfuls of bubbling brown stew, served by an older, dowdier waitress. They ate in silence, absorbing the warm, restorative goodness of it, looking up now and then only to take another slug of coffee or slosh more whiskey into their cups.

'What I don't get is why you were after this Madden guy anyway,' Sullivan said, pushing his bowl aside at last and reaching back behind him in an arching, knuckle-snapping stretch. 'And don't go pulling that confidentiality bull on me. You owe me that much.'

Getting up from the table, Tom walked over to the coat rack and pulled the pack of Chesterfields from his pocket. He held one out to Sullivan, who took it, struck a match from the table set and offered it to him before lighting his own, drawing in a deep lungful of smoke.

'So maybe I should have told you this morning,' Tom said, sitting down again, his voice low across the table. 'But between you and me, I've been doing some digging around on Mack Sennett's behalf.

You know, Normand is his biggest box-office earner, and he's been busting a gut over how all the bad press about her and the Taylor murder will hit his bottom line. He's got a half million bucks tied up in her new movie.'

Sullivan was all attention now. 'You're not saying Sennett thinks she had something to do with Taylor's murder?'

'No, absolutely not. He's worried about her. And his business.

'So, what's he think you can do about it?'

Tom gave him the bones of it. Then, 'He wanted me to find something solid to prove Normand had nothing to do with the murder. So he'll have something to throw at the papers if they go after her. But then she went to ground. It's like she dropped out of sight completely since your guys spoke to her yesterday, so he asked me to track her down, make sure she's OK.'

Sullivan leaned forward himself now. 'You want to be careful, Tom. Sennett's a dangerous a man to be involved with right now. For Chrissakes, he was one of the first people we talked to.'

'You questioned him?

'He didn't tell you?' Sullivan asked, his eyebrows up, a hand clamped on the back of his neck.

'No, he never mentioned it.'

'Funny, don't you think? You two being so intimate and all. He didn't mention hiring you, to us, either.'

'Plays his cards close to his chest, I guess.'

'Sure he does. In more ways than one. Says he was out in Santa Monica Wednesday night, playing poker with that movie director guy, Tom Ince, and his buddies at the time Taylor was killed. Know anything about that?'

Tom shook his head.

'Do you know Ince?'

'I've met him. He's a good guy. One of the best. If he runs a poker school, it'll be high stakes, so, sure, I could see Sennett wanting a slice of that.'

'Which could rule him out for doing Taylor himself. But like I said about Normand, just because we can't place them at the scene doesn't mean he or she didn't have a hand in it. What do you reckon?'

Tom laughed. 'For Chrissakes, Thad. I'm working for Sennett.'

'All the more reason for you to know. I'd say you're not someone to go into a thing like this blind. So, come on, if you have an opinion, out with it.'

Tom sighed and rubbed the bridge of his nose. 'OK, for what it's worth, I just can't see it. Mack was jealous of Taylor's friendship with Miss Normand, for sure. Him and her go back so far history barely covers it, and there's a lot of high feelings involved. But it's a jump from that to murder. He'd have to be a hell of an actor to pull off all that concern for her while covering up his own hand in the deed, wouldn't he?'

'It's not like he's not used to acting.'

Tom brushed away that suggestion with his hand. 'Yeah, and there's a reason why he gave it up years ago to concentrate on making movies and not ruining them. Bluster's the best he can do these days. And, anyway, why would he hire me if he was behind it? It doesn't make sense.'

'Not much does, so far,' Sullivan said. 'Could be he's using you to draw us off the scent.'

'Well, he's not exactly advertising it, is he?' Tom said, exasperated. 'I mean, you didn't even know about me until I told you myself a minute ago.'

Sullivan had to concede that, but no way was he ready to throw in the towel. 'Like I say, for me he's still in the frame. But I'll tell you something: the DA's office is not interested. Those monkeys – anything to do with the movies, they steer us clear, so the organ grinders don't get upset. It's like the studios are becoming untouchable now.'

'You said.' Tom pulled himself up short, knowing that if they went off on that tack, they'd never get back. He lit another cigarette and sluiced some more whiskey into their cups. 'Look, we're getting way off the subject here.'

'Right.' Sullivan nodded guiltily as if he too was losing the thread due to the lateness of the hour and the potency of the Powers. 'So what's the connection between this Madden guy and Sennett?'

Tom exhaled impatiently. 'There is none, far as I know. The connection is with Taylor. That's the connection you guys need to nail down.'

'Why would Taylor even know the guy? A low-life bootlegger?'

'You can't take a wild guess?'

'Well, sure, I suppose it must've been for booze. It's just that knowing what I know about Taylor, I'm surprised he didn't patronize a more fashionable supplier. Seems to me, Taylor was all about the way things look. I can't imagine him wanting the likes of Madden anywhere near his fancy digs.'

'Correct.' Tom smiled, wheeling his hand as though he was unspooling a line. 'Or anywhere near Miss Normand's digs, to be more precise.' He let that one hang in the air.

'Miss Normand?' Sullivan's eyes lit up.

Tom was too tired for a guessing game. So he told him straight out about Normand's dope habit and how he got Madden's name and whereabouts from her driver.

'I would've thought she needed to be even more discreet than Taylor,' Sullivan said at last.

'Maybe she's past caring. Remember, this girl's one serious hophead. She has to get her supply somewhere, and Madden's front office, Hannigan's, was only a block north of her studio on Effie Street.'

'Tell me more about this driver guy. What's his name?'

'Davis. You should have a word with him. But go easy. He got a bellyful of shrapnel over in France. Real bad, poor schmuck.'

Sullivan sat there absorbing it all, a grinding of his jaw betraying the intensity of his rumination. 'I still don't get where Taylor fits in to all this.'

Tom told him what Davis said about Taylor being desperate to get Normand to quit cocaine, and how he offered Madden money to stay away from her. 'But she was too good a customer. Madden couldn't afford to lose her. They came to blows over it.'

Sullivan's eyebrows arched like cat backs. 'Blows? Taylor and Madden? Are you serious? You're only telling me this now?'

Tom shut him up with a hand in front of his face and asked how the hell he could have told him, since he'd been in custody since he found out. It wasn't strictly true, but it would do for the moment.

'So why the hell did Madden spill this to you?'

'He didn't. Not in so many words.'

Sullivan scratched his head, unable to believe what he was hearing. 'But you're still saying you might've cracked this thing. That maybe Madden shot Taylor because he was getting between him and his best customer.'

'It's got to be a possibility,' Tom said, putting his hands up. 'On the other hand, Madden didn't deny any of it. Not even the fisticuffs in Normand's yard. If he was going to stay out of the frame, he'd have to deny that at least. Far as I can see, once he knew Davis had blabbed to me, he reckoned it couldn't be long before the cops heard, too. What he wanted was to get out of town until the heat died down. Like he was mostly concerned about being pinched for something he didn't do, and by some cops desperate to make it stick. Frankly, I can see his point.'

Tom studied Sullivan's reaction but all he got was a blank expression.

'The guy was a street rat,' Tom continued. 'If he was going to murder someone, you would expect he'd do it himself. But he fits the description of the killer about as well as Normand does. He wasn't a big guy. Not at all. And if he did shoot Taylor, why in hell is he lying cold on a mortuary slab himself right now?'

'You tell me, Sherlock,' Sullivan said in an oddly peevish tone. 'Maybe he overstepped the mark? Street guy like that, maybe someone higher up doesn't like the dust kicked up by taking out a swell like Taylor. That's got to draw heat his way.'

'So why draw even more attention by killing Madden?' Tom said. 'Apart from anything else, I can't see Madden passing up the chance to rob the place while he was there, if only to cover his tracks. You said yourself none of Taylor's valuables were disturbed. There's got to be something else going on. Something we're missing.'

'Well, it's a hell of a new direction, Tom; I'll give you that. I'll get the boys to follow up on it straight away.' Sullivan slapped his two hands down on the table and heaved himself out of the seat. 'You look all done in. I'll drop you to yours, and then I need to call this in before I head for home myself.'

Tom stood up, wincing as a twinge arrowed through his lower back. He checked his wristwatch. It was getting on for four.

'When're you on duty again?'

'At ten a.m. sharp, would you believe it!' Sullivan snorted. 'Do you want me to stop by on my way in, give you a lift to Tenth and Hill?'

The address rang a bell way at the back of Tom's memory, but why it did refused to come to him. He put his hands up, wondering at the grin spread across Sullivan's face. 'Why would I want to go to Tenth and Hill?'

'I thought you wanted to find Miss Normand.'

'Of course I do, but . . .' Tom shot a tired, frustrated glance heavenwards. 'Look, just tell me, Thad, would you?'

Sullivan grinned. 'Because that's where Gab Ramirez told me the Taylor inquest is being held, tomorrow morning.'

Tired as he was, the surprise managed to jerk him upright. 'An inquest – so soon? On a Saturday? Are you sure?'

'Darn right. I told you they want to bury this quick. And guess what? Your Miss Normand has been subpoenaed to give evidence. What do you think of that?'

'They served her?'

'Must've,' Sullivan grinned. 'Looks like we managed to find her when you couldn't. Maybe you're not such a hotshot Sherlock Holmes after all.'

Sullivan looked so pleased that Tom had to give him that one.

'Look, don't sweat it,' Sullivan said. 'Thing is, Ramirez says Woolwine wants it kept as hush-hush as possible. So there's no guarantee you'll get in without a badge or a subpoena. But with me, you'll sure as hell have a better chance of getting through the door.'

SEVENTEEN

Aglow of yellow light in the window. He pushed through the unlocked door and there was Colleen on the sofa, a blue-and-white plaid blanket around her and the table lamp lit on the floor beside. Looking up sleepily from an old copy of *Captain Billy's Whiz Bang* he must have left lying around.

She sat up, wrapping the blanket closer, eyes widening as he stepped further into the light. 'Oh my, what happened to you? Your face, it's . . .'

'Scarred for life?' He laughed, touched by her concern. 'I don't think so.' But he stepped across to the overmantle mirror to be sure, wondering if he'd really done such a poor patch-up job at the Hibernian. What he saw was reassuring. 'Some might say it's an improvement.'

'Who did this to you?' She was on her feet now, standing beside him under the mirror, her nose wrinkling as she smelt the whiskey on him. 'Were you in a fight?'

'No, not exactly.' He frowned at his reflection in the glass, incongruous, his ill-used features accentuating the difference in their ages, stirring something long distant within. 'I got jumped. But don't worry. It's a hazard of the job. It looks worse than it is.'

She accepted that and sat down again, tucking her legs under her. He turned and stared at her without saying anything, his eyes slowly roving her face.

'What is it?' she asked, embarrassed, tugging at a loose lock of hair. 'It's gone four, you know.'

'I had a kid sister looked a little bit like you, back in Ireland. You kinda remind me of her, you know, your smile.'

'I heard that one before,' she said smartly. 'And I bet her name is Colleen.'

The hardness in her voice took him aback momentarily, then he got it and laughed. 'No, really, I mean it. Her name's Mary. God's honest truth.'

He thought better now of sitting down on the davenport beside her, but the tiredness was beginning to overwhelm him so he pulled a straightback from the table and sat on that.

'So where is she, this sister of yours, now?' she asked.

'Don't know. Back in Ireland, I guess. Lost touch with her. I was only fourteen when I left. Had no choice. My ma died. Da was gone years before. Maybe your folks told you: Ireland's a stone-hard place, land and people. My brother Pat, he took the boat a year before, got a good job as a rigger in New York, said I should come over, he'd take care of me.'

'And did he?'

'Sure he did. Sent me the ticket. Got me work, made sure I kept up my reading and writing, didn't let me squander my pay on booze like all the other lads on the job. He was a good, kind man.'

'Was?'

'He's gone too. Fell from the one of the towers we were rigging. Metropolitan building on Madison Avenue. I never could look at it after without feeling sick to my stomach. He was tapping off rivets on one of the outside beams, lost his footing. Stumbled out into the air like you would off a sidewalk. Except it was twenty floors up. Didn't stand a chance. I still hear him scream, in the night, sometimes.'

He stopped and looked up, realized the whiskey had turned him maudlin. Knew for sure he wasn't talking only to himself when he saw the horror in her expression.

'I'm so sorry,' she said, 'I didn't mean to . . .' In the lamplight, he saw the glint of tears brimming on her eyelids.

'It's OK. It was a long, long time ago.' He pushed his hands through his hair and stood up, wincing as he caught the wound at the back of his skull. 'Look, I'd better be hitting the sack. Anyone call while I was gone?'

'Sure, loads of 'em. You're popular, ain't'ya?' She reeled off a list of creditors he'd been avoiding for weeks. 'And a lady called, too, after hours.'

'She leave a name?'

It couldn't be Fay. She wasn't due back for a week yet. Unless he got it wrong. But he'd been counting down the goddamn days.

'I didn't catch what she said first. Sounded surprised there was a girl in your place taking calls. Fay, I think she said. Then changed her mind and made it Mrs Parker.'

'Long-distance?'

'No. Said I should tell you she was back in town. Made some crack about the trouble she's taken to come back early. I didn't catch it. Put the phone down real hard. My ears are still ringing from it.'

'Really?' That didn't sound like Fay.

He looked up, saw Colleen smiling wide at him, barely able to control her laughter, teasing at the concern on his face.

'No, not *really*,' she said. 'She was all nice and polite. Said she'd try again in the morning. A real lady, I guess.' She halted there, but couldn't resist asking the obvious question. 'She's your girl, right? Your sweetheart?'

He nodded, cautious.

'So how come she goes around calling herself Mrs Parker? She a widow or something?'

'It's complicated.'

'Yeah?' She was all interest now. 'How?'

EIGHTEEN

For an establishment more accustomed to the reverent hush of death, the Overholtzer funeral parlor was abuzz with activity. Outside the white stucco building on Tenth and Hill, a determined band of newsmen jostled for position, competing with a growing congregation of stargazers. As each in a succession of shining limousines and landaus disgorged its passengers, the throng convulsed and surged. Fans ogled at the movie folk dismounting the machines. Reporters held notebooks aloft, waving, yelling questions. Photographers thrust their cameras out – no need for flash pans this dazzle-bright morning – beckoning and pleading. Every now and then, these efforts paid off and, forgetting this was no premiere or gala dinner, a famous face would stop, smile and pose for the photographers. But most played their assigned roles, hunched and silent, eyes unseeking, hurriedly mounting the steps, pushing through heavy doors that closed behind them with a dignified thud.

Tom and Sullivan shouldered through the crowd. The patrolmen manning the doors stepped aside to let them enter, satisfied by Sullivan's badge and a growl of 'he's with me'. Inside, the atmosphere was quieter, but only just. A hum of gossip passed from lip to ear and on again as information was gathered and relayed, and the latest rumors compared, about the death of a colleague whose propriety had been the rarest kind in Hollywood – almost entirely unquestioned. The inquest had been convened at the request of District Attorney Woolwine, and most of those attending had been summoned there expressly by telephone call from his office late the previous evening. Why it couldn't have waited until Monday, nobody knew, though it certainly was a godsend for the Sunday papers.

Tom stood alone to one side, self-conscious now, aware from one or two disapproving looks that his sunglasses looked out of place and didn't entirely disguise the bruising round his eyes. Sullivan had gone off to consult with his colleagues from the detective squad, but there were plenty more faces he recognized, acquaintances as well as those whose regular appearances in the fan magazines and gossip columns made them known to half the world. He forced himself to smile and nod at one or two who greeted him, but there was only one person he wanted to talk to, and he wasn't about to miss his chance with her, if and when it came.

He felt a tap on his shoulder.

'Hey, Tom, sad day, huh?'

It was Harry Fellows, a director he knew from Lasky's, and who had worked with Taylor on and off. They chewed the air a while, catching up, when the sounds of a commotion emerged from a room on the far side of the lobby.

'That's the room where Mr Taylor's laid out,' Fellows explained. 'That negro valet of his, he's in there now. I saw two bulls take him in. You should see him, rigged out like he's going to—'

Before he could finish the sentence, the door of the inquest chamber opened and an usher called those assembled to take their seats. Fellows hung back, saying he might be called to testify, so Tom went in alone, making for an empty place at the aisle end of a rapidly filling bench near the door. He had a momentary standoff with a thin, birdlike woman, impeccably coiffured and fitted out in the fabrics and furs of a studio executive's wife. But he held his ground, knowing he might need to get out the door quickly if all went according to plan, and the woman pushed past to take a place further in as the coroner and two assistants entered from a side door.

Coroner Frank A. Nance looked like a man begrudgingly sacrificing his Saturday morning lie-in. A squat figure with a prominent gut, spectacles and the carmine flush of a drinker, he strode across the room and took his seat ill-temperedly, fussing over the documents he placed in front of him, then looked up for the first time at the packed room. The chatter dwindled.

'We are here for one purpose only,' Nance announced formally. 'That is to establish the circumstances in which William Desmond Taylor met his death. Witnesses have been called here today to testify on the facts alone. Speculations as to responsibility, motive or guilt will not be tolerated.'

A murmur rippled through the assembly, which Nance rebuked with a sharp clack of his gavel. As he and his clerk went through the preliminaries, Tom looked round, saw Sullivan sitting amid a bunch of detectives crowded on to the police benches. Beside them, sectioned off behind a rail, sat six anxious-looking jurors, most of them fidgeting and sweating, eyes sweeping from person to person, awed by the famous faces and heavy fug of power. Apart from the cops, the hacks and the court officers, the jurors were about the only non-movies present. Sullivan caught his eye, crossed his arms and pointed discreetly at a dark-haired, pug-faced cop sitting to his right. That had to be Ramirez.

Nance called the room to order and asked that the first witness be called. When the clerk announced Mabel Normand's name, heads turned, necks craned and, despite the coroner's clacking disapproval, another murmur rustled through the room, rising in volume as, second by second, no Miss Normand came to answer the summons. Looking the least surprised of anyone, the coroner issued an order to the clerk, who dispatched an officer from the room. Clearing his throat, Nance himself then called for Charles Eyton.

Tom watched intently as the familiar trim and well-tailored figure made his way to the plain wooden chair at the front of the room. His former boss was looking good, a slate-gray suit setting off the pomaded gleam of his black hair and sun-tanned skin. The flat nose, high cheekbones and powerful shoulders gave a strong impression of pugnacity. In the good times, Tom regularly shot the breeze with him about the fight game, impressed by his knowledge. As he took the oath, an air of power radiated from Eyton, permeating the crowd, setting them on edge.

'State your name,' said the coroner, an extra purr of gravity in his voice.

'Charles Eyton.'

'Where do you reside?'

'Nineteen twenty Vine Street, Hollywood.'

'What is your occupation?'

'General Manager, Famous Players-Lasky Corporation.' Eyton settled back in the chair but didn't relax, squeezing his hands into fists in his lap.

'Mr Eyton, have you seen the remains of the deceased in the adjoining room?'

'Yes, sir.'

'Do you recognize them as one you knew in life?'

'Yes, sir.'

'Who was it?'

'William Desmond Taylor.'

'Where was he born?'

'He was born in Ireland, to the best of my knowledge. He told me so.'

'What was his age?'

'Forty-four, I should judge.' Eyton eyed the coroner to see whether this would be contested.

'Was he married, single or a widower?'

'He was married.'

A low gasp went through the room. Only that morning, news-papers reported rumors of a woman claiming to be Taylor's abandoned wife in New York. What now of his supposed engagement to Mabel Normand? But Nance seemed determined to question none of it. It was more usual, Tom knew, for a cop to be called first. To establish the facts, the wheres and whens, the whos and hows. But for some reason, Nance was taking Eyton's authority as a recorder for granted. Which was hardly credible, given his, or at least the studio's, vested interests. Taylor was on the cusp of fifty and had claimed to be single for years, regardless of what the studio deemed it best for the public to believe.

'What was the cause of his death, if you know?'

'Well, Mr Taylor's assistant rang me up at my residence about eight o'clock and told me Mr Taylor had died suddenly; so I imme-diately went over to his residence and he was lying on the floor on his back. Detective Ziegler was there.'

Here Eyton broke off to nod towards the detective in question, before resuming.

'He had called the doctor prior to my arrival and the doctor told me Mr Taylor had died from a hemorrhage of the stomach. Douglas MacLean told me he thought he heard a shot the night before, and his wife also thought she heard a shot. He wanted the body turned over; they didn't want to turn it over until the coroner came. The deputy coroner came after a while, and I told him he had better turn the body over to make sure, and he put his hand under Mr Taylor's body and he found a little blood on his hand. Douglas asked him what that was, and he said it evidently had run down from his mouth, but I noticed that there was no trail of blood – Mr Taylor's head was in a pool of blood – there was no trail of blood running down.'

'There was a pool of blood under his head?'

'Under his head, yes – a little pool of blood. I immediately opened up Mr Taylor's vest and looked on the right-hand side, and there was no mark. I looked on the left-hand side and saw some blood, and then I told the deputy coroner I thought that evidence enough to turn his body over to see what would happen. I sent for a pillow to put under Mr Taylor's head, and we turned him over – the deputy coroner and myself – and we pulled his shirt and his vest up and we found the bullet wound.'

At this point, Eyton directed his gaze towards the room, which had rippled with a collective intake of breath. Tom watched his green eyes slowly sweep the room, assessing the reaction, calculating its worth, preparing to present the next exciting instalment. But Eyton's anticipation was short-lived. Nance trundled on, seeming not to notice that anyone had been shot, instead asking if the body had been stone cold, where it was lying with reference to the front entrance, and who else had been present.

'Did all of those persons live there in the neighborhood?'

'That I could not tell you,' Eyton said. 'Mr MacLean did, I know, because he showed me where his apartment was.'

By now it was becoming clear that Eyton was frustrated with this tedious line of questioning. Like everyone else present, all he wanted to do was get back to the body.

'The place Mr Taylor lived was in a court?'

'In a courtyard setting, yes.'

'These other buildings were nearby?'

'Well, yes, obviously, there are several apartments all the way around. It being a court.'

The sarcasm elicited a laugh from the room and drew the coroner irritably up from his note-taking. 'Did Mr and Mrs MacLean, or either of them, tell you about the hour that they heard the gunshot?'

'Yes, Mr MacLean told me it was about eight or a quarter after eight, and Mrs MacLean thought it was a little later.'

'That night?'

'The night before.'

'You didn't make any definite measurements as to the position of the body?'

'No, sir, I would not have regarded that as my role.'

'So what you have testified to is only an estimate, and nothing definite about it.'

Eyton's shoulders went up as he took a deep breath. Everyone in the room held theirs too as he glared for some seconds at Nance, before responding in a voice clipped with disapproval. 'Yes.'

'Now, how long has Mr Taylor lived in this place?'

'That I could not tell you. He lived in it before he went to the war, I believe.'

'When did you last see him alive?'

'The day before – Wednesday.'

'Now, did he have any firearms of his own?'

'I believe he had a revolver. I believe the revolver was in a drawer upstairs; in fact, I know it was there because Detective Ziegler and myself went up there and saw it.'

'Did you see any firearms in the room where he was?'

'No.'

'What was the name of his valet or attendant there?'

'Peavey, the colored cook. I never knew him or saw him.'

'Was he the one who called you?'

'As I said, Harry Fellows, Mr Taylor's assistant director, was the one who called me.'

'You have no independent knowledge of the manner in which he met his death?'

'No, sir.'

Coroner Nance let out a long sigh and turned his attention to the startled jurors. 'Have you any questions, gentlemen?'

One, eager as everyone else to hear more of the dead man, put a hand up gingerly.

'Was his clothing ruffled in any way, showing any violence?'

'No, not at all,' Eyton said. 'It looked like he just walked in the door and was shot in the back; that's the way it looked. Neither the room nor the body showed any evidence of a struggle. He had on the same suit as the day before when he talked to me.'

Eyton looked back at Nance, expecting the coroner to grab the out-held baton and run with it. But it was not to be.

'Is there any other question? No? That is all, you may be excused.'

Eyton rose and left the stand, shaking his head, eyes checking that the crowd also thought the questions he'd been subjected to were something in the line of a farce. The whispers of discontent rippling through the ranks confirmed it. But already Nance was rapping his gavel and ordering the next witness to be called. Dr A.F. Wagner, county autopsy surgeon, was duly sworn in.

'Doctor Wagner, did you perform a post-mortem on the body of the deceased?'

'I did.'

'Will you state your findings?'

'I performed an autopsy on William Desmond Taylor here on February second, 1922 and found a bullet hole in the left side. The bullet entered six and a half inches below the armpit, and in the posterior axillary line, and passed inward and upward, passing through the seventh interspace of the ribs, penetrating both lobes of the left lung and emerging on the inner margin of the left lobe, then traversing the mediastinum . . .'

NINETEEN

For Tom, the testimony that followed seemed largely irrelevant. The appearance of Taylor's butler, Henry Peavey, who'd been first to come across the dead body and was the most visibly distressed person in the room by some margin, caused a particular stir. A heavy-set man with the build of a bare-knuckle boxer, he cut quite a dash in an outlandish costume of checkered plus-fours, canary-yellow silk shirt and maroon bow tie. Speaking of the circumstances in which he had found Taylor's body, he burst into tears and it was some minutes before he could be calmed enough to resume. Many in the room were unable to decide whether horror or glee was the more appropriate reaction, and opted for snickering of the lowest kind instead. At least three reporters dashed for the door, much to Nance's annoyance. After more questions and a deal more commotion, Peavey was excused.

Detective Ziegler's evidence was notable chiefly for its brevity. Eyton had clearly satisfied all Nance's curiosity regarding the scene. When Ziegler told him of Faith MacLean's encounter with a stranger outside Taylor's door just after the gunshot was heard, Nance moved on hurriedly as if this information was of no consequence. Again, it was left to a juror to elicit the useful fact that the caliber of

Taylor's revolver and that of the bullet found in his body were
different, and that therefore he hadn't been shot with his own gun.
Tom was beginning to wonder how long this slow torture would
continue when he heard Ziegler dismissed and Mabel Normand's
name called again. Immediately, a cop pushed into the room and
held the door open behind him.

This time, everyone gawped. If Mabel Normand knew anything,
it was how to make an entrance. She was tiny, barely over five foot
tall and slightly built, although her wide-brimmed green velour
fedora and button-over high-heeled shoes added extra inches to her
height, and her brown-and-white three-quarter-length coat, with
fox-fur collar and cuffs, imbued her with still more presence. It
wasn't until she reached the stand and turned to sit that Tom saw
her demeanor for the first time and realized what had made the
people further up the room gasp. The beautiful, animated face that
had brought Normand worldwide fame was pale, spent and haggard.
Her huge, usually laughter-lined eyes were dull and lifeless, rimmed
with sorrow. The personification of grief.

As she was sworn in, she barely looked up, concentrating on
folding and unfolding a lavender silk handkerchief in her gloved
hands. Coroner Nance rapped the desk and the babble ceased, the
silence and expectation as complete as when a great conductor taps
his baton. Here was the moment everyone had come to witness –
one of movieland's royalty come to explain in public her involvement
in the murder of the man she loved.

'Please state your name.'

'Mabel Normand.'

'Where do you reside.'

'Thirty eighty-nine West Seventh.'

'What is your occupation?'

She hesitated, searching for an adequate description. 'Motion
pictures.'

'Miss Normand, were you acquainted with Mr Taylor, the
deceased in this case?'

'Yes.'

'Did you see him the evening before his death occurred?'

'Yes, I did.'

'Did you see him at his home?'

'Yes.'

'And you were with him about how long on that occasion?'

'I got there about seven o'clock and left at a quarter to eight.'

'And when you left his place, did you leave him in the house, or outside?'

'No, he came to my car with me.' Her voice trembled, aware of the fateful significance of that final act of gallantry.

'Where was your car?'

'Right in front of the court.'

'On Alvarado Street?'

'Yes, on the hill.'

'Was he still there when you drove away?'

'Yes, as my car turned around, I waved my hand at him.'

She raised a gloved hand towards the jurors to show them how. A tear spilled down her left cheek, transforming a gesture of innocence into one of overwhelming sadness. While she dabbed at her tears, two or three sympathetic sobs broke out in other parts of the room. Tom looked round at all the faces transfixed, wondered whether this was the greatest performance ever given or simple unadulterated truth. He for one was convinced. She looked to be close to breaking point. He would have to go gently when he approached her. Meanwhile, Coroner Nance considered she'd had sufficient time to compose herself, and forged on.

'At the time you were there, was anybody else in the house?'

'Yes, Henry, his man.'

'Henry Peavey?'

'Yes.'

'Do you know whether Mr Peavey left the house before you did?'

'Yes, he did. He left about, I should say, fifteen or twenty minutes before I left, but stopped outside and spoke to my chauffeur. We came out later.'

'No one else except Peavey was there?'

'That was all.'

The coroner hesitated, apparently lacking for anything more to ask, and for the first time since she had taken the stand, attention shifted away from Normand and on to Nance. Reddening slightly, he coughed to cover his confusion.

'And what time was it you say you left him – drove away from his place?'

'I left him on the sidewalk about a quarter to eight.'

'Did you expect to hear from him later that evening?'

'No, I went to bed; when I am asleep, he tells my maid not to disturb me.'

'Was that the last time you saw him, when you left at about a quarter to eight?'

She looked up at the coroner directly for the first time, eyes wide, her voice faltering. 'That was the last time.'

'Have you any questions, gentlemen?'

To a man, the jurors looked horrified that they should be expected to intrude on such sorrow. Unable to muster a 'no' between them, they shook their downcast heads.

'That is all, then; you may be excused.'

As Normand rose, the court broke into another rush of whispering and half a dozen reporters made a break for the door. But what came next stopped everyone in their tracks, as the coroner rapped his gavel and spoke up above the noise.

'That is all the evidence we will take in this case. All but the jury will be excused.'

Tom, already half out of his seat, just had time to whip round and catch the look of confusion on the faces of Sullivan and his fellow detectives. Surely that couldn't be it? The proceedings had lasted barely forty minutes. Not even half those subpoenaed had given evidence. The room was swept up in pandemonium, everyone jumping to their feet. Over their heads, Tom could see a green velour fedora bobbing towards the main door amid a clamor of reporters. Struggling against the tide of people surging for the door, he saw DA Woolwine and his deputy, William Doran, push through the press to Miss Normand, take her by the arm and whisk her through the small side exit, an officer barring access to the following mob. Meanwhile, Tom was swept out into the lobby. He shouldered his way to the edge of the crowd, and through a service door that promised access to the interior of the building. The corridor behind was wide and curved round, skirting the inquest chamber. Doors led off on one side, the smell of embalming fluid harsh enough to make him glad they were all shut. Ahead, he saw a passage leading to the left. Reaching it, he caught the last eclipsing light of a door closing at the far end – and ran towards it.

TWENTY

The glare of daylight dazzled him momentarily. Then he saw them, standing atop the steps leading down to the service yard behind the mortuary, black hearses parked all round. DA Woolwine could have passed for an undertaker, his suit a severe black, buttoned-up three-piece with starched wing collar and black bow tie. Doran, his deputy, was more modern, his suit slate-gray, his shirt collar snap-down, his copper-colored tie silk and perfectly centered in the V of his vest. The two men stared at him, daring him to approach. Between them, Mabel Normand stood, turning uncertainly at Tom's sudden appearance, then away again, uninterested.

'Miss Normand is not giving interviews,' Woolwine said, an impressive rumble of authority in his strong Southern accent.

'I'm not press.' Tom sidestepped to his left, and addressed his next words directly to her. 'Please, Miss Normand, may I have a word? Mr Sennett wants you—'

At this, Doran stepped between Tom and the actress. 'What in heaven are you doing, man? Can't you see this lady is upset? Leave us now, before I call an officer and have you removed.'

But Sennett's name had done the trick.

'No, wait, please,' Normand said, placing a restraining hand on Doran's arm, turning to face Tom. There was a hauntedness in her expression, a quaver in her voice. Her jaw seemed to fight against the effort of speaking. She took a step closer, and in the harsh light Tom could see her huge eyes were ringed by dark circles under the caked-on make-up. 'Mr Sennett sent you?'

'Thank you, yes,' Tom said, disconcerted by the feverishness of her manner. 'Mr Sennett wanted to be sure you're well. You haven't been home. He was worried.'

She put a hand up, cutting him off. 'You tell him he shouldn't worry, not one bit.' Her voice was shrill with anxiety, the muscles in her neck taut with the unrepaid effort of keeping a level tone. 'Tell him that I'm just dandy, thank you. Just dandy. And I . . . I need some time to be alone now.'

Her eyes were no longer meeting his, no longer fixing on anything. It was as if she were retreating inside the shell of herself for protection. All he could do was try to call her back. 'I'm sorry, but Mr Sennett is genuinely very concerned. He needs to see you. Can I at least tell him where you can be reached?'

She stiffened as though she'd been struck across the back, but her eyes remained strangely blank. 'I don't want to be reached,' she spat back at him. 'Not by him. Not by anybody. But especially not by him. You be sure and tell him that. *Especially not him.*'

Before he could say any more, Normand began making her way awkwardly down the steps towards a black limousine reversing into the yard and drawing to a halt. Tom went to follow her but was stopped by Doran, his arm barring the way. A moment later, the chauffeur Davis dismounted the automobile, pointing up at Tom, angry. 'He's the one, Miss. He's the one I told you about.'

She turned, her face empty of everything but fear as she glanced a last time at Tom before disappearing into the limousine's curtained interior.

Woolwine strode over to Tom and poked him on the chest with an elongated forefinger. He wasn't a big man, but the finger carried a surprising weight, and his cheeks were puce with anger.

'Would you like to tell me what in tarnation's going on here?' he roared, the Tennessee in his voice coming out now. Tom watched the auto speed away before pushing off Doran's restraining arm.

'Nothing. Absolutely nothing's going on. I wanted to talk to her, that's all.'

'Well, she very clearly did not want to talk to you, now, did she?'

Receiving no reply, Woolwine barked again at Tom, demanding his name.

'And you are in the employ of Mr Sennett, are you, Mr Collins?'

Tom said nothing. He wasn't getting himself in any more trouble.

'Very well, Collins, you stay silent. But heed this: if you go near Miss Normand again, I'll have you behind bars quicker than you can blink. You may depend on that. And when you see Mr Sennett, tell him the same goes for him, too. Direct from me. He has many questions to answer in this affair, and I won't have him intimidating my witnesses. Do I make myself clear?'

'Why would he want to intimidate her?' Tom said. 'All I was aiming to do was help.'

Woolwine regarded him with open contempt. 'I assure you she needs no help of yours. My office has the situation in hand. Now remove yourself before I lose patience.'

Woolwine wheeled on his heel and headed back into the building, followed smartly by Doran, who pulled the door shut behind him. Alone now in the yard, Tom cursed volubly, bitterly, with no one and nothing but the empty hearses to hear him. He'd had it up to his neck with this stupid affair. But Normand's anguish and Woolwine's words were already itching away at him. He said Mack Sennett would have questions to answer before this was finished. No surprise there. But what had he meant when he insisted his office had everything in hand? Tom hadn't even mentioned the murder investigation. Was he talking about Normand, too?

TWENTY-ONE

'Hey, Collins? Tom Collins, wait up a minute, brother.'

Hearing his name called, Tom looked back up Hill Street towards Overholtzer's. The crowd outside had swollen. Pushing against the wall of spectators, hailing him with a raised notebook, was the scrawny figure of Phil Olsen. Tom waited while Olsen wriggled free and scuttled up beside him. The wire-framed spectacles perched on a hawk nose and the constant curl of knowingness on his lips marked him out as a newsman as effectively as the police press badge pinned to the frayed silk band of his boater. The hat had seen a skirmish or two too many, but Olsen's navy-blue suit was clean and pressed, a detail Tom noted not only for its rarity but also its contrast with his own. Even the red bow tie Olsen sported looked new.

'They must be paying well at the *Herald* these days, Olsen. You're looking flush.' Tom held out a hand in greeting.

'Aw, you Irish, always with the charm.' Olsen grinned and pumped his hand enthusiastically. His eyes roved Tom's face, checking out the bruises and the split lip. 'I wish I could say the same for you, brother. Jeez, you've been through the wringer. I thought I might run into you at the fights in Vernon last night, but I never thought to look for you *in* the ring.'

Tom laughed. He always found it hard to resist Olsen's line in patter. 'No, business isn't that bad – yet.'

'So how'd you come by the thick lip? And don't tell me you slipped on some orange peel. I've tried it, it don't work.'

Tom looked away, back up the street. 'Questions, questions. Don't you ever stop, Olsen? I would've thought the big story was back up there with the movies. Isn't that supposed to be your beat?'

Olsen flapped a hand at him. 'I saw as much as I needed of that. What a farce, brother.'

, 'I didn't see you in there.'

'Sure I was there. And very fascinating it was too, especially the contributions of your former boss. I thought him in splendid form – one of the best performances I've seen in years. Pity so much of it deviated from the truth. I mean, they didn't even get the name right. Don't these guys ever read the papers?'

'How do you mean?'

'Didn't you see it either? Jeez, why do we even try?' Olsen threw his hands up in only partially mock horror. 'Actually, it was the *Times* got this one, but it's a beauty all the same. Turns out Bill Taylor's name isn't Taylor at all but Tanner. And the Desmond was fake, too. So he wasn't William Desmond Taylor; he was William Deane Tanner. Yeah, Mr Deane Tanner, late of New York, where he abandoned a wife and daughter fifteen years ago. The guy was a total phoney.'

It was news to Tom, but hardly a surprise. Name changers were a dime a dozen in the colony. Lots of folk did it, to sound more euphonious or attractive. Or maybe to turn their back on an undesired past. It was a non-starter and he said so to Olsen.

'It's still a good story,' Olsen said. 'Eyton must have known. And I don't care what you say; Nance should've picked up on it. Still, could be it's a minor sin compared with the rest he missed out on. And with all those movie stars on hand, too. What a waste.'

'No doubt that's exactly what you'll be saying in your news report,' Tom laughed.

'Yeah, right. As you know, I'm contractually obliged to embroider the truth and salivate suggestively wherever possible in my reporting. So I'll be leading in great detail on what Hollywood's foremost comedienne Miss Normand was wearing, and how sorrow was consuming her already frail figure. And pondering whether her uncharacteristic aversion to being photographed today had less to do with grief than guilt. Over her allowing the intruder an opportunity to enter the house, of course. Nothing else implied.' He rolled his eyes before continuing. 'If I toe the line with that, I might get to slip a few inches in about what a fine upstanding character our investigating coroner is and how admirable it was that he could dispose of the most controversial inquest ever to come his way in under forty-five minutes.'

'But you'll lead on Normand,' Tom said, feeling duty-bound to defend her. 'What did that woman ever do to you guys? Sounds to me like somebody has it in for Hollywood's foremost comedienne.'

Olsen tipped his boater back, scratched his forehead and gave Tom a penetrating stare. 'You might have something there, you know. Look, I've got a bit of time before I file my story. Join me for a coffee? You look like you could do with one.'

They walked around the corner to Van De Kamp's, a bakery with a Dutch-style windmill above the door and an enormous display case in the window with stacked trays of plaited breads and pretzels, candy-colored cakes and pastries of all kinds. It had a new, modern feel indoors – all scrubbed tiles and no tables, only neat padded swivel stools lined against brushed steel counters – apart from the waitresses, who were decked out in Dutch maids' uniforms.

Tom and Olsen sat at the counter and a strikingly pretty girl took their order, a sharp Texan twang at odds with her Hollandish cap and plaits.

'Everyone's an actress in this town.' Olsen licked his lips as she walked away.

'Still helping young hopefuls get that first foot on the ladder?' Tom asked.

Olsen grinned. 'One of the benefits of a city that attracts a multitude of good-looking gals seeking fortune through fame, not marriage. So many are content to start at the bottom.'

'And that'd be you, Olsen, would it?'

'You got it in one, friend. You'd be amazed how thirsty some of these lovelies are for a drop of ink.'

'Sure, or a taste of the camera,' Tom grunted. He'd seen enough of that for a lifetime.

Olsen nodded, then narrowed his eyes. 'Speaking of which, Tom, have those gentlemen at Lasky's realized the error of their ways and asked you to rejoin their ranks?'

'What makes you ask that?'

'Oh, nothing.' There was a slick of disingenuousness to Olsen's reply. 'Only I saw you sitting in on the inquest and I was, you know, wondering what you were doing there if you didn't have nothing to do with Lasky no more. That's all.'

'Just a casual observer,' Tom said. The invitation to coffee was always going to have an ulterior motive.

'Yeah,' Olsen said. 'But I had to sell my grandmother to get a pass for that inquest, and I had every reason to be there.'

'So maybe I knew somebody who got me in. You press guys can't have all the perks, you know. I was interested, that's all.'

'So you knew Taylor? You being Irish and all. You were part of his circle?'

'No, not at all. Barely knew him. Other than his reputation as a decent guy and a capable director. And seeing him around the studio, from time to time. Spoke to him on a couple of jobs I did over at Realart, but I wasn't there very often. He played in a different league. Seemed a nice fella, though.'

'What about Mabel Normand?'

'What about her?' Tom said, letting a note of irritation flavor his reply. 'Christ, don't you ever give up? Quit giving me the shakedown, will you.'

'OK, OK. You can't blame a fellow for trying. I was just fishing. Kind of hoping you might be able to give me the inside track on something.'

'You must be hard up, coming to me. What track?'

'Just something I heard happened round at Taylor's, Thursday afternoon. Thought you might have been there. That being your line of work, or used to be. You live out that way too, no?'

Tom frowned without meaning to. How the hell did Olsen know where he lived? 'I wasn't anywhere near Taylor's on Thursday.'

Olsen pushed on regardless. 'Well, somebody told me a certain starlet paid a visit to the death house, and created quite a scene while she was there. Word is, she claimed Mr Taylor and her were engaged to be married.'

'That's hardly news. Miss Normand's already made a statement denying it.'

'Sure she did. And you should listen more carefully, Collins. I said starlet, not star. I'm talking about the young lady your Mr Zukor says will be the next big thing. I'm talking about that erstwhile *Anne of Green Gables*, the one and only Mary Miles Minter. You ever hear anything about her and Taylor swapping rings?'

He kept his eyes on Olsen, recalling now the inscribed photo of Minter in Taylor's front room and Sullivan pulling himself up when referring to Taylor's age. Had he known more than he said? Tom prayed his expression gave nothing away. 'I thought the press line was he was engaged to Normand?'

'My point exactly. It's what makes it a good story, no?' Olsen's grin was feral. He leaned in towards Tom and dropped his voice. 'That's not all. I heard also that, upon leaving the house, the lovely Miss Minter sped straight down here to Overholtzer's and bribed a staff member to leave her alone with Taylor's cold dead bones for a half-hour.'

Tom's jaw didn't quite drop, but Olsen was delighted with the reaction. 'Put it another way, here's the sell: "Well-known youthful movie actress of flawless complexion and national renown, distraught at the death of a much admired senior director, requested and was granted a private audience with the lifeless remains at Los Angeles' premier funeral parlor Thursday evening last."'

'You can't be serious.'

'Oh, but I am.' Olsen swept his left hand across and made a 'ding' before continuing. 'New paragraph. "The golden-ringleted actress was heard to weep copiously and make numerous – sadly muffled but manifestly passionate – declarations of undying love on said director's unbeating breast. She was further observed draping her lithe and much admired young figure all over his, uh, too-solid flesh. Such was the ardency of her grief, it was said, she had to be detached forcibly from the late director's remains by members of the mortuary staff."'

'Jesus, Olsen. You can't put that into print?'

The reporter gestured disconsolately. 'That's the god-awful problem. It won't get halfway to the typesetters if I can't find something solid to back it up. The morticians are all keeping schtum – or staying off the record, anyhow. As an erstwhile oil-the-wheels man yourself, you'll appreciate what tidy sums Eyton and his cronies must've paid out for their discretion. Nothing I can

match, that's for sure. I thought you might . . .' He paused only to
turn his palms up. 'Well, obviously not. I got most of this straight
from one of Overholtzer's embalmers in exchange for a steak supper
last night. Then she got scared of losing her position and denied it
just as straight.'

Tom hardly knew whether to be disgusted or annoyed. 'See, that's
what I don't get. How come you guys can splash any trash you like
over the front pages about Normand, but when it comes to Minter
you've got to give it the velvet glove? Why is that?'

Olsen grunted in disbelief. 'Oh, now, brother. You ain't that dumb.
How long did you work for Eyton? You've seen enough of this stuff
to know how it works. Only the right rumors ever get into print in
this town. I've done my damnedest to get this Minter story past my
editor and he put it straight on the spike. Worried about his annual
pension contribution from Adolph Zukor and Jesse Lasky. He told
me to my face: Minter is off limits for now, unless it's copper-
fastened. 'Course, everybody out at Lasky is clammed up tighter
than a pigmy's ass about it. All they're interested in is Mabel
Normand. But I'll be damned if I'm not going to get something in
about Minter.'

'I don't know how you sleep at night, Olsen. I really—' It had
taken a second or three to register. 'Hang on. Back up a second,' Tom
said. 'What do you mean, they're only interested in Normand? Why
would the Lasky guys have anything to say about Normand at all?'

Olsen's lips flickered fractionally and his eyes locked and glinted.
There was a lot going on behind them. He sat back in his chair and
clasped his hands behind his neck. 'You know, I had a feeling you'd
be grabbed by that.'

For Tom, it felt like falling into a trap, only he wasn't sure what
kind. 'Why are you telling me this?'

Olsen's smile broadened. 'Oh, just a hunch. I've been in this
game long enough to spot a ringer. I saw the way you were looking
at Normand back there.'

'Wasn't everybody?'

'Yeah, but not everybody sneaked in the back of the building
after her. I was tempted to follow you but I had to finish the job
and grab a few workable quotes from the famous folk. Gotta keep
the boss happy or I'll be shown the door myself.' Olsen paused for
dramatic effect. 'I figured maybe you're working for Normand.'

'Don't be crazy.'

'Because, you know, I'd be real eager to hear about it if you are.'

'Sorry to disappoint you, but that's not how it is.'

Olsen wasn't so much dissuaded as wholly skeptical. 'Now I know why a handsome guy like you never made it the other side of the camera, Collins. You're one lousy actor. C'mon, what're you doing for her? Tell me. I could maybe give you somethin' that you want to know.'

Tom laughed out loud to cover his unease. This conversation was way out of control, but he was intrigued as all hell by it. 'What makes you think I want to know anything from you?'

Olsen grinned, his sure sense of a story evident in the flush blooming on his cheeks. 'OK, Tom, quid pro quo, yeah? I spill, you spill. We got a deal?'

'Depends on what you got,' Tom shrugged.

'I can tell you why Normand's coming in for so much stick and how it's being engineered. I can give you a name.'

'Are you saying someone at Lasky is running some kind of smear campaign against her?'

'Maybe I am, maybe I'm not. Do we have a deal?'

Tom hesitated. Sennett was convinced somebody was out to get Normand. Confirmation of that, and a name, might get him off his back. It had to be worth a shot.

'OK,' Tom said, 'but you didn't hear any of this from me. Agreed?'

'Sure thing,' Olsen nodded encouragingly.

'Right. I'm not working for Normand, but somebody asked me to look into her involvement in the Taylor case.'

'With a view to what?

'With a view to exonerating her.'

'Who hired you?'

'A friend.'

'Who? Sennett? Mickey Neilan?'

Tom showed him the flats of his palms. 'Wait. First tell me about the smears. Who's running them?'

'Ain't it obvious? All these stories coming out of the woodwork about her; nothing about Minter. Who would have access to all that information about her and Taylor in the first place? Who's most concerned to divert attention away from rumors about Taylor's involvement with Minter? Go on, you figure it out; it's not so hard.'

He was right. It wasn't. 'Eyton? All this is coming from him?'

'Eyton, Jesse Lasky, J.J. Fine in the publicity office, whoever.'

'You're certain of this?'

'Not a hundred percent. I'd only stake the one year's salary on it, no more.' Olsen held his palms out at the obviousness of it. 'It could be Eyton or even Zukor who's behind it, but it's definitely coming from the studio. The Lasky press boys have been working flat out – and it ain't because they've got any good movies premiering next week. It's a smoke screen. I got three calls yesterday giving me juicy little nuggets about Normand and Taylor's love trysts. I know other guys on my paper, at the *Times* and *Examiner* as well, all getting the same. Supposed to be anonymous but, you know, these publicity guys we speak to most days of the week. We know their voices.'

'So what did Normand do to bring this on?'

'You're missing the point, brother. It's not about who they're trying to hurt; it's what they're trying to protect. You of all people should know how jittery everyone at Lasky is since this Arbuckle debacle. I'm told you have painful personal experience of how ruthlessly they protect their assets – when it suits them.'

Tom's eyes must have widened at that remark, as the curl on Olsen's lips tightened in response. But there was no way Olsen could have knowledge of what had happened between himself and Fay, or the deal they had been forced to do with Eyton. Was there?

'So enlighten me.' He said it cautiously. 'Who are they trying to protect?'

'I already told you.' Olsen laughed as if he'd got one over on Tom, then leaned in towards him, his voice dropping lower. 'Minter, of course. You know Zukor put millions into her. Sure, so he was wrong about her being the new Pickford, but she still does great box office. He can't afford to have that tainted. But it's not just her. This Taylor thing, coming so soon after all the bad juice about Arbuckle? Lasky's is drawing all the heat. Think how much there is at stake: jobs, reputations, big money. You think they would overlook a ready-made headline-grabbing distraction to draw attention away from their door? What better than a dope-fiend crowd-puller from a rival studio who's been jumping in and outta the sack with the murdered man. She's a gift to them, brother. No way are they gonna pass on that.'

TWENTY-TWO

T he traffic on Sunset was all snarled up, so a block west of Gower he swung the Dodge into the curb and walked the rest of the way. His route took him past a cluster of small independent studios, a general hubbub outside. Throngs of extras and bit-parters milled about, lining up at the cheap food stalls that spring up like weeds outside all studio walls – a hallucinatory mix of war-bonneted Navajos, raven-haired juanitas and bow-legged buckaroo boys fresh off the latest horse operas. Chow time in Gower Gulch.

It was all too tantalising. Crossing the intersection, he bought a couple of soft, spicy tacos and iced sodas from a stand run by a Mexican boy at the entrance to the Steiner building. Heady aromas of garlic, cilantro and peppers wafted from the warm wax-paper wrappers. He was most of the way through the first by the time he reached the top floor and shouldered through a door with *Efficiency Secretarial* etched into the frosted glass. Inside, a brunette with spectacles and a frown of intense concentration was barely visible behind a desk stacked high with mail and paperwork. The clatter of typewriter keys ceased as she jumped up, adding no more than nine inches to her height and revealing little more than a good string of pearls and the shapely upper portion of a pale blue tweed jacket.

'Don't you go spilling food on my floor, you big Irish ape.' Her voice was more redolent of Brooklyn's smoke-clogged avenues than the cool, clean air of the City of Angels. 'The mop's still recovering from the last time you were here.'

Tom sucked a teetering drop of salsa from the end of his taco. 'Good to see you, too, Betty. Here, I got one for you. And a soda.'

Betty removed her glasses and emerged from behind the desk. 'This what you meant by buyin' me lunch? Well, thanks, I ate already. But I won't say no to the soda.'

She ushered Tom the few steps towards a small table and chairs by the side wall of the office. 'Sit here. It's all I managed to clear today. Wait a sec . . .'

She pulled the table out an inch or so from the wall before setting the soda down and motioning Tom to be seated. The telephone rang. She gave it a dismissive wave and sat herself down.

'Busy?'

She directed her brown eyes heavenwards. 'The stupid lunk's only gone and taken on another eight clients. Can you believe it? I keep on saying, "Paulie, I can't cope with the ones we got already." But it's like I'm not even in the room with him for all the attention he pays. Maybe I'll join a union one of these days.'

'A one-woman strike?' Tom laughed. 'He wouldn't last a day without you.'

She reached across and squeezed his wrist. ''Cept for special clients of course. The rest of them, they can drop dead for all I care. He'll soon get the message when the checks stop coming.'

'I always said that man doesn't deserve you,' Tom said, starting in on the second taco.

Betty shot a coy glance back at him, fanning her neck with a hand. 'Ooh, Mr Collins. If only I wuz unencumbered.' Her East Coast drawl crossed more than a continent and wrapped the final vowel in a veil of smoky sensuality it was never intended to bear. Tom held her eyes for just a little longer than he should. Another image of her, high on a flickering screen, drifted into his mind – a close-up in a Fairbanks costumer, high point of her brief career in motion pictures. Now this.

He looked away, unsure of what was being unsaid, and nodded towards the paper stacks. 'So is there anything for me? Any calls?'

'Well, nobody could say you weren't getting value for money from us, honey. There's a stack of mail, and the telephone's been ringing off the hook for you all morning. Your beloved Mrs Parker was after you, more than once.'

His pained expression caused one of Betty's tweezer-thinned eyebrows to rise, ever hopeful for a crumb of gossip. The truth was more prosaic. He had called Fay first thing but her maid rebuffed him saying she was asleep. Doubtless exhausted by the three-day journey. He hadn't had a chance to try again since.

'And that awful Mack Sennett,' Betty breezed on, since he wasn't elaborating. 'Jeez, but he's an unpleasant man. You can tell him from me, I ain't never going to watch none of his stupid movies again.'

'What did he want?'

'He didn't say. Just keeps calling to "apprise" you of his whereabouts. This may be a small town, but that man sure knows how to get around every inch of it. Last I heard, a half-hour ago, he was over in the Hollywood Hotel and wanted you there too. Fast.'

'I better get on, then. Before he busts a gut.' Tom gulped back the last of his soda and stood, pulling on his coat.

Betty rose too, a hand unconsciously kneading the small of her back as she walked to her desk. 'Need any typing?'

Tom shook his head and she handed him a small stack of mail and handwritten messages. Taking them, he gave her hands a squeeze and pulled her towards him. There was no resistance as her body curved into his, her lips opening a fraction as he bent and sidestepped at the last moment, his lips just shy of her ear.

'There is one thing you could do for me.' He laughed then and nodded towards the telephone on her desk.

She stiffened in his arms, feigned a look of disappointment and put a hand round her back, untangling herself from his clasp. 'You're such a dope, Tom Collins. I don't know why I let you get away with it.'

Slipping on her shoes, she reached across the desk for her purse and gloves, and headed for the door. 'Ten minutes, no more. And you be sure you hang up proper this time when you're done.'

TWENTY-THREE

'William was called away on urgent business for the bank,' Fay yawned, happy. 'He insisted I take the private car with him to Chicago. I couldn't pass up the opportunity to come back early. And in such comfort. I grabbed it.'

Her voice had a breathy energy that never failed to ensnare him. It was the first thing he had known of her, other than an imperious tap on his shoulder, interrupting a deep-and-meaningful he was having with Al Krexler about whether radio would ever be powerful enough to relay big fights all the way across America. Like it had the Dempsey–Carpentier bout in Jersey the week before to a handful of cities on the East Coast.

'Mr Collins?'

Was it that tap on his shoulder or the elegance of her voice that had run through him like electric shock? At the time – July the previous year – he was working for Lasky. He knew who she was, and had been expecting her. Fay Parker – *Mrs*, not Miss, he'd been warned. A small but promising splash in a surprise hit out of Zukor's New York operation had seen her sent West to take a more prominent role in a new DeMille costumer. She wasn't getting the royal treatment – Lasky himself, or DeMille at a pinch, would have been at the railhead for that. Even so, she was having it better than most, with Tom deputed to show her the studio ropes, see her settled in and iron out any problems. He had seen the reel that made her name and thought she looked pretty good up on screen, if no more than that. Which is why he was unprepared for the jolt of raw want that struck him square in his chest when he turned and saw her.

'You're looking at him.'

Something kicked in her, too, because she took a step back and flicked her clear green eyes away from his. Later, she claimed it was to stop herself laughing at the stupid expression on his face, but he knew he'd turned with his usual confident smile. Knew, too, without arrogance or expectation, that since that moment something animal bound them together.

It wasn't so much her beauty, although in a town awash with good looks she had no trouble holding her own. That wasn't what he saw, or felt. Or what asserted itself in the hours that followed. He took one of the best studio cars, a big McFarlan Six, and gave her the tour, out around the lots, up to the viewing spot above the Cahuenga Pass, the whole of Los Angeles spread out before them. By the time he was to drop her off at the Garden Court Apartments where the studio had boarded her, they knew they would be spending the night together. So he drove on, to his place, away from the whispering spotlight of Hollywood.

He had never been with anyone like her before – bright, funny, glamorous, at ease in any company, charming everyone she met. Lying together in the gathering light of dawn that first time, she answered his questions about what she was doing in Los Angeles plainly, simply. Her husband, William Parker, was a charming man who had confessed, after a not especially unhappy first three years of marriage, that he had come to the realization that he preferred to share his bed with men. His social standing, his position on the board of a venerable New York banking firm, ruled out divorce or scandal. However, he did not want Fay's life ruined as a result either, and wished her to pursue her own interests and ambitions, and to repay her discretion in any way he could. She spent money for a period until she found it didn't satisfy her, opened a jazz club, then returned to her career on stage – although more selectively than before. She was visited backstage one evening by an associate of Mr Zukor who invited her to test for the screen. She found she liked it. William tolerated it. Hollywood beckoned. She was happy with the freedom the arrangement gave her, more than any she had previously experienced in life. It also meant Tom's unresolved marital status bothered her not one whit. If anything, it drew them closer together.

The months that followed had been for Tom among the busiest, and happiest, of his life. His work at Lasky was going well. He heard whispers Eyton was considering him for promotion. Fay made three movies with DeMille, and although she hadn't quite taken with the public, Zukor remained convinced of her talent and determined to find more suitable material for her. Meanwhile, with an energy as seemingly inexhaustible as her funds, she set up the Oasis, a small supper and dance club at the western end of Sunset, to keep herself occupied and, two or three nights a week, display the one talent she couldn't get across on screen – her singing. Tom never felt he was in her shadow, and what it was she saw in him, apart from a total contrast with herself and her past, he didn't care to wonder about. For him, this was what Hollywood was all about. Nobody cared about the old hierarchies. You made your own way and were judged by what you had to show for it.

Which was fine, as long as you were on the up.

Now, holding the mouthpiece close to his chest, he realized just how much he longed to see her again, to hold her close. Over the telephone, he always struggled for an intimacy to match hers. The words would never come to him. So he asked her how her journey coast to coast had been, and she told him how much she loved that second leg out of Chicago, rattling through countless miles of sagebrush, desert, mountain, rock and range – the iron-heavy heat, the beauty so epic in scale.

'I don't think I could ever be bored by it,' she said. 'Especially with so much to look forward to this end. I thought we could celebrate by doing something nice tonight.'

'Great. You don't need to be at the club?'

'They're doing fine without me. How about supper at the Palm Court?'

'Sounds good.'

'I reserved a table for seven. For two, I should say, *at* seven.'

'Thanks for the clarification. I was worried.' He laughed. 'So you're not mad at me?'

'Mad?'

'About the girl? Colleen. She said you called.'

The pause was minimal. 'No, I'm not. I mean, I *have* just come back from visiting my husband in New York. And she's your niece, right? Strange how you never mentioned this family you have stashed away in Idaho. Or was it Ohio?' Her laugh was so knowing, so self-assured. 'Especially as she's such a pretty little thing.'

'Smart with it, I reckon—' He stalled, had to reel it back a foot or two. 'Pretty?'

'Yes, very. I had to be downtown this morning, so I stopped by yours on the way back, to see if you were home. Well, like you say, she's smart for sure. Didn't bat an eyelid. Invited me straight in, said I was welcome to wait. Seems you told her all about me. Once we got talking, she confessed what had happened. What you did for her.'

'Right,' he said, unsure how much Coleen would have told her. 'She's a good kid, I think. Just needs a push in the right direction. I thought maybe you could help. You're always on the lookout for table staff at the Oasis. Or you could introduce her to Delores Tamlin and get her a place at that rooming house of hers. Be a start for her, wouldn't it?'

This time the pause was longer. 'You're right. Why not call her now and ask her to meet me at the club in an hour and I'll get something set up with Eddie. Even if Delores's house is full, she'll know someone else to send her to. Somewhere away from the likes of kindly lonesome heroes like you.'

She laughed again, and this time he told her exactly how much he'd missed her, and how the hours couldn't beat by fast enough until he would hold in his arms what he'd been hungering for so much while she was away.

TWENTY-FOUR

Long before the movies came to town, the ramshackle old Hollywood Hotel was a retreat for wealthy consumptives in need of winter sun. A resort for folk who liked good manners, plain food and polite conversation. The lobby still bore a sign pronouncing 'No movies, no dogs', though only as an amusing museum piece. Yet despite the largesse rained down on it by those selfsame movies for almost a decade, the interior was looking jaded now. Still the old hotel soldiered on as one of the colony's principal daytime watering holes, even if the evening trade had vanished to more fashionable venues. It was especially favored by those who thought of themselves as being among the small elite band of pioneers who had recognized this light-drenched patch of California for the movie-making idyll it could be, and made it their home.

Mack Sennett had every right to claim a place in that select group. Seated on a plush settee in the center of the lobby, he was surrounded by a clutch of chattering young women, all exceptionally pretty and à la mode in pleated skirts and cloche hats, hair poking out in artfully looped kiss curls and bangs, face paint generously applied. Sennett's Bathing Beauties, a scattering of new signings among them, to judge by the whiff of flash pans in the air and the handful of newsmen flirting and firing questions.

Tom waited until the last of the newsmen had gone, each with a sawbuck folded into his palm to squeeze an extra inch or two of ink. As Tom approached, Sennett raised his jaw and every face in the circle flashed towards him, glittering eyes, parting lips – a broadside of pulchritude.

'Tommy boy, at last. I was beginning to think you'd gone to ground on me. Sit down, man, here, here.' He signaled for space to be made beside him. 'So, what have you got for me? Did you talk to Mabel?'

Tom embarked on a full account of his morning at Overholtzer's, Sennett's forehead furrowing ever deeper but remaining silent for the most part, grunts and sniffs the sole indicators of his thoughts until Tom recounted the details of his brief exchange with Normand.

'I'll be honest, Mack, they hustled her out of there so fast, it was probably for the best with all those newspaper boys buzzing around. What she did say to me was that you don't need to worry about her. "Just dandy" were her exact words.'

Sennett was unimpressed. 'So where can I reach her?'

Tom hesitated, looking for the right words.

'You did ask her, I presume?' Sennett prompted impatiently.

''Course I did. Only problem is, she insisted she doesn't want to be reached.'

Sennett's face flushed. 'What the hell's that supposed to mean?'

'I'm sorry, Mack. There's really no good way of saying this. Miss Normand said she doesn't want you calling. Or being anywhere near just now. There was no mistaking what she meant.'

'But that's, that's . . .' Sennett's coloring took a trip towards purple, and a scramble for words that would not come did nothing to alleviate it.

Tom took his chance to get the rest out while he could. 'That's not the worst of it. The DA doesn't want you contacting her either. Woolwine said to tell you that straight.'

'What are you now?' Sennett growled at last. 'The DA's messenger boy? Christ in heaven, I expected you to come back with more than this.'

'Look, Mack, don't go laying the blame for this at my door. I did what you asked and spoke with her – and I haven't told you half the mess I had to go through to do that. If Miss Normand doesn't want to see you, it's no fault of mine. But if you just keep your hair on for a minute, you'll see it's not all bad news. At least we know she's safe. And we know now the DA's not viewing her as a suspect.' *You, maybe*, he considered adding, but thought better of it.

Sennett seemed to relax a little and leaned in towards him, his voice even lower than before. 'That's all fine and good, but what can we do to make sure she stays safe until they clear her name?'

'That's just it. I'm not sure you need to do anything. I got a feel from Woolwine that, somehow, Miss Normand is under his protection right now.'

Sennett looked up, sharp as a tack. 'In what way?'

'I don't know. Just that him and that deputy of his, Doran, they were behaving real protective towards her, as if she was in their care. Woolwine even said it: "My office has the situation in hand."'

'What situation? Why would she need their protection?'

Tom wondered if he had said too much. But what choice did he have? Either way, Sennett getting jumpy again would not help anyone.

'Look, I have no idea, Mack. All I'm saying is, if what Woolwine says is true, Miss Normand is safe. She can't be out on the razzle all night with his guys by her side.'

'Shut up,' Sennett hissed. 'I told you before I didn't want you repeating those lies. And don't think for a minute I can't see what you're up to. No way are you pulling out of this now. Here's how I see it. You say Mabel's not a suspect, but every newspaper I read is screaming the exact opposite. They're the ones we need to convince, and you're going to go out and find something that proves it to them.'

Tom threw his hands up. It was like talking to a wall. 'For Chrissakes, Mack, what the hell more can I do? You can't control what the papers say. Even if you could, the cops won't like me poking my nose in deeper, and Woolwine says he'll stick me in a cell if I go near Miss Normand again. How the hell am I supposed to prove anything when I can't even talk to her?'

'Know what?' Sennett was rubbing his hands together as though he'd settled the matter in his own mind and wanted to move on. 'That's your problem, Tommy boy. All I know is, you're seeing this through whether you want to or not. Otherwise, you'll find yourself without a roof over your head and with a debt collector on your back. Do you understand me?'

Tom got to his feet, his eyes fixed on Sennett's. 'I understand you, Mack. I'll do what I can. Just don't expect to hear back from me anytime soon.'

TWENTY-FIVE

By the time he got back to the house, Colleen was gone. The empty house wrapped round him like cold comfort, his body yearning for rest he had not realized he wanted or needed. It couldn't hurt to lie down for a minute, pull that neatly folded blanket over him, breathe in a faint scent of . . .

Two hours later he woke. Only then did he see the note on the kitchen table, his name in Fay's handwriting. All it contained was the same invitation she made him on the telephone – to meet at the Palm Court at seven – and a pair of crossed kisses. A hint of jasmine drifted up from the notepaper, her scent raising the ghost of green eyes, full lips, the warmth of silk-smooth skin. A jolt of inspiration. In that moment he saw as clear as the day outside what it was he needed to do. And Phil Olsen was the key to it. He checked his wristwatch. Plenty of time to arrange things before he headed downtown.

He thought it through again while he dressed, pulling his favorite gray mohair from the wardrobe, a cobalt tie, and a new Mullen and Bluett's shirt he had been saving for an occasion. If he did this right, he might get shot of Sennett, Normand, the whole shebang. No way could he afford to be dragged any further into their mess. Not with the DA on his back. Even Olsen had hooted like a barn owl when Tom hinted who he was working for.

Palming his hair into shape with a lick of pomade, Tom grabbed his hat and coat and walked out into the crisp afternoon, swinging the door shut behind him.

He didn't notice the enclosed Nash tourer parked opposite or the men in it, who had been sitting staring at his door for some time. First thing he knew about the punk behind him was the poke of a gun barrel hard in his lower back as he pulled the key from his pocket.

'Christ, what now?' Tom said, as much in anger as surprise.

'You keep your hands where I can see 'em. Not another move.'

A voice masking youth with almost comical gruffness. Who the hell this was, Tom had no idea, but he was damned if he'd let some young hothead boost his auto.

'Look, kid, if you want money, OK, but you're not getting the—' As he began to turn, he was silenced by a vicious prod in his kidneys.

'Shut up. Not a move, I said – that means your mouth, too.'

There was a feral snarl to the voice now and Tom froze, arms out, as the boy frisked his pockets, belt and ankles, the gun barrel all the while digging in sharply.

'Get in the jalopy.' The kid pushed him in behind the wheel. 'You'll be doing the driving, I'll be keeping you on the right road. See those guys across the street?'

Tom turned his head cautiously in the appropriate direction, saw two apes in the Nash glare at him as they pulled into the road, and got the picture.

'Get after them.'

The kid climbed in, kept the gun on his lap out of sight but at the ready as they trailed the other auto down the hill, past the lake and west on to Wilshire. Tom risked a glance at his captor. Pale pitted face, wiry with an ill-cut suit, no collar and an oversize bakerboy cap that looked like it had put in some hard miles on someone else's fatter head. Seventeen at best, he reckoned; a hard-bitten air already.

'Look, kid, would you at least tell me where we're going?'

'You need gas or something?'

'No, I—'

'Then shut up and drive. You'll know when you know.'

The boy twitched the gun at him. An ancient, rust-pitted Colt, like something passed down from Camp Drum. He saw how the boy clasped it hard and close to his leg, itching to use it, to prove himself. Saw enough to pray it had a good strong hammer spring and alert him to every crack and dip in the road ahead.

Twenty minutes later, Tom watched the Nash turn off the seafront in Santa Monica on to the ramp leading down to the municipal pier. He steered the Dodge down the decline, wondering what in hell awaited him there. Below and to his right, another road led off to the wide shore under the bluffs, where movie stars and millionaires built beach houses as elaborately appointed as the mansions they inhabited in the folds of the Hollywood Hills. Between the row of wooden houses and the ragged hem of surf was a sweep of flat yellow sand dotted with strolling couples and picnicking family encampments. But the Nash ignored the beach turnoff and proceeded onwards, thudding off the ramp and on to the wooden boardwalk where the pier began its advance to the horizon.

Tom followed, carefully negotiating the throngs of Saturday-afternoon walkers drawn out by the salt sea air and the attractions of Looff's amusement park on the pier's south side. Out there, up and under an intricacy of wooden scaffold, the Blue Streak roller coaster was doing a brisk trade, a chain of cars rocketing round the fearsome elbow twist, shooting riders out high above the surf before whipping them back inland again. The buffeting wind served up their screams in snatches.

'We're going to the amusement park?'

The kid's mouth broke into a broken-toothed grin. 'Yeah, maybe we take you up on the high ride, mister,' he cackled. 'Let you down the hard way.'

The car ahead drew to a stop by the Hippodrome, in the lee of which the breeze dropped off. Tom pulled in and killed the motor. For a moment all he heard was the wheeze and whoosh of a carousel organ grinding out a jaunty tune, caught the hot, sickly-sweet waft of candied popcorn belching from an open window. The two goons had already dismounted the Nash. They lumbered over, and the smarter-looking one – brow like a dead caterpillar, jaw like a black-smith's hammer block – pulled the door open.

'C'mon, outta there, this way.' He crooked a thick, hair-backed finger and strode off, leaving his mute companion to urge Tom on with a shove in the back like a jackhammer. The kid stayed in the Dodge.

TWENTY-SIX

Out along the boardwalk they walked, past food stalls and day-trippers, shrieking children, hucksters sharping from suitcases. Out beyond the shelter of the buildings and the crowds, out to where the full arc of the blue bay came visible either side. Silent but for the wind whipping about their ears and their own footsteps echoing more and more hollow as they went. Past fishermen trying their luck, courting couples doing much the same, gulls wheeling above, waves slapping and gurgling against the pilings underneath. Out above the water to the distant pier-head, where two men stood alone, leaning on the sea-rail, gazing at the shimmer on the water and the haze far out on the horizon.

The taller, more athletic of the two, turned to observe Tom's approach for the final twenty yards.

'Collins, right?'

He didn't put a hand out, didn't introduce himself. Didn't need to, his face plenty familiar from the newspapers. Still in his twenties, Tony Cornero was already a man of notoriety and substance, a hustler made swiftly rich and powerful by a single fall of the legislative axe: the Volstead Act. Thirty months down the line, he was one of the best-known bootleggers on the West Coast. Admired from afar for his panache and swagger in the face of the dry squads, splashed in the press for his daring coups, he was feared by anybody smart enough to recognize the ruthlessness of his operation and the other, less visible avenues into which his criminal enterprise extended. Up close, he looked the perfect gentleman. The English look he sported – immaculate cream Oxfords, white cashmere sweater, gleaming tan brogues – suited his strong Italian features, the nod to Valentino so obvious it ached. A platinum and diamond watch, brilliant against the black hair on his wrist, completed the picture, but nothing glittered sharper than his eyes.

'Thanks for taking the time to come out here.' He smiled, surprising Tom with the warmth of his manner.

'No need,' Tom said. 'Thank your goons here. They do an irresistible line in abduction at gunpoint.'

'I wanted to be sure you'd accept my invitation.' Cornero gave an entirely Latin ripple of muscle from his neck to his wrists, signifying anything from apology to indifference.

'You know who I am, no?'

'Sure, I do.'

'This is my associate, Jimmy Sanchez.' Cornero gestured at the squat, brick-built Mexican beside him, who didn't look round but tossed his head back in acknowledgement while maintaining his gaze seaward. 'We share some business interests.'

Not a name or face Tom recognized. 'I'll take your word for it. But I don't see what it's got to do with me.'

'No? Well, we can help you with that.' Cornero clicked his fingers and a goon stepped forward, slipping a fistful of brass on his knuckles. Tom took an instinctive step back and felt something solid behind him. The other ape. He put his hands up, as close to pleading as he thought wise, taking the opportunity to point out his existing bruises.

'OK, fellas, let's stop right there, can we, please? This has to be some kind of mistake. I may look like a punchbag to you right now, but, believe me, that's not by choice.' The next line he addressed to Cornero direct. 'Just tell me how I can help you. I don't know what you think I did, but I assure you, I didn't do it. I've been too busy getting the stuffing knocked out of me somewhere else, OK?'

Tom pointed again at the evidence on his face, and Cornero, curious, flicked a finger up. The apes stepped back. Now Jimmy Sanchez, too, turned round for a look, easing back, elbows on the rail, real cool.

'Lot of people saying you killed a good friend of ours, last night.'

'Excuse me – what?' It wasn't that he hadn't heard; it was simply too much to comprehend.

'Shorty Madden,' Cornero said. 'You trying to tell me you didn't have anything to do with that?'

'Jesus H. Christ.' Tom felt the color blanche from his cheeks as a cold rush of fear filled out his understanding. He looked around wildly, seeing nothing, not even the backhand slap that snapped his head back round and brought him back into focus.

'Is that all you got to say?' Cornero didn't look any angrier, but an imminence of violence had settled on him like the still, metallic air you get before a lightning storm.

'No, no . . . I mean, I know about it, uh, I was . . .' Tom's thoughts piled up and tumbled out in no particular order. 'I mean, I was there. But I didn't do it, I just saw it. That's all. Why in hell would I want to kill Madden?'

'That's what we want to know,' Cornero said calmly. 'Why would you do that? I know he wasn't always the sweetest of guys, but he was good at what he did. Made money for me. How much were you into him for?'

It was a better motive than the cops had come up with, but now was not the time for compliments. 'Nothing. I didn't owe the guy a cent. I never even met him until last night. Look, you have got completely the wrong idea here. I didn't do it. Even the cops can't pin it on me, and God knows they want to.'

Cornero shook his head again and tutted melodramatically. 'Wally here says you did.' He flicked his head towards the larger of the two apes, but all Tom could do was stare uncomprehendingly at him.

'What?'

Then it clicked: the iron jaw, the grunting brute at Hannigan's. It was him, all right, only minus the stupid derby.

'Wait now, wait,' Tom said. 'He, he . . . Wally was on the inside door, right? He must know I left Hannigan's a whole half-hour before Madden, right?'

Cornero looked to Wally, who nodded.

'So what were you doing still outside when he got shot?' Cornero asked.

'I asked Madden to meet me outside. I was there when he got shot, sure, but I didn't do the shooting.'

'So you lured him out. Same thing. My question was why? Who are you working for?'

'Christ!' Tom roared, so loud it took even him by surprise. One old fisherman, a good fifty yards off, looked round and waved vacantly, then turned away again. But that was the only response it elicited and a lurch of fear washed through his gut as he noticed Sanchez reach inside his jacket.

'Wait, no, please. Look, I didn't have any beef with Madden. It was some other guy, in a Packard tourer. They had an argument, and he blasted Madden in the back. I even tried to warn him, but it was too late.'

Nothing but cold hard stares, an expectation of more.

'C'mon, look, the cops didn't find a gun, right?' Tom pleaded. 'How would I have got rid of it, out in the street? I couldn't. Soon as the shooting started, a crowd ran out. Somebody would have seen me with a gun. But they didn't, because the gun was off down the street in the goddamn Packard, along with the guy who fired it.'

Tom broke off, out of breath, out of ideas.

Cornero looked over his shoulder and rattled off something that sounded like Mexican. Sanchez barked out a short, hard reply, and impatiently brushed some invisible object from the palm of his left hand, then turned back to the ocean and took up staring again.

'Maybe there's something in what you say,' Cornero said. 'Jimmy here thinks we should kill you anyway. In that respect, you're lucky, because he follows my lead, not the other way round, and I like to remind him of that every now and again. So I'm giving you a chance to convince me. What was it you wanted with Madden, if not that?'

Tom didn't mean to give it all away but, once he began, pretty much the whole story came out. Cornero settled back against the rail, the sun bouncing off his snow-white slacks and sweater, the swirling wind failing to unsettle a hair on his head, listening carefully to every word. The goons stood by, Sanchez stared at a ship steaming out across the bay, and Tom Collins, stuck in the middle, sweated like a spit-roast hog into his brand-new shirt as he talked. About Normand, Sennett, Taylor and the rest.

'So you decided it was Shorty shot Taylor,' Cornero interjected. 'Why not tell the cops instead of you going after him?'

'No, that's not it,' Tom insisted. 'Like I keep saying, all I wanted was a line on Miss Normand. I never believed Madden shot Taylor, especially not after I met and spoke with him. I couldn't see it, no way.'

'What made you so certain?' Cornero was more relaxed now. 'Even I thought it might've been Shorty when I first heard. And I was mad as hell because I already told him to leave Taylor alone. The man was a pompous old fool, poking his nose in where it wasn't wanted, but he didn't need killing. I had to stop it getting out of hand.'

'You stepped in?' Tom stared closely at Cornero. There was something here that either made perfect sense or none at all. And he hoped, for his own sake, it would be the former. 'Why would you get involved over a stupid punch-up? That's one thing I can't get my head around. Why is Miss Normand so important to you all?'

Cornero shrugged again, less convincingly this time. 'She ain't. Least, not to me. To Shorty, sure, she was a gravy train. But there was more to it.'

'Like what?'

'Like things you really don't wanna know,' Sanchez interjected loudly, his back still turned to them.

'Oh, I want to know,' Tom said, his annoyance getting the better of him. 'Everybody going round sticking a murder on me – you're damn right I want to know.'

Cornero put out a hand to stop Tom from saying more. 'Jimmy's right. All you need to know is soon after those two tangled a big slice of Shorty's action died off, and he blamed Taylor for kicking up dust about it. I was worried he would do something stupid. So I put a stop to it and told him to back off. Taylor fancied himself a crusader, maybe, but he had no clout. To single him out was stupid. There had to be another reason for Shorty's problems. Like someone trying to muscle in, maybe.'

'The cops know nothing about this?' Tom asked.

'Of course not. And you better make sure they don't get to know it either, or I'll know where it came from.'

'So why tell me?'

'Because you're going to put that knowledge to work, for me.'

Tom looked up. The sky was just as blue as before, but he could feel the storm coming. 'What do you mean?'

'What do I mean?' Cornero scoffed, pushing himself away from the rail. He wasn't as tall as Tom but he gripped him by the upper arms and stared hard in his eyes. 'I mean, if you say you didn't kill Shorty, then you better find out who did, and quick. You're the one playing detective, so go do some detecting. If you're so smart, you find out who put Shorty on the slab and tell me.'

Tom's protestations fell like feathers on stone.

'Somebody's got to die for Shorty, Mr Collins. That's how we do business. Life for a life. Yours will be acceptable, if it comes to it. But as you're already in trouble with the cops over this, you'll be pleased to have a chance to clear your name. Either way, you don't have a choice. You find Shorty's killer or I get Jimmy here to take you for a one-way trip out there.'

The Mexican half turned from the rail again and rasped what sounded like a well-used punchline at him. 'An' he ain't talkin' Hawaii.'

Cornero laughed out loud, a deep goose-like honking that didn't sit well with the pressed-white gentleman image. Probably didn't get much practice.

'Wally,' Cornero said, 'give Mr Collins one of our cards.' The goon produced a calling card from his pocket, bearing the name and telephone number of the Stralla Shipping Company of San Pedro, Southern California.

'You can call me there any time. Leave a message, I'll get back to you quick. But don't take long over this. Couple of days, it better be done.'

Cornero turned away, the audience over. Tom felt one of the apes grab his elbow, but this time he shook it off and started back down the boardwalk on his own steam. He'd gone just seven paces when he heard Cornero speak again.

'Hey, Collins. This cop who came last night and messed up your face. His name Devlin, maybe?'

Tom turned, no longer surprised by Cornero's omniscience.

'Yes, it is. Why?'

Cornero ignored the interrogative, nodded thoughtfully and turned his back again, leaning in towards the Mexican, talking in low Latin tones whipped away by the wind.

Tom lowered his eyes and walked away, the glare of the sun washing the boardwalk red with the dazzle of the dying day. All he could think of was putting as much distance as humanly possible between himself and those men, yet every footstep seemed an effort. Finding himself back amid the happy tourist throng brought a crumb or two of comfort, but not enough. People were crowding against the sea-rail, young and old alike, staring out in wonderment as sun, sky and ocean staged a gloriously flaming color play on the horizon.

The wind caught a young woman's murmur to her beau as they held each other tight, entranced. 'Ain't it heavenly.'

Thoughts tumbling, all Tom saw were the flames of somewhere else entirely, licking at his feet.

TWENTY-SEVEN

The kid was gone but he had left a parting gift: a glob of spit on the wheel side of the seat and the unsettling memory of his gap-toothed cackle. Tom wiped it away with an oil rag, drove off the pier as quick as he could through the throng and didn't pull over again until he was well outside the Santa Monica limit. Only then because he remembered a shack near the old veterans' hospital in Sawtelle where a man could procure a shot of such throat-ripping rye it didn't so much steady the nerves as stick 'em to the canvas.

By the time he hit Spring Street, it was dark, the home-time crowds thinning, a smattering of storefronts still spilling light on the sidewalk. At the Alexandria he tipped the washroom boy a buck to have his rig sponged and pressed. He emerged twenty minutes later looking reasonably well spruced, considering. The hotel's famed marble lobby was crammed with Saturday-night revellers, milling about beneath glittering Italian chandeliers on the so-called million-dollar carpet – that being the amount of business done on it every day. Movies made up a good part of the crowd, and Tom soon found himself surrounded by a circle of merrymakers from Lasky. From all the backslaps, handshakes and agreement on how swell he looked – despite the evidence to the contrary – it was clear they were already full to the foaming brim with fellow feeling. A consequence of being kicked off early from a shoot they had worked on for weeks under some new German director.

'Stap mit the laffing, I insist you!' Herb Bascom japed, aping the director's fury and sending the group careening into one another, laughing.

Chuck Havers, the soberest of them, told Tom their release came after the director had a volcanic crack-up, trashed the set and walked off the picture when one of his players didn't turn up a second day running.

'Leon Mazaroff was the guilty party – y'member him?' Havers asked. 'Good guy, but a real Muscovite. So serious. Always with the long face and how he's an *artist*. Not your unreliable type. Or not usually.'

'Sure. A dance man, isn't he?' The name rang a bell. Pale face, sharp features, thin limbs. 'Moves like he's walking on crushed velvet. Worked over at Realart—'

'Vo ist that ferdamte Russischer? Ay kill heem!' Bascom howled, lurching drunkenly in on them. 'Goddamn Kraut was poppin' blood vessels by the second, Tom. I never saw nothin' funnier since the war.'

Bascom swayed away, topping up his high spirits a mite too openly with a flask pulled from his pocket. By then another bell was clanging for Tom.

'Wasn't Mazaroff a regular on Bill Taylor's list?'

Havers' face clouded over. 'Jeez, poor Bill. You heard about that?'

'I'd be a dumb ox if I hadn't.'

'No, I mean 'bout him and Mazaroff,' Havers said *sotto voce*. 'About them two being – how's that song go – "bachelor buddies so gay"?' A hefty elbow nudge and he looked down as Havers crudely circled the thumb and index finger of his left hand and wagged another through.

'Taylor?' Tom was so taken aback he coughed. 'You can't be serious? The whole world says he was with Normand.' But he wasn't even certain he believed that anymore.

'Why not her too? And the Minter girl,' Havers leered. 'Taylor wouldn't be the first to run both ways. Maybe if he kept it in his pants, he'd still be alive. All I'm saying, that's the word goin' round. Explains why Mazaroff's so grief-stricken he can't work, don't it?'

'You really are serious.'

'Sure I am. It's not like I ain't sad for the guy.' Havers was getting defensive now and Tom had to wonder if he knew more than he was letting on. Either way, Havers shut down the subject with a grunt and a sideways glance as a burst of laughter drew their attention back to the main group. One of the guys had returned from the cloakroom, hair slicked down with soap, doing a mincing impersonation that could be of nobody other than Valentino.

'Speakin' a pansies,' Havers laughed, 'damn wop's shooting on the stage next to ours. But they're on nights so we never catch a glimpse – just the whiff of his perfume when we come in mornings.'

Tom watched the heaving shoulders, the streaming eyes as the others lapped up the Latin-lover routine, thinking he'd just about had enough of it. His wristwatch read ten after seven. Fay was being fashionably late. Even as he was thinking it, a thunderous slap landed on his back and he barely managed to stop himself from pitching forward into the others.

He whipped round, hands bunched, automatic.

'Whoa there, Tom – it's me, Mickey.'

Blinking, he saw red hair, a high brow, wide cheek bones and a mile-wide smile resolve into the handsome, bespectacled features of Marshall 'Mickey' Neilan, arms wide, palms up, inviting an embrace.

He dropped his guard and found himself engulfed in a bear hug.

'It's good to see you, y'big Celtic brawler. Where you been?' Neilan said from the tangle of limbs.

'You want to watch who you go thumping like that, Mickey. Someday it'll come back at you.'

Neilan stepped back, palms up in mock innocence, his accent a thick brogue. 'Ah, go on, Tom. Sure it was only a little tap.'

He had to admit it was mild by Neilan's standards. His reputation as a prankster was second only to that of Fairbanks on the lots. He got away with it by being one of the colony's best-known directors. That and his irrepressible Irish charm, of course – or so he liked to put it about. In reality, he was one of few in the colony who was born and raised locally, in San Berdoo, albeit of Irish stock. Over the years, Tom had worked with him, played cards, got drunk with him, and if Neilan's star was rumored to have dimmed a little of late, he was still regarded by many – most of all himself – as the life and soul of every party.

But for once Neilan displayed no interest in joining the fun. He was already backing away, pulling Tom with him.

'You seen the Swan here, Tom?' This a whisper in the ear, although Neilan made no secret of the fact that the latest in his long line of marital indiscretions was with the colony's most glamorous rising star, Gloria Swanson.

Tom admitted he hadn't. 'It'd be hard to miss her, Mickey. But I've been busy getting my ear poisoned about Bill Taylor.'

The pale blue eyes narrowed and Tom belatedly remembered Neilan was one of Taylor's best friends – always going off for boozy weekends to a lodge house at Mount Lowe with Tony Moreno, Jimmy Kirkwood and that gang. He'd been invited to join them once or twice, but something else had always come up.

'Christ, I'm sorry, Mickey. I forgot you and Taylor were close . . .' He stopped, lost for words, until something more obvious at last occurred to him. 'Can I ask you a question, though? You being so tight with him and all. Have you any ideas about who was behind it?'

Neilan regarded him sadly, then shook his head. 'Come on, Tom. What do I look like – the cops? Why ask me that?'

'Every gossip in town is competing to blacken Taylor's name. Not ten minutes ago someone was telling me . . .' Tom repeated what Havers had said, without revealing the source.

Neilan cursed, but kept a hand on Tom's arm. His exuberance had fallen away completely now and he was clearly upset. 'I never heard anything so dumb. Bill was straight as a die. I never met a more stand-up fellow. Too goddamn concerned for other people for his own good, if you ask me.'

Tom was about to ask if he was referring to Mabel Normand – she being, he knew, another great pal of Neilan's – but stopped. The director was staring off into the middle distance, having some kind of a brainstorm.

'You know, it's a coincidence seeing you here, Tom,' he said, his tone hushed. 'Downright strange, now I come to think of it. Not two weeks ago, right here in this room, Bill was asking me about you.'

'Taylor? I hardly knew him.'

'Well, he knew you.'

'Did he say what it was about?'

'I'm not sure. I forgot it until now. Must've had a few too many cocktails that night, I guess.'

Every night, Tom thought. 'So?'

'So, we were fixing to go to the lodge at the weekend when out of nowhere Bill asked if I could recommend someone to make some discreet inquiries on his behalf. I guess he thought with my track record I'd know the score. A matter of honor, he said, all stiff and proper. You'd laugh if anyone else put it that way, but not Bill. So I told him about you, how you'd gone out on your own, and how he wouldn't find a better man for the job. Straightaway he remembered you from the lot. Said he always liked you.'

'You tell him where to reach me?'

'Sure, I think so. Like I said, I had a few. He didn't get in touch?'

'Isn't that obvious? Did you tell the cops about this, Mickey? Can you remember anything else he said?'

Neilan began shaking his head, then thought better of it. 'No, but hang on . . . Yeah, I asked him if it was to do with that valet of his. You know the one – Sands – who ran off to Mexico last year with his auto, then tried to bilk more money from him?'

'The one every cop in the state is searching for? Of course I know, but only since I read it in the papers, Mickey.'

'Right.' Neilan looked up, surprised at his vehemence. 'Bill was mortified over Sands, you know. Took it real personal. But this wasn't about that. He told me straight it was' – Neilan pulled his shoulders back, adopting Taylor's fake English accent – '"Another matter entirely. Too close, too dangerous". That's how he said it, exactly like that.'

Tom could hardly believe his ears. 'And you haven't told the cops?'

Neilan shook his head.

'But you have to, Mickey. It could be important. I know someone on the detective squad you could talk to.'

'No, Tom. No cops.' Neilan raised his hands, defensive. 'I can't. You don't know what it's like at Lasky right now. Everybody's terrified they'll get drawn in by this, pulled under. Eyton called us over, said Zukor insists anyone with a public face, anything we got to say about Taylor has to go through them from now on. On pain of dismissal. I got a big one set to roll next week, Tom. My first in eight months. I need it. I *really* need it. Bill was a great man, but I've done what I can. He's gone. I got to go on living.'

'But that's crazy,' Tom insisted. 'How could telling the cops hurt?' He was doing his best to keep his exasperation under control, but it hardly seemed to matter. Neilan was too self-absorbed even to notice.

'I don't know, Tom. I just can't risk it. Any taint at all, Zukor will shut me down. Charlie as good as told me to my face.'

'You told Eyton about this?'

'Not about you, no. I didn't see the point.' Neilan looked away, awkwardly.

'But about Taylor being worried?'

'Of course, couple of days ago. He said he'd get it to the right people.'

Whoever the right people were, it seems it didn't include the cops.

'Jesus, what in hell are they trying to do?' Tom said, thinking out loud.

Neilan laughed harshly, mistaking his meaning. 'Good question. I never saw them busier in publicity. Wearing out the phone lines, churning out pap for the papers. Keeping the panic at bay, I guess. All I know is I'm pulling my neck in till the storm passes.'

With that, he gave Tom an odd look, as though he had just dredged something else from the alcohol-soaked recess of his memory. 'You might want to think about doing similar yourself, Tom. You better be careful. There's a lot riding on this. You don't want to be the one gets in the way.'

Tom took a step back. 'What's that supposed to mean, Mickey? What are you saying? Or not saying, more's the point?'

Neilan laughed as if he should know better than to ask, but said nothing. It was too late anyway. Neilan had spotted something over Tom's shoulder and was walking away. 'Just remember what I said. Watch your step.'

He strode away, arms extended, bellowing a welcome to a mass of people moving through the lobby, at its center a woman so short she would have been invisible but for the cascades of flaming color flashing off a headdress that could only have been borrowed from a DeMille costumer.

'When Gloria Swanson enters a room, all the guys go into a swoon.' Half sung, half whispered in his ear, Fay's voice wiped all other thoughts from his mind as he turned to find her behind him.

He caught his breath as she leaned into him and proffered her lips in greeting. He threw his arms around her, kissed her, consumed by her proximity. So much, he had to break off, hold her at arm's length, drink in the sight of her. A gown of sea-green silk stitched with whorls of silver beadwork and pearl. Her auburn hair, pinned up, glimmered under the light of the chandeliers. She looked like an earthbound deity. As she took a step back, delighting in his admiration, half a heaven of reflected light scattered across her tall, trim figure.

'Checking out the competition?' She nodded back towards the clique surrounding Swanson but kept her cool green eyes fixed on his, a smile playing on her lips. 'She's out of your league, you know.'

'Sure she is. I'm not bothered. What worries me, if *she's* out of my league, what chance do I stand with you?'

'I guess it couldn't hurt to encourage you a little.' Fay put a gloved hand up to his cheek, noticing the bruises for the first time. 'What happened to you? Have you been sparring at Jeffries' Barn again? Honestly, I can't leave you alone, can I?'

He smiled at that. 'Maybe you better not leave me alone.'

She turned away, laughing, surveying the fashionable throng and drawing glances from half the men in the lobby. From a good few women, too. Tom caught the eye of Louis, the Palm Court's maître-d who was standing by the entrance to the dining room, and received a friendly nod in reply.

'Come on, let's go in,' Tom said, steering Fay towards the door. 'You're making me very hungry.'

TWENTY-EIGHT

Louis gave them a good, comfortable table off to the side, promising to move them closer to the dance floor once they finished eating. Already the high vaulted room, with its exquisite yellow and blue Tiffany roof light, intricate stucco panels and frieze, was filled to capacity with chattering diners. For now the dance floor was deserted, the stage empty but for three tiers of straightback chairs with a purple Paul Whiteman banner draped behind, and a journeyman quartet cranking out some old-time tunes to fill the room with sounds more melodious than the clatter of cutlery and the babble of other people's voices.

Tom watched how Fay accepted the waiters' attention. In a town more awed by fame than wealth, Fay reckoned she had come about as far as she was ever likely to go and was happy to enjoy it. Tom drank in the calm of her presence like cool water on a desert walk. She nattered happily across the table, telling him the tattle from New York, who she'd seen and how they'd been, what was in the theaters, and the scandal caused even there by the Taylor murder. Tom updated her on all things West, including his involvement with Sennett and Taylor, skirting the more unpleasant details.

She could no more see a pattern in what had happened than he, and through her eyes it all seemed suddenly, reassuringly, absurd. He loved how she was amused by the scrapes he got into, and often wondered how he would have coped without her support. It was Fay who convinced him he had the wherewithal to set up on his own. It was she who provided him with the best and only reason to stay strong, to make sure he didn't fail.

As they were finishing their meal, he saw Fay look up in surprise across the rim of her glass at something over his shoulder. A buzz of excitement was sweeping the room and he turned to see a compact figure bounding like bundled electricity in the direction of their table, beaming a smile that occupied half his deep-tanned face. Douglas Fairbanks, the biggest movie star of them all, was heading towards them, arms outstretched in greeting.

'Tom, old man.' Fairbanks took him by the hand and worked his arm like a rusty old water pump. 'I can't quite believe it. I was singing your praises to Mary only this morning.'

'Doug.' Tom struggled to his feet. 'I didn't think they let you out on your own anymore.'

Fairbanks hooted. 'Ha-hah, too right, old man. Only when I succeed in giving them the slip. The slip, you remember?'

Tom laughed. It was a shared memory, a reference to a shoot they worked on together long before the great star left Lasky and set up an independent operation. Even as Fairbanks' eyes were darting towards Fay, he made the introduction.

'I am more than usually enchanted, Mrs Parker, I assure you.' Fairbanks lived up to his reputation as the industry's most charming man. 'Regrettably, I am in a greater hurry than usual also. Would you allow me to tear Tom away from you briefly? I need a word in private. Just a moment or two, I promise.'

Nothing would please her more, Fay said. As Tom turned to follow Fairbanks out of the room, she dropped her jaw at him, her expression the zenith of impressed.

Outside in the lobby, Fairbanks swished a tall wall curtain aside and ushered Tom into an alcove he'd never noticed before, containing a small table, a telephone and a chair. Fairbanks closed the curtain but remained standing, his energy as ever giving an impression of barely contained excitement.

'I can't tell you how pleased I am to bump into you, old man,' Fairbanks began. 'I heard that fool Eyton let you go from Lasky's. A scandal in itself. But I was unsure how to get in touch. Now here you are in the flesh. It must be fate.'

Tom let Fairbanks have the floor, batting away the commiserations on his joblessness by repeating that he had struck out on his own, reaching into his jacket for a business card.

'That's most admirable, old man,' Fairbanks said, pocketing it after the briefest of glances. 'You know how big I am on self-reliance. But honestly, could this give you and that charming lady of yours the life you deserve?'

Tom wasn't sure how to take that. Fairbanks thrust on regardless. 'Which is why Mary and I want to talk to you. Would you be free Monday to come see us? At Pickfair? I appreciate it's a long way out, but we have a proposal I'm certain will be of interest to you. After lunch, say, at three? Will you come?'

Tom was so baffled he could barely get the words out. 'Of course, I will, Doug. If you want. But what's this about?'

Fairbanks tapped his nose and beamed the trademark grin. 'Can't tell you more for now, old man. But suffice to say, it will be very much in our mutual interest. If you could keep it under your hat for now, too, I'll be grateful. If anyone asks, just say I want you to join me on a shoot at Lake Arrowhead. We're up there next month. OK with you?'

'Sure, but won't you stay and have a drink with us? We're staying on for the dance. Louis always gives us a good table.'

Fairbanks was amused by that but declined. 'Alas, no, Tom, thank you. As I said to your lovely lady, I cannot dally. I must get over to the Lasky studio. You know I hate to be late.'

'Lasky's?' Tom was surprised. Fairbanks had not left the studio's employ on amicable terms when he broke free of his contract in 1919, to go set up United Artists with Pickford, Chaplin and Griffiths, and he had never been welcomed back. 'What could you want there at this hour, on a Saturday?'

It was a casual inquiry, but Fairbanks appeared dumbstruck by it. Even his celebrated tan seemed to pale a tone, his eyebrows drawn in consternation, as though he had let a cat out of a bag.

'I, eh . . . I shouldn't have told you that, old man,' he said hesitantly.

A reaction like that, Tom thought, with anyone else would have to involve a woman. An illicit liaison on an empty stage. But not Doug 'the faithful' Fairbanks, surely? His devotion to his wife, Mary Pickford, was legendary. Tom couldn't bear to watch the man flounder and, remembering what Havers said earlier, laughed.

'It's OK, Doug. I get it. Valentino's shooting nights out there, and Fred Niblo's directing. He helmed you in *Zorro*, didn't he?'

Fairbanks eyes widened further, then he grasped the rope Tom was throwing, his face flooding with relief.

'Yes, uh, yes, that's exactly it, old man.' The grin reappeared like the sun after an eclipse. 'You always were quick, weren't you? Yes,

Fred's a good friend, and we are very keen to witness young Valentino enact his art in the round, if you will. You know what it's like for us. Couldn't be done by day without a fuss, but on a Saturday night with nobody else around, Fred thought we might slip in unnoticed. You won't tell on us, will you?'

'You can rely on me, Doug.'

'Good man.' Fairbanks seized him by the hand, working the pump again. 'I knew you'd be the one for us.'

Tom hadn't the first clue what in heck had just passed between them, but he was darned if he'd mess with it now the significance of Fairbank's invitation to his home in Beverly Hills was beginning to dawn on him.

'Until Monday, then. Toodle-pip!'

With that, Fairbanks threw back the curtain and launched himself out across the hotel lobby, the sea of guests parting before him as if he was some kind of Moses. Except Moses never worked a crowd like that, grinning and saluting all round, good will surrounding him like a halo, as he made his way out into the night.

TWENTY-NINE

'**M**an alive,' Fay said, when he rejoined her, pretending to drag her jaw off the floor. 'You never run out of surprises, do you, Tom Collins? So D'Artagnan is your best pal now?'

'I liked him better as the dashing blade,' Tom said, doing his best to mimic the blinding Fairbanks grin. 'We go back. He's like that with everyone. Always the charmer. Even with me.'

She wagged a finger at him amiably, then linked him again, her excitement palpable wherever their limbs touched. 'Come off it, Tom. You're no slouch and you know it. Fairbanks, for heaven's sake. What did he want?'

'He has some work for me.'

'United Artists? They would be good to get in with,' she said, her pragmatic head on.

'Yeah, next month, a location shoot up at Lake Arrowhead. Wants me to organize a few extra hands to ride shotgun, keep them all safe.'

'You said yes, I hope.'

'Absolutely, I'm not going to pass on that. He's good to work for. Said he might have more for me, too, but couldn't be sure of it.'

He considered whether to hold back or not, but knew she'd wheedle it out of him anyway, he was so excited by it. 'He wants me to meet him Monday. And Mary. Out at Pickfair.'

Again she was seriously impressed. 'My word, a royal summons.'

He had never seen her truly starstruck before, and he liked it. If she couldn't be awed by the King of Hollywood, then she couldn't be awed by anyone, and nobody needs that. Fairbanks's shower of stardust seemed to have hit the waiters too, as solicitous to Tom now as to Fay while they were escorted round the Palm Court dance floor to a booth.

Settling in, Fay was not letting go. 'Did he say what about?'

'No. But I heard last week someone bought the old Hampton Studios out on Santa Monica Boulevard. You know it?'

'I think so. Out past La Brea. Big old place, not much else around?'

'Not yet,' Tom said, thinking ahead. 'A couple months ago there was a rumor Doug and Mary were sniffing around out there. I heard before that they wanted to set up a production arm, together – somewhere to produce movies by themselves. So, look, all I'm saying is . . .' He hesitated, not wanting to get carried away. 'Well, put that together with tonight. He was like a coiled spring. More than usual. Like he couldn't wait to get started on something.'

He leaned in closer to lower his voice. But she got there before him.

'They will need someone to run security.' She laughed, unself-conscious in her delight. They had to wait a moment for the curious glances from a nearby table to die away again.

'But that's wonderful,' Fay whispered. 'If he takes you on, you'll be much better placed than you were at Lasky's.'

'*If*,' he emphasized. 'Could be they just want me to man the gate.'

'Not the way he shook that mitt of yours,' she said. Her hand was on his shoulder now and she pressed in, lips feathering against his ear. 'Never be afraid to want, Tom.'

The hunger in her eyes was intoxicating. They both thrilled to it, acknowledged it, and knew that here, in public, they had to pull back. She looked away, anything to break the intensity.

'So when did you work with him before? Was it anything interesting?'

He laughed, heady with lust and optimism. 'We've done some things together. I met him years ago. When he was still under contract with Zukor. Before United Artists. Even before he and Pickford were an item, officially.'

She caught the qualification. 'Officially?'

It wasn't as if she didn't know the story. Or half of it, at least. Fairbanks and Pickford had the squeakiest clean image of any couple on the silver screen. Him the tanned athletic hero, her the curl-clad virgin bride. For years their immense popularity was considered dependent on it. Yet everyone in the business knew the reality was shabbier: that Doug and Mary had met and fallen in love while married to others. Shortly after the end of the war in Europe, their secret had come out in the press but it had been well managed, and they had survived more or less intact. What never came out was how long they'd been seeing each other before they put it right.

'That was one of the reasons Zukor sent me out here,' Tom said, pleased with the double take this provoked from Fay.

'But you told me you came out in 1917,' she said.

'Sure. You know Pickford was married to Owen Moore then?'

She nodded eagerly. 'I met him at a party, back East, not so long ago. He seemed a nice enough man, not at all as rough as I'd heard.'

If only she knew, Tom thought. 'I heard he cleaned up. Back then he was wed to the bottle more than Pickford, a regular mean-minded bum. Couldn't cope with all the "America's Sweetheart" commotion around her. I'm not kidding; the more famous she got, the more he looked like a train wreck. Nasty with it – not shy of dishing it out some.'

Fay leaned in closer, aghast. 'He beat her?'

'Right.' He checked the tables around. No one was paying any attention. 'She left him, but no one got to know. Zukor moved her out to Hollywood with her mother and the rest of the family; Moore stayed in New York. Then somebody let slip about Fairbanks and it was like a bomb went off. Moore came storming into Zukor's office at Paramount, waving a pistol, screaming, "I won't have it! I'm gonna kill that climbing monkey! I'm gonna rip the grin off his face!" He was crazier with the drink than jealousy.'

'You were there?' Fay's laugh was so scandalized he had to shush her.

'I was having my own troubles,' he said. 'I'd gone to see Zukor, to make good on a promise he made me once. We were only talking five minutes when Moore burst in. I knocked him one in the gob and he dropped like a baby.'

'But he had a gun.'

'I dealt with worse than him every day of the week in New York. Real men, hard as nails.' Tom accompanied that with a wink. 'Or so Zukor reckoned anyhow. Next day I got a note from him to come in again, and when I got there, Allan Dwan, Doug's director back then, was in the room. They were all set to start shooting *A Modern Musketeer* out here, but Zukor was afraid Moore would follow Doug out to Los Angeles, and do God knows what. So he packed them off to Colorado to shoot the outdoor scenes, and begged me to go along in case Moore discovered where they were. What an adventure. We were up by Grand Canyon filming for most of a month, the whole company camping out in tents. We moved on to a Navajo reservation in Arizona. I never saw anything like it. I'd never been west of Philly before. And Doug – he couldn't have been friendlier, or done more to make me feel a part of it.'

'He had good reason to stick close,' Fay said. But he could see she was touched by the idea of it.

Tom slipped into familiar reverie. The parched landscapes of rock and ravine, like nothing he had ever dreamed of before, the freedom and good humor of the company, his wonder at the Navajo and their ways. Had any dumb Irish cop ever enjoyed such great good fortune?

He felt the soft tug of Fay's stare and brought himself back. 'Doug came straight out to Hollywood after, to see Pickford. Zukor suggested I go with him, keep a discreet eye out. Couple of weeks later, asked me if I liked the sunshine. Said he needed a reliable guy to beef up security at "Famous Players". He never once called it Lasky's.' He laughed at the memory. 'I jumped at it, naturally. Would've bit his hand off for it at the time, situation I was in.'

Fay took a sip and wrinkled her nose. 'So Moore never came after them?'

'Like I said, Moore was a drunk. And a coward. He knew it was all over with Pickford and that even Doug, who was only half his size, could probably flatten him quick as a blink if he tried anything. But all Zukor cared about was the scandal, the reputations of his two biggest stars going up in smoke – along with their guaranteed half million bucks a year each, which he'd have to pay even if nobody wanted to buy tickets to see them anymore. Moore knew how to rattle Zukor, all right. He probably got well paid for his silence.'

'Always the money with Zukor, isn't it?' Fay said, her mood altered, distaste tugging down the corners of her mouth. 'And reputations.'

The last thing Tom wanted was to dig over all that again and put a maudlin turn on the evening. Not on her first night back. He caught a waiter's eye, flashed him a bill and asked if he could bring them something warming. Colony speak for an under-the-table brandy. The waiter nodded and went to see what he could do. Fay flashed her approval and he thought he had got away with it. But it was obviously a night for not letting go.

'I never get that thing you have for Zukor,' she said quietly. 'What is it between you? You're always so crazy loyal to him. Even now, when he threw you out on your ear, still you won't hear a word against him.'

'You know it wasn't him who sacked me. It was Charlie.' A pointless distinction, one he knew she would not let him get away with.

'Oh, come on, Tom. You know all Zukor need do is click his fingers and you'd have been back in there like a shot. Point is, he didn't. After all you did for him, it's shameful. I never liked the man. Even when he was fawning over me to sign my contract. It was like all he ever saw in me was dollar bills and useful connections. You know what the girls in the New York office call him, yes?'

'Yeah. Mr Creepy,' he laughed, thankful for the release.

'Most don't credit him with the Mister,' she said.

'Come on, he's not that bad. Sure, he's a shark, but he doesn't try to hide it. And you're right about the money. It's all he dreams about. Given a choice between a buck and a fu— fabulously nice girl' – he winked again – 'he'd go for the buck every time.'

'You are incorrigible, Thomas Collins,' she laughed. 'It's just as well you have a facility for making friends.'

The waiter arrived with their drinks in coffee cups, which they chinked like the old days and drank a toast to the future. Whereupon they were distracted by a new commotion, a big party arriving loudly across the floor. Swanson and her coterie attracting a swarm of waiters.

Fay grinned. 'Something else for the tourists to talk about back home.'

Tom looked on as Neilan tucked a cushion under Swanson's bead-encrusted behind, her thanks a flash of those extraordinary eyes. The sight of them together brought something of what Neilan said to him earlier bubbling up in memory. Something about the publicity department. Something that wasn't right. Or was it what Fairbanks had said? Hollywood royalty visiting Valentino's set under cover of darkness – any publicity department in Hollywood would kill for a story like that. No way would they let that go. But it was actually what Fairbanks said about nobody else being out there. An opportunity? Maybe it could be for him, too.

'Is everything quite all right, Tom?' He turned, startled by Fay's inquiry, the concern in her voice. He hadn't realized he had drifted so far away.

He apologized, told her an idea had occurred to him about the Sennett job he was working on. He thought it through quickly, adding Olsen to the picture forming in his mind, realizing he might not get another chance to act.

He leant across the table and took Fay's hand in his. 'Look, I know it's our first night back together and all, but I need to ask a favor.'

She pursed her lips, eyes afire. 'Depends on what you're asking for, I guess.'

'That too, believe me,' Tom said. 'But later. Thing is, if this Pickfair job turns out like I hope it will, I'll need to have the deck clear. Doug'll want me to start straight away. And I can't afford to have Sennett stomping around, complaining I let him down. Much as I can't stand the old bastard, I don't want him bad-mouthing me.'

'I can see that,' Fay said. 'But what can you hope to do about it tonight?'

'Do you have your studio pass with you?'

'Oh, Tom. Really? Do I look like I came out to work? Do you see pockets on this gown?'

'OK,' he laughed, appreciating anew the perfect lines of the dress, its daring neckline and back. 'I guess we have to go via your apartment. You can change there.'

For a moment Fay looked uncertain, then her smile broadened, getting into the spirit. 'But why? Where are we going?'

It was what he found most attractive in her. Curiosity. Mischievousness. Her willingness to play along.

'On an adventure,' he said.

'Well, I do like the sound of that,' she said. 'But can't we stay for a dance or two first?'

THIRTY

Through the coachwork he heard a muffled exchange of voices. One male and imperative, the other Fay's, bright and confident. Curled up in the trunk, he felt the shift of the clutch, a meshing of gears. But the acceleration, when it came, was not in the expected direction. Instead, the machine reversed in what felt like a sweeping arc, and it was all he could do to stop himself being pitched around the cramped, lightless luggage space like an egg in a box before the brakes squealed sharply and the auto came to another bone-crunching halt. Disoriented, he braced himself for another stab of pain. Instead, he heard Fay's voice outside and a rumbling male response, more amiable this time, and they were on the move again, slower now. They were in.

'What happened there?'

The raising of the trunk lid revealed the moon sharp and yellow above the soaring glass walls of one of the Lasky studio's gigantic covered stages, Fay's face radiant alongside it.

'They wouldn't let me in on Vine,' she said. 'Nobody in or out. Had me come round to Argyle instead. The gate guy waved me through soon as I mentioned Niblo.'

He clambered out. Fay had picked a good dark spot for surreptitious work. Back at her apartment, she had changed into a close-fitting two-piece riding suit. It looked just the ticket for an actress on her way to film an actioner with Valentino. Enough to convince the Lasky gate men, who knew her well.

'Come on, hurry. While there's no one about,' she whispered, with the urgency of one whose reputation, and contract, was on the line.

Although she had been redirected on to the Lasky backlot, Fay had driven deep into the studio's muddle of passages and alleyways to get Tom as near as possible to where he needed to be. But it would still take time to pick his way back through the dark, prop-strewn maze that lay between the stages and the long, low executive block that fronted the studios on Vine Street. He looked around, getting his bearings. Through the muslin-draped glass of the stage building beside them, he saw a familiar glow of lights on the other side of Argyle. Either Klieg lamps or the emanation of Valentino's ego.

'OK, if anyone spots you here, they'll know something's up. You head over to the stage and I'll come find you once I'm done. You'll be OK?'

'If they ask, I'll say I got an urgent casting call. Let them figure it out.' She hesitated a moment, then grabbed his coat sleeve and tiptoed up to kiss him. 'Be careful.'

And she was gone, climbing into the machine again, pulling away, a discord of jasmine and gasoline dancing in the air.

He stuck to the edge of the shadows, threading through the industrial heart of the studio, a labyrinth of blacksmith and carpentry shops, hangers brimming with scaffold and scenery flats, the costume factory and store, long, narrow film-processing sheds that reeked worse than tanning factories. In five years working here, he could not remember the lot ever being this still, this eerily quiet. Jesse Lasky and Charlie Eyton were no respecters of time or custom; if a thing needed doing, it needed doing now. Even weekend nights, something was always being torn down or rebuilt, forged or recast, spliced or pushed through. But tonight? Nothing.

It was a good ten minutes before he reached the executive compound. Amid quadrangles of low-slung, shingled bungalows, darkness and silence reigned where lights usually glimmered into the morning hours. Cautiously, Tom made his way to where the bungalows stopped a few feet short of a back wall rising blank and imposing. It was only two floors higher, but built of solid brick and stucco in an altogether grander style, accentuating the gulf between the bigwigs and the casually employed.

He made for a door he knew gave access to the back stairs and up to the executive quarters. Snicking it open with a creak, he stepped inside with all the familiarity and misgiving of a thief breaking into the home of an old friend. This building had been his life once. He'd watched it constructed from the foundations up, was present when the ribbon was cut with cheers, streamers, flash pans and brass bands. Now, up stairways and along dark corridors, he threaded his quick and quiet way. An open window in one stairwell revealed a glow of light from the suite of rooms below. Something was going on down there, but he didn't need to know what.

He pressed on.

At last he reached the third-floor apartments where the publicity teams toiled day to day. Everyone knew Famous Players-Lasky spent millions more dollars than any other studio lavishly promoting its stars and movies. But few would have dreamed the true cost, the legions of publicity men hired to churn out oceans of press-friendly boosterism on every scrap of news from the latest starlet signing to the next DeMille extravaganza. No one in America had a keener understanding of the value of publicity than Mr Zukor. And it repaid him well. But underhand projects had to be done discreetly, away from the mainstream. Tom made his way to the suite of offices occupied by publicity director J.J. Fine and the handful of private staff he used for his most sensitive operations.

Tom's heart beat faster as the glass-panelled door yielded to a twist of the handle. Inside, a quartet of desks squared off against each other. A fifth protected access to Fine's inner sanctum. This was where he would find what he was looking for, if it was anywhere. He took a flashlight from his pocket. All four desks were piled with newspapers and fan magazines, mimeographed check-off lists and handwritten notes. The first two desks yielded only puff pieces about top stars – Tommy Meighan, Pauline Frederick and Blanche Sweet among others. A handwritten note from Fine was attached to a bundle of magazine cuttings hinting at Marshall Neilan's affair with Gloria Swanson, listing editors to be telephoned and threatened.

Others related to Artcraft leading man Wallace Reid and rumors of his dope addiction.

On the other desks Tom hit pay dirt. Stacks of papers and cuttings devoted to Taylor's murder. It was too soon for the weeklies to have published anything, yet piles of magazines – *Photoplay*, *Motion Picture News*, *Variety*, *Captain Billy's Whiz Bang* – lay open at articles speculating on whether Mabel Normand had a new man in her life, and whether it could be Taylor. Many featured large studio portraits of Mack Sennett looking moody and forlorn, their captions hinting at loss, sorrow, the pain of unrequited love. Lies returning to haunt him.

There was too much for the flashlight's restrictive beam. Tom risked switching on a desk lamp. Laid out in rows were clippings and articles about Taylor, gushing homilies about his seriousness and artistry, his war service in Europe, his achievements as head of the Directors Association. Newspaper reports speculating on the reasons for his murder. Attached was a handwritten list of names – well-known reporters – a tick beside each. Another stack of cuttings related to Mary Miles Minter, slurs hinting at her friendship with an older man. Beside them a mimeographed batch of ecstatic, high-flown romantic pieces topped by rotogravure portraits of Minter, all innocence and golden curls. Again the lists: editors, reporters, publications – suggested stories and rumor bait. Everything Olsen had suggested earlier, laid out like a storybook.

Even so, Tom could find nothing that amounted to outright slander. Least of all against Normand. Despite the material on the desks, the enigmatic notes and jottings, lists of tips and whispers, there was no hard proof he could simply slip in his pocket and take back to Sennett. Unless . . .

He was down on his haunches, attempting to pick the lock on J.J. Fine's office door when he heard a noise. Shoe leather on linoleum, approaching along the corridor outside. He froze, glanced over his shoulder at the glass panel door, then at the desk lamp. The footsteps kept coming, and with them some jauntily whistled bars of 'Hallelujah, I'm a Bum'. Only one thing for it. He took a breath, concentrated on the metal prongs in his hand and willed the tumbler to turn. A click. The lock yielded and he scrambled inside, heart thumping, back to the wall, just as the outer office door was flung open.

The whistling stopped abruptly, then a loud tut and the desk lamp was doused with a peremptory click, and another lit opposite. Through the barely open door, Tom glimpsed a gangling, carrot-haired figure in a tan check suit and brown-and-white brogues. Jed 'Red' Peppard, the youngest member of Fine's inner circle and not the brightest. In the same glance, with a nauseating lurch of his gut, Tom spotted his flashlight on the floor outside the door, left while fishing the lock picks from his pocket. It was switched off, but no less a beacon for that. If Peppard saw it, there was no way he wouldn't investigate.

Eons passed, or so it seemed, before Peppard found what he was searching for, the light was doused and the slam of the door was followed by the pad of receding footsteps. Quickly, Tom retrieved the flashlight and turned its beam on J.J. Fine's carved oak desk, so large it had to be placed crosswise in the room. Its surface was bare but for a leather-trimmed ink blotter and a pen stand. Behind stood a pair of tall file cabinets. Locked, but it took Tom seconds to unpick them, and three drawer pulls later his eyes fell on something he knew instinctively should not be in there. A bulky manila file folder with *M. Normand* inscribed on the tab.

He laid it open on the desk. Saw yet more clippings, sheaves of private memos from sources in the studio containing every variety of scurrilous rumor regarding Normand's dope habit, poor health and relationships with men. At the back were four blurred photographs of a muscular, buck-naked man squiring a tiny woman whose disheveled black curls and outsize, glazed-over eyes might well have been Normand's, though little else could be discerned. The reports were far too many and thorough to read through. Tom considered his options, urgency and excitement quarreling. To take the entire file would be too risky – he could never talk his way out if he were stopped. The cops would be called. And, just up the Boulevard, Hollywood police station was one place he really couldn't afford to land in again. Not if he wanted to stay alive.

What he needed were one or two sheets of paper that would say it all. He laid the file on the desk, preparing to rifle through it again, when he noticed a note pinned to the inside front of the folder, a scrawled memo from Charlie Eyton, dated the day of Taylor's discovery:

Feb 3

J.J., regarding matter so urgently discussed, see attached from
New York, congratulate your perspicacity and agree best way
to proceed is turn all light on Normand. Most everybody on
lot has some story to tell.
     Yours, Charles E.

Unpinning the memo, Tom unfolded the telegram attached, shocked
by the simple ferocity of the sparse words laid out in two strips of
green type, datelined Paramount, New York:

***IMPERATIVE SUPPRESS MMM RUMORS ANY
COST=STOP=SPOTLIGHT MN AS SUGGESTED WITH
ALL SPEED=STOP=ZUKOR=STOP***

Even as Tom slid the folded papers into his pocket, a lingering,
irrational sense of loyalty made him sicken at the thought of what
he was about to do.
     But what more proof could be wanted?

THIRTY-ONE

All he had to do was retrace his steps, locate Fay and get
over to Sennett's, and he would be done. But as he descended
the stairs, a landing door thumped open right in front of
him, near taking his nose with it. Red Peppard halted like he'd been
knocked back, more surprised than Tom, his pale eyebrows mounting
almost to the copper curls above.

'Holy moly, Tom . . . Tom Collins, how the heck you doin',
friend? We ain't seen you in—' The penny dropped, and the eyebrows
knit together now for a slow-witted glance up the stairs.

'Red, hey, that's what I call lucky.' Tom leaned forward to seize
him by the shoulders, as if this unexpected renewal of acquaintance
was all he'd ever wished for. 'You wouldn't think a guy could forget
the layout of this place in six months, would you? I lost my bearings, coming back from the can.'

He wiped his hands together as though he had just washed them, mostly to let Peppard see they were empty. It was a ludicrous excuse for being there and, slow as he was, the boy probably wouldn't buy it. Tom slipped his hand in his pocket and gripped the heavy flashlight. He was a nice kid, but even so . . .

'Oh, yeah,' Peppard blurted, his cogs finally getting in a full turn. 'Sure, I heard you were working for Dick Rowland now, but I didn't see your name on the list. Rush job, was it?'

What Peppard was talking about, or what the president of Metro Pictures had to do with it, Tom had no idea. But he went along with it.

'Sure, you got it now, Red.'

Peppard's mind seemed to be engaged on other business anyhow.

'Look, Tom, ol' buddy, I don't want to get you in trouble, but you know the rules. Hell, you probably made 'em, for all I know. Stick to the meeting rooms, no wandering.' Peppard's tone was admonishing, but conciliatory. For whatever reason, he didn't want a confrontation. 'You best get back in there and rejoin your people before you're missed. They're wrapping it up now anyway.'

Still Tom had no clue. But at a guess some kind of pow-wow was going on downstairs. Something big. Enough for Peppard not to want to rock the boat.

'Sure, Red. You know how it is. I'll hold it in next time, OK?'

The kid grunted. His eyes darted back up the stairs. He was in a hurry. 'Bottom of the stairwell, left through the doors, and no straying. Yeah?'

The gratitude in Tom's handshake did not need to be feigned. He made his way down the last two flights. At the bottom, he pushed loudly through the swing door, then stopped, waiting, until he heard Peppard skipping upwards again. He peered out, ran straight across the stairwell and into the corridor opposite. Two minutes later he was out in the air again, in the gap between the buildings, breathing in deep gulps of relief and leaning his forehead against the cool stucco of the wall.

Whatever Peppard had been talking about, it had saved his neck. Now he had time to, he wondered what Dick Rowland and his 'people' from Metro – one of Lasky's biggest rivals – could be doing right here at the heart of the Lasky operation? A secret deal, maybe? Some kind of merger? That kind of business usually got done in New York, not out here. Still, it would explain all the cloak and dagger, the block on the Vine Street gate, the total shutdown. Something major enough to merit all that.

A roar of automobile engines and a flare of headlamps drew his attention to the far end of the passage. The smart thing, he knew, would be to get straight back across Argyle, find Fay and get the hell off the lot. But the idea that he might have stumbled across something secret spurred him on. Some folk would pay well for a tip-off about a deal between Lasky and Metro – not least of them Phil Olsen.

Out front, the night air was thick with noise. Limousines lined up in two curving rows, engines running, liveried chauffeurs standing by. From his vantage point, Tom had a direct line of sight to the portico of the executive building as a lone figure in a dinner suit emerged, pushed a fat cigar between his lips and struck a match on one of the pillars. Tall, balding and possessed of a nose that would not have looked out of place on a punchbag, there was no mistaking him. Still, Tom had to blink three times before he convinced himself it really was one of Lasky's biggest, most powerful business rivals. Joe Schenck. Standing there, puffing away, like he had just bought the place.

Tom had no time to think it through. The door swung open again and a stream of voluble men in black dress coats emerged on to the portico and began signaling to the waiting drivers. Again, Tom was dumbstruck. Every one of them was a name of national importance. There was Dick Rowland, as Peppard had said. Beside him the still more eminent Marcus Loew, and the diminutive figure of 'Uncle' Carl Laemmle of Universal, William Fox, Sam Goldwyn, Lewis Selznick, Hiram Abrams of United Artists and – godammit, there was good ol' Doug Fairbanks strolling out alongside him. So much for the stupid story about Valentino, even if he had known it was bunkum from the get-go.

What could have brought all these men together, so many of them known to despise each other? The only ones missing were the Lasky contingent. But then they too emerged: Jesse Lasky and Charlie Eyton and last of all – impossible as it might seem that no news had leaked of his arrival from New York, yet there he was – the president of Famous Players-Lasky and the Paramount Corporation, the most powerful man in movieland: Adolph Zukor.

What in hellfire and damnation was going on?

THIRTY-TWO

B ack on the far side of Argyle, things couldn't have been more different. Drawn by the umbrella of yellow light, Tom found himself by a luxuriously appointed set, a three-wall interior – open to the night sky apart from the rigging and a broad sweep of muslin hanging from it to diffuse the glare from the Kliegs ranged above. Outside, chalk marks on the timber flats identified the movie as *Blood and Sand*. He smiled at the seductive cruelty. How many careworn hearts would flutter back to life at the sight of Valentino in a toreador's skintight suit of lights. The young Italian had stormed the box office in *Four Horsemen of the Apocalypse* and *The Sheik*. Every production he could be levered into was in overdrive; this must have been the fourth in as many months for Lasky. Nothing – not even a meeting so secret it shut down the rest of the lot – could halt the money machine that was Rudy Valentino.

The open stage was an island of opulent luxury, an ornate Moorish salon, all pencil-thin columns and sinuous arches, cascading silks, embroidered wall hangings suspended from the rigging above. On the floor, an artfully configured profusion of Persian carpets, animal skins and furs. Tables strained to support bowls of abundant fruit, flowers and baubles. At the center, the principal point of focus for lighting and lens, a grand divan smothered in lustrous folds of silk and satin cushions.

'Tom, over here,' Fay called out, hand raised aloft as if she had every right to be there. She was standing by the camera platform with a short, plump, homely-looking woman dressed in a slouchy, old-fashioned fur over a severe three-quarter-length dress. The waved bob cut she wore was a sole concession to fashion. The plain face it framed seemed unlikely to have graced a screen, but it was familiar.

'Have you met Miss Mathis?' Fay asked.

He knew the name. June Mathis. Recognized her now from magazines. Valentino's chief promoter and scenario writer, a former executive at Metro who had pushed so hard for this Italian unknown to be given the role that made his name – she had resigned her position to go with him when he turned his back on Metro and moved to Lasky.

'We haven't met but, yes, of course—' Tom stopped short as the woman extended a gloved hand, sweeping frank, black, polished-pebble eyes up and down him as he made his introduction, before beaming her approval to Fay.

'Miss Mathis is kind enough to patronize the Oasis occasionally,' Fay interjected. 'We have become such good friends.'

'I heard Mrs Parker sing and, of course, I was enchanted.' Miss Mathis ran her eyes over Tom again. This time he detected a diamantine hardness in them. 'But I think our friendship is more probably founded on shared dislikes. Such as that dreadful Swanson woman. I'm told me she was putting on a scandalous display at the Alexandria earlier. So unnecessary, Mr Collins, don't you agree?'

He had no opportunity to reply. Amid a general murmur, a switch was thrown and the set lit up in a brighter blaze than before. Something stirred on the richly upholstered ottoman at its center and, for the first time, Tom noticed a sinuous female form draped upon it, her face buried under silks until now.

A shout went up. 'No, Nita. No! For Chrissakes, stay still. We've only just got the light right. You wanna look good, don't you?'

Tom looked up and saw the familiar figure of Fred Niblo striding to the edge of a scaffold platform beside a big, twin-reeled Bell & Howell camera. He was clothed in the standard movie-director outfit of jodhpurs, riding boots and tailored safari jacket, and appeared entirely unconcerned by the stream of muffled invective directed at him from the actress lying face down on the bed.

'I'm roasting my tush off under these lights, Fred. I don't see Rudy being subjected to this torture. If you don't get started, I'm walking. I mean it.'

Niblo rattled down the scaffold and, ensuring he didn't disturb the lie of the props, leaned over the divan and stroked the actress's mounded black hair and bare shoulders. 'OK, sweetheart, lift your head and get your breath for a minute. We can't let you move just yet as we need that close-up of you when Rudy comes into your lair for the first time. We can't let the fans miss the flash of those fiery eyes of yours as you rise and catch sight of him, can we? We need the long lens for that, so we need to get the lights spot on.'

Tom looked on in silence as screen siren Nita Naldi raised her head from the fabric in which she was buried. Sultry, raven-haired, as she shifted slightly, the curve of a voluptuous white haunch, previously blended perfectly into the hillocks of surrounding silk, came visible through the translucent veil of near-nothing in which she was attired. Niblo's expression changed to barely controlled ecstasy.

'Are you getting that, Alvin?' he shouted to the lensman above and got a double thumbs-up by way of reply. 'OK, let's go for the shot. Musicians, you strike up something hot. And Norm, tell Mr Valentino he's up next. Let's roll 'em now.'

As Niblo stepped carefully out of frame, a trio of musicians in the wings struck up a slow-burning Latin rhythm on viola, bass and piano accordion. Under the director's shouted encouragement, Naldi began to writhe sensuously on the divan, her urgent desire speaking eloquently from dark-rimmed eyes gazing straight into the camera. Tom wondered how many present knew that Naldi, this epitome of Eastern promise, was in reality Mary Dooley, progeny of impoverished Irish immigrants in New York, whose sloe-eyed beauty and curvaceous form won her first a place in Florenz Ziegfeld's Follies, and then a ticket West to immortality.

As for her Italian leading man, there was still no sign. Once Niblo had captured his siren's luminous flesh and flashing eyes in a variety of poses, he uttered a string of curses at Valentino's failure to appear and stormed off in the direction of the dressing area. With that, Miss Naldi erupted from the bed in a flurry of cushions and fabric, and walked off, too. Whatever sizzling moment Niblo had carefully planned to capture for the delight of the movie-going public was lost for ever.

'Miss Mathis tells me she knew poor Mr Taylor very well,' Fay said, turning away from the scene. 'And like you, Tom, she believes his death was most peculiar.'

'I would hardly be alone in that, my dear,' Miss Mathis objected with considerable hauteur. 'He *was* murdered. What I meant you to understand was that I could agree with none of the accounts offered hitherto as to why. Certainly none of those concocted by the authorities, or by this city's nincompoop newspapers, are in the least credible. Is this your opinion, too, Mr Collins?'

It was not so far from his own opinion, although he would have expressed it differently. 'You're not wrong there, Miss Mathis.

Nothing about his death makes sense to me. But then, I only knew Mr Taylor slightly. You were close?'

'I knew him professionally.' She swept a hand around the set. 'And we dined occasionally as friends. More so recently, as I was preparing a scenario for Mr Valentino to play in under his direction.'

Tom offered condolences, and wondered whether Miss Mathis had noticed her friend behaving any way abnormally or fearfully in recent weeks.

'There were one or two occurrences, since you ask,' she replied. 'I did not set great store by them before, but now I'm not so certain. As you doubtless know, all of Mr Taylor's leading ladies adored him. Worshipped the ground on which he walked, in fact.' With this, she struck a vaguely tragic pose. 'A very attractive man he was, too. But there were two in particular about whom he was quite concerned. To the point of distress, I fear.'

Apparently under a professional obligation to dramatize, Miss Mathis made a meal of trying to look hesitant, but also seemed very eager to get something off her ample chest. Tittle-tattle, Tom didn't doubt.

'Obviously, I can reveal no names,' she continued. 'Mr Taylor was the very soul of discretion and I would not wish to sully his reputation. But perhaps, if you knew him, you already know the two ladies I'm talking of?'

'Perhaps,' Tom said, with as much knowingness as he could muster.

'Well,' Miss Mathis said, 'whatever they say, or don't, about the *young one* in the newspapers, Mr Collins, I believe Mr Taylor was genuinely anxious that she was trouble. She was infatuated with him, you know – a case of youthful *amour fou*, I imagine. She insisted on calling at his quarters in the evenings, shamelessly begging him to, well, to make love to her. There's no other way of putting it. It's not as if he encouraged her. He had to get that manservant of his to demur and tell her he was out. Even so, the child turned up at three in the morning only two weeks ago, out of her wits with ardor and threatening to injure herself unless he consented to wed her.'

'Really?' Tom said, unprepared for Mathis to so comprehensively back up everything that Olsen had suggested to him about Minter and which J.J. Fine's memo had all but confirmed. 'You think she might have acted violently against him?'

Mathis gave him a derisory glare. 'No, no, Mr Collins, not Mary. That crazy mother of hers – the dreaded Mrs Shelby. It is she who would have delivered the *coup de grace*. Just think of her, alone in that big house, fearful she might lose her daughter, lose control of all that money, her only source of income, after she'd fought so fiercely to establish her child's name, and to drag her family up from abject poverty. Only to lose control of it to Mr Taylor? If they had married, Mother Shelby would have been cut out entirely – finished, for ever. The young lady made that consequence quite clear. Mother couldn't afford to let it happen, could she? In fact, she said as much to someone of my acquaintance.'

'She did?' Tom asked, as surprised by her powers of imagination now as anything else. 'And have you reported any of this to the investigating detectives?'

Miss Mathis was taken aback by the suggestion. 'Well, I didn't feel it was my place, but I certainly advised my friend to do so.'

Tom rather doubted it and was about to ask straight out who this friend was when he got a kick on the ankle from Fay, who had a question of her own.

'Which is all one could expect,' she interjected. 'But what about the other woman, Miss Mathis? Tell Mr Collins what you were saying to me about her *condition*.'

Tom arched his eyebrows at this, a response Miss Mathis took for skepticism. She began to look uncertain about continuing the conversation.

'Well, I'm not sure it's appropriate, my dear. It is only hearsay, and whatever one might say among we ladies, I'm not sure Mr Collins . . .'

In the event, she was saved her blushes. Their conference was interrupted by a shout from the wings as Niblo darted out from the curtained cubicle and marched straight across to where they stood.

Puce-faced, bursting with indignation, he demanded Mathis's adjudication at a crisis meeting in Mr Valentino's dressing room, post-haste.

'He's gone mad, June. It's just too much. How are we ever going to get this picture made with these constant, unreasonable, ridiculous demands?'

Without a by-your-leave, Miss Mathis was away, swept up by the tornado of angst that was the director of *Blood and Sand*.

'What did you kick me for?' Tom asked. 'I was about to ask her who this friend was. Now she's gone.'

'You can see she would never have told you,' Fay insisted. 'But me, on the other hand—'

'She did?'

'Yes,' Faye laughed. 'But that's not all. I was hoping she would repeat what she confided to me about Mabel Normand. It is scandalous, Tom. I wasn't sure you would believe it coming from me alone. I still don't know quite what to think.'

Fay looked around guardedly. 'She said there's no question but that Miss Normand is hopelessly addicted to cocaine. By her own witness.'

'Come on, Fay. That's hardly news.'

She shushed him, her own voice low and confidential. 'Not entirely perhaps, but then she said Normand only started using the dope after' – at this she dropped her voice to a whisper – 'after she was forced to engage the services of an abortionist.'

'Miss Normand? You're kidding? She was having a baby?'

Fay frowned at his response. 'Poor thing, she must have been so distressed.'

Tom's racing thoughts were taking him through less compassionate territory. 'Did she say who the father was? Was it Taylor?'

Fay shook her head. 'She wouldn't, or couldn't, say more. I gather Miss Mathis heard this not from Taylor but a mutual friend – a Mrs Ivers, she said her name was. Do you know her?'

He thought hard on it, his mind churning. There was so much conflicting information about Taylor. How much of it was reliable? Credible even? The problem with movie folk was that their lives were bound up in fantasy. Writing, acting, their business was dreams. Some of them would believe anything. Then it hit him: the lady in blue.

'Do you, Tom?' Fay repeated, taking his arm now and starting away from the set.

'Maybe I do at that,' he said. 'At least, I think so. Not to speak to, but once or twice I saw Taylor hanging around the lot late in the evening, talking with a little old lady. She was always dressed the same, in a long blue dress – old-style, you know? He asked me to arrange a studio pass for her, and that's the name he gave: Mrs Ivers. I'm sure of it. Said she wrote scenarios for him, and came in at night to advise him on details for the sets and all. Hours at a time, just talking. He said they worked together something like five or six years. They looked close.'

Fay raised the inevitable eyebrow.

'No, not like that,' Tom said. 'She was much older, and if what I've been hearing is true, Taylor liked his fruit on the green side if anything. From what I remember, though, he sure loved talking to her.'

Rocking his head back, Tom worked the tension from his shoulders. The moon was still so bright that there was barely a star to be seen. 'There must be someone around who knew Taylor well. Maybe this Ivers woman is the one to ask. Otherwise, all the random trash that's coming out about him, it's crazy. One fella at the Alexandria tonight wanted me to believe Taylor didn't go for women at all. Said he knew for a fact Taylor liked men. What're we supposed to believe?'

'Well, it's not impossible, is it?' Fay ventured.

'Maybe not, but you've got to admit it is unlikely, given what we've just heard. It's just one secret life too many – even for Taylor. Nobody could live like that and keep quiet about it. Not out here.'

Fay was not convinced and Tom lapsed into silence as they walked.

'I forgot to ask,' she said. 'Did you get what you wanted for Sennett?'

He tapped his pocket but couldn't quite raise a smile about it. 'I think so. I just hope it'll be enough. There was something crazy going on over there, too. Some studio pow-wow, a gathering of chiefs of some kind.'

'So that's why Vine Street spurned us. Any idea what it was?'

'No.' He held his hands up. 'Whole place's gone mad, far as I can see.' His voice dipped on the final phrase, the last of his energy draining from him.

She leaned in, squeezed her arm against his and pulled him close. 'It's been a long day. We should get out of here and have ourselves a nightcap. You look like you could do with one. And I know I could. You might as well sit up front with me now. I can't imagine they'll check us going out.'

Without his realizing it, Fay had steered a course back to her automobile. The sleek Cadillac roadster stood out among the jalopies parked along the backlot wall, facing out across Argyle towards the commissary and studio clinic across the street. As they reached it, a movement across the street caught his eye. He watched intently as a man in a dark coat, hat brim low across his face, emerged from the clinic, pulled the door shut and locked it. Tom mounted the machine, sitting heavily in, mesmerized by the indistinct figure beyond.

'You're some gent, Tom Collins,' Fay complained, climbing into the driver's seat. 'Thank heaven for electrical starting, that's all I can say. A girl wouldn't want to be in need of a crank with you around.'

She turned to him, saw his face slack with concentration and followed his line of sight. Across the street, against the darkness of a far wall, she barely distinguished the shuffling motion of a man, walking the shadow line. Together they watched him climb awkwardly into a dark tourer and start the motor.

'Someone you know?'

Tom seemed not to hear, transfixed as the other machine pulled away from the curb and exited the Argyle gate. An arm waved out of the guardhouse window, acknowledging its departure.

'Tom?' Fay shifted the gearstick and nosed out into the street,

'It's nothing.' He shook his head wearily. 'Reminded me of someone I knew once, a long time back. I'm so beat, I'm imagining all sorts now. I'll be seeing ghosts rising next.'

Fay slowed as they passed the guardhouse. No one so much as looked in their direction, let alone raised an amiable arm to speed them on their way.

THIRTY-THREE

In contrast to other venues out that end of the Boulevard, the Oasis was all about discretion. It was Fay's take on the New York cabaret clubs she had frequented and fallen in love with after the war. Situated in a suite of rooms beneath a mixed commercial and residential block, the club's existence was signaled only

by a green canopy bearing the simple monogram of a tent picked
out in three curved gold vertical lines topped by a pitched fourth.
The door was manned by an urbane army veteran, Herman Sutter,
who combined good manners with a formidable demeanor, greeting
patrons not in the usual livery of a doorman but a midnight-blue
double-breasted and a necktie picked out in tiny gold tents. It was
a theme continued in the apparel of all the floor staff, even the
cigarette and hat-check girls.

One of the latter stopped Tom in his tracks passing the booth at
the bottom of the stairs, a beaming young woman with a halo of
blonde hair lit from behind. 'Good evening, Mr Collins.'

'Colleen?' He couldn't believe the change wrought in so short a
time.

'I'm plain Mae here.' She bowed her head. 'At Mrs Parker's
suggestion.'

Nothing plain there, he thought. Hair waved and crimped, face
fresh, devoid of rouge or powder, a shirtwaist and vest that couldn't
quite impose on her the contours of a boy. The same girl, only
prettier, more radiant.

'You're quite the surprise.' He glanced back up the steps to where
Fay was still engaged in conversation with Sutter. 'Fay said she was
getting you settled, but I never suspected it would be this quick.'

'Oh, they were short-handed. I said I'd dive in. Glad of the
opportunity. And it's not like I was busy with anything else.'

He could see no obvious signs of the sickness on her. Must be
she wasn't so deep into dope as he had thought. They talked for a
couple of minutes more, until Fay appeared beside him. Her manner
was pleasant, but there was distraction beneath her smile and an
urgency in how she drew Tom away from the booth and through
the leather-padded doors into the elegantly appointed club room.

There the decor created the mood of a dark and smoky desert
encampment. The walls were covered in pleated cloth of rose pink
and celadon, the ceiling tented in the same fabrics. Hanging lanterns
cast a low light that barely penetrated the dimmer recesses where, here
and there, the walls glowed with tiny backlit tent motifs. The room
was busy but not crowded, an air of elegance and complicity marking
the murmuring parties occupying most of the thirty or so tables and
booths that ringed the modest dance floor, and a small stage occupied
by a weather-beaten pianist playing a soft, seductive rag.

'Would you like to have something here or go straight up to the apartment?' Fay asked, waving a greeting to a table of regulars across the room. Fay usually insisted on fulfilling her duties as the Oasis's charming proprietress for an hour at least, while leaving the hosting to her manager, Eddie Solomons.

'You've been away from me three weeks,' Tom said. 'You know the answer to that.'

'You're bad, Tom Collins.'

'I'm probably too beat to be bad. But I'll give it a try.'

She laughed, reached up and kissed him on the lips. 'You go on up, then. I need to have a word with Eddie. I'll be just a minute. Five at most.'

Again he sensed her anxiety. 'Is there a problem?'

She shook her head, her attention still mostly on the room. 'No. It's something Herman mentioned. I need to check a payment went out while I was back East.'

She slipped out of his embrace and threaded her way towards the far side of the room where he could just about discern the club's tall, impeccably groomed manager conversing with a young woman robed in a glittering evening gown. The next act, Tom supposed. He backed out the door and trotted up the outside steps, nodding goodnight to the doorman before changing his mind and turning on his heel.

'Any trouble here tonight, Herman? Mrs Parker seemed a little upset.'

'No trouble, Mr Collins.' The doorman was unruffled. 'Just some cops pushing their weight around. I told them we don't admit non-members.'

'They accepted that?'

'No. They tried to push in anyway. But I can smell the law a mile off. I sent them on their way.'

'They weren't in uniform?'

'Long ulsters and homburgs, if I 'collect right,' Herman said, warming to the subject. 'Tough guys, or so they thought. Insisted on having a look inside. Dug out their badges when I said I'd call the cops. Big mistake. I pointed to the corner there and told them that's where the city line stops, and they were the wrong side of it.'

Tom laughed to himself, admiring the man's pluck.

'And they left?'

'Sure they did. Once I told them we paid our dues to the county sheriff and he wouldn't be long putting a sock in their traps if they didn't push off.'

'You're one cool customer, Herman.'

Sutter rolled his shoulders, as if to say he wouldn't disagree with that estimation but modesty forbade him to admit it.

'They weren't happy, Mr Collins. But you know what they can do about that.' The doorman bunched his fingers in a gesture that, for all its swiftness, was replete with obscenity. 'A big fat fistful of nothing. That's what.'

THIRTY-FOUR

Downtown was quiet even for a Sunday morning. The one streetcar he saw, rumbling off towards Hill Street tunnel with a clang, looked to be carrying no passengers at all, and the wide thoroughfares of the business district were mostly empty. The few folk he passed were either disheveled young men stumbling home from late-night revels or well turned-out families strolling down to mass at the Pro-Cathedral on Pershing Square. He wondered what his mother looking down from heaven would think of his fancy American ways when he hadn't seen the inside of a church in three years or more.

The sun was high above the campanile of the old City Hall by the time he pulled up out front of the Chamber of Commerce building further north on Broadway. On the huge plate windows right of the pillared entrance, the *Evening Herald*'s masthead was gilded in fancy letters four feet high. Inside, he could see the sprawling newsroom was deserted, apart from one or two dedicated souls in vests and visors hunched over desks by the windows.

Of Phil Olsen, though, there was no sign. Tom checked his wristwatch. Ten was what he had said. It was that on the dot. Across the street, the marquee of the Mason Opera House advertised the arrival of the Russian Grand Opera Company, on its first American tour. *The Tsar's Bride. Eugene Onegin.* Seven-night run. Lingering sensations of the night before were strong enough to ripple on his skin and make him smile like a boy. Russian opera would be Fay's kind of thing. If all the tickets hadn't sold out already, it looked such a plum.

He pulled on the parking brake, glanced up and down the street, then at his watch again and wondered whether he should go ask after Olsen inside. It would be worth it just to walk through the lobby and breathe in the scent of the exhibit kept there of all the fine produce bursting forth from this vale of Eden, this Southern California. Piled pyramids of oranges, lemons, olives, peaches and figs. All kinds more – potatoes, cotton, every kind of grain. At the center, dominating everything, a life-size elephant fashioned from, so the sign said, eight hundred and fifty pounds of walnuts. Man, that was something to behold.

About to cut the motor, he heard his name called and turned to see Olsen exit the building by a side door down the street. The reporter had exchanged his boater for a wide-brimmed fedora, but the suit looked the same as he'd worn the day before, as did the shirt and tie. Olsen's smile hadn't changed either, switched on full, teeth running back almost to his ears.

'Hey, Collins, keep that motor running. You had breakfast yet? Couple of blocks over on Spring's a new joint does the best pastrami ever.'

'Pastrami, for breakfast?'

'Got a problem with that?'

His stomach yawned like it hadn't been fed for days, so he shook his head, swinging the door out for Olsen.

'Guess not. Let's go.'

Olsen clambered in, hat and all. 'See Davis has been brought in to fight Colina next week in Vernon? You Irish boys'll be down there for that one, I guess.'

His voice sounded thinner over the engine clatter as Tom turned the corner. For a little guy, Olsen sure loved his boxing.

'I heard Kid George was up against Colina,' Tom said, knowing Olsen was a big fan of the Kid. 'He running scared now or something?'

'Not likely. He got a chance to tangle with Johnny Lotsey out in Oakland a couple days earlier. Guess he thinks even if he wins it, he'll take too many hits to fight again next week. Should be a barnstormer. Me and the boys are making a party of it. Stick a pencil behind your ear, Al Treloar will get you in on the press ticket.'

Olsen broke off and pointed at a drab, brick-front store in the row ahead. 'Hey, pull in – see this sign right here?'

Inside, the place looked less promising than out: mean and empty, with long tables and benches like an army commissary. But it was clean and wafting a rich aroma of roast meat and spices.

'Enough to make your belly fall flat in love,' Olsen said, as he hailed the guy lounging behind the counter, threw his hat on the table nearest the kitchen and ordered pastrami for two. His enthusiasm was borne out as soon as the sandwiches arrived, steaming hot, dripping juice and mustard over the plate. So good even Olsen couldn't talk for a couple of minutes for chowing down, breathing fire out through his nostrils.

'So, tell me, what's so important you gotta prise me from the arms of Morpheus before noon on a Sunday?'

Tom wondered if he'd heard right. 'You got a squeeze now, Olsen?'

Olsen hacked out a cough, eyes watering from the mustard or something else. 'Actually, it's a . . . Ah no, forget that. C'mon, out with it. What's happened you need to ask me about?'

Tom hesitated, not wanting to give too much away straight off. 'You heard of any studio pow-wows in the pipeline?'

Olsen gave him an assessing stare while taking another, smaller, bite of his sandwich, then wiping his lips with the tablecloth as he swallowed. 'You know how this town works, Collins. There's always something going down that line. What kind of pow-wow we talking about?'

'Big one. All kinds of rival chiefs sitting down to suck smoke together. You got no word on it?'

Olsen put the last corner of his sandwich carefully down on the plate, his chewing winding down in speed now.

'You saying you heard this, or you seen it?'

'I don't recall saying either way.' Tom leaned back from the table, folding his arms. 'But for a man who's just put a quarter pound of pastrami in his gut, you're looking hungry, Phil.'

The reporter sat in, eyes intent across the table. 'Sure I am. Always. Why else would I be here? Question is, you got something for me or not?'

'I do, but I want to know what I'm giving you. So tell me why
your jaw flapped open just then, and I'll give you something to
close it up. You've heard something, right?'

Olsen ran a finger round the inside of his celluloid shirt collar,
considering. 'OK, so maybe I have. But so far it's just whispers
and I ain't been able to get anything solid on it. You give me that,
I'll get you to Oakland – ringside, if you want.'

'That's not what I'm after. Anyhow, tell me about these whispers
first.'

'You spill this to anyone, I'm coming after you with a bayonet.'

'You won't need to sharpen anything but your quill, Phil. Go on,
tell me.'

Olsen glanced into each shadowed corner of the empty room
before answering. 'Did you see the story yesterday about this politi-
cian, Hays, being brought in to reorganize the movie distribution
racket?'

Tom had seen it all right: a dull little squib about plans to use
the Railway Express Company for a new movie distribution service
to major cities led by a nest-feathering friend of President Harding
called Will Hays. No other city in America would have had it for
front-page news.

'Sure, but what's that got to do with anything?'

'Rumor is, that ain't the half of it. All this rumpus over Arbuckle
and now Taylor, it's got the money men sweating their socks off.
You heard about those God-botherers down south setting fire to
theaters showing Arbuckle flickers, yeah? Well, it's started up again.
Ticker today says four cowboys rode into a movie theater in
Cheyenne last night, tore down a screen showing *Mollie O*, and
threatened to do the same to any other movie house in Wyoming
that dare put Mabel Normand up on screen.'

Tom shook his head in disbelief. Sennett had the smarts to see
it right from the outset. No wonder he'd been worried. 'I still don't
get why folk are taking against Normand in particular.'

Olsen darted him a look like he was some kind of ignoramus.

'C'mon, Collins, keep up with the story. Like I said yesterday
– it's because they're being told to. And that's the whole point. This
is not about Normand – it's about everything. All this muckraking
in the Eastern press about the movie colony being the wickedest
place since Babel, it's beginning to stick. Arbuckle was bad enough,

and maybe if the second verdict had'a gone the other way last week, things would be different. But it didn't, and now this baloney about Taylor and his drinking, doping, panty-sniffing, starlet-shtuping habits – it's like a call to arms for all those vigilantes and mothers' union handwringers who haven't tasted blood since Volstead was passed.'

Tom couldn't resist a snort at that. 'But most of what's in the papers is bull. You should know – you write half of it.'

Olsen grinned. 'Not me, friend, I'm a crusader for truth. One of the good guys. I mean it. Anyhow, you never heard of public opinion? You should see the letters we get at the *Herald* every day from ordinary, decent Angelinos who'd happily tar and feather half the movie folk in town for their corrupting ways. And all they got to do is look out the window and see it ain't really like that. What hope they got in Biblesville, Kentucky?'

Tom sat back again and put his hands up in surrender. 'OK. So folk are angry. What about it? I still don't see what you're saying.'

Olsen leaned right into the table and dropped his voice. 'What I'm saying is, this situation has every major movie producer from here to New York quaking in his boots right now, worried that all these scandals are gonna bring the dream factories they spent years building up – and making millions outta – crashing down around their ears. For now, Lasky is drawing the fire, what with Arbuckle and Taylor both belonging to them. And like I told you yesterday, they're doing all they can to stop it spreading to the Minter girl as well. On past form, you'd expect Meyer, Goldwyn, Loew and all the other boss men to stand back rubbing their hands while Zukor and his whole Paramount–Lasky outfit goes up in flames. But – and this is what I'm telling you – the business world says no, there's too many chips in the pot. For everybody. If Paramount and Lasky go down, the banks will get the heebie-jeebies and start pulling their money out from other studios too. Are you with me?'

'That's crazy. Why would they do that? If the whole industry goes bust, the banks'll never get a penny back.'

'But it ain't only the banks. It's the stock market, the shareholders, the nickel-and-dime investors. Nobody wants to lose their dough, not even a little bit. So they all try to get their money out before the next guy. It's a house of cards – if one goes, the whole caboodle comes crashing down.'

The creak of the kitchen door opening made them both turn. The pastrami guy, coffee pot in his hand, asking if they wanted more. They said no in unison, waiting till he went back the way he came before speaking again.

'So, what you're saying is all these studio heads are burying the hatchet and coming together to do something to stop this happening?' Tom said, low.

'That's the million-dollar question. Personally, I reckon this Hays is up to his neck in it. You know he resigned as postmaster general for this job? This guy's no small-timer. He ain't gonna play penny ante with distribution. There has to be something bigger in it for him.'

'Sounds like a story. How come I didn't see anything on it already?'

Olsen's laugh was as sharp as a guillotine. 'You kidding me? Like I said, this is just a hunch. I bring it to Klegg, my editor, he says, "What've you got to back this up?" Then he tugs my ears off for wasting his time.'

'I don't see them being so careful with the other bull they print.'

Olsen shook his head impatiently. 'C'mon, we've been over this already. We don't print it unless someone says it to us. Anyhow, movie stars are one thing, but movie business is a whole other ball game. Get the industry side of things wrong and you soon find yourself looking for another job – compliments of Mr Hearst.'

'Mr Hearst? What's he got to do with anything? The *Herald*'s always screaming about how it's the only independent paper in Los Angeles. It's your motto, ain't it?'

'Yeah, and you're old enough and ugly enough to know better. Hearst has good as owned us five years or more now. He's been buying up stock on the sly so long, it's only a matter of time before he gobbles us up whole. Then you'll see what "independent" means in this burg. Same as it always did – sweet Fanny Adams.'

Tom was still trying to get his head around that one, but Olsen had already switched back to the only thing interesting him at that moment.

'Look, Tom, forget about that, will'ya. I been chasing this story weeks now and every door's been shut in my face, every lip sealed. Then you come telling me about pow-wows and peace pipes. So, for the love of God, if you saw any of those guys in a room together, you gotta tell me – because you know as well as I do, they wouldn't've been in there to exchange pleasantries.'

Tom put his elbows on the table, bunched his fists under his chin and let out a long slow breath. If what Olsen said was right, the last thing the studio needed now was him blabbing to a newspaperman. But maybe they made that choice six months ago when they sacked him. Or yesterday, before he found that telegram. He had his own life to live. That it would be cut a damn sight shorter by Tony Cornero if he didn't get what he needed from Olsen was enough to push him on.

'OK, Phil, you can stop begging. I've got what you want. But you'll have to go somewhere else if you're looking for proof. I was over on the Lasky lot last night – unofficially, you understand. And I saw the biggest mob of studio big shots ever come together in one place.'

'Hang on, gimme a chance to write this down.' Olson was transformed, a live wire again, the grin a mile wide, one hand digging in his jacket pocket for a notebook, the other for a pen. 'You gotta give me detail. Names and times. Everything you got, OK?'

Tom sat back, rubbed his chin with his hand. 'I'll give you names, big ones, and while we're at it, you're going to tell me everything there is to know about Tony Cornero. OK? That's the deal, or I walk out the door.'

Olsen's jaw was back to flapping.

'Cornero? What the hell's that biggety boot got to do with anything?'

THIRTY-FIVE

The dark mesh fly screen clacked sharp against the doorframe as another of Sullivan's brood shot out from the house, ran barefoot across the stoop, down the white wood steps and across the yard, whooping like an Indian brave. Either 'little' Eamon, 'little' Sean or 'little' Donal. Or could be it was Thad junior. Tom never could tell with certainty any of Sullivan's seven sons from the others, save for the eldest, Patrick, whose height and erect carriage even at fourteen years of age bore the stamp of a born leader. Otherwise, all of them, irrespective of years, appeared to have sprung fully formed from Eleanor's womb, each with massive limbs and jaws, and topped by yellow hayseed sprouts of hair.

Tom watched his friend's calm eyes track the boy's progress until he disappeared from sight, crashing through the line of brush that marked the yard's northern boundary.

'The little scamp,' Sullivan said quietly, almost to himself. 'I told him he'll be sorry if he steps on a rattlesnake.'

'Not so sorry as the rattler,' Tom laughed. 'You breed 'em big, friend.'

Sullivan responded with an appreciative hoot. 'They're eating me out of house and home. I'll have to make detective sergeant or go on the take if they don't stop growing.'

The house was a pretty timber-frame bungalow on a good-size, elevated lot west of Brentwood, the yard dotted here and there with cottonwoods, orange blossom and one elderly pepper tree. Sullivan purchased the land in the spring of 1919 when the arrival of yet another child meant their already cramped apartment in Elysian Park would no longer take the strain. It was a good time to buy. California's land speculators were falling over themselves in readiness to fulfill war-weary dreams of sunshine, health and prosperity with a flood of new subdivisions and fresh-graded patches of paradise. Sullivan got in early, had his pick, and at a good price. Three years on, he was the proud owner of the best-situated home in a colony of little white houses that spread across the hillside like mushrooms on a damp October night back home.

They had been outside a good half-hour now since Sullivan suggested a breath of fresh air – his euphemism for a drop of the hard stuff. But, so far, none had appeared. Instead, Sullivan had embarked on a rambling jeremiad triggered by a report in the newspaper about the looming civil war in Ireland, which he had taken, quaintly, to calling 'the Old Country'.

'He's nothin' but a blackguard and a traitor,' Sullivan said bitterly of Michael Collins, leader of the fledgling Irish Free State, cursing his betrayal of the 'cause' in accepting Britain's decision to partition the island. Tom kept his own counsel other than to point out his namesake's political pragmatism. From what he heard, Sullivan's alternative, the rebel leader Eamon de Valera, was a cold, heartless stick of a man who cared more about ideals than people's lives. Tom was only too happy to turn his back on all that bloodletting and strife. But a large part of Sullivan's heart remained wed to his birthplace, and Tom didn't like to offend that sentiment, except occasionally in jest.

'Speaking of blackguards, you'll never guess who I thought I saw last night.'

Sullivan, knowing his flow was being deliberately diverted, rose from his cane chair and padded in long, loping steps towards the far end of the stoop. 'Go on then, who?' he said at last, bending to fiddle with a loose board.

'Mikey the Grapes.'

Tom had woken with a start in the early hours of the morning, felt Fay warm beside him, his dreams haunted by the shuffling figure he'd seen coming out of the clinic on the Lasky backlot. Now it was clear as day who he had been reminded of: Mikey 'the Grapes' Ross. A nasty piece of work, one of Devlin's chief confederates back in New York. A ludicrous thought. He had quickly drifted off to sleep again, but a trace remained, haunting his dreams.

'Where was this?' Sullivan squatted, thrusting his hand into the void beneath the boards.

'Is that not kind of beside the point? Anywhere west of the Bowery would be a miracle, no?'

Tom had expected dismissal, or a note of derisory disbelief. Ross was one of the lowest criminals they encountered in New York. He was said to have fallen under a streetcar as a child and suffered terrible injuries to his legs. But it was Sullivan who gave him the nickname that stuck, mockingly attributing the man's twisted gait to hemorrhoids. To the delight of those whose lives he made a misery.

'I wouldn't be so sure,' Sullivan grunted, his shirt close to splitting across his back as he scrabbled deeper under the stoop. 'Not with Devlin out here now. Them two were always tight as arsecheeks. Can you imagine one without the other? It's not like Devlin wouldn't have plenty to set him to work on, with a whole new port at his disposal.'

The thought crawled round in Tom's head until Sullivan gave a sigh of victory and pulled something free from the void.

'Ah, there you are, *a ghrá mo chroí*,' he said, cradling in his arms like a new-born infant a bottle of tobacco-colored whiskey, three-quarters full.

'Bushmills?' Tom laughed. 'Where in Christ did you get that from?'

'Father Doran.' Sullivan's grin was beatific. He snatched two tumblers from the sill and blew the day's dust from them. 'He was most appreciative when I helped a nephew of his who turned up in rags at the railhead last week. The Santa Fe fellas wanted to chuck him in pokey. I persuaded them to be more charitable.'

'Trust in the Lord, and do good,' Tom intoned.

'And he will give you the desires of your heart.' Sullivan laughed, uncorked the bottle with his teeth and poured two generous measures.

'One thing's for sure, you can always rely on a priest to have the best of what drink is going. *Sláinte mhaith.*'

Tom raised his glass to the toast and drank deep. Here was a kind of nationalism he could appreciate. He paused a moment before continuing. 'If Ross was out here, what would he be doing at Lasky's? And coming out of the clinic of all places? Since the war you see a lot more men around in his kind of state. Maybe someone's making a flicker about it.'

'No matter,' Sullivan said, settling back again. 'I'm sure Ross's not the reason you graced us with your presence today. Are you going to tell me or do I have to drag it out of you?'

Tom grinned and held out his empty glass. 'I could do with another stoke of the fire before I do.'

But the bottle stayed where it was. 'I was hoping you came to tell me how it went with Ramirez.'

Tom shook his head. 'I haven't had a minute. I've been up to my—'

'I don't care what you've been up to,' Sullivan growled. 'You better get down to Central and talk to him damn quick. He was chewing my neck about you when I got in last night. He's not a man to mess with. If you don't watch your step, he'll get a warrant served, and I might not be around to save your skin next time. I went out on a limb for you, Tom. Don't let me down.'

Tom muttered an apology, but it washed over Sullivan.

'Look, just do it. I don't want to have to ask you again.'

Sullivan grabbed the bottle, tugged the cork and poured himself a tot before pointing the neck at Tom's empty glass. 'Are you going to have another or not?'

As Tom held his glass out again, he leaned forward and lowered his voice. 'Listen, I'm sorry. I will see Ramirez, but it's got even more complicated now. I haven't told you all of it. I'm in trouble, and I'm not sure what to do.'

Sullivan's brow furrowed, and Tom stretched out a hand and placed it on his friend's forearm. 'It's not what you think. You're not harboring a fugitive. Not yet.'

Sullivan poured him another slug of liquor, saying nothing.

'I was hijacked outside my house yesterday,' Tom said, 'and taken to see Tony Cornero. Out at the end of Santa Monica pier.'

'God almighty,' Sullivan muttered under his breath in disbelief. 'What did that dago good-for-nothin' want with you?'

In detail, Tom described what had happened, from the moment he'd been jumped by the kid to the threats Cornero made on the pier. Sullivan, who had punctuated his listening with attentive grunts and queries, finally admitted, 'Christ, I'd forgotten how much trouble you can get into in a day.'

'So long as it's less than I can get out of, I'm OK,' Tom said. 'Problem is, I can't see an out from this one yet, other than to fold and do what the man says. Maybe he'll leave it at that.'

He looked up and caught Sullivan's skeptical glare.

'Don't be fooled by the clothes, Tom. He may be smooth on the surface, but he's a vicious greaseball at heart, and slippery with it. Downtown's been all over him like a swarm, but never got the sting in. You know that's why you had to go to him, don't you? He almost never leaves Santa Monica. He's got every man in the local PD paid off, from brass to beat. So long as he stays there, he's untouchable. If he wants a jaunt down to Tijuana or up to Monterrey, it's by boat – and he's got plenty of 'em. They say he even has a Pierce Arrow that's never been outside the Santa Monica city limits. Never seen a dirt road.'

Tom drained his glass. 'That's what this newsman pal of mine said earlier, while pointing out that the rest of Cornero's mob are under no such constraints. He says Cornero had it easy so far because he got in early and built up the muscle to force out competition this side of Frisco. But it's just too tasty, and there's all sorts of punks and small-timers piling in again, snapping at his heels, trying to grab his action, there's so much movie and oil money washing round out here.'

'He's not wrong about that.' Sullivan shook his head slowly. 'A prohie I know said they smell a war on the way. Told the morgue to buy in extra gurneys. Nobody's going to do anythin' to stop it.'

'So that's what happened to Madden, right? Business?'

'Got to be the likeliest,' Sullivan nodded. 'From what you say, Cornero seems convinced enough of it. Only question for him, probably, is who was the shooter working for? And you stepped right in and churned up the mud even more. Their heads must've been fairly throbbin' trying to figure it out. Can't rightly blame 'em for leaving it to you to clear up.'

'Ha-ha,' Tom said, scathingly. 'All of which gets us precisely nowhere. What I need is a plan.'

'What more can I say? Follow your gut and go with it as far as you dare. See how it works out. Failing that, I hear Vancouver's nice this time of year.'

'Not funny, Thad. I like the weather here just fine.'

They lapsed into silence again, gazing out towards the bright blue strip of ocean lining the horizon in the still afternoon. Nothing to be heard but the chirrup of birdsong and the homely sounds of housework leaking from the kitchen. Tom wondered how it must be to live so, envisioning his own house built, his own yard to sit in, his own brood to watch with care and pride. Somehow, the picture wouldn't come clear.

'Whatever you do,' Sullivan broke in on him, 'don't go telling Ramirez about Cornero. He'll have your ass in the slammer double quick.' He threw his hands up, unwilling to contemplate it. 'Holy Jesus, what a mess. I guess your Sennett thing's had to take a back seat with all with this going on?'

'No, not at all,' Tom said. 'I mean, I'm damned if I can see how Taylor and Normand tie in with the rest of it anymore. But one thing I know for sure is Sennett's being set up like a sap.'

'How so?'

Tom batted the question away. 'It's movie stuff. Nothing to interest you.'

'Anything to do with them two interests me.'

'You don't seriously still see either of them in the frame for it?'

'Indulge me,' Sullivan said.

Skirting the details of how he obtained the information, Tom told him what he had uncovered about the Lasky studio using Normand to divert press attention from Minter.

The big man tutted. 'I guess they have to protect their own. Maybe they're right to. I mean, what is this thing with Normand and Taylor? Why does she deny she was engaged to him, if she was?'

'Come on, Thad. They're movies. Maybe it was no more than fantasy to her. Or him, for that matter.'

'But he *was* banging her, right?' Sullivan's color was rising again, the frustration clear in his voice.

'From what I've heard, yes, almost certainly.'

'And Minter?'

Tom shrugged. 'Who can say? Everything I've heard says she was crazy for him. *Crazy* being the word. But there's no way of telling if he was feeling it back. Why so interested again?'

Sullivan sighed heavily. 'Woolwine's latest is Taylor could've been a homo. Secret, like. I mean, how crazy is that? But you know this Sands – the ex-valet, took Taylor to the cleaners? Well, Woolwine and Captain Adams put two and six together and got the hots for Sands blackmailing Taylor, then murdering him when he refused to cough. Except there's not a shred of evidence Sands has been back in town since he ran off. You know the guys at Lasky's, Tom. Ever hear anything about Taylor being a fairy?'

'No,' Tom laughed. 'Never a word. Until last night.'

Sullivan's eyes widened with anticipation, but Tom put his hand up. 'Don't get excited, old pal. It was one of a hundred stories, each one dumber than the last. Four days ago, no one had a word to say against Taylor. He was a living, breathing, exceptionally well-tailored saint. Now, if you listen enough, he was into every vice known to man: boozing, doping, gambling, pederasty, Crowleyism, bestiality – even had a thing for sniffing women's undersilks, according to some. You name it, all of a sudden Taylor wasn't just into it, he wrote the goddamn guide book for it.'

Thad snorted. 'It's the same for us. Every time we speak to someone new, the story changes. One guy swore on his life Taylor only went with men. When I told him we tracked down a wife and child Taylor abandoned in New York, he didn't bat an eyelid. "Well, we all know why he left them, then" was all he said, and flapped his goddamn wrist at me. I'm telling you, the more we hear, the less we actually know. I'm beginning to think we might never get at the truth.'

'Not unless . . .' Tom trailed off. A glint of sunlight on the sea, a tiny sail tacking in the distance, drew his gaze further west and an image bloomed in his mind of Nita Naldi's milk-white haunch, and Fay and June Mathis deep in conversation on the set of *Blood and Sand*.

'Not unless what?' Sullivan said impatiently.

But Tom was already getting out of his chair, knocking back the last of his whiskey, reaching out to Sullivan, pulling him to his feet.

'Listen, Thad, I know I said I wouldn't ask any more favors, but this could be important. Can you call Central for me? Get them to dig out an address I need?'

THIRTY-SIX

The road trailed off into a jagged expanse of rocks, red earth and brush. Tom stopped and scanned the rising ground to either side. Searching for evidence of a track or habitation. But there was nothing. The only thing to do was reverse the Dodge to a point where he could turn without busting the wheel springs. Doing so, he caught a flash of alien white in the sunlight. It looked like the painted upright of a signpost twenty yards behind. Sure enough, that's what it was, complete with a hanging arrow snapped off and pointing directly down at the loosened dirt below. He tilted his head and read aloud what he had been looking for.

← Casa Duende ½ mile

Five minutes later, he crested a rise and below saw the white walls and terracotta rooftiles of a lone old hacienda situated in an oasis of lush green land nestled in the head of the canyon below.

He pulled up in a wide and shady stone-paved courtyard. The cool air hit his skin as soon as he stepped down, a welcome relief. Large-leaved trees and palms cast great gouts of shadow randomly across the rough-hewn slabs. Sprays of purple, pink, red and orange blossoms beckoned and blushed from beds laid out at the back of narrow strips of well-watered grass. Even the ivy looked carefully arranged, straggling up the rough white stucco facade towards a pretty second-floor balcony, the dark wood rail overrun by honeysuckle.

Tom approached the iron-studded oak door, but before he got a hand on the black bell-pull, it opened and a short, gray-haired woman emerged. Close up, she was not as old as he remembered. In her late fifties at most, a face youthful other than a wide, thin-lipped mouth that wrinkled at the corners. She had shears in one hand, a watering can in the other, and beneath a soiled canvas apron that covered most of her clothing, she wore a well-worn dress. Once it would have matched exactly the pale blue of the eyes staring intently up at him.

'Mrs Ivers?'

She nodded, more formal than friendly. 'Mr Collins?' Not so much a question as an assertion of fact. Her clear, confident voice again threw doubt on his assessment of her age.

'Yes, like I said on the telephone, I need some information about Mr Taylor. I know you and he were good friends, and—'

'Just a moment, Mr Collins,' Mrs Ivers cut across him. A note of agitation in her voice did not bode well. 'Before you proceed further, I would like to get something straight. When you telephoned, you led me to believe you were an associate of Mr Charles Eyton's and that you were making your investigations on his behalf. Which, I can assure you, is the only reason I agreed to let you come out here to my home. But I have spoken with Mr Eyton since, and he informs me that you are certainly no employee of his, that he dismissed you six months ago, and that I should have nothing whatsoever to do with you. So unless you have a very good explanation why you lied to me, I will have to ask you to turn around and remove yourself from my property.'

Wrong-footed, Tom scrambled to remember exactly what he had said to Mrs Ivers on the telephone but couldn't see where he had gone wrong. That Bushmills of Sullivan's was still working on him when he had called but, even so, he would never have been dumb enough to lie to her about working for Eyton.

'I–I really don't understand, Mrs Ivers. If I misled you in any way, I apologize. That wasn't my intention. I know you work with

Mr Eyton over at Lasky. I mentioned the connection only to introduce myself. I never meant to imply that I work for him now, and
I'm sorry if I gave you that impression because we really haven't
been on good terms since he let me go. But please believe me, I
have sound reasons for wanting to talk to you about Mr Taylor.'

'Are you working for a newspaper, Mr Collins? Is it some sala-
cious story that you are after?' Her voice was harsh and superior
now, and together with the pain he already had in his behind from
the dirt-road drive, the suggestion that he was here under false
pretences began to nettle him.

'Certainly not. Look, Mrs Ivers, I don't know how you got the
wrong end of the stick, and, like I said, I'm sorry if you got it from
me. The truth is I'm a private investigator working for an associate
of Mr Taylor's, in pursuit of which I have stupidly succeeded in
putting my own life at risk. The reason I'm standing here right now
is that I'm real keen to stay alive. Now, I know that is no concern
of yours, but someone told me yesterday that you knew Mr Taylor
better than anyone, and I just thought you could help me clear up
a couple of things. That's the honest-to-God reason I've dragged
myself all the way out here on this fine Sunday afternoon. If you
don't believe me, or don't want to help me, then I'll turn around
and take myself out of here just as soon as you say. But that is the
truth of it, and I would be very grateful, and relieved, if you would
talk to me.'

She stood in the doorway, making no move to close it. 'That's
most intriguing, Mr Collins. I'm not sure I could come up with a
more enthralling movie scenario myself.'

'That's real nice of you, Mrs Ivers, but, believe me, nobody could
wish more than me that this was not real life. Apart from Mr Taylor,
maybe.'

It was a low blow, he knew, but it struck home. She flushed to
her high hairline and immediately dropped her gaze to the floor,
blinking rapidly. He stood there, staring at her, wanting her to feel
it keenly. It took her a good half-minute to regain her composure.

'You do an impressive line in truth-telling, Mr Collins.'

'Excuse me?' Awaiting another insult, he didn't recognize her
compliment for what it was.

'You're the one Charlie sacked over Roscoe Arbuckle, aren't you?
I thought I recognized your name.'

Tom felt the confidence drain out of him. There was no way she would let him in now.

'There was a little more to it than just Mr Arbuckle, ma'am. But yes, it was around that time Mr Eyton let me go.'

She looked him in the eye, steadily, the blue of her gaze as piercing and authoritative as a searchlight. 'I don't require details, Mr Collins. But I do recall Bill saying he thought you were shabbily treated. So, in his memory alone, I suppose I should give you a hearing.'

That was the second time in two days that his name and Taylor's had been connected. He never thought, as gossip-ridden as all studios were, that his sacking would have been noticed, let alone a cause for comment by the likes of this woman and Taylor. But he wasn't going to let that get in his way, so he kept his mouth shut and waited.

'And now you've taken an interest in Bill's death,' she said. 'Don't you think we should leave the investigating to the police department?'

'They haven't done a great job of it so far, have they?'

Somehow it was enough. She smiled weakly at him and patted the back of her hair, still unable fully to meet his gaze.

'Very well, Mr Collins.'

She turned and entered the house, making no further invitation. Inside was a high, airy vestibule that rose two floors to a dark wood ceiling supported by carved beams. From the centermost an ancient, black iron chandelier hung on thick chains, its cartwheel fitment a good eight feet across, its outer rim bearing a garland of electric light bulbs. The room was sparsely but gracefully decorated, the walls of rough white plaster interrupted by a vast framed portrait of a proud old Californio striking a military pose. Mrs Ivers was a woman of taste as well as substance.

'You've certainly got a beautiful place here, Mrs Ivers. Driving that final stretch, I wondered how you get the water here to keep everything so green. You can't have it pumped all the way out here?'

She turned to him, smiling again, her defensiveness banished.

'No, indeed. We are blessed in having a subterranean watercourse running beneath this hill on which we sit. We take water from it year round. Otherwise, it would be quite impossible. It is a gift from the Lord for someone with a passion for growing and tending plants, as I have. It was why I fell in love with the house, which was rather dilapidated when I took it on. But the prospect of all that life-giving water in the barrenness around, it was irresistible. Do you like to garden, Mr Collins?'

'I think I would, Mrs Ivers. But in my scrap of yard over in West Lake, weeds are all that're dumb enough to survive.'

He got the smile he expected for that and was considering how to turn it to his advantage when Mrs Ivers's thoughts converged with his own.

'I'm sure you want to get down to business, Mr Collins. I had thought to conduct it here, but perhaps it would be more pleasant to go out on the terrace, where you can enjoy more of my gardens.'

She led him through a wide doorway that opened on to a court-yard bordered on three sides by wide, shady arcades, cooled by a three-tier fountain tinkling at its center and crowded with the same profusion of pots and flowers as out front. But it was the open fourth side that took his breath away, framing a magnificent view of a green canyon running down to the glittering Pacific a mile or so in the distance. He had not realized the journey had taken him so high into the hills, or so far west.

'Bill loved it here,' Mrs Ivers said, wistful. 'He would sit for hours, working, talking, sipping tea and staring out. He said it was like being gifted a glimpse of eternity. He had such an appreciation of subtlety. But then, I think you Irish have a more emotional response to the ocean than most.'

'Maybe because the sea only ever brought us enemies or exile, Mrs Ivers.'

She liked that, and he felt she was warming to him. Maybe it wouldn't be a wasted journey after all.

'Will you sit down, Mr Collins, and take some tea?'

He sat and stared out across the ocean, struggling to wrest his mind back from the enchantment of his surroundings. Mrs Ivers struck a small gong on the table before them and a Chinese houseboy, done up in immaculate starched whites, appeared from nowhere, running, to take her very precise instruction on the tea he was to bring to them. The boy ran off again.

'I might as well tell you, Mrs Ivers, I am truly desperate to find someone who can help me out. As I said, I'm pretty sure Mr Taylor's death is connected to another matter I'm investigating. But so many people say so many different things about him, I feel I'm going round in circles. I thought maybe you might set me back on the right track.'

'I'll do what I can, Mr Collins, but I'm sure you won't expect me to break any confidences.'

They parried like this, falling over each other with politeness, laying out the rules for a while, until Tom got tired of it and went in for it straight.

'Look, Mrs Ivers, I wouldn't want to shock you, but . . .' He paused to get his words right, and she mistook it for a continuation of the game.

'Please go on, Mr Collins, and you needn't worry about shocking me. Nothing could shock me more than the sight of my dear friend Bill lying white as a sheet on the floor of his apartment last Thursday morning. It was an effort to make myself believe he was dead. He might as well have been asleep.'

He wondered if he hadn't misheard her and had to bite his tongue as the houseboy arrived with the tea on a bamboo tray and silence reigned while Mrs Ivers fussed over warming the cups before pouring the tea. But eventually it was done, and he put the question to her. 'You mean to say you were present when Mr Taylor was discovered?'

She nodded, seemingly unaware of the import of what she was saying. 'Well, not exactly then, of course. It was his boy, Peavey, who found him, and Doug and Faith MacLean and others from the court. But we arrived soon afterwards, before any police. You see, I was staying over with my son, Jimmy, in his apartment around the corner from Alvarado – I sometimes do that if my work at the studio keeps me late. Well, it seems Mr MacLean telephoned Charlie Eyton, and Charlie telephoned Jimmy and asked us to hurry round to Bill's, to ensure there was nothing embarrassing or compromising lying around. Like liquor, letters – anything the newspapers might whip up scandal with. I suppose Charlie knew the MacLeans would be required to stay on by the police. You must understand, Mr Collins, at that stage we all thought Bill had died of heart failure, or some other natural cause. That's certainly how it appeared. There was no sign whatsoever of a disturbance. He looked so peaceful, lying there on the carpet.'

She paused, brushed a hand across the tip of her nose, before continuing. 'It sounds so shocking now we know he was murdered. But ever since Mr Arbuckle was arrested, that's how it is in the movie business. Everyone is simply obsessed with scandal. Even the police department cannot be trusted. They sell everything they find to the newspapers, with no regard for how it might be interpreted or whom it will hurt. So, you see, upset as we were, all we wanted was to protect Bill's reputation. Jimmy went upstairs to see what he could find while I gathered what letters and bottles of spirits were downstairs. We were leaving with them as the first policeman pulled up on Alvarado.'

'And he didn't see you? They never found out about this?'

'Well, I don't know, exactly. Later, when we saw in the paper that Bill had been murdered, I became concerned. I contacted Charlie again and he spoke to the District Attorney's office and had everything we removed from the house delivered to them. Charlie said he begged them to be discreet, and I suppose they must have been because I have heard nothing about it since.'

Tom cursed to himself and recalled what Sullivan had said about the right hand not knowing what the left hand was doing. Eyton must have got to Woolwine and called in a few favors. One thing was for sure: the DA's office wasn't passing all the info down to the cops on the ground. Looking up, he noticed Mrs Ivers wipe a tear from her eye, and wondered what else she knew but wasn't telling.

'Do you have any idea who might have wanted to kill Mr Taylor, ma'am? A lot of folk are saying it was Mabel Normand. Would she have had reason, that you know of?'

Mrs Ivers stiffened visibly, and the look of skepticism came galloping back across her features. 'That's all newspaper trash. Why would you even repeat it?'

'Well, I would hardly be the first. One of the reasons I came here was to clear up a doubt over Miss Normand.'

'What doubt?' she snapped. 'What possible reason could Miss Normand have had for wanting to hurt Bill? He was entirely devoted to her.'

Tom, surprised by the ferocity of her conviction, saw how to use it.

'That was the impression I got, too, Mrs Ivers. But there are so many shocking stories coming out. Most of them contradictory. I mean, can you believe someone told me yesterday that Miss Normand had got herself with child. And that she turned to dope afterwards, because she was forced to get rid of it. The suggestion was it had been Mr Taylor's child.'

Mrs Ivers paled, regarding Tom with a cold anger crackling in her eyes. 'Who told you that?'

'It doesn't matter who told me. The question is whether it's true or not.'

'I have never heard anything so preposterous in my life.'

Her voice faltered slightly and he searched her face for signs of doubt.

'Haven't you, Mrs Ivers? That's a real shame. Because I was also told that you were the source of this story and more about how Miss Normand acquired her hop habit.'

Tom gave her his hardest, most disappointed stare, and in return saw the first flicker of uncertainty in her eyes before she turned away from him.

'Look, my position is very simple, Mrs Ivers. I don't believe Miss Normand had anything to do with Mr Taylor's murder. Leastways, not intentionally. In fact, I'm convinced she had nothing to do with it. But so long as she could have had any motive what-soever, such as having her life or career ruined by Mr Taylor, she can't be ruled out. Certainly, that's the view the cops are taking, and if the only way I can get to the truth is by passing this informa-tion on to them, then I will have no choice but to do that.'

He let it sink in a moment, watched her chew her bottom lip as she glared out towards the ocean, tears welling in her eyes.

'The reason I came here was to avoid that, Mrs Ivers, because if it is not true, that line of inquiry will be a big waste of police time. And it would be an even bigger shame to draw Miss Normand further under suspicion, and to have such a delicate part of her life exposed to public scrutiny. It wouldn't surprise me if you found a troop of detectives on your doorstep too, asking awkward questions of you and your son. I'm sure Mr Taylor would not have wanted that.'

He knew he had taken it to the limit, but he didn't want to leave with nothing. He could smell the truth hanging like the scent of lilacs in the air. It was here, he was sure of it.

In the event, he hadn't even got halfway out of his chair before she put out an arm to stop him. Her thoughts were way back behind her eyes now. He'd seen it often in precinct houses, the blankness of deep decision-making that presages a confession. He waited a beat, two, and then it came, heralded by a deep exhalation of breath.

'Very well, Mr Collins, perhaps you are right. Perhaps, I should help you. For Bill's sake, if not my own. But, please, promise me that none of this will reach the newspapers. You must assure me of that, at least.'

THIRTY-SEVEN

For years, Mrs Ivers said, she had acted as confidante to Taylor, working with him closely ever since the movie company her late husband founded for her was taken over by Adolph Zukor and absorbed into Famous Players-Lasky. As an experienced scenario writer, she had recognized in Taylor a true nobility of character and the potential for creative vigor. With her help, he gained his first job as a director in 1915, and she had worked with him ever since, forming a bond that, she admitted, went beyond the role of mentor – caring for him when he was unwell, as he often was with nervous exhaustion, and talking, always talking, loving him as a spiritual, artistic soulmate.

'Such a rarity this side of the continent,' she sighed.

As far as Tom could tell, hers had not been a romantic love. She expressed nothing but admiration for the women Taylor had been involved with. The suggestion that he had relations with men, she said, was risible. Of course, he knew such men – who in Hollywood does not? – yet it was entirely characteristic of him to befriend them as he would any others. At the same time, she was convinced no woman would have shot him. He had such a keen understanding of the female psyche, she said. And Mary Miles Minter had, indeed, become hopelessly infatuated with him.

'The poor child confused Bill's paternal, professional interest for some *grand amour* fantasy of her own invention,' Mrs Ivers explained. 'Mary could not be blamed – brought up by that witch of a mother only to work, never to know anything remotely like love, fed an unvarying diet of crude ambition and moving-picture fantasy. No wonder she mistook what Bill was offering. He was a fifty-year-old man for heaven's sake, and she barely nineteen. What could she seriously hope would happen? No, Bill felt sympathy for her, but that was all.'

'Some people are saying the mother shot Taylor to prevent him from taking the girl away,' Tom said.

'No, that is impossible. Her mother was far more concerned about that young director fellow, James Kirkwell. You must know him.'

'Jimmy Kirkwood?'

'Yes, Kirkwood, that's it,' Mrs Ivers corrected herself. 'And rightly so, to my mind, because not so long ago Mary did actually threaten to run off and marry *him*. Until her mother got wind of the plan and put a stop to it. Not with a pistol either, Mr Collins, but with a telegram to Mr Zukor threatening a suit if he didn't act promptly to protect Mary from the young hound. Naturally, one word from Zukor was more effective in damping his ardor than any gun blast. Poor Mary, abandoned, found Mr Taylor a consoling presence and clutched at him instead. Bill, understandably, was horrified.'

She stopped and flushed a little at that, not quite sure whether she'd said the right thing. Tom took a surreptitious look at his wristwatch. This was sounding more like movieland gossip than he had hoped for. He felt Mrs Ivers's gaze shift on to him again and met it. She smiled apologetically.

'I'm sorry, Mr Collins. I'm rambling. You must forgive me.' She swept her arm past the panorama laid out before them. 'For all its beauty, this house can get lonely sometimes. You desired to know about Miss Normand.'

'Yes, that in particular.'

'Well, with Miss Normand I'm certain Bill was convinced he had found contentment. They made an unlikely couple, but I believe he loved her. What she felt for him, I cannot say. But he had hopes that his feelings were returned. The difficulty was the poison she insisted on running through her veins.'

'He told you about that?'

'Oh yes. According to Bill, she could be a fiery inferno of passion one day, then cold as ice the next.'

'Because of the dope? He told you about her problems with it?'

'Well, it is hardly a secret, Mr Collins. Everyone in the business knows it, do they not?' There was an edge to her voice again now.

'Well, I guess it was strongly rumored. But did Mr Taylor tell you why she had the problem in the first place. Is it true about the baby?'

Mrs Ivers flinched perceptibly but seemed determined to go on. 'Please, you must not tell a soul, but yes, according to what Bill confided to me, Miss Normand did have trouble of that kind. But it was some time ago and the child most certainly was not his. He said it occurred two or three years before they met, when she was working back East, and that she had been destroyed by it. Body and soul. It seems the man who performed the operation was more butcher than doctor, and she suffered horribly in the months succeeding. For a woman whose life was all for laughter, it must have been intolerable. Apparently, a theatrical acquaintance told her that cocaine would take the pain away. And it did. But it threatened to take her soul away, too.'

Mrs Ivers pressed the back of her hand to her lips briefly before continuing. 'Bill confided in me that Miss Normand confessed her dependency on this narcotic shortly after they became intimate, and begged him to try everything in his power to save her from its grip. Naturally, he did all he could. He believed that helping her overcome it was the only chance they had for happiness together. For a time he even believed that she had conquered it. Until he found evidence that she had lapsed and was more in thrall to it than ever. He was greatly downcast by the discovery. But Bill was such a very generous, loyal, courageous man. He would have paid any price to bring about her cure. And it appears he paid the highest. The dear man lost his life because of it.'

A tear spilled down her cheek, and Tom reached out and placed a hand lightly on the back of hers. 'You're not suggesting she shot him?'

'No, as I said before—'

'But you are saying you think his murder had something to do with the dope?'

She sniffled, searching in her shirt cuff for a handkerchief with which she politely dabbed her nose. 'Surely it must be entirely likely. He had a number of confrontations with her wretched supplier, and though I understand violence was exchanged between them at one point, I also know Bill believed he was getting somewhere with the man. But then someone else became involved.'

'Someone else?' Tom hardly dared draw a breath, willing her to go on.

She nodded, then dabbed at her nose again. 'Someone higher up. Some more powerful peddler. A bootlegger. Don't ask me who or how, because Bill never shared that information with me. He said that events had moved on. That it had got somehow bigger, but I never heard in what way. That was a week ago, ten days at most. All I know is that he was very excited when I last spoke to him on the telephone. Triumphant almost, saying something about ridding the studio of "parasites", but how, exactly, he didn't say.'

'The studio?'

'Yes, that is what he said. Next I heard of him, he was dead.'

She plucked at her shirt cuff again, and her tears began to flow, this time in earnest. Tom found no words to comfort her, but her sobbing did not last. Her dignity quickly reasserted itself. His attempts to probe further about what Taylor meant regarding the studio were unsuccessful.

'Didn't you think the police should know about this?' he asked eventually.

'But of course,' she replied, embarrassment turning to chagrin. 'Charlie Eyton offered to see to it, as he had with the letters and liquor. But this time I insisted on going to the District Attorney's office in person, and so he came with me. I repeated everything Bill had said regarding the narcotics peddlers, but I felt they didn't lend me much credence. I was assured the information would be passed to the investigating officers, but they sent me away feeling like a silly old woman making a fuss over nothing. Even after I told them about Leon Mazaroff.'

'Mazaroff, you say?' Tom looked up. That was the man Chuck Havers had so gleefully maligned the night before in the lobby at the Alexandria.

'Yes, do you know Leon?' Mrs Ivers delivered this inquiry with the same soft smile she had adopted when reminiscing about Taylor.

'Only by reputation,' Tom replied. 'How does he come into it?'

'Well, Leon had a most troubling encounter with Bill, not so long ago.'

'Troubling, how?' Tom's head was beginning to spin. He'd been talking to Mrs Ivers for over an hour, and now she was hitting him with all the good stuff in the space of a couple of minutes. 'I'm not sure I follow. Was this to do with narcotics?'

She spread her hands, her expression one of genteel mystification. 'Well, I don't know it exactly myself. Leon said a man behaved in a most threatening manner towards Bill. Out in Griffith Park. He was disturbed by it at the time, I know. Then when Leon heard poor Bill was dead, he was very shaken indeed. He is still not quite recovered.'

'Really?' Tom could barely contain himself, wondering if and why Sullivan might have held out on him over this information. Or whether, as seemed more likely, none of it had been passed on to detectives. 'Did Mr Mazaroff get a good look at this guy, then?'

'Well, yes, I assume so. He was right there in front of them. But why not ask him yourself? Come, I will call him and you can speak with him.'

She was up and out of her seat before he could say anything further, retreating indoors. Tom would want to talk to this Mazaroff all right. He might be the only man able to point a finger at the killer. But not over the telephone. Face to face was the best way with this kind of thing. He rose and followed Mrs Ivers into the house, but she was nowhere to be seen. He searched one room after another until he finally found her clutching the telephone in a well-stocked library – the sort that looks as if the books were bought by the yard. Mrs Ivers had already cranked the machine and was speaking into the mouthpiece.

'Leon, darling, yes, did you succeed in getting some rest? . . . Excellent, that must be a relief. My dear, do you think you could come up to the house, please? Yes, to me. There is a gentleman visiting me whom I believe you should meet. Don't go worrying now, it is quite safe.'

THIRTY-EIGHT

M r Leon Mazaroff, actor, dancer, formerly of somewhere deep in the frozen wastes of Russia, was indeed right on hand. He being the current occupant of Casa Duende's 'little cabana', as Mrs Ivers described it while pointing a bony finger out the library window at a guesthouse, half hidden amid exotic foliage further down the gardens, that looked twice the size of his own small home.

While they waited for him to walk up to the house, Mrs Ivers informed Tom that ever since the news broke of Taylor's murder, Mazaroff, a regular visitor, had been nervous of returning to his own quarters, an apartment he rented in Echo Park. Appreciating that, as a dancer and player of rare artistry, Mr Mazaroff was not one for the rough and tumble of life, she had insisted he stay under her roof for as long as he considered necessary.

'Leonid Mazaroff, allow me to introduce you to Mr Tom Collins,' Mrs Ivers said grandly as he walked into the room. He was a smallish man, mid-height but short on flesh, with a long nose that flared wide at the base on a face so thin it could haunt. His black hair was worn longer than was fashionable, and his clothes – a tweed suit and plain white shirt with some kind of neckerchief underneath – were cut rather looser than was usual. Tom could believe he was a dancer. Every step he took looked like it was individually weighed.

'Mr Collins is a private investigator looking into poor Bill's murder, Leon. I thought it might help for you to speak with him. He seems to think it possible that Bill was shot by dope fiends, as we suspected.'

Tom stuck out his hand and Mazaroff, looking none too certain of the safety of this gesture, extended his for a surprisingly firm shake.

'Mrs Ivers tells me you witnessed someone making threats to Mr Taylor out in Griffith Park. Is that right?'

'Yes, that is correct.' The voice was thick with the land of his birth and Tom had to lean in nearer to understand. 'We work in

Griffith Park last month, re-filming scenes for one of Mr Taylor's productions. We took a break, to talk about Chekov.'

'Chekov?'

'A great Russian writer,' Mazaroff said impatiently, wafting a withering sideways glance to Mrs Ivers. 'No matter. For some minutes we walk away from others along a trail, not so far, when a man jumped out from behind bushes. So sudden, you know, it was frightening. Yes. And he stands there and says nothing, does nothing, but looks hard at Mr Taylor. Like I say, frightening.'

Tom got the picture, but it wasn't making much sense to him. 'He didn't make any threat or gesture?'

Mazaroff shook his head. 'No.'

'And you never saw him before? Not at the studio, or hanging round the shoot?'

'No, I never saw him before. He was not a movie type. But Mr Taylor, he knows him, for sure. I know from the eyes, the way they look at each other, they are thinking bad things, dangerous things. You know how I mean?'

'Sure, I think so,' Tom said, picturing the scene entirely. 'So what happened?'

'Nothing more. It is most exceptional. One minute – less – they stand, stare, no speaking. Then this man, he turns and walks away, back towards town. Mr Taylor takes my arm and turns me quickly, you know, and we go back to the camp, hurry, hurry. I ask Mr Taylor what is happening, but he does not explain. I worry, so later, when we finish, I ask him again. But he tells me, don't be concerned. "We will not be deterred by dirty dope peddlers." His exact words. Then, when I hear Mr Taylor was killed, I think of this again, and worry again.'

Mazaroff threw up his arms for emphasis, but Tom had already figured from his expressions during the story that he wasn't using them for empty dramatic effect. The Russian was telling the truth as far as he could tell.

He pushed himself off the desk and paced out a step or two, thinking hard. Mrs Ivers, meanwhile, gave Mazaroff's arm a reassuring squeeze.

'Do you think it could be relevant, Mr Collins?'

'Yes, I do, Mrs Ivers. I certainly do. But I think it's too big for me to handle, so here's what I can do. I have a good friend on the detective squad who I'm certain will be very keen to hear this. If Mr Mazaroff will come downtown with me now, I will—'

But Mazaroff was already saying no, getting excited, and Mrs Ivers was shushing him and calming him and assuring him he wouldn't have to go anywhere he didn't want to. Finally seeing him settled in a chair, Mrs Ivers turned and looked at Tom with pleading eyes.

'You will not force him if he does not want to.'

'Look, I'm sorry, Mrs Ivers, but the cops really need to be told this. It is irresponsible to keep such important information from them, for any reason, even fear. There is a murderer on the loose.'

Mrs Ivers and Mazaroff gave Tom the combined force of two blank stares before exchanging glance between themselves. It was she who spoke up.

'But Mr Mazaroff has already informed the authorities, only to be accorded the same response that I received.'

Tom looked at her, unable to believe his ears.

'The DA's office again?'

'Well, yes, of course. I thought Leon's evidence might make them think again about what I had told them. But they dismissed it. Said there had been no threat, and that it was most likely some hobo or tramp who stumbled across their path by accident. Leon was most offended. Weren't you, my dear?'

Tom wasn't sure Mazaroff entirely understood, but he got the gist of it.

'I know difference between tramp and threat, between drunk man and dangerous man. This man was very frightening. Even how he walk is bad.'

Tom froze. 'What was unusual about how he walked?'

'One of the legs did not work good. It pulled on the ground, you know?'

'Like a wounded animal,' Mrs Ivers ventured. 'That's how Leon described it to me, Mr Collins.'

'Wait, I show.' Mazaroff jumped up from his seat again and mimed the distinctive perambulatory action of the assailant.

'You're one hell of an actor, Mr Mazaroff,' Tom said, his mind spinning. 'You've got that off to a tee.'

THIRTY-NINE

N ight was full down by the time he left, but the moon was bright and Tom had no trouble making his way quickly back to the canyon road. Fifteen minutes later, he was on San Vicente, heading towards the city at a clip, thoughts turning over fast as the engine now. Had Sullivan been trying to protect him again? Their conversation earlier about Devlin's old ally Mikey Ross had seemed confined to the realm of dreams and banter. But Leon Mazaroff's vivid little mime had changed all that. So chillingly precise, it hadn't so much persuaded him as knocked him off his feet.

Ross really could be in Los Angeles.

The more thought he gave it, the more it made sense. Sullivan had even put it into words earlier. Devlin and Ross. Rubbing together like two limbs of the same beast. Ross always worked under Devlin's protection and instructions. A machine, a meat grinder. Because Devlin was the smarter, the stronger, you could see him moving away. Moving on. And where better than Los Angeles, booming bigger than any other city in America thanks to oil, land speculation and the movies? Compared with New York, mired in layer upon layer of competing corruption, this was virgin territory, ripe for the plucking. Devlin would never be dumb enough to think he could do it alone.

But what could be their link to Taylor?

The streets were no more than a blur now, his foot on the gas, the sparse late-Sunday traffic yielding to his urgency. Lights and streetlamps were liquid trails of color as San Vicente melted into Wilshire and the built-up boulevards and avenues of downtown beckoned. Tom's thoughts surged, too. Mrs Ivers said Taylor told her he thought he was getting somewhere with Normand's supplier, until someone bigger got involved. A bootlegger, she'd said. Tom assumed that was Cornero, and the man himself had seemed to suggest it out on the pier. Said he'd been forced to take matters in hand. But he also said there was a whole lot more to it, too.

What if Taylor had been talking about someone else entirely? Someone new on the scene, who had already stolen Normand's custom away? Maybe she found herself a new supplier, even kept it from her driver, Davis, who she must have known was in Taylor's pay already? Sure, it was a heck of a leap from there to a terrifying encounter with Mikey Ross in Griffith Park. But how many other explanations were there?

No more than a million or so, Tom reckoned, pushing the idea away. Ahead, he spotted the yellow swag-like chains of electric bulbs picking out the block-deep driveway leading in to the Ambassador Hotel. He checked his wristwatch and decided to drive on. He had thirty minutes to get back home and telephone Sullivan to tell him what he'd uncovered. Plenty of time left to freshen up and grab the note he took from J.J. Fine's office, then double back to the Ambassador to meet with Sennett. Last time for a while, with any luck.

The thought of Sullivan's jaw dropping to the floor on hearing Mazaroff's story made Tom smile as he turned the Dodge on to Coronado. A grin wiped away in a trice when he spotted a Big Six parked outside his house.

What now?

He pulled in to the curb a couple of houses back, let his head-lamps linger on the machine in front. Not one he knew – a shiny new Studebaker, canopy down, empty. He cut his engine, anger mounting as he became aware of a crack of light seeping through the drapes in his front window.

Someone was in his house. That auto was too good for a house-breaker. Not for the mob, though. Which could only mean Cornero had sent his trouble boys round for an update. Damn their eyes if they thought they could march into his home any time they liked.

Tom jumped down, ready to go in swinging. A touch of the Studebaker's hot hood told him his visitor was recently arrived. Inside, there was nothing to give a clue to its ownership, but a heavy hickory ball bat in the rear footwell did not bode well. Tom stepped through the gate as quietly as he could, a colder kind of rage grip-ping his stomach when he saw the front door all stove-in and hanging from its hinges. Why the hell did they go and do that?

It was a move dumb enough to make him hesitate and put a clamp on his temper. Some nagging instinct of self-preservation made him hold back. If they hadn't felt the need to smash his door down before, why would they now? When he had already agreed to work with them. It made no sense. He forced himself to cut away instead across the small patch of dirt that was his front yard and peer in through the crack of bright yellow in the drapes. The little he could see was enough to leave him dumbstruck.

Bent over the sideboard, searching with such concentration that the burned-out cigar butt between his lips stood almost erect, was not one of Cornero's apes but a man he had seen just once before. In the same gray trench coat and trilby he'd worn at the inquest, it was Sullivan's colleague from the detective squad, Gab Ramirez. Tom shifted position for a clearer view and saw the plundered contents of his cupboards strewn around Ramirez's feet. Again, a pang of violation twisted his gut, but the impulse to protest was stayed when Ramirez glanced up in response to a shouted summons from elsewhere in the house. There were two of them in there.

'You got something?' Ramirez asked and got a muffled response.

Tom watched him turn as though someone else was entering the room. Shifting his position again, he peered from the other angle now and felt the blood slow in his veins. There in the parlor doorway, taking up most of it, was Al Devlin, all done up in his Port Inspector's uniform.

Under one arm he carried the steamer trunk from beneath Tom's bed, cradling it in the crook of his elbow like a toddler's toy box. He thumped it down on the table and called Ramirez over as he flipped the lid open, dug a hand in and removed with the tips of his fat fingers a long-barreled revolver. The window glass was cheap enough for Tom to make out every word that followed, though he could probably have made up most of it himself.

'The slugs they dug out of Madden were thirty-eights, right?' Devlin said with conviction. 'I'll give you any odds this is the iron that fired them.'

As he watched Devlin hand the gun over to Ramirez, a glint of gunmetal under the parlor lamp sparked a memory of a long barrel poking out into the wet night from the rear window of a Packard. As set-ups went, it was a doozie. The gun was an old, six-inch Police Positive, just like the one Tom was issued with back in New York, and had handed back when he left the police department. There were tens of thousands of Positives in circulation, but Ramirez would believe the evidence presented before his eyes, even though the gun couldn't have been in the trunk five minutes. He saw Devlin smirk as Ramirez snapped open the cylinder breach and held it up to his nose.

'Couple of days, most, since it was fired,' Ramirez said obligingly.

Sure enough, Tom was being trussed up like a turkey. At a guess, Devlin had contacted Ramirez and not only convinced him to have Tom picked up, but offered to help him do so, personally. Maybe he'd even bypassed Ramirez and gone straight to the DA's office for a warrant, then forced Ramirez to execute it for procedure's sake and ensure he had an unimpeachable witness to the discovery of the planted gun. But how had he convinced Ramirez, or the DA, that Madden's murder was any of his concern?

Tom turned his attention back to the conversation, the subject now being where the fugitive Collins might be found. Devlin was taking a little too much delight in suggesting that Thad Sullivan was probably up to his neck in it and harboring his old pal.

'Not a chance,' Ramirez said, bristling at the suggestion. 'Sullivan is straight as an arrow. One of the men in the squad we can absolutely depend on. If you knew him like I do, you'd know that already.'

'That's not how he was when we had Collins in custody,' Devlin scowled, but said nothing about knowing Sullivan better than Ramirez knew.

'Anything else in there might give us an idea?' Ramirez asked, motioning towards the trunk. Devlin tutted dismissively and shoved it across the table to him. He'd never been one for paper trails. Words were too much trouble. Instead, he rumbled over to the disembowelled dresser, studying the framed old lady on the wall beside it. Then, with more interest, the inscribed portrait of Fay.

'Any idea who the whore is?' Devlin said over his shoulder. 'Collins always fancied himself a ladies' man.'

Ramirez glanced over at the picture, then at Devlin, his eyes narrowed as if there was something wrong with that remark.

'You know him so well?'

Devlin, realizing he'd said too much, stared Ramirez down. 'Do you know her or not?'

'Some two-bit starlet, I guess,' he shrugged. 'Enough of 'em about.'

But Devlin wasn't letting it go. He plucked the photo frame from the dresser, studying it closely. Tom felt the bile rise in his stomach as Devlin's eyes greedily roamed the contours of Fay's features, his spittle-flecked lips mouthing the inscription: 'For my dearest Tom, forever yours, Fay.'

It wasn't until Devlin flipped the frame in his hands, his fat stubs of fingers scrabbling to undo the pins and remove the backboard, that consternation set in. It was a publicity shot taken for distribution to the press, not adoring fans. Stamped on the back of the print were Fay's name and studio details, the address of the Oasis and the telephone number of her publicity man should further interest be expressed. Further interest? No way could he let Devlin get sight of that.

To make matters worse, in that moment he saw Ramirez dig his fingers in the trunk and pull out the very papers he had come back to retrieve for Sennett. Surely they couldn't mean anything to him? But with the Lasky studio letterhead on them, and a telegram from Adolph Zukor dated just a couple of days earlier, they were sure to grab Ramirez's interest. And so they did.

He had to do something.

As Devlin's fingers pulled Fay's picture from the frame and Ramirez's brow furrowed over the telegram, Tom cast about wildly for something – anything – with which to cause a distraction. But there was nothing, only dirt and weeds, within reach. All he could do was rap his knuckles on the windowpane and roar through the glass at the top of his voice, 'Devlin, you've never been anything but a fat bastard crook, no matter what coast you're on, or what uniform you wear.'

Inside, he saw the two men stiffen in unison, then react – Ramirez making for the window, Devlin for the door. Tom had barely made it out the gate before Devlin barreled out, bellowing like a bull moose, fragments of the smashed doorframe flying as his bulk burst through it, into the night.

Tom stood still, stared him dead in the eyes, just long enough for Devlin to cast the photograph aside as he went for his gun, fat fingers fumbling with the holster catch. Then he ran. Ran with Devlin's apoplectic roars ringing in his ears. Ran like he'd never run before, with the zip and rip of a bullet whipping past, the crack of discharge sounding fractionally behind. He ran zigzag into neighbors' gardens, vaulted picket fences, ducked behind shrubs, anything that would ruin Devlin's line of sight until he was beyond the range of a dependably fallible police revolver.

As he ran, he lost all sense of what was real. His fear was replaced by something cold and lonely, yet ecstatic. Glancing back, he saw Devlin in the growing distance behind, arms out, steadying himself to take another shot. Saw Ramirez hurtle on to the sidewalk and deliberately careen into the fat man, knocking his aim off, screaming at him to lower his weapon and cease firing. All Tom felt was the night air cold on his face as he sped down the hill towards the park on legs oblivious to fatigue. All he heard was the blood pounding in his heart and in his lungs, and the living city rushing past his ears like a locomotive.

All he knew was he was running.

FORTY

Reaching the broad thoroughfare of Sixth, he sprinted across through the sparse traffic and stumbled into the concealing vegetation of Westlake Park. He caught his breath in great gulps of fragrance-laden air, eyeing every vehicle and intersection to assure himself that he wasn't being pursued. The park boundaries appeared like a ring of pale fire, the surrounding street lamps and house lights delineating the gloom. Behind him, the lake glittered black in the moonlight, wavering reflections of small fires burning along its edge, a popular spot for hobos to congregate after dark. A good place to lie low for a while. But he didn't want to. Within the hour, every cop in the city might be looking for him. His house would be watched. He couldn't risk going back to grab the Dodge.

The spirit of defiance that possessed him back at the house abandoned him now as the enormity of what had happened opened up to him. That Devlin had been willing to shoot him brought a new clarity to his situation. As did Ramirez's desperate efforts to prevent it. In the wrangling confusion of his thoughts, two probabilities were blindingly clear. For whatever reason, Devlin was prepared to go to any lengths to frame him for Madden's murder. And if he ended up in a police cell in Los Angeles, there was a greater chance than ever that a confederate of Devlin's would ensure he didn't make it through the night.

He had to get in touch with Sullivan and fast. He needed to get to a telephone, but that didn't have to be a problem. He'd been on his way to see Sennett at the Ambassador, and there were plenty there. The booths in the lobby were too public to risk, but he was on good terms with the manager of the Cocoanut Grove supper club, Jimmy Manos. Whatever else he knew, Manos was no friend of the cops. He would be sure to help.

Dusting himself down, Tom set off across the park, heading for the exit on Seventh. Years spent getting movie folk out of trouble had taught him the quiet ways in and out of all the best places. So, keeping to the unlit streets, he made his way to the rear of the hotel, then in through a kitchen delivery door. It was a route he had used a year or so before, but in the opposite direction. Getting Tommy Meighan out quick after he thumped some bozo in the lobby over a girl. The memory was still strong enough to raise a smile as he negotiated the maze of the service basement, confident enough not to be challenged by staff.

Emerging into a mirrored hallway, his feet hit carpet and the syncopated beat of 'Wabash Blues' echoed in his ears. Sunday nights at the Grove were always busy, a last chance to blow off steam before the hard slog of living began for another week. Checking his reflection, he reckoned he just about cut the mustard. Most men in the place would be in evening rig, but seeing as how he would not be asking for a table, he could probably get away with it. He waited as the swallow-tailed head waiter snagged a money-dripping couple ahead, seeing them in personally. Slipping in unnoticed, he saw Manos leaning on the balustrade that separated the dining area from the dance floor, watching the dancing below.

'Hey, Jimmy,' he said, hoping to keep the hurry out of his voice.

'Tom.' Manos didn't turn or show a sign of having seen him come in. Wearing the best-cut dinner suit in the room, with dark good looks and hair slicked back to a patent leather shine, he liked it put about that Valentino based his Latin-lover look on him. Folk might have swallowed it if he hadn't been built like a blockhouse mauler, his girth unvarying from shoulder to knee. 'Good to see you, buddy. It's been a while.'

'Too long,' Tom agreed. 'Lasky's not paying the checks anymore.'

'Your credit's good here any time. You know that.'

On the bandstand, Abe Lyman and the boys were striking up 'April Showers' and couples were crowding on and off the dance floor, women glittering head to toe, men all stiff and starched. Tom eyed the room, the exuberance of the decor, from the sparkling night-sky ceiling and arabesque arches right down to the paper monkeys hanging from fake palm trees that Manos bought straight off the set of *The Sheik*. This was one of the few nightspots in town that lived up to the myth of movie glamour.

'Look at this crowd,' Manos snorted. 'Handsome guy like you could make it back in a'hour, easy. Take one or two old girls for a flap round the dance floor. They'd cover your expenses for sure. Worked for Rudy.'

He glanced round at Tom with a teasing grin that promptly fell from his face. 'Or maybe not. What's this?' He flicked a hand at Tom's crumpled lapel. 'You can't afford a decent suit even?' He looked again, this time concerned. 'You OK, Tom? You in trouble?'

'No. Not yet. But I need a phone and a place to rest up for a half-hour. I thought maybe you could let me—'

Before he could finish the sentence, Manos was ushering him around the dance floor and out along a corridor leading off.

'Like I say, Tom, any time.'

Manos opened the door into a small office, mostly taken up by a carved walnut desk, a tigerskin rug and a couple of overstuffed leather armchairs. 'Take as long as you need. There's a washroom at the back, towels and fresh shirts in that cupboard by the side.' He looked at Tom appraisingly. 'They should fit fine now you slimmed down a bit,' he grinned. 'Gimme the jacket and I'll have one of the busboys press it.'

'Thanks, Jimmy, but I'll pass on that. I've got to be ready to go.'

Manos liked the sound of that. He smiled again and pointed towards the washroom. 'There's a private door back of there, leads down to the delivery yard. You know, if you don't want to show your face on the way out. Give you a chance to check out my new motor, too.'

Tom raised an eyebrow. 'Yeah?'

'You betcha. Mercer Raceabout. One heck of a machine.'

'You going up in the world, Jimmy?'

'Where else?' Manos chortled, then reached into the desk drawer, drew out a key fob and laid it on the leather top, stroking it delicately like a lover's hand. 'You oughta take her for a ride, Tom. Like I say, she's a beauty. Goes like the wind. Ain't nothing gonna catch her.' He pulled his hand back, leaving the key, his palm out flat, an unspoken offer.

'Thanks, Jimmy. You're a pal.'

Patting the side of his nose with two fingers, Manos turned to go. 'I gotta get back out there. I'll send a boy in with something reviving. And don't you worry about the bad guys. We'll head 'em off.'

As soon as the door shut, Tom grabbed the handset, easing himself into the chair behind the desk, clicking for an operator. Waiting to be connected, he took in the framed photos hung like trophies on the wall behind, all featuring Manos, arm draped around members of the movie colony's elite: Jimmy acting the fool with Doug Fairbanks. Jimmy with Wally Reid, with Charlie Chaplin, Tom Mix, the Gish girls, Tony Moreno. None with Valentino, although the one of him shadowboxing with Jack Dempsey was impressive, and in pride of place.

'Hello, Central? Yeah, I need to speak to Sullivan in the detective squad. It's urgent.'

Urgent or not, Sullivan had not yet arrived, though he was expected shortly. Tom declined an offer to speak with the duty officer, checked the apparatus and left his number but not his name, saying only to tell Sullivan it was an emergency and had to do with 'our friend Ross'. He prayed that would be enough. He removed his jacket and dusted it down with a brush he found in the cupboard. He washed his face and hands, ice-cold water as good as balm, and helped himself to a crisp new shirt and a couple of dabs of Manos's personal pomade worked in with a pair of tortoiseshell brushes whose inlaid silver initials made him wonder about the source of such a generous gift.

He was sitting at the desk again when he heard a rap on the door and automatically answered. Manos's head turtle-necked in, his face a picture of strained apology, a rumpus coming from behind.

'I'm sorry, Tom—'

He hardly had time to react before Manos was levered out of the way as the door opened fully and in burst Mack Sennett, crimson-jowled, white tie askew, apparently the beneficiary of a skinful of bootleg hooch.

Tom breathed a sigh of relief, of sorts. 'Jesus Christ, Mack—'

'I thought you said meet in the lobby, Tommy,' Sennett brayed. 'What the hell were you up to with Jimbo? He good as flung himself in front of the door when I said I seen you two sneaking off down here.'

Manos strode in behind him, still off kilter and attempting to compose himself. A man in his position couldn't get on the wrong side of a studio boss, not even a loose cannon like Sennett – it would be bad for business. But he wasn't the type to lose face either.

'Mr Sennett, I must insist—'

'It's all right, Jimmy,' Tom interjected. 'My fault. I thought I was meeting Mack later. I got it wrong. Are we OK to conduct our business in here, just for now?'

Manos got the message, gave him a skeptical glare, nodded curtly at Sennett and swung back out of the room. Not happy, but in possession of his honor at least. It would be a while before the balance of this particular favor could be paid.

Sennett made an obscene gesture in the direction of the closing door and lowered himself into one of the armchairs. 'Who made him Grand Vizier all of a sudden?' He fumbled, arranging himself better in the chair. When he looked up next, his mood had changed. He looked around approvingly. 'Nice digs. Jimmy got a private supply in here?'

'You look like you've had plenty, Mack,' Tom said, settling back again. 'What has you so excited, anyhow? Miss Normand get in touch at last?'

Sennett laughed, but there was little amusement in it. He smoothed his suit with his hands, brushing off his inebriation like rain. 'Funny you should ask. She telephoned before I came out. Said she was sorry for being so "elusive". She was real upset.'

'I guess she has a right to be.'

'Oh, don't fool yourself,' Sennett said. 'It wasn't Taylor she was crying over. It was herself, as usual. Got all bawly to soften me up, then asked straight out if it was me set the private detective on her, poking into her private affairs.'

'I'd have thought I was the least of her problems,' Tom said, restraining himself from laughing in Sennett's face. 'I haven't seen her since the inquest.'

'You tell her you were a private man then?' Sennett asked, eyes hard now, no trace of the drink he had seemed consumed by moments before.

'No, not as such.' Tom cast his mind back. 'All I said was you sent me to make sure she was doing all right. DA Woolwine was right beside her at the time. Maybe he told her what I do for a living. Does it matter?'

Sennett batted the idea away with his hand. 'I guess not, now. But I reckon you must'a hit a nerve somewhere along the line. She was mighty perturbed. I know her well enough to be certain of that. But she wouldn't tell me the cause, or even where she was. Who else you been talking to?'

'Who *wasn't* I talking to?' It occurred to Tom that maybe Mrs Ivers had contacted Normand after he left Casa Duende, to confess what she had divulged to him about the abortion. It was one heck of an indiscretion.

'You have no idea?' Sennett pressed. 'She mentioned you by name, more than once. Whatever it was, you made an impression.'

Tom kept his poker face in place. But that settled it for him. It had to be Ivers. She was the one who focused on his name. And Normand would rightly be appalled if she thought Sennett would discover her secret. That information might destroy what little remained between them. However scarred and buried deep, the man had a heart. And no matter how poisoned and contorted the bond with Normand had become over the years, that heart was still fused to hers with a ferocity Tom would never understand. No way could he tell Sennett what Ivers had revealed.

'I kinda assumed it was what you wanted to see me about tonight,' Sennett continued. 'One way or another, you better tell me now. Because Mabel says she'll only come back to work if I get rid of you.'

'Get rid of me?' The pitch of Tom's voice betrayed him, but Sennett misinterpreted it as shock.

'Sorry, Tom, but if that's what it takes. She's still my little money-spinner. And all-round light of my life, in truth. I need her back.'

Sennett said it so gently that Tom had to wonder what else had passed between him and Normand during that call. The man had always been putty in her hands, and his mood had certainly lifted. Had something more significant happened?

'I'll pay you for the time you've put in, of course.' Sennett leaned back, pulled a money clip from his pocket and lobbed a wad of bills on the desk. 'And how about as a bonus we write off what you owe me on the house, and the next three months' rent as well? That ought to see you settled. Enough to lease an office room off the Boulevard, get yourself set up proper. Gotta have an office of your own if you're in business.'

Tom had done it enough to 'friends of Lasky' to recognize when he was being bought off. And none too subtly either. He just wasn't sure why. Had he got it wrong? Did Sennett already know about Normand's abortion? Or was he just wrapping things up on her orders, the only way he knew how?

Either way, it made no difference. He was so overjoyed at the thought of finally being rid of this mess, it was as much as he could do to disguise it.

'You know everything I do for you is confidential, Mack,' he said, picking up the cash and putting it in his pocket. 'That's guaranteed. I'll take your money – and your bonus. Because I did the work. But you need to hear what I found out, because this could be seriously bad for your business.'

Sennett had closed his eyes and put a hand up, he was too tired to hear any more. But at the mention of his business the eyelids snapped open again. The hand ceased to be a stop signal and, palm up, became a demand.

'Meaning what?'

'Meaning what's going on over at Lasky's, and how you might want to do something about it. They're selling you down the river big time, Mack. You and Miss Normand. And they're making a dirty job of it.'

Sennett leaned forward in his chair, the color rising in his neck as Tom outlined what he had uncovered about the negative press being run against Normand out of the Lasky studio, and the indisputable evidence he had removed from J.J. Fine's office.

'Those bastards,' Sennett exploded. 'And I had Charlie Eyton call me only yesterday, consoling me over being barred from exhibition in Kentucky. The little jerk must have been laughing up his sleeve all along. I'm gonna make him sorry. I'm gonna sue the goddamn shirt off his back. And Jesse Lasky's, and Adolph goddamn Zukor's as well. I'm gonna make 'em rue the day they crossed me. They want to spread muck? I'll make 'em eat it by the wagon load.'

'You'd be better off calming down, Mack,' Tom said when he finally got a chance. 'You know what they say. That particular dish is best served cold.' He could have pointed out that litigation would succeed only in giving the press a field day: the perfect excuse to rake out even more dirt about Miss Normand. But his job was done, and he was not going to risk getting caught in the fallout.

'Forget that claptrap,' Sennett said. 'Where's this telegram you say you have? I'm gonna set things going with my attorney right now.'

Tom felt his cheeks burn, the image of Ramirez poring over the papers in his front parlor clear in his mind.

'I don't have it with me.'

'So let's go get it.'

'I can't. Not right now. I told you I'm only in here cos I'm waiting for a call. It's too important to miss.'

Sennett blew some steam from between his lips, exasperated. 'So let me go. Where is it?'

'Somewhere safe, OK? Look, Mack, you're just going to have to trust me on this. That's just going to have to wai—'

The telephone bell lopped off his words like an axehead, and both men turned to the apparatus as if a stranger had burst in on them. Tom hesitated but knew he couldn't risk missing Sullivan. As it sounded again, he plucked the earpiece from the cradle and put his hand over the mouthpiece.

'You do what you have to, Mack. But I'm taking this call. Now leave me to it, please. I'll bring over the proof to you in the morning.' *If I make it to then*, he thought.

Sennett began to say something but checked himself. He flapped a hand angrily at him, but Tom was already turning away, all his attention taken by the buzz of Sullivan's frustration echoing from the earpiece.

'Hey, Thad . . .'

The rest of his greeting was drowned by Sennett storming out, slamming the door behind him so hard that Jimmy Manos's gallery of stars shivered on the walls.

FORTY-ONE

At the other end of the line, Sullivan was busy berating Tom. He had heard on the grapevine that an arrest warrant had been issued. It served Tom damn well right, he said. He'd given him enough warning about making that statement.

Tom let him blow off some more steam before challenging him. 'And you know for sure it's Ramirez who did it, Thad, do you?'

'Well, who the goddamn hell else would it be?'

It took Tom a further five minutes to calm Sullivan down and bring him up to speed with what had happened since he'd seen him just a few hours earlier: about Devlin and Ramirez, Mazaroff and Taylor, and Mrs Ivers, too. But most of all about Devlin and Ross.

'And you're certain it's Devlin, not Ramirez, who was behind this?' Sullivan asked finally.

'Well, no, how could I be? But come on, Thad, would you go to the trouble of issuing a warrant just because someone didn't make a statement?'

'Damn right I would – if the ungrateful malcontent had already been brought in on suspicion and subsequently disappeared into thin air.'

'But I didn't, did I?' Tom insisted. 'I mean, Ramirez was happy to let you vouch for me. Why would he go disturbing a judge on a Sunday just to throw some worry my way, when he hasn't even tried to get in touch with me before now? It doesn't make sense. Or risk getting on the wrong side of you, for that matter? You know he would've have tipped you the wink first, just like you would him.'

That seemed to clinch it for Sullivan. He couldn't see one cop treating another so shabbily, not even as queer a fish as Ramirez. Devlin, of course, was another matter entirely.

'OK, but even if you're right,' Sullivan finally conceded, 'why in hell would Devlin go to so much trouble over you? Why not frame someone easier?'

'I don't know, Thad. I mean, at first he must've just reckoned the gods were smiling on him when I was brought in for Madden's murder. He said as much to me that night at the station. But I'm thinking maybe he since figured out – assuming it *was* Ross who killed Madden and I'm the only witness – that I'm also the only one who can link it all back to him. So he wants to get me out of the way, fast as possible. You have to admit it would've been pretty neat if he'd managed to plug me earlier. How much better would that have been for him? No messy loose ends to tie up. A fleeing suspect shot. It would have been impossible to challenge. Even for you.'

Sullivan grunted a nominal doubt. But he knew as well as anyone how cops close ranks over such things, regardless of circumstance.

'All right, so maybe what you're saying makes some sense,' Sullivan said, dropping his voice even lower. 'But that doesn't get us away from the fact that, right now, as far as the law is concerned, you're a fugitive from justice and I'm risking my badge talking to you.'

Sullivan's frustration crackled down the line, and Tom knew he'd have to say out straight the danger he was in.

'I know, but what the hell else can I do? I'm dead meat if Devlin gets his hands on me. I reckon I'm lucky I even got to pass any of this on to you. That's about as far as I've thought it through.'

There was a silence on the line as both men sought to come up with a plan, until Sullivan said, 'I reckon there's one move we can play and keep you alive long enough to get at the truth. You'll have to give yourself up.'

Tom could not believe his ears. 'Jesus, Thad, haven't you been listening? That's the one thing I can't afford to do.'

'Wait now. Hear me out,' Sullivan said reassuringly. 'I don't mean to just anybody. I mean to me. Place yourself in my protective custody. It's the only way, don't you see? That means we get you straight to somewhere safe, and Devlin can't touch you on the way.'

Tom wasn't convinced. 'Yeah, very nice, old pal. I'll be locked up while Devlin mixes the ingredients for a nice frame-up in court. No, I don't think so.'

'Ah, don't be ridiculous. It will give Ramirez and me time to crack whatever he's got going on. Look, I don't see you've got any choice. If you don't do it, you'll be on the streets and on your own. You're long in the tooth enough to know you're not going to last long at that lark.'

Tom groaned. He didn't want it to be true but he could see it was probably his best hope of getting out of this mess alive. Sullivan didn't even need to hear it from his lips. His silence was eloquent enough.

'Good lad. Now, come on; speed is important here. Let me come and pick you up before any of the boys go and get too enthusiastic. You can be sure Devlin will have let it be known how grateful he'll be to any officer who nabs you. Where are you? On Wilshire from that number, I guess?'

It near killed Tom to tell him. 'Yeah, I'm up at the Ambassador, in Jimmy Manos's office in the Grove.'

'Christ!' Sullivan laughed. 'You do well for yourself even when you're in trouble. No bloody hole in the wall for Tom Collins, eh? Look, I'm going to put a citywide bulletin out on Ross to make sure the boys on the street keep an eye out and nab him as soon as he's spotted. At least he's recognizable with that gait of his. As for Devlin, we'll have to go easy for the moment, play him at his own game until we have Ross in chains, OK? Now, you hang tight. I'll be there in ten minutes, right?'

'Yeah, all right.' Tom heard a sharp rap on the door. Thinking it must be Sennett coming back, he put a hand over the mouthpiece and shouted, 'Come.' But nobody came. 'Thad, you need to speak to Manos when you get here, yeah? I'll tell him I'm expecting you. Hang on a sec first, though.'

He put down the earpiece and ran over to the door and opened it a crack, but there was nobody there. He opened it wider, then saw, down the corridor, out on the dance floor, a flurry of flying fists and Jimmy Manos attempting to break up a rumpus between two men. One of them was definitely Sennett. The other . . . Christ, was that Charlie Eyton? What the hell was he doing out there? Sennett must've gone off like a powder keg on seeing him.

He clicked the door shut again. Thinking hard. It could be only a matter of minutes before Sennett had the bright idea of dragging him out of Manos's office to back up everything he was throwing at Eyton.

He picked up the telephone again, held it to his lips.

'Listen, Thad, there's some trouble kicking off outside. I can't stay here. I'll have to make a bolt for it. I'll see you over at Fay's place instead. The Oasis. You know it, don't you?'

Without waiting for a reply, he hung up, placed the telephone back on the desk and, hooking a finger round the fob that held the key to Jimmy Manos's auto, shouldered past the washroom and slipped out the back.

FORTY-TWO

As soon as he skidded to a stop outside the club, he knew something wasn't right. The door was wide open and one of the awning poles had been knocked out of true, giving the canopy a drunken, woozy tilt. Still more concerning was the fact that Herman was not in his usual spot, no burble of music leaking up from the club below. Inside was no better – the carpet scuffed, an electric light bulb smashed, glass fragments littering the floor. Tom dashed down the stairs. Cloak hatch shut. Silence ominous as a storm cloud. Through the padded doors the club was almost empty, lights up eye-ache bright, stale smoke loitering in the used-up air, a couple of waiters righting chairs and tables as if closing time had come and gone.

Across the room he spied Herman sitting on the stage edge, Colleen standing beside him, mopping at his face, a blur of dark red on the front of her cream shirtwaist that could only be blood. A couple of steps further and he saw it: Herman's face gray, smeared from a gash on his hairline, suit pocket torn at the lapel, the buttons all popped.

'What the hell's happened here?'

They looked up as one, hadn't heard him approach. Colleen stood quickly, her face a stew of fear and relief, and reached out, pulling herself in towards him for comfort. 'Oh, thank God you're here. Herman's hurt. His head won't stop bleeding. He needs a doctor.'

Tom repeated his question, leaning in to take a closer look at the ragged cut on the doorman's forehead. He knew enough about head wounds to know most bleed worse than they are. Where the hell was Fay?

'Is Mrs Parker out back?' he asked.

Herman was mumbling something that wouldn't make it past his split and swollen top lip. Colleen glanced away, and back, tears spilling from her eyelids as she shook her head.

'They took her,' she said. 'They took Mrs Parker away with them. It was awful.'

'Who did?'

Herman was still struggling to talk, frustrated, but got it out, the effort loosening his lip for a whole sentence. 'Prohies, Mr Collins. Barged in with some cops. Too many for me to keep out.'

Tom looked to Colleen for confirmation.

'I heard shouting,' she said. 'I looked out the hatch. Herman was coming down the steps backwards, whole gang of big guys on him, shouting, "Raid, raid!" and "Stay where you are!" I tried to see in the main room after them, but folk started screaming and rushing out. Then they came out again, dragging Mrs Parker by the arms. Real rough, they were.' She looked away, ashamed to say it.

'Just her?' Tom asked. 'Where was Eddie?'

'He don't work Sundays,' Herman said.

'And they arrested her?' He couldn't believe the night could get any worse. 'How long ago was this?'

'Twenty minutes, maybe,' Colleen said, still looking scared, uncertain, her gaze flicking to the door and back all the time. 'They weren't here long.'

Tom looked around for something to anchor him, to convince him that any of this felt right. But it didn't. The room had barely been turned over. 'Did they go in the back at all? Take any crates and cases, books, ledgers – anything like that – away with them?'

She shook her head. 'I didn't see any. Only Mrs Parker.'

He really did not like the sound of that. A glance at his wrist-watch. Sullivan, surely, would be arriving any minute. He wondered if Herman would be more forthcoming about what happened if the girl wasn't there.

'Colleen, in the office, on the shelf, there's a box with bandages and iodine. Has a white cross on top. Go get it; we'll patch up Herman.'

Once she was out of earshot, he leaned down, looked Herman straight in the face. The man looked all in, eyes struggling to focus. 'I'm sorry, Mr Collins,' he mumbled. 'They caught me on the hop.'

'You didn't try to stop them?'

'Sure I did, but there were four of 'em and big with it. Caught this early on.' Herman tapped the gash on his forehead gingerly, looked at his finger to judge the drying blood. 'Didn't notice much of anything after that, except Mrs Parker arguing with 'em, telling 'em she already paid her dues to County and to get the hell out. Must've realized she was the boss then, cos they just laid hands on her and dragged her out. No need to be so goddamn rough about it, I said. And got another tap for my trouble.'

'They the same cops as last time?'

Herman shook his head. 'I ain't sure of nothin' right now.'

'But they had a couple of prohies with them, you said? Did you get a look at their badges?'

Again the desultory headshake. 'No chance for that, Mr Collins. They come in swingin'. All nightsticks and mouth. Shouting about liquor violations, yelling all round 'em.'

'But only four-strong?' He scanned the room again. The damage was minimal. Could be as much the fault of folk climbing over each other to get out as those coming in. Not like any booze raid he'd ever seen.

Again he examined the gash on Herman's head. The flow had stopped. Didn't look like the kind of wound you'd get from a night-stick. He might have said more but Colleen was coming back, bandages in hand. He squeezed Herman's shoulder.

'I'll leave you in Florence Nightingale's hands. I got to get some air.'

But Herman was holding him back, pulling at his arm with unexpected strength. 'I suppose, now you say it, Mr Collins, they didn't look much like Feds. The one in charge, he was real rough-house. I know they took in war veterans in the bureau, so many come back from Europe. And this guy, he could handle himself. But I don't see how he could perform all his duties. Not with that injury. No way could he chase down no bootlegger on the run.'

'What're you saying, Herman?'

But Tom knew exactly what Herman was saying, and his gut had already wrung itself into a knot, his mind emptied out of anything but fear for Fay.

Now he needed air like a dope fiend needs the needle. He

stumbled out on to the sidewalk, bent over, hands fixed on his thighs, heaving in lungfuls of night air, trying to fight the shake that had taken hold of him head to toe, desperate to get the memory of Devlin ogling Fay's photograph to release its grip on his gut.

Between each gulp of air he cursed out loud. Cursed his own stupidity and his loser's bad luck. He ought to have known Devlin would check the photograph again. Ought to have known he would send Ross. Soon as he got away, he should have telephoned Fay and warned her to make herself scarce. Instead, all he'd done was waste time taking care of himself. If he'd called her, she might have got away.

The Mercer sat like an accusation by the curbside, mocking its own effortless speed minutes before. He wanted to get in it, race off to the rescue, be the dashing hero. But where to dash to now? He knew already what Sullivan would say when he arrived: 'Give yourself up, lad. Leave it to us. She'll be fine. Ross won't get far.' Every pointless reassurance in the book.

The thought of Fay in Ross's clutches sent waves of anxiety and anger crashing in upon him. Jesus, how could he have been so dumb? He bent his head again to rub his aching temples. If he hadn't, he would never have seen it coming. Would never have caught the flash of movement reflected in the Mercer's gleaming coachwork, or gained the split second that allowed him raise his shoulder and deflect the blow that came rushing out of nowhere at his head.

The bat glanced off the muscle of his upper arm, wrong-footing the attacker swinging at him wildly from the darkness behind. Only instinct made him twist and lash out, putting his weight on one leg as he swiveled round and smashed blindly up and back with his elbow. He felt the hardness of bone connecting with a smack against a face, followed by an agonized gasp. But even as he twisted round to see his attacker, and saw him stagger back clawing at a ruined nose, another came at him, a lead-filled sap hurtling straight at his face.

It caught Tom like a hammer square above his left eye. He could have sworn he felt his brain hit the back of his skull as he went down. Somehow he had sense enough left to pull in his shoulders and roll, saving his head from hitting the sidewalk, and arch away again – just enough for the boot that came after to whistle past his face.

Now he was on his back and his knee was up, and through the blur of pain he sighted how to do most damage. As the figure looming above drew his boot back for another stamp, Tom slammed the heel of his brogue up into the undefended arc between his legs. And amid the heaving and retching that followed. Tom rolled away again, trying to see where the first assailant was and whether he was coming back for more.

Scrambling to his feet, he heard a squeal of brakes and he saw a shadow duck into the alleyway behind, the thud of shoe leather echoing as he ran. A second later Sullivan was on the sidewalk beside him helping him up, pushing him back, getting between him and the goon writhing on the ground.

'Are you trying to take on the whole town now? What the hell's the matter with you, Tom?'

Unable to see straight out of his left eye, Tom was peering and pointing into the alleyway. 'There's another one down there. Get after him, will you! They jumped me. They got Fay as well, for God's sake.'

Sullivan cursed and ran. Tom turned his attention back to the one on the ground, now attempting to crawl away on all fours. Tom sank a heel hard into the back of the guy's thigh and he went down again, moaning and exposing his belly to the kick that Tom walloped into it next. He doubled up like a baby, wheezing and hacking, barely able to draw breath. Tom stepped round him, predatory, unsure of what to kick next, so spoiled was he for choice. Instead, he spotted the fallen bat, its owner long gone, and picked it up.

'You're no Fed,' he said, poking it into the man's gut. 'Who the hell are you? Who sent you? What have you done with Fay?'

The guy was yelping with each jab, but not ready to open up yet. Tom was raising the bat to strike when Sullivan emerged from the alley, palms up.

'You sure there was another one?' he said, striding over and pushing him back from the man on the ground and plucking the bat neatly from Tom's shaking grasp. 'C'mon now. You don't want to go killing anyone for real. Get your breath back. Tell me what's this about Mrs Parker.'

Tom told him.

Sullivan, cursing low and mean, began twirling the heavy bat in his hand with the ease of a drum major. 'And you're sure these guys aren't Feds? You got a badge on you, show it to me now,' Sullivan said, taking a poke at the guy. He only shook his head, in too much pain to care.

'He ain't no cop.' It came as a blurt from behind them, a voice high and angry. Colleen, standing in the club doorway, was staring wide-eyed at the man on the ground. How long she'd been there watching, there was no knowing. But her face was white as a corpse, her gaze tracking from the blood on Tom's face to the guy cringing on the ground. Her words a tangle as she struggled to explain. 'That's . . . I mean, he's—'

'He's one of the guys who took Fay, right?' Tom asked.

She shied back, he barked it so sharply. 'I came to tell you. I didn't say before cos I couldn't be sure when I saw them go past, inside. It happened so quick, I took fright, I had to hide. But now I see *him* again.'

'You saying you know this man, sweetheart?' Sullivan asked.

She nodded, crossed her arms and drew her shoulders in protectively, clutching at the collar of her shirtwaist as though she'd caught a sudden chill. When her answer came, it wasn't addressed to Sullivan but to Tom alone.

'At the house on the hill,' she said. 'They were the ones brought the dope in. I seen them – him, too, opening the packages, parceling it out.'

It took Tom a moment to get his head round it. How long had she been up there, to see all that?

'This guy was in charge?'

She shook her head. 'I only seen them come and go.'

Tom reckoned she was lying about that, but it was not his concern now. 'He hurt you?'

She lowered her head, the shame returning in a whisper. 'Not like that.'

'And you're certain they were the same guys?'

'You think I could mistake them?'

FORTY-THREE

They sent Colleen back inside and dragged the goon round into the alley, taking it in turns encouraging him to talk. He was a big guy and didn't give easily. If they hadn't been so worked up, they might even have admired him for holding out so long. But they did what they had to and at last he coughed out a name along with a snarl of submission.

'Ross – he's the boss, he got us out here.'

Tom glanced across at Sullivan, his eyes a glare of I-told-you-so. But any sense of triumph was undercut by the certainty that Fay was now in the worst danger she could be in. And it was his fault, no one else's. His response was fierce enough to ensure the goon spilled the rest. He and the boys were playing cards when Ross got a call and they all piled into the Packard and raced out here; supposed to make it look like a liquor raid and have a good smash-up for themselves.

'Ross was only after this guy.' He nodded towards Tom. 'Got us out quick when there was no sign. Lady wasn't giving nothing away but she got in his face about some protection she pays the sheriff, and he said he'd have her for bait. Told Joey and me to hang back, see if Collins here would take it.'

'What were you supposed to do when you got me?'

'Take you back. Mikey told Joey – the other guy, who ran – not me. I don't know what the plan was.' The goon's glance bounced nervously between them, not wanting to say any more, his fear of Ross returning to the fore.

'Back where?' Tom growled at him. 'Where in hell did he take her? Was it to that goddamn fun palace on the hill?'

The goon's eye's narrowed, but he was beyond the point of lying. 'No, not there. Too much going on. But not far. Mikey's got a place he takes marks to work 'em. A construction site. Nobody else there. Nothing but half-built houses since the owner went bust. It's quiet. Good place for that line of work.'

'Where?'

'It's not like it has an address. He only ever takes us there when he needs the muscle.'

Another couple of slaps jogged his memory, and eventually he described a spot out the east end of Franklin, on the edge of Griffith Park.

Tom had an idea where it was and glanced over at Sullivan who nodded.

'I know it.'

'OK, let's get him in the Mercer. I've got to run back in and—'

But Sullivan had a hand up, blocking him. 'No, hold on now, Tom. I know you're worried about your girl, and rightly so. But remember what he said. She's bait. What Devlin wants is you. He won't let Ross touch her. Not yet. We'll sort this out together, right? Let's at least get this one off our hands first. There's a Gamewell down the block. I'll go call someone out to pick him up.'

'No way. What if he's lying about where they're at? We'll have nothing.'

'He's not lying, Tom. He's told us what he knows. What you got to think is how many more of them are out there. We're going to need help. Do you think Mikey Ross is dumb enough to let us just come in and take her?'

He gave that idea short shrift. No way was he being taken out of the picture by calling out Sullivan's pals from the detective squad.

'Dumb is what Ross does best, Thad. You know what he's like. He won't keep his hands off Fay, not if he thinks she has anything to do with me. He's going to hurt her. And I'm not sitting here letting that happen. We have to move now. Stick this guy in the roadster and we'll take him with us. At least he can point out the right place.'

Sullivan had to admit he was right about Ross. Together, they dragged the goon over to the Mercer. Stared at the pair of neat little bucket seats, and the bulk of Sullivan and their captive.

'That's not going to work,' Sullivan said. 'C'mon, we'll have to take mine.'

Tom didn't so much as glance at Sullivan's flivver. No way was he going in that – he'd be quicker running.

'You go ahead in yours, Thad. Cuff Bozo to the door or something. I gotta run in and ask Herman something. I'll catch you up in no time.'

Ignoring Sullivan's scowl of displeasure, he ran back into the club.

Colleen was already on her way up with two glasses brimming with bourbon. He knocked one back, then took the other and had that too, laughing grimly as she drew breath at the torn and bloody knuckles on his hand. He told her was going to get Fay and not to worry but to lock up after him and stay safe with Herman, giving her a key to Fay's apartment above, telling her to stay there until he got back. He didn't wait for her answer, but went straight into the back office and shut the door.

He didn't want to think too long about it, but he knew for sure that Ross would be armed, and there was no way now, even if he lost this battle, that he was prepared to lose the war. He dug his wallet from his pocket and slid out a business card and laid it beside the telephone on the desk. Then he opened the second drawer down, removed a rosewood box, tipped the contents out. A small, flat pocket automatic lay in the bottom, two full clips besides. He took all three, slapping one of the clips in with the heel of his hand and slipping the spare into his pocket. The gun he stuck in his waistband at the back. No point upsetting Sullivan. Then he rested his hip against the desk edge, running his fingers through his hair, before he made his decision.

He picked up the telephone receiver, clicked for the operator and asked to be connected to the Santa Monica number on the card. A voice answered with a gruff 'Yeah?'

'Is Cornero there?' A request met with rebuff and denial. 'I don't have time for this,' Tom said at last. 'He's the one gave me his card. You go get him, bud, tell him Tom Collins wants to talk, and it's now or never.'

FORTY-FOUR

Tom hit the gas pedal as if wildfire was scorching his boot-straps, hitting seventy as he hurtled down a deserted Hollywood Boulevard, up Los Feliz and out past the Mount Hollywood turnoff where the paving ran out. A heavy bank of cloud drifted across the sky, diminishing the moonlight to a hazy glow. But even at full tilt on the ungraded road, the Mercer's huge head-lamps cut yellow through the night, the featherlight suspension gobbling every bump in the roadway, churning up a billowing tail of grit and dust in its wake.

Tom was beginning to think Sullivan must have made it to the rendezvous ahead of him when his lights picked out the dusty old Ford pulled in at the roadside ahead. The goon was sitting in front, cuffed to the canopy strut, Sullivan standing at a telegraph pole by what had to be the last police box out this side of the city, receiver pressed to his ear, tapping on the cradle. Tom braked hard and drew up, cutting the engine. A gap in the cloud cover leaked enough light to reveal a track climbing to the left, then disappearing over a rise.

'That's it?'

The goon nodded, glum, defeated.

'So tell me, how far?' Tom growled at him. 'What's there?'

'Like I said, it's a construction site. Just beyond that rise. Nine or ten houses, half built. Only one's got a roof on – older, been there a while, I reckon. That's the one you want, off to the right.'

'Who else is there?'

The goon shrugged. 'We were four before. Who knows? Depends if they went looking for you, I guess.'

They were interrupted by a string of imprecations from Sullivan, tapping furiously on the Gamewell. He gave up, put the receiver back in the box and locked it. 'Something's broke on this one. I'm not sure they even heard me,' he said, coming around and stepping up on the footplate.

'I'm not waiting,' Tom said.

Sullivan wasn't happy with that. 'Hang on, man. We can't take the machines any closer. We'll sound like a cavalry charge heading their way.'

'So we go on foot.' Tom jumped down and squinted at the track up ahead. 'Way I see it, there's not much point doing much else until we know the lay of the land. Ross might not be there. Maybe he has a small army with him. And if he hasn't got Fay, what's the point of calling in help? Best thing is you stay put with bozo here, while I go scout the place.'

Sullivan began to protest, but Tom cut him off. 'Look, it's the only way. You stay here; he won't try anything. I'll run up the trail, check it out. Fifteen minutes at most, I'll be back and between us we can make a plan, a good one. If I'm not, or if you hear anything bad up there, you come get me. Gallop on up in the auto if you like; that'll give them something to worry about.'

'OK, but no heroics, Tom. You have enough black marks against you, you can't afford any more. Me neither if anyone questions why I came out here instead of taking you in. So you be careful and come right back.'

Tom set off at a trot. Another break in the cloud showed the twisting track a ghostly white in moonlight, the rolling landscape a sea of dry, windblown grass with little in the way of cover. He felt no fear, the thought of Fay being hurt or scared spurring him on. Cresting the hill, he saw the cluster of half-built houses below him, looking out over what must be a bend in the Los Angeles River, though he couldn't see that far beyond. What he did see was that amid the half-built lot of A-frames that snaked down the falling ground, only one off to the right had a shingled roof. A glimmer of light seeped from its windows. But he could see no auto outside. He would have to get closer.

He covered the remaining distance hunkered down, using his hands to steady himself against the slope, skirting piles of discarded lumber, stacks of shingles and flooring, making for the rear of the house. Close up, he could see it had been there a while, now in disrepair. A smoking, black iron chimney pipe poking out through the gable looked like an afterthought. Tense as he was, he couldn't help wondering what catastrophe had befallen the owner to leave the lot in such disorder.

Two windows looked out from the back of the house, by which he approached, a dim glow emanating from each, though the one closest to the chimney was brighter. He sidled up to glimpse inside. A bleak living room, its gloom punctuated by a scattering of storm lanterns. His heart thumped loud enough to wake the dead when he saw Fay, his view partly obscured by a cast-iron stove with a coffee pot on top. She was sitting in a straightback chair beside a heavy hewn table, her hair mussed, but otherwise she looked unruffled, defiant, incongruous in a shimmering jade evening gown, one hand in her lap. His anger flared up seeing the other handcuffed to the table. But so did hope, seeing no sign of Ross or anyone else inside. Had they gone back into town?

He didn't dare signal her. Instead, he crept towards the second, smaller window and peered in. A bedroom, empty but for a couple of grimy mattresses on the floor, heaped with rumpled blankets. Slowly, he inched forward to peer around the corner, and froze when he saw a dark Packard parked hard up against the front of the house. How had he not seen it before? But that shock was as nothing to the chill of ice-cold fear that shot through him at the touch of cold gunmetal to the nape of his neck.

'Don't move a muscle, not even the one in your lip.'

Tom complied, heard the ratcheting click of a revolver being cocked.

'You oughta get silencers for those feet of yours.' Mikey Ross's rasping voice was unmistakable. 'I heard you comin' a mile off. Here to rescue your lady love, are you? Well, I'm not sure she's worth it. No tits, and a mouth like a boxcar slut on her, if you ask me.'

Ross gave out a low, breathy cackle that had more animal than man about it. Tom flinched and got the gun barrel jabbed still more painfully in his neck. 'I told you not to move. Now, do not make me pull this trigger. Do not make me.' In silence, he patted Tom down and immediately found the little automatic in his waistband.

'What's this? A peashooter to take me down?'

Again the low cackle. Tom had the impression now that Ross was hopped up to the eyeballs, so jittery, so breathy, so agitated in his movements. As he shuffled round him to finish the frisk, Tom saw, in the dull yellow light from the window, Ross's face close up for the first time in years. He was shocked by how wasted and aged he looked, the skin on his face a slack, sickly gray that even darkness couldn't disguise, the tendons in his neck taut like cables, his veined eyes black and empty at the center.

'I guess we won't be needing this no more,' Ross said, making to throw the automatic out into the darkness, then pulling back. 'Or maybe not.' He laughed. 'It's a gun for a lady, right? So maybe I should use it on one. Or on the both of you. Make a nice story for the papers. "Killer takes own life and movie player lover's", eh? Al can have some fun setting up the evidence for that one. I bet it makes the front page.'

Ross slipped the gun into the pocket of his black overcoat, motioning Tom forward with his own long-nose Colt. 'But that's for later. Let's go visit your lady friend inside. That's what you came all the way out here for, no? Move now.'

Heading for the door, Tom wondered why Ross hadn't called out to any of his cronies or stood them down. Could he be alone here with Fay, the others out on the prowl? He sneaked a look at his wristwatch to get a fix on how much time had passed. Ten minutes since he left Sullivan. Add another five for worry time, and five at most to get here in the auto. He had to make it through till then.

The expression on Fay's face when she saw him coming through the door pulled his heart to pieces. A surge of hope, then a crash of disappointment when she realized Ross was shuffling in behind, gun in hand and in control.

'Oh Tom, what's happening?'

Instinctively, she rose from the chair, but was jerked back by the cuff securing her wrist to the leg of the heavy table beside her, and her eyes filled with pain. Ignoring Ross's threats, Tom ran over to her, held her, assuring her everything would be all right. She was too smart to believe it, but he also knew she would be too proud to let Ross see the fear she was feeling.

'Help's coming,' he whispered as he pressed her to him. 'Did he hurt you?' He pulled back, enough to see her shake her head. 'Is anybody else here?' Again, a negative.

'Shut your trap and get away from her.' Ross grabbed his collar from behind and pulled them roughly apart. 'Get that chair over there, put it by hers where I can see you both, and don't get any ideas. This is the end of the road for you two, so get used to it.'

He should have been scared by that threat, or at least as scared as when Ross first got the drop on him outside. But if the plan had been simply to kill him, it would have been done by now. Ross was a creature without compunction, but never the sharpest card in the pack. He'd already let slip that he was in it with Devlin, acting on his orders. That had to allow for some leeway. A cold and remorseless clarity descended on Tom, like some kind of absolution. This was all his doing. If he hadn't lost his job, he'd never have been at Sennett's beck and call, never got himself drawn into this ungodly mess. Now his past in New York was rising up before him like a demon from hellfire, dragging Fay into the conflagration. But she had done nothing. She was blameless. Whatever it took, no matter what he had to do, all that mattered to him now was ensuring she came to no harm.

'Let Fay go, Ross,' Tom said. 'You took her to get hold of me. She's got nothing to do with this.'

'Yeah, like that would be a real smart thing for me to do.'

'C'mon, you've got me now. What do you need her for?'

Ross cackled as though Tom was the best gagman in the business. 'Yeah, right. And I'm guessing she'll promise never to mention any of this to nobody never again. I'll say one thing for you, Collins: you're still as big a dope as you were back East, and that's saying some.'

'Take the cuff off at least. You can see it's hurting her.'

Fay leaned across and squeezed his arm with her free hand. 'It's OK, Tom. I'm all right,' she whispered. 'Don't rile him; he'll turn on you.'

'Listen to the lady, Collins. It's good advice. And don't worry, I got enough cuffs to go round. I got a friend in the business, remember.'

Ross threw his head back at this inimitable wit. Kicking a chair out from the table, he told Tom to sit. His own agitation kept him on the move, shuffling from one wall to the other, over and again, the peculiarity of his gait emphasized still more by his left shoulder rising in response to a nervous tic of the neck. Something had to be going on behind the blankness of his eyes to account for such absorption.

'So what you been saying to that cop pal'a yours?' he eventually asked, barely breaking stride.

For a moment Tom wasn't sure what he meant. He thought of maybe playing the innocent, playing for time. Then it struck him clear. Whatever Devlin's plans might be, Ross was not fully in the know. That could buy him an edge when the time came, as it had to, soon. Tom shared a glance with Fay, which he hoped said *Go with me on this*.

'I told him the truth, Ross. I told him, as God is my witness, I saw you shooting Shorty Madden dead on the street, out on Virgil, from the back seat of that Packard parked out front here, and that your old puppet-master Devlin was dumb enough to try and put me in the frame for it.'

He felt Fay stiffen beside him. But Ross's reaction was the one he was waiting for: stopping in his tracks, eyes locking on to Tom's, jolted into anger.

'The hell you did.'

That he might have been officially identified in the case was evidently a concept new to Ross. He strode over to the stove, held his hands out above it, rubbing them hard, thinking harder. His pretence of calm betrayed by the flicker in his gaze when he looked back at them over his shoulder.

'Nobody'll believe that,' Ross said. 'You're the only suspect they got. You ain't around no more to deny it, that'll be it. They got nothing on me.'

'You're wrong, Ross. Didn't Devlin tell you? I spoke to Sullivan less than an hour ago and he said they got the goods on you. There's a citywide call out. They're coming for you. And not only over Madden.'

Ross rounded on him now. 'What the hell you talking about?'

Tom felt something close to pleasure course through his veins. He had him on the run now. Surely Sullivan must be here any second.

'The Taylor murder,' Tom said. 'What else? They're on to you for that, too. A witness identified you threatening Taylor in Griffith Park. Not so far from here, now I think on it. Said he'd never forget that crooked walk of yours. Had it off to a tee, he did. Even saw it for myself. Devlin must've said he'll cover for you, but you know how far that goes. If it's a question of you or him, he'll throw you to the wolves. And right now every cop in Los Angeles is getting in line to kick your ass straight into Old Sparky, make no mistake about it.'

It was stretching a point, but there was nobody there to contradict him. And it was having the desired effect on Ross whose gray pallor was now invigorated by a carmine flush of rage. Fay was tugging gently with her free hand at Tom's sleeve, urging caution. He covered her hand with his and squeezed a silent plea for trust.

But Ross responded only with a laugh. 'Oh, very good, Collins, you almost got me going there.'

Tom knew he had to keep him on edge, to find another way to keep the man distracted. 'You think it makes no odds, Mikey? Am I right? One way or another, despite those banjaxed legs of yours, you'll always outrun the law. Is that it?'

Ross's brows knitted together at another mention of his legs. Tom managed a glimpse at his wristwatch. Where the hell was Sullivan? There was no going back on this. He had to go for it while Ross's guard was down.

'I know one thing for sure. You'll never outrun Tony Cornero.' Tom waited a beat, to be certain the name hit home.

It did.

'I gave you up to Cornero, too, Ross. Straight after I told Sullivan, I called Cornero and told him you were the one killed his boy Madden. And do you know what I enjoyed most when I did that? Hearing him say how he was going to rip your stupid head off your neck with his bare hands.'

Ross might as well have been hit with a bullwhip. His chin shot up, shoulders rearing back. The room went absolutely still for a second. Then he flipped. Gun up, he ran at Tom and slammed it sideways into his temple. Only the grip caught him a glancing blow as he ducked, but it was enough to knock him to the floor.

'Tell me, now – now, before I blow your brains out.' Ross loomed above him, face flushed with rage, gun barrel bearing down. 'What's Tony goddamn Cornero got to do with anything?'

Tom heard Fay emit a low moan of fear as Ross pulled back the hammer and it was all he could do not to scream himself. Every instinct in him begged to prostrate himself at Ross's feet, take it all back. Except for the iron-hard ball of fury in his gut that told him to keep on going, that he was on the right path. That this was the only way out. He screwed his eyes shut and forced himself to raise the stakes again. Sullivan, surely, had to be here any second. He had to find the right words. He had to keep Ross in a spin.

He had to go all in.

'That's the problem when you're in a town you don't know, isn't it, Ross?' he taunted, at last finding the air in his lungs to spit it out. 'You don't know the ground for yourself, do you? Or who owns it. Are you such a chump you didn't know Madden was Cornero's man? Did Devlin not tell you who he was sending you out to kill? Whose pips you were really squeezing? No? Well, the cops are looking for you, for sure. And you better hope they find you first. Because Cornero's gonna rip you limb from limb – one crooked leg after the other. That's the truth – and you better believe it.'

The gun was aimed at Tom's forehead, but the hand that held it was shaking like a palsy now. The mind behind it apparently divorced, somewhere else entirely, a muck sweat breaking out on his brow. Tom didn't dare move a muscle. A hair's breadth lay between life and death, time itself suspended in the awfulness of possibility.

And then it came. Into the silence dropped the longed-for miracle. A rising rattle of engine noise approaching at speed, a vehicle kicking up dirt as it swept to a scraping handbrake stop outside.

Ross whipped round, his eyes wild. 'One move and I'll ice the both'a you.'

In a shambling run he made for the window. Ducking down on his haunches, peering out like a man already under fire, it was clear that he did not like what he saw outside. Which could only mean it was Sullivan. Tom glanced across at Fay, the closest to a smile he could raise to alleviate her fear, to communicate that help was at hand. But now more than ever he had to keep Ross on the run, too.

'That's probably Cornero and his boys,' Tom said with vehemence.

Ross showed no sign of hearing him, but it had to be what he was thinking, too, as he crouched, shoulder to the wall, and checked the rounds in his revolver, sweat glistening on his gray face.

'I don't reckon Cornero's boys'd drive a wreck like that,' Ross said, glancing again through the clearing dust outside, a breathy confidence creeping back in his voice as he ranged the gun at the darkness. 'I'm thinking maybe you told that dumb Irish bull of yours where you were heading, and here he is, hoping to take me in. Well, I got a welcome for him he ain't expecting.'

Rummaging deep in his coat pocket, Ross drew out an apple-size black metal ball and, with a smirk of malice, held it up for them to see. From the pineapple grooves in its cast-iron casing, it was, all too clearly, an army-issue hand grenade.

'See, Collins, you're wrong. I make connections real quick. I got friends down Fort MacArthur pass me on beauties like this.'

Tom felt a bitterness of nausea flood his gut. Ross let loose a cackle as he clutched the lever to the grenade's raised metal head, and with his right hand pulled on the pin. But then he stopped midway, pushed his face closer to the window pane, and a leer of pleasure lit up his features, followed by a grunt of surprise. With a twist of the thumb, he pushed the pin back in the grenade and returned it to his pocket. Shuffling the two strides to the door, he swung it open.

'Where in hell'd you get that ride?' Ross called out. 'And who's that you've got—' He cut off the end of his sentence, replacing it with a long guttural laugh. 'Aw, man, you ain't serious.'

FORTY-FIVE

Unable to see beyond the door, Tom strained to hear as a creaking of auto springs and a scuffling in the dust outside was accompanied by an angry shout.

'Would you come out from there, Mikey, and give me a hand with this almighty sack of shit, for Chrissakes.'

Whatever Tom's gut had suffered before, a double edge of anguish twisted in sharp as he recognized the voice. High, breathy and whining, it was Devlin's. There could be no doubt. But how?

The answer became painfully clear as, seconds later, the shuffling restarted and, with a grunt of exertion, Ross appeared again in the doorway. This time staggering under the weight of Thad Sullivan's barely upright form. As they came through, Sullivan's shoulder smacked against the doorframe and a moan escaped from lips that, like much of his massive face and head, were already streaked with blood. His eyes flickered open and took in the room, coming into focus on Tom's face, his expression of shock transparent enough.

'I'm sorry, lad,' Sullivan said, exhausted from the effort. 'I never thought it'd be—'

Whatever Sullivan said next was lost in Ross's bellow at him to shut up. Tom turned and met Fay's eyes, which were alive with horror.

'Oh my Lord, is that . . .'

Tom nodded and put a hand out to comfort her. But she pulled away, lost in her fear as the implications hit home. In any case, he was barely able to control the confusion coursing through his own bloodstream, his own mental processes now. Especially when the corpulent figure of Aloysius Devlin, still in his Port Inspector's uniform, squeezed in through the doorway behind them.

'Dumb fuck thought I was his backup – until it was too late,' Devlin said to Ross, a half laugh in the back of his throat. 'Had to leave Billy on lookout in the Studebaker down there – though those two done him in good.' He glared across at Tom and snarled, 'You'll get it back a hundred times, Collins. Any minute now.'

He emphasized his point by jabbing his fist into Sullivan's unprotected lower back, with such force that Ross cursed and stumbled under the impact. Unable to bear the weight any longer, Ross lurched forward and unshouldered Sullivan on to the floor with a joist-cracking crash. Blood scattered across the dusty bare boards, but Sullivan just lay there, moaning, attempting to crawl away.

Tom inched over to see if he could do anything but was met with a thump in the chest from Ross which sent him reeling back.

'For heaven's sake!' Fay cried, caught between stepping back in horror and reaching out instinctively to help. 'Stop it, you animals.'

'You stay where you are, lady, unless you want some of the same,' Ross scowled at her.

She gave him a defiant jut of her jaw. 'You wouldn't dare.'

'No? You just watch me.' He reached a hand out, grabbed for her throat, the other arm raised to strike. Tom scrambled to his feet and got between them, forcing Ross back as the blow came down, enough to take its force. A second later, Ross wasn't even there, pulled out of reach by a mighty tug from Devlin.

'Leave it, Mikey, leave it,' Devlin said, spinning him round and shaking him urgently by the shoulders. 'We'll have plenty of time for that later. We need to get out of here. Like I said, this one's called in this place to Central. Least that's what Billy says. They'll not be much longer. So come on, let's get the job done and get the hell out of here—'

As if the gods themselves had been listening, Devlin's words were cut short by a sharp percussive crack echoing in from the distance outside.

'What the fuck was that?' Ross wheeled around.

But everyone in the room knew it was a gunshot. And where it had come from. Tom took advantage of the others' distraction to check on Sullivan, who opened a fluttering eyelid and struggled to sit up, but, failing, slumped to the floor again.

'It's Billy,' Devlin said. 'He said he'll do what he can to buy us some time. There's another road out, down to the river, right?'

Ross nodded, wiping away the sweat breaking out on his brow. He jerked his head to where Tom was now crouched between Fay and Sullivan on the floor 'So, what we gonna do with them, then?'

'Like I said, we finish it here, now, then go. Like we planned. But we got to hurry. So get on with it, now.'

But Ross was not buying that. Thinking he heard another noise outside, he stiffened and turned, panic suffusing his features again. Pausing only to run a sleeve across his nose and mouth, he pulled the Colt from the pocket of his black coat again and ran to the window, peering intently out into the moonlit night outside.

'Seein' as you're so keen, Al,' he said, glancing back, over his shoulder, 'why don't you take care of it? I didn't sign up for no cop killing.'

Devlin's response contained more anger than surprise. 'What dope-addled shit are you talking, Mikey?' He took an anxious glance at his watch. 'You been telling me for years how much you want to put these two in a hole.'

'Yeah, and, like I said, I changed my mind. You do it.'

Devlin shook his head ruefully as though he and Ross had been arguing over nothing more consequential than cracking eggs. Then, with an undulating roll of fat folds, he turned and grinned at the three of them.

'Looks like the pleasure will have to be all mine.'

He pulled a familiar-looking Police Positive from his holster.

'Y'know, Collins, I think I'll do the girl first – just for the pleasure of seeing the look on your face.'

With the same surprising nimbleness Tom had marked in him before, Devlin was across the room in an instant, grabbing Fay and dragging her towards the center of the room until, eventually, he heeded her scream of pain and saw she could go no further for being cuffed to the table.

Ignoring Tom's cry to let her go, Devlin swore under his breath and pulled at the table roughly, knocking Tom back against the wall with a clout of his forearm when he tried to get between them. With a leer of delight, his eyes on Tom all the while, Devlin was raising the gun to Fay's temple when a roar of engine noise breached the night and a sweep of light broke across the crest of the hill above them. Devlin let go of the table, pushed Fay back and ran towards the window, head down, in a waddling, rolling motion. A convoy of powerful vehicles, as many as five or six, was racing down the incline towards the house, sweeping to a halt outside, the dim interior ablaze now with the light from their headlamps. Tom pulled Fay down beside him, feeling the shudders ripple through her as he pulled her head and shoulders into his chest, whispering he knew not what to try to calm her.

Outside, the sound of doors slamming, feet shuffling, weapons rattling and being readied. Inside, Devlin was struggling to restrain Ross, trying to stop him from loosing off with the gun.

'No, Mikey. Go easy. Don't let them see the iron,' Devlin whispered furiously at him, holding his gun arm down. 'Leave it to me, would you? I outrank them all. I'll just go get rid of 'em.'

But it was a confidence Ross did not share. 'Are you fuckin' crazy?' he screamed at Devlin. So panicked now, he'd forgotten who was usually in charge. 'They ain't no goddamn cops. Just look at the motors they come in.'

'What the hell are you talking about?'

'What he said – Collins, there,' Ross said, whipping his head round to nod quickly towards Tom, and wiping his spit-flecked lips with the back of his hand. 'It's Cornero's boys. He says he called Cornero, told him we were here.'

For the first time ever, Tom saw a flush of real consternation on Al Devlin's face as he turned and stared bitterly across the room at him. It took every ounce of courage in his soul to crack a bitter grin back at him.

'You better believe it, Devlin,' Tom said. 'Your time is up.'

As if by way of confirmation, the lower pane of glass in the window nearest Ross shattered as a bullet whipped through the room. Everyone tried to get closer to the floor except Ross, and Fay, who could only crouch beside the table, trapped there by the cuff. Tom reached across her, lifting the table leg an inch, and slipped the cuff out from under it, freeing her arm and pushing her flat on the floor beside Sullivan, shielding her body with his own as two more shots thumped into the woodwork.

No one moved a muscle in the ringing silence that followed. Then a voice from outside the broke the stillness. A voice rich in authority, with an underlay of menace.

Tony Cornero. In person. 'We know you're in there, Ross,' he shouted, 'Now, you come on out and nobody gets hurt. You hear me?'

In the silence that followed, Tom risked raising his head. Devlin had retreated a few feet to the stone chimney stack, his gaze on the ceiling, thinking through his options, or the odds. Ross was crouching by the window, the stove his only cover, breathing hard, his eyes flicking over and back to Devlin for guidance, but too jittery now to wait any longer.

'You're the one's gonna get hurt, y'wop bastard,' Ross roared out. 'You won't take me without a fight. Not now, not never. I don't give a goddamn how many you are.'

'Don't even think about it, Ross,' Cornero replied, gruffer now. Impatient. 'And the same goes for that crooked shitbag boss'a yours. We know you're in there, too, Devlin. Your boy Billy got real helpful once we hurt him. So, tell you what. I'll let you live if you muzzle up that mad dog of yours and hand him over. What you say? Give up Ross and walk out alive.'

Even as he was saying it, Ross was panicking, eyes wider than ever fixed on Devlin, clearly believing his old confederate and mentor more than capable of selling him out.

'You know that's not going to happen, Cornero,' Devlin called back, his voice a high, reedy contrast to the others. He crept close to Ross, his enormous belly brushing the floor yet not impeding his progress, and whispered something in his ear, enveloping him in a fold of fat in the process. Ross reared back, disgusted by his smell or touch – it was impossible to tell. But he didn't appear to be listening too hard anyway. Devlin darted a malign glance towards Tom and the others.

'If you're wanting a deal,' he shouted out again, 'you should know we got your pal Collins in here. With his movie whore, and a bull from the detective squad. You fire another shot, Cornero, and they die. You want to be responsible for that? Even Santa Monica ain't gonna give you refuge if they think you killed a cop. You'll have every patrolman in the state of California out gunning for you.'

The silence in which that information was digested lasted a long three seconds, punctuated eventually by Cornero's honking, goose-like laugh.

'I don't give a rat's ass if you've got Tom Mix and the Queen of Sheba in there with you. I only came for Ross. But y'know, if it comes to it, one dead cop or two ain't gonna make a lot'a difference – in case you're forgetting you still are one, you fat fuck. I'll take my chances.'

A clatter of firearms being raised and cocked underlined the threat for him, then a brief silence ached by before his voice rang out again.

'Give them a taste, boys. Show 'em we mean business.'

An instant later, it was as if the room was erupting from within. First came the handgun and rifle fire, then the terrifying staccato chatter of what could only be a Thompson machine gun thumping great gouts of wood and sprays of glass from the walls and windows and the roof beams above. A hurricane lamp was blasted off a shelf and crashed to the floor, bursting into a pool of flaming oil at the far end of the room. Tom did everything he could to cover Fay, arm and shoulder shielding her head, his back and legs barricading the length of her body, a hand clasped in hers around her belly, whispering hope into her ear as much, in truth, for his own comfort as for hers. The onslaught roused Sullivan to a kind of conscious-ness where he lay, hugging his head in his arms, seeking to make his giant frame as small as possible, a massive ball of humanity curled beside them. Tom steeled himself for the hit that must come any second, but then, sudden as it began, the barrage ceased.

Tom raised his head, looked round, saw Devlin flat, or as flat as he could be, to the floor, uninjured, and Ross apparently the same. It had been as Cornero said: a taste. They'd been aiming high.

Again Cornero shouted, 'This is your last chance, Ross. Throw any irons you got out ahead of you, then come out with your hands where we can see 'em.'

'Are you seriously gonna get us all killed here, Devlin?' Tom whispered with ferocity, nothing left to lose now.

'You maybe, but not me,' Devlin snarled. But before he could do anything about it, Ross, pinned by the window, raised himself up on his haunches, weapon poised, preparing to fire. Outside, they were ready for him. As soon as his gun breached the window, a shot came in reply, the slug spinning a jagged hunk of wood from the frame hard into Ross's temple, just behind his right eye. He leapt back, cursing wildly, stumbling against the wall, rubbing madly at the wound with the heel of his gun hand. Seeing the blood there, he emitted a strange keening wail, low at first but gaining a strength and shrillness that drowned out all of Devlin's attempts to calm him from the cover of the chimney stack.

'Get down, Mikey. Don't be crazy. They'll nail you quick as they see you.'

Cornero's voice followed on hard from outside, full of fury now. 'I told you not to try that. You get no more chances. Throw your goddamn weapons out. Or you die. All of you.'

But Ross was beyond hearing, beyond reason, as, gun aloft in one hand and fumbling in his pocket with the other, he made a dash across the open floor to the chimney stack, a look of frenzy on his face, eyes fixed on Devlin.

'You do what you want, Al,' he muttered furiously. 'We're done for anyhow if we stop here. I'm gonna take my chances.'

Tom felt Fay's grip tighten on his. Devlin blanched and reared back as Ross pulled the grenade from his pocket and held it up just inches from his face.

'Where the fuck you get that?' Devlin whispered frantically. He didn't get an answer, only his outstretched hand palmed off as Ross stumbled onwards to the door.

'I'll give 'em a taste of this, Al. Then go for the Packard. You follow if you want.' Ross lumbered towards the door, pulling the pin from the grenade with his gun hand. Devlin could only stare balefully after him as he crouched down, opened the door a crack and called out again.

'Hey, you out there, it's me, Ross. Don't shoot, I'm coming out.'

'Throw your iron out first.'

It was enough for Ross to get his bearings. He swung the door open and rose up under cover of it, his black greatcoat billowing, his gun hand out straight, firing, the other back behind him like a knuckleballer about to pitch. From the dark outside came a ragged volley of shots. Ross stopped in his tracks as if he hit an invisible wall as he took a slug to the middle of the chest. Two more sent him toppling back through the doorway, his face a mask of almost childish surprise, twisting and falling.

Tom saw panic strike Devlin's soul at precisely the same moment it struck his. Out of Ross's hand, the black metal ball tumbled and spun back into the room, hitting the floorboards with an unearthly thud as the thin zinc lever pinged from the pineapple top like a sprung watch cog, the cast-iron casing skidding and rumbling into the center of the room, the sputtering fuse a breath-halting harbinger of the horror coiled inside.

Time slowed to the pace of a childhood prayer. He knew he had
five or six heartbeats left at most. Beside him, Fay was already on
her feet, gesticulating, shouting, willing him to see what she saw,
as she reached for the far side of the table

Holy Mary . . .

and he understood at once, was one in mind and body with
her as

mother of God . . .

together they lifted, thrust, tilted the massive slab of wood up
and over,

pray for us sinners . . .

its knot-hard iron weight missing Sullivan's skull by a hairsbreadth
as it

now and at the hour . . .

crashed on its side and, after it, two bodies diving, twisting, arm
in arm

of our death . . .

over the rough oak edge in a rolling, desperate lunge.

Ame—

FORTY-SIX

'**W**here are they now?'
It wasn't the the only thing Sullivan demanded to
be told when he opened his eyes. But it was close
enough to it.

Having learned from Tom with his first, hoarse-throated inquiry
that all three had escaped the blast with nothing more than cuts
and bruises, his second, directed with a bitter scowl at Cornero
who was standing behind, was barely audible in the muffled world
of sound that Tom now inhabited. It went entirely ignored in any
case. Sullivan's third inquiry, delivered as he heaved himself
upright from the slump in which he'd been left since being dragged
out into the night air, was this one: the whereabouts of Ross and
Devlin.

Tom understood it as much by reading his lips as by hearing.

Before he could reply, he felt a steely hand grip his shoulder and Cornero stepped in front of him to supply the answer.

'They got away.'

'The both of them?' Sullivan glared at Cornero with a furrowing of the brow that wedded shock, disbelief and anger. Cornero replied with the heels of his hands and his best Italian shrug, apparently just as perplexed himself.

'Into the night, like ghosts. We have no good idea how.'

Tom said nothing.

'But I saw it with my own eyes. He went down, the gren—' Sullivan broke off, pushing gray hair back off his brow, clenching his eyes shut as if determined to dredge the moment up from memory. 'Didn't he?'

'Down, sure. But not out, detective,' Cornero said, brushing his hands free of nothing and turning to walk away. 'Don't rightly know how. But they vanished. You don't believe me, ask your pal here. Thin air. Ain't that right, Collins?'

Almost the first thing Tom had seen when he came round, his sight resolving slowly from post-blast blur into a pin-sharp shock of recognition, was Devlin, tattered and bloodied, a bloated man-whale in moonlight, being dragged across the dust-blown lot and hauled into an open touring car.

How he himself had got to be outside, or came to be propped up beside Fay on the chromed footplate of a big Hispano-Suiza, attended by a gorilla-sized goon with a first-aid box, he had no idea. Fay, he was relieved to see, had suffered not a scratch beyond a ragged wound across her left shoulder that the goon was dabbing at, gentle as a junior nurse, with a wad of white cotton. Tom reached out a hand and took hers, and she turned and spoke to him but he couldn't hear a word. He tried to say so, but his own voice was so damped he simply stopped. Something thick and god-sized had inserted itself between his hearing and the outside world. He knew then that Fay was suffering the same from the way she was pointing to her ears and laughing, and crying, without seeming to notice she was doing either. So he bent and cupped her perfect face in his hands, smeared the dirt and dust from her cheeks with a wipe of his thumbs, and kissed her and held her to him so hard the goon had to turn away, all bashful.

Tom walked back towards the house, surprised to find it still intact. Not collapsed or burned or anything else he might have expected, though an eight-foot gap had been blown through the wall at the front. It was through this that Devlin, leaking blood, nearly every stitch of clothing blown from him, was hauled on his back from the dark interior, two big goons pulling on each of his pink shredded legs, his big arms flailing, his eyes wide with pain or terror, unable to scream for the gag rammed hard in his mouth. Getting his unwilling, corpulent enormity into the waiting car took Cornero's muscle boys a mammoth effort, a mesmerizing thrash of fists and boots and remorseless intent, a muted shadow play of grunting and cursing that ended with the roar of a motor, a kick-up of dust, and a sense of screaming yet to come.

It was then that Cornero strolled back across the lot and drew Tom aside, a comradely arm around his shoulder, an inquiry as to his wellness. Tom indicated he was having trouble with his hearing. Cornero grinned a big grin, then pushed his face hard up against Tom's ear to be certain he understood, and explained to him in an exaggerated drawl exactly how things would have to be. How things could only be, if he wished his beautiful girl to make it through another day on earth. And, more imminently, if he wanted his detective pal to make it to the dawn of this one.

There could be no other way. No discussion. No negotiation. No recalcitrance or reluctance. No word of what had happened on this night to Devlin and Ross could ever be disclosed or discussed. Not to the detective squad. Not to the studios. Not to the newspapers. Not to any other ears. Silence was the price, and all that was required. It was for Tom to make it happen, and make sure it stayed that way. Or the cost would be their lives. A simple deal. All three or none. And that was how it had to be.

Silence. Silence. Silence.

FORTY-SEVEN

Tom knew Sullivan had been itching to tell him something since they met, two hours before, to attend Bill Taylor's funeral service together. But whatever it was, he hadn't found the moment. Arriving downtown, they were repulsed by the vast crowd gathered at St Paul's Pro-Cathedral, gawping in their thousands, heaving and swelling outside the great Gothic facade on Olive and spilling deep into the formal paths and flower beds of Pershing Square opposite. Even with a phalanx of patrolmen pushing back the throng, the limousines of the invited mourners struggled to make it to the cathedral steps without adding to the body count.

Satisfied by now that the whole world really was going mad, Sullivan suggested an alternative way in. They worked their way round the crowd to a side passage where, badge in hand, he secured them entry via the vestry door. From there they made their way out through the packed chancel, past the closed casket that appeared to float on a sea of extravagant wreaths and a bier bedecked with roses, up a side aisle to where, eventually, some of the less esteemed members of the congregation took pity on Sullivan's limp and cane, and shuffled in to make room for two more on their pew.

Up front, everyone who was anyone in the colony was present. Valentino. Doug and Mary. Swanson and Mickey Neilan. Wally Reid and the DeMilles. There was no sign of Zukor, who was probably back in New York by now, though the Laskys and Charlie Eyton were present, the latter scowling as he spotted Tom across the nave. Mrs Ivers, in midnight-blue, had persuaded Leon Mazaroff to break cover. As the minutes passed, the hubbub from the crowd outside got louder, the moment of crisis coming when Mabel Normand arrived, veiled in deepest mourning and unable to proceed without support from her lady companion and a police officer. Such was the press to catch a glimpse of her, the police cordon split and a section of the crowd surged up the church steps. Only the quick thinking of two officers, who heaved the great cathedral doors shut behind her, prevented inundation by the mob.

Not until after the litanies were intoned, the ceremony concluded, the haunting strains of Handel's *Largo* died away and the coffin was shouldered up the aisle and back out to the waiting hearse and clamoring crowd, did Sullivan pull a newspaper from his coat pocket.

'I'm guessing you didn't see this?' Sullivan said, pushing the rolled-up paper into Tom's hands.

Tom took it, nodding, expecting to open the same *Evening Herald* he had grabbed on his way downtown earlier from a newsboy hollering with even more fervor than usual. *Hays To Clean Up*

Hollywood, the headline spanning the front page. Beneath it, Phil Olsen's byline, and photographs of Will Hays and Zukor over columns declaring, *Exclusive: Studios to appoint czar to save movies from censors*. And: *Sweeping reforms in wake of Arbuckle, Taylor.* This was the goods all right, a humdinger of a scoop. Olsen had it all mapped out: how Zukor had strong-armed every major studio boss into accepting his plan to draft in Hays to censor the industry from inside rather than risk the federal government imposing something from without. For now, Zukor was refusing to comment. Hays, too, although Olsen's sources claimed it was because he'd quibbled over the salary offered – a staggering $100,000 a year. Tom stared at Hays's photograph again, judged him every inch the rat he looked, a pocket-filling politician to the core, and felt deeply uncomfortable about his own role in the affair. So much so that he'd flung the rag in the first trash can he passed.

To his surprise, though, the newspaper he unfolded now was not the *Herald*. Instead, he found himself staring uncomprehendingly at the densely inked advertising columns at the back of that morning's *San Pedro Star*.

'What is this, Thad?'

Sullivan flipped the paper over in his hands and stabbed a finger at a three-paragraph stub in the Late News section in the bottom corner of the back page, its bold headline ringed in pencil: *Point Fermin Mystery.*

Still it held out no meaning for him.

'Just made it into the late edition,' Sullivan said. 'They're going wild about it in Central.'

Tom skimmed the story: a report of the discovery of a body on the rocks under the cliffs beneath the lighthouse at Point Fermin, round the bay from Los Angeles port, so shattered by the fall as to render identification difficult, though perhaps not entirely impossible. It was as if the mass of people pushing past, elbowing their way to the door and the procession behind the hearse outside, were no longer present. Tom was instantly alone as the final sentence hit him with full force: *Local sources speculate that the remains are those of deputy port police chief Aloysius Devlin, reported missing two nights ago.*

'Christ. Is this for real?' Tom stared blankly at his friend, certain that most of the blood in his face had just drained down into his boots. He steadied himself, grabbing at Sullivan's arm. A gesture mistaken for quiet jubilation and responded to in kind.

'I thought you'd be glad to hear it,' Sullivan said. 'The word from San P is it's him for sure, but the body's a mess. Looks like sharks got at it. They're waiting for a statement from the county coroner to confirm it. Seems he for one is dumb enough to think it could have been an accident. But I know which wop bootlegger my money would be on. And yours, I'm guessing. Not that I'm gonna help anyone out on this, mind. Let the fat pig roast in hell and have the justice he deserves, eh?'

'With Mikey Ross there, too, on a spit beside him, right?'

A residual anger flared up in Tom but subsided just as quickly. He couldn't help wondering what horrors Cornero's men had subjected Devlin to before they finished him off. And what they'd done with Ross's shattered body. Dumped him in the sea, too? Or left him in some remote canyon for the coyotes and buzzards to pick apart? Questions Tom found it easy enough to put away again unanswered. Sullivan would not bring it up again.

'Amen to that . . . with bells on,' Sullivan said, looking up into the cathedral's vaulted roofspace. From the tower a plangent peal of bells was resonating down into the church, joined by carillons from all across the city.

'If there's one thing this town does well,' Sullivan added, 'it's giving a man a send-off as big as he could ever dream of. You can be sure Taylor never would've guessed he'd be so honored.'

Making his way outside, Tom leaned with both hands against the carved wood balustrade at the top of the steps, felt a fresh breeze on his temples and breathed in a lungful of cool Los Angeles air. He thought of Fay at home in her apartment awaiting his return, the windows open to the balcony, knowing that she too would be feeling the warmth and hope of this beautiful Californian day.

Below him, the crowd was already withering away. The show had moved on. Only true mourners would follow the hearse six miles out along Santa Monica Boulevard to the Hollywood Cemetery where Taylor would be interred among more celebrated peers. Inside St Paul's, only a small cluster of people remained, circled around a tiny seated figure, her weeping echoing in the great empty drum of the nave, too distressed and exhausted to go on.

'Poor woman,' Sullivan said, joining Tom outside. By now even he was convinced Mabel Normand was not putting on an act. 'I hope she has someone at home to take care of her.'

Tom knew she had, but whether they or anyone else had the means to heal as bruised a soul as Normand's he doubted very much. But he was free of her, and her friend Sennett, now. Her concerns were no longer his.

'This will all be gone a month from now,' Tom said, waving a hand at the boarded-up shop fronts, office buildings and rooming houses lining Olive on the west side of the square. 'They're tearing this whole block down. That requiem was as much for St Paul's as it was for Taylor. The wrecking crews are moving in this week.'

'And they say the devil hasn't got the upper hand in the City of Angels,' Sullivan grinned. 'C'mon, let's go get a drink. We deserve one.'

Tom shook his head. 'I'd love to, but I have to see a man about a job.'

'Yeah?' Sullivan said, giving him the eye. 'You kept that very quiet. Things looking up for you again, are they?'

'A big storm's about to hit the movie business, Thad. And this city with it. The studios, they've got all the connections they need at the top. But men like you and me, working the low end, we're what they'll need more than ever. Men who know the worth of keeping their mouths shut.'

Sullivan frowned at him as though he was talking in riddles. 'Well, you be sure you don't go bringing any of it to my door. I've had enough to last a lifetime.'

'All I'm saying is that change is coming. Someone's got to benefit. Might as well be us.'

And with that, Tom Collins tipped a hand to his hat in salute, and made his way down the steps into the clear bright dazzle of the morning.

THE END

AFTERWORD

A century on, the murder of William Desmond Taylor remains unsolved. Theories abound but none could ever be proved, the waters were so muddied from the outset by vested interests. But the crime sparked a US-wide obsession that continued for decades. Mabel Normand's health, career and personal life went into a tailspin that ended with her early death in 1930. Mary Miles Minter could not escape the taint and was quietly dropped by Zukor, never to work again. Of those implicated, Sennett alone soldiered on until the talkies put him out of business. Within weeks, Will H. Hays, the Harding administration's chief political fixer, was confirmed in the new post of 'movie czar'. Hays's solution to avoid state-controlled censorship was to impose an industry-wide reign of terror that eventually evolved into the infamous Hays Code of the 1930s – a system that suited autocratic studio bosses very well, and kept Hollywood in check for the next forty years. The silent-era's age of innocence and excess was over.